Mob Boss

The O'Rourke Brotherhood

Sabine Barclay

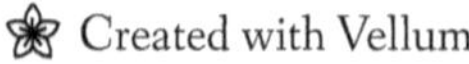 Created with Vellum

Here's health to your enemies' enemies!
~Irish Proverb

Find me writing Historical Romance as Celeste Barclay.

Happy reading,
Sabine

Subscribe to Sabine's Newsletter

Subscribe to Sabine's bimonthly newsletter to receive exclusive insider perks.

Have you read *The Syndicate Wars*? This FREE origin story novella is available to all new subscribers to Sabine's monthly newsletter. Subscribe on her website.
www.sabinebarclay.com

The O'Rourke Brotherhood

Mob Boss

Mob Star

Mob Princess

Mob Saint

Mob Bride

Mob Knight

Do you also enjoy steamy Historical Romance? Discover Sabine's books written as Celeste Barclay.

Chapter One

Dillan

I hate meetings like this. I don't need to wear pants from some shitty off-the-rack suit that are too tight to *try* to make my dick look bigger. I'm secure in my cock size, and I don't need to show how big my balls are for people to know I run this part of the city. I loathe strip clubs too. I'm past the point where naked women make my jimmy do jumping jacks. I can appreciate a hot bod and gymnast level strength, but it does nothing for me. These douchebags? They're practically ready to come in those cheap arse pants. Why am I here? I keep asking myself that.

Seamus and Shane are doing just fine with these negotiations. I'm just here to look good. I'm the muscle today. Or rather my name and my position. Who the fuck thought— way, way back in the day —that giving the mob hierarchy nautical names was a good idea? Fucking Skipper. This isn't motherfucking Gilligan's Island. None of these numb nuts are the Professor, even if they think they're fucking Mr. Howell.

But who is that? If this is *Gilligan's Island*, then she's Mary Ann.

I glance at Seamus, but he's focused on the Albanian he's trying not to lose his shite at. Shane smirks at me when I dart my gaze to him. I cock an eyebrow as the waitress walks over. She's definitely not a dancer. She has too many clothes on. But you can barely call the pieces of thread she's wearing clothes. She's got on a bikini top that's barely more than pasties, and the skirt she's wearing would make my Catholic grandmother do somersaults in her grave.

It's the standard uniform for this place, but somehow it doesn't look right on her. Not because she doesn't have a banging body because she does. Not because she's a butter face — but-her-face —as in great bod, not so great face. She's beautiful in a super understated way. That's part of what makes her look out of place. She has next to no makeup on. I think those are even her real eyelashes. The natural beauty is drawing way too much attention.

"'Scuse me."

She tries to step around Zef Hoxha, the *kyre* of the Albanian mafia here in New York. When he reaches out to grab her wrist, I'm out of my seat with my hand around his. He never gets a chance to touch her because my hold is so tight he can't bend his fingers. I keep squeezing until it must feel like I'll snap the bones.

"No touching."

Zef drops his arm as much as my hold allows. I let go and stare at him before I tilt my head toward the waitress. I narrow my eyes, and he knows what I expect.

"I apologize, miss."

"That's all right, sir. Here's your drink."

She's polite as she hands him his glass. Unfortunately, to put down the rest, she has to bend forward, giving everyone a view of her glorious cleavage. Tits and arse are what sell here, and she has them in spades. I'm certain it's why my cousin hired her. If I sit down, everyone will know I'm just as guilty as these fuck nuts because she's made my dick do something that hasn't happened in a strip club since I was like twenty-three. I'm now thirty-three.

If we were alone, and she were a dancer, I might indulge. But neither is the case. The strippers might give lap dances, but patrons aren't supposed to touch them during those either. Doesn't mean they don't. Doesn't mean they don't try to get a little more. And doesn't mean some women don't indulge—which gets them fired. We have cameras all over the place. Someone reviews the film every night after we close. By morning, if anyone fucked a customer, they're done. We don't run a prostitute ring.

I see her nametag says Molly. I'm not convinced she looks like a Molly. Not that I know exactly what would make her a Molly. There's something about her that's sorta girl next door. Mary Ann from *Gilligan's Island*. But when she looks up at me before straightening, all I see is Ginger. And that's what my balls see, too. Apparently, they have x-ray vision through my pants. When she backs up, she bumps into Shane. He puts a steadying hand on her waist— her bare waist —and chuckles. I want to snap that hand off my cousin's wrist just like I nearly did to Zef. Shane looks over at me, and his smirk is even more obvious than before. The fecker is taunting me. It's a good thing we're close family and actually friends— that's why he's a fecker and not a fucker. I might have to kill him otherwise. He can read me too well. He knows I'm inexplicably territorial about Molly.

I cock an eyebrow and return my attention to Zef. I want this meeting over, and not just because I want to go to the office and learn everything there is to know about Molly— because that's not stalkerish at all —but because there are other things I need to do right now to finish this deal that's taking forever for Seamus to negotiate. Shane's keeping Zef's bodyguards occupied, plying them with drinks, and they are way overindulging since they know we're footing the bill.

I wish we could do business somewhere respectable, but for the head of the Irish mob to meet with the head of the Albanian mob, we need a place that's a little less noticeable when it comes to the acceptable parts of society. We do a lot of our deals in our strip clubs. The lighting sucks except for the spots shining on the stage, which means we have some sense of anonymity. Hence, the cameras all over the place. *We* might want anonymity, but we aren't giving anyone else that. It's a mostly cash business, so it's easy to launder. If we get raided, it wouldn't be shocking to find a large stack of cash in the safe. And we can liquor up fuckers like this.

As I turn my attention back to Seamus and Zef, it sounds like they're getting somewhere. Not where I was hoping we'd go, but maybe on the path. I don't fucking know at this point. The Albanians are too fucking unpredictable.

"We aren't doing business with those pussies. The Poles want to play nice, so the Ivankov bratva doesn't take away jobs from their community. Fuck Maksim Kutsenko. Fuck his family."

Zef's accent is so heavy that, along with the Albanian mafia's reputation, it scares the shite out of most people. Maybe it would me if I hadn't gotten into my first knife fight when I was ten. I wasn't even supposed to be carrying one, but luckily I was. It was actually against Zef's now dead cousin when he wanted a baseball card I had. He nearly lost his index finger for touching what didn't belong to him. He tried to gut me for it. I left a scar across his chest that never faded. So, listening to Zef go on and on about the Polish does nothing to move me.

Seamus feels the same way, and I know he'll make sure Zef understands. I just sit back as the muscle and listen. I'm reigning over my fiefdom by overseeing this little tête-a-tête.

"You can want to fuck the bratva into next Sunday, but that doesn't mean doing business with the Polish is a bad thing. Maybe they are pussies, but they're pussies who are doing a damn good job at loan sharking. *They* don't kill everyone the first time they slip up. *They* understand that intimidation makes for lasting customers. Death does not. I have drugs, and they have money."

"Bah. In a city this size, there's always someone else to get money from. If you're weak, then they think they don't have to pay. It just makes more work convincing the next person to learn from the last motherfucker if they think you'll forgive them. Leave a head on their porch, and people in the neighborhood learn fast."

You'd think he was some old school Sicilian mafioso. Even Salvatore Mancinelli is more refined than this goon. I may be the mob boss, but even I know there are times when you win more people with honey than with vinegar. But Zef wasn't the brains of the family. That was Ardit until he got himself killed. Which reminds me, I owe his counterpart up in Boston a call. Let's see what Seamus has to say to that.

"And it takes one little granny screaming on her stoop to bring way too much attention."

Seamus shoots Zef a pointed look. That's how his cousin wound up dead. Ardit tried to strong arm the wrong person—his rival up in Boston —by lopping a guy's head off who was in town visiting his grandmother. The victim's brother was supposed to find the head in a paper bag on the stoop. Instead, it was the grandmother who screamed, had a heart attack, and died on the stoop. Who was the brother meant to find the head? His Boston rival.

My full attention drifts to Molly, who I've been watching while listening to Zef and Seamus. My cousin— because nepotism is the secret to a long life —is growing impatient. Even if no one else can tell, I can. He's reining in his temper by breathing slower. If he were angry like most people get, he would breathe more rapidly. It would be a tell. Molly's trying to make her way back up to our table, but one of Zef's guys is giving her a hard time. He's standing at the bottom of the stairs up to the mezzanine level where the private boxes are. I look over the railing as my other cousin, Sean, steps in front of the giant. Sean weighs at least thirty pounds less than these motherfuckers, but I still have my money on my cousin.

Yes, Sean, Shane, and Seamus. We're that fecking Irish. Sean and Shane are twins. Those who know, know to look for a freckle on Sean's throat to tell them apart. Close family has no problem doing it. We just act like we can't. It's useful. Seamus is our mutual cousin.

Molly skirts around Sean and the arse fuck and hurries as best she can with the bottles. Vodka and whiskey. May as well stick with all the stereotypes tonight. This time Zef leans back and keeps his hands to himself, but he conveniently moves his right foot to look like he's trying to give her room. Instead, it boxes her in between his legs. When she starts to lose her balance, I'm on my feet again to snatch the tray and shove it at Shane. I wrap my arm around her waist and draw her next to me. She's tall, but not so tall I can't see over her head to Zef. The fucker's laughing until he realizes my cousins and I don't think he's funny.

I keep my voice low. "Are you all right?"

"Yeah, thank you, Mr. O'Rourke. It would have been a disaster if I'd spilled all of that."

"I would have tripled your tips tonight if you'd dumped

those drinks all over his lap. I just didn't want you to fall onto his lap."

"Definitely not somewhere I want to sit."

She curls her nose up at the idea, and I'm certain she knows it's because he wanted her to land on his hard on.

"If it happens again with any guy, make a fist as you fall."

She looks up at me, wide-eyed. Then she laughs. Little lines bracket her mouth like sets of dimples. If I don't let go, everyone is going to realize just how attracted I am to her. That's not safe for either of us. As I drop my arm, she takes a step back. A step right onto Zef's foot with her near stilettos. She isn't wearing the platform heels many of the dancers do. They're more like backless slip-on things my sister's Barbie wore. I don't think of Colleen often, and even four years later, it still rips a hole in my heart to. I focus on Molly, who lunges forward, bumping into me. I wrap my arm around her waist again, but she spins in it.

"I'm so, so sorry, sir. I didn't realize— I'm so sorry."

I tighten my hold on her, pinning her to my side. It's my turn to smirk now, and I direct it to Zef as I speak.

"He could have moved his foot. No need to apologize."

"I..."

She snaps her mouth shut. I don't know what she was about to say. I let go of her, but she doesn't step forward as fast as she could. She looks at the floor, but it feels more like she's not in a rush to move away from me than being careful about where she puts her high-heeled foot next. She glances at Seamus and Shane, deciding to go around the table that way. We wait until she's gone again, and now it's my turn to speak up. Strong, silent type is done.

"Zef, either you work with the terms Seamus offered, or we take it all. I don't give a shite which it is. We have the men to take all your drugs and all the Polishes' as well. We're doing you a courtesy to cut you in. A sign of good faith that we're on your side when the Mancinellis come for you again. But if we aren't going to get our fair share in return, then I couldn't give two fucks about courtesy. I'll take what's ours and walk over your balls and your face. Decide."

He springs out of his seat to get in my face. We're about the same size, but I'm not worried. The bodyguards Shane was distracting notice their boss is pissed, so they try to get to me. Seamus moves to block them on the other side of the table from Shane. It also means he boxes Zef between him and me, who now tries to intimidate me with his words rather than his size.

"I could take my business to Maks. We're getting along."

"I wouldn't."

I sound casual, and I know it grates on his nerves. He tries to wait me out, but I know he's too damn curious.

"Oh, and why's that?"

"Because Maks didn't care when Ardit died. He thought Ardit was the only one involved in the human trafficking ring that got his sister-in-law's sister. Misha sure as fuck is going to care because that's his wife's sister. I can guess how they'll react when they find out you were the one who gave the woman's address to that psychopath who grabbed her. You thought your hands looked clean, but you didn't look under your nails. All the evidence is right there. You didn't clean up so well."

I've been holding onto that piece of information for a rainy day. It's not even the best thing I know about him. I have something that would interest the Colombians and the Italians. So, I have leverage in all directions. This is the nugget I wish to trade right now.

"I'm not fucking scared of Maks. I told you. He can go fuck himself."

I get out my phone and unlock it. I hold it, so he can see me pull up my contacts, then tap Maks's name. He shifts uneasily.

I'm about to hit the call button when he reaches out his hand. But he snatches it back when he realizes what he was about to do. That wouldn't have been good for his health.

"No need to get more hands in the cookie jar. Maks'll just want a cut. Then you'll get less, Dillan. That's not a win for you."

"But having you as one less competitor is." I put my finger to the screen.

"Wait! Wait. Fine. We'll find a way to get along with the Poles. It might drive me nuts, but I'll play nice."

Sure he will. For about five minutes. I'm counting on that. I want him to fuck it up with the Polish, so they shift their attention to their revenge. While they do that, we'll not only slip in and take over their loan sharking, but we'll get in on their fencing. In this case, the stolen goods are lists of compromised bank accounts and Social Security numbers. We'll resell them through a middleman to the Russians. We'll just make a couple calls to the FTC. It won't take the bratva down, but it'll be a headache. I've been cleaning up my predecessors' mess for nearly four years. That's the shitshow they left me. Despite what I've done, Maks and his family are still gunning for my head. I'm over it. I played nicely like Zef claims he will. Now I'm done.

"Good. Stop wasting our time. Agree to our terms. We entertained your negotiation to stroke your ego. But I'm not giving an inch. Take it or leave it."

Zef looks at me, then Shane. Finally, he looks at Seamus who's watching his guards from the corner of his eye while facing Zef. Our Albanian pain in the arse extends his hand to Seamus, who practically crushes it. Seamus makes Shane, Sean, and me look like kids. He's massive. The Irish aren't usually known for height, but he and his brother are close to six-feet-six. They carry their two-hundred-and-fifty pounds well. It's all lean muscle. When they plow into someone, that person isn't getting back up. Mind you, Shane, Sean, and I are all somewhere between six-three and six-four and well into the two-twenties to two-thirties range. None of us are hefty, either.

Seamus's arrogance is his trademark. He grins at Zef as he lets go. The guy's palm is bright red, but his fingers are white. I've arm wrestled with Seamus. I know how much that guy's hand hurts right now. Good. He shouldn't have been a dick during our conversation, and he definitely shouldn't have touched Molly. I haven't forgotten about her. I've still been keeping an eye on her. I don't like how Zef's guys have been watching her, too. That ends now.

"We expect to hear from Bartlomiej by noon tomorrow. If the Polish don't have good news, then it'll be your head in a bag on your mom's stoop. Fuck me over and find out, Zef. Do not even think about coming back here or going to any of our clubs unless you're invited. I told you not to touch, and you still tried to, anyway. You know the rules. You want to go to a brothel, then go to one of your own places. The women at ours dance and serve drinks. Nothing else. Get out."

My cousins and I watch the Albanian entourage go down to the main floor. Molly noticed them and went in the opposite direction. Good girl. Since we're all so tall, we don't need to approach the railing to see Zef and his men leave. My guys at the door will make sure they get in their cars and drive off. The ones I have trailing them will ensure they don't cause any trouble for us tonight.

"Good job, Shay."

Seamus nods and rolls his eyes. It's more about not gutting any of them instead of getting the terms we want. I look at my other cousin.

"You too, Shane."

All three of us would gladly have stuck our knives in those

guys. All of us carry at least one at all times. Call me paranoid, but I have one under my pillow. I have topnotch security, but I take no chances. Especially not after the shite my predecessors got us into.

This meeting took longer than I realized because I hear the bartenders say last call. That means a half hour before we close for the night. There are groans from the men around the stages. Now, they're either out of money and feeling pathetic. Or they're in a hurry to spend all their money because they think it might get them a few extra minutes. Even the fucking regulars do it. Dumb sons of bitches. It never works. It's my turn to spend the next few hours skimming the security tape. I don't mind. There's someone I want to get to know better.

Chapter Two

Greta

I didn't hear nearly as much of that conversation as I wanted. That fuck nut either is smarter than he looks and intentionally distracted everyone by trying to grope me, or he's an idiot to touch a woman in an O'Rourke club. I've only been here three days, and I already know the O'Rourkes have no patience for any of the women getting harassed. Who knew? Certainly not what I've heard about their family. Certainly not what their family history suggests. Whatever the reason, it kept the conversation from going on around me. The asshole ruined it. Then again, maybe an O'Rourke would have paused it if they got to stuff they truly want no one else to hear. Either way, the tips were too shitty to make not getting any info worth another night with my ass hanging out of my skirt.

The lack of info and Mr. Grabby Hands would have made this assignment completely blow for yet another night, but Dillan O'Rourke is fucking fine. Like holy hot damn. Like come in my panties just looking at him hot. And when he pulled me against him and away from the Albanian piece of shit, his body felt as good as I guessed it would. All hard muscles. I don't know if he noticed, but I put my hand on his stomach to brace myself. Ripples upon ripples of muscle. He held me close, but I didn't feel trapped. I felt safe. Which is fucking bonkers, considering he's a mobster. Not just that. He's the fucking mob boss.

Maybe he was watching a girl on stage before I came up the second time, but I'd like to think it was me. I'm pretty fucking certain I felt his hard on. If that was his cock at rest... Goddamn sledgehammer. Thinking it was because of me is ridiculous. Men like him do not go for women like me. Women who work for him. In a strip club. With next to no clothes on, so every other man can see me. I'm not some seven-figure corporate star, and I'm not even remotely glamorous on my best days. I—

"Molly?"

Oh, shit.

I look up from the table I'm wiping down. He commands each and every space he's in. It would be arrogance if it weren't justified.

"Yes, Mr. O'Rourke."

"I'm Dillan. There are at least six of us who will respond to Mr. O'Rourke. Unless you want all of us, you'll have to be more specific."

I only want you.

There's something in his gaze that makes me think he's testing me. Testing me to see if I admit he's the one I want to fuck on this table. Or something about me wanting all of them. Like a sevensome? Or that I'd take whoever approaches me, indiscriminate of them as individuals.

"All right." I stand up with my rag in my left hand, and my tray pressed against my thigh and belly with my right.

"I'm sorry about what happened tonight. He shouldn't have

tried to touch you either time. That's not how we run this place."

"I know. Thanks for coming to my rescue."

He looks at me for a moment too long before he answers with a casual smile.

"Always. Did you drive today? I don't want you walking out to the parking lot alone."

"I did. I'll go with some of the girls."

He doesn't look away, but I'm certain he knows where each girl is right now. He shakes his head.

"Most of them carry mace or pepper spray, but the guys who were here tonight aren't easily deterred. I don't think there's any reason to fear walking out there with the others, but I'd feel better if I escort you out."

"Thank you." I glance toward the door. This job just gets worse by the hour. No info. An asshole who tried to get me onto his lap twice. And his henchmen who might try to assault me on my way to my car. The fucking things we do for work. And not work like I need the money to survive. Though I'm not turning it down.

"Let me know when you're ready to go. I'll be in the office. I already let Sean and Shane know you'll be going down the hall."

So fucking certain of himself that he's certain what I'll do. Presumptuous. But he's not wrong. I nod. He takes a step around the table as though he'll walk past me to the hallway no one goes down unless they're an O'Rourke. It has the office and the liquor storage rooms. He shifts to stand next to me, so we're standing nearly opposite shoulder to shoulder.

"If anyone ever gives you a problem here, you come straight to me. My cousins will know."

I look up at him. I don't know what to say, so my brow furrows.

"Molly, I don't think I overreacted. But if that man or any of his bodyguards decide to strike back, I don't want them taking it out on you. If I caused you to get more attention than you want, then I'll take care of it."

I raise my chin and look him straight in the eye. Something passes between us, but I have no idea what to call it. Maybe it's some defiance on my part. Why should I only go to him? Any of the other men who work in this club could keep me safe. If he's the cause, then I should stay away. Maybe it's me wanting to show him I don't scare easily.

He heads toward his office, and I'm left behind. After being in his arms even once, it feels so fucking disappointing to not be there again. To have him walk away. I don't want to look back at him, but I could since there's no way he'll look back at me. I hedge my bets and look at the mirror behind the bar. Holy shit. He's doing the same. He flashes me a quick smile before looking where he's walking.

I take twenty minutes to finish my tasks. I traded wiping down more tables and sweeping the bar area for mopping around the stage. I just can't. I know there's nothing on the floor over there except napkins, cups, and spilled drinks. But it still skeeves me out to mop the floor. When I'm serving, I'm not thinking about what else might have landed on there. I'm definitely glad I'm not responsible for mopping the stage. I have nothing against the ladies. But the sweat. The lotion. The any and everything else. I'll mop the shit out of my place. And I'd do it here if I had to. But I'm happy to trade. I put the broom away and grab my coat and bag in the dressing room. I pull out my jeans and sweatshirt. I'm quick to change. There's no way I'd feel safe going out in public in my uniform. And I'd fucking freeze my tits off if I did.

I smile at Sean— or is it Shane —one of the hot twins. And he lets me pass. There's no other sound in the hallway, so I move quietly. I'd love to poke my nose around in the store-rooms, but a: they're locked, and b: whichever twin would see me. The hallway gets really dim in between the liquor storage and the office, so I'm not as worried about the twin noticing I take my time. I strain to hear anything.

"*Is cuma liom. Ba mhaith liom a guys ón oíche a leanúint. Cuir sa sceideal é, a Chormaic. Níl muinín agam astu timpeall uirthi.*" I don't care. I want his guys from tonight followed. Make it fit in the schedule, Cormac. I don't trust them around her.

Fuck. I'm still fluent in Irish Gaelic. My full name is Gaelic, and I spoke it as a child. But I don't use it frequently. Something about following guys. Someone named Cormac—that's another cousin. And not trusting her.

Not trusting me? Another woman?

I hurry to pull my phone out and attempt to look casual as I listen to Dillan's half of the conversation.

"*Uirísliú mé air os a chomhair. De ghnáth ní bheadh cúram orm, ach tá sí nua. Níl a fhios agam cad atá ar eolas aici fúinn. Níl a fhios agam an féidir léi aire a thabhairt di féin nó an bhfuil a fhios aici teacht chugainn. Níorbh í seo an oíche cheart dá seal. Deisigh sin freisin.*" I humiliated him in front of her. I normally wouldn't care, but she's new. I don't know what she knows about us. I don't know if she can take care of herself or knows to come to us. This wasn't the right night for her shift. Fix that, too.

He's uncertain whether I know what type of man he met with. He must know I've guessed who he is. Or rather, if I didn't know before, I've guessed by now. I know exactly who Dillan O'Rourke is. And that's why I'm here.

I keep swiping my phone screen as though I'm reading as the men's conversation continues. I've got to knock soon, or else the twin will wonder why Dillan and I aren't walking out.

But I need a natural lull, so he doesn't fear I overheard something.

It'll be tomorrow. I want Jacek. Zef will wait until the last minute to tell Bartlomiej about what we arranged. Jacek will go ape shit. He won't be able to help himself. He'll come looking for me because a phone call won't be enough. Bartlomiej can't muzzle his brother any better than Ardit could muzzle Zef. Jacek knows where to meet. He'll assume Finn will come with me. You and Seamus are going instead. Don't kill him. Just make him wish you had. But no internal bleeding that requires a hospital. We don't need anyone asking about his last known associates.

Bartlomiej and Jacek Nowakowski. Bartlomiej heads the Polish mob, and his younger brother, Jacek, is his chief henchman. The first is cunning as fuck. The second is straight up psycho. I've seen his mug shots. Fucking crazy eyes. The man left the Polish army more fucked-up than he went in. I don't know his whole back story, but my guess is the TBI in his medical records accounts for a lot. Yes. I've seen them. And no, I don't feel guilty for how I got them. No more guilty than I do eavesdropping now.

I don't know what Cormac said, but it was quiet for a while. I should have used that as my chance. Now I can hear Dillan again.

Pick Jacek up again next week. Drop him off with Bogdan at Ivy. Let them deal with it. Merry fecking Christmas. They can owe us.

It goes quiet again, so Cormac must be speaking. I knock and take a step back. I quickly lock the screen as I knock and shove my phone in my back pocket. As I hear his hand on the doorknob, I change my mind. I drop my phone in my bag.

"Hi. I'm all done. If you're working, I can ask one of the other guys to—"

"No."

I wait for him to say more, but he doesn't. I take another step back as he walks out. He shuts the door, and I hear the lock click. There's a punch code to unlock it, so it won't be as simple as stealing a key. I need a reason to see someone unlock it and memorize the code.

"Let me help you."

I almost answer, huh, until I realize he's reaching for my coat. I hand it to him, and he holds it out for me. I slip my arms in, and he settles it on my shoulders. When we get to the door, he opens it, holding it out for me. I sense more than feel his hand hovering at my lower back. Someone's cleared the snow and ice on the sidewalk, but more ice has formed in the parking lot. I should have changed my fucking shoes. I have my sneakers in my bag. I was in too big a hurry to snoop. When I nearly misstep, his hand moves from my lower back to holding onto my forearm.

"Thanks. I won't make the same mistake twice. I won't think I can just slip out to my car without changing my shoes."

"I'm glad I'm here to help."

He has no coat on, and we can see our breath. Yet he isn't even close to shivering. Just the opposite. His hand is warm through my coat and sweatshirt sleeve. At least it feels that way. Maybe it's just from him holding my arm. The moment my right foot starts to go out from under me, he picks me up in his arms. Like the way a bride gets carried over the threshold. He did it as though I'm a feather. I am not. The club specializes in curvy girls, so the dancers and the waitresses are hardly what most people would expect at a strip club. I'm hardly what someone would expect at a strip club.

"Which one is yours?"

"The Jeep."

It's not a fun Wrangler. I wish. Those aren't winterproof for New Hampshire, where I went to college and got my first job straight out of school. I'd paid it off by the time I moved back down to the city. I fumble for my keys and hit the remote start. He puts me down and opens the front door. I don't sit though. I need to clear my car off. There's a dusting of snow, and there's ice.

"Get in and defrost it. Change your shoes. I'll take care of the windows. Where's your brush?"

I have shit from work on the backseat. I don't need him seeing that, so I reach back and grab the scraper. While he clears off the car, I need to gather all the papers and hide them. The way he spoke to me. It wasn't like he was barking orders or telling me the obvious. It was more like a don't worry. I'll take care of you. I'm reading way too much into it. But that's how it felt. Just like his hand at my lower back. His hand on my arm. Then carrying me. I feel safe.

But the fact that he's the least safe man I could be with is why I'm spying on him.

I watch him start with the rear window. Good. I twist in my seat and scoop up the folders, quickly getting them into a pile that I shove under the front passenger seat. He's already done the rear passenger side window, but it's dark in the car. I don't think he noticed me hiding anything. Maybe he'll think I have a messy car and am trying to hide that. My interior isn't spotless, but I keep it clean. It's the secret to making things last. I have no interest in leasing and getting something new every three years. I'm interested in not having another car payment for like ten years.

I'm letting my mind wander as I wait for him to finish. It's really chivalrous, and I appreciate it. I would have changed my shoes and done it myself, but this is much nicer now that I have the heater on. That reminds me. He told me to change them. It's not that I feel like I must comply. I want to. The way he said it was more like let me do this, so you can stay warm and safe. Once again, Dillan O'Rourke is the last man I should fool myself into thinking I'm safe with. I know shit that went down with his family. I know the danger that goes along with them. Some of the dirt I found, but that only happened because a highly reliable source told me. And if I don't get something useful soon, I'll break my deal with that source. I don't want them to doubt me, or that fount of information will dry up.

I finish tying my second shoe as Dillan comes back to the driver's side. He brushed off the light dusting on the roof and scraped all the ice from the windows. He didn't just do a quickie to make holes in the ice and snow for me to see through. He scraped every single bit off. It took him nearly ten minutes. Thorough. Again, it feels like he genuinely cares about my safety. That's so at odds with what I know about him. But he's cunning. They warned me about that. Does he suspect something about me? Is that why he's paying attention to me? I didn't see him offering to walk any of the other girls out. Does he suspect me? Is he trying to lure me into telling him why I'm at 4Play? It's called that for the obvious innuendo, but they also have four stages. Smart.

"There you go." He passes the scraper to me through my open window.

"Thanks. That was really sweet of you. I appreciate it. Luckily, there wasn't too much snow." Maybe I can strike up a conversation since the man doesn't appear to notice it's early December, and New York remembered it's winter.

"Molly, I was serious. If anyone bothers you, come to me. You can tell my cousins, but I don't want to hear it from them. I want to know exactly what happens. Those men should be smart enough not to come near you. But if they aren't, it's my club, and I'll deal with it."

I can imagine what that means. I didn't need to overhear his earlier conversation to guess. "I'm sure they won't even remember me by morning."

He watches me before he nods and steps back. He's assessing me, and I don't know whether I pass.

"Goodnight, Molly."

"Goodnight, Dillan."

Chapter Three

Dillan

Something's off about Molly, but I can't put my finger on it. I forced myself to review the footage before indulging in my stalking. It's not really stalking since I own the club, and she's an employee. But I have next to nothing to do with the daily operations. That's all Shane. He loathes coming to these clubs, but all the syndicates own them. Our night clubs are also largely cash too, but we keep those for research. It's a great way to know what's going on with drug sales. It's a great way to upcharge, making more money on the booze and cover charge, and find out how much people will pay to play.

We also watch the low-level gangs and wannabe syndicates do deals. We see and hear it all. Dumb fucks don't check for the bugs under the tables or the cameras in the walls. We get the rich dicks who want to see and be seen. That makes the average person hope they can get far enough forward in line to make it in. It keeps our clubs at the top of the lists of places to go in New York. Of course, we vie with the other syndicates to be at the top. Nothing like buying bots to drop five-star reviews. It's not like we don't all do it.

And that's why we have security footage at all our clubs. I watched Molly walk down the hallway to my office, then I saw her get out her phone. She didn't get a call, and it didn't look like she was sending a text. Maybe she got one or an email and decided not to respond then. Still, I know what I was talking about, and it wasn't something anyone outside my family should hear. Red flag number one.

Margaret McDonnell

That's the name she wrote on her application. It looks like she's waitressed in a few places outside the city. She lived in New England, probably during college from the looks of it. Yup. Dartmouth. What the fuck is she doing working some place like this? Red flag number two. Though she has a nice Irish name. My grandmothers would approve.

I move onto her tax form. What?

Mairghráid MacDonnell

Red flag number three. That just got old country Irish. It's still Margaret. I'm third generation on one side and fourth on the other, but still grew up speaking Gaelic. I learned it before I learned English. My parents still insist that's what we use the majority of the time we're at their home. Same with my aunts and uncles. They fear us forgetting it. I don't know why. They know we speak it with one another because next to no one else does too. Great for private conversations.

Maybe her parents like the traditional name, but to make it easier, she goes by Margaret or Molly. Understandable. Mine in Gaelic is Diolun. My parents chose to spell it with an "a" instead of an "o" because that's the default for most Americans. O'Rourke is super Irish on its own. My deep red hair and freckles are Irish enough, too. They didn't need to add anything that might draw more attention to how Irish I am. Not that it helps now, considering my role.

She used her driver's license and Social Security card to verify her eligibility to work legally. A lack of either of those or other documentation that says someone is legal to work in the U.S. is hardly an impediment. But we balance it out for tax reasons. We need to have enough legal employees to justify the taxes we pay on our legal businesses. We aren't going down for tax evasion like Mickey Cohen, the Irish version of Al Capone. We keep the outside of our noses clean. Never mind what goes up some of our clients'.

Three red flags, but none are really serious enough for me to raise the alarm. I'll keep an eye on her. Gladly. Willingly. Eagerly. She fills out her uniform in a way that gets me hard just thinking about her. Seeing her in it? Well, it's just fucking uncomfortable to have a hard on for that long. The commercial says if you have an erection lasting more than four hours, seek medical attention. That's if you take the little blue pill. What the fuck do you do if it's natural? The things I want to do to her. The places I want to put my fingers, then my tongue, and finally my aching cock. Goddamn. Just thinking about this right now makes me want to get off. If I were home, I'd jack off with an image of her in my head. I draw the line at taking a photo of her on the sly to use pathetically alone. But Lord, it's tempting. She's tempting. I want excuses to touch her, but I know that's masochism.

Despite her hotness, she needs watching because those red flags won't go away just because I'm hot for her. It might mean I volunteer to come in to watch the tapes more often than I'm on the schedule to. I'll take shite from the guys for it. But as much as I want to fuck her, something still doesn't feel right.

Three weeks of torture. At least, I've had legitimate reasons to be at 4Play. Of course, shite would go sideways with the Albanians and the Polish, except it was the fucking Polish who screwed us. We prepared ourselves because the likelihood of them trying to fuck us over was so high. But it just makes it inconvenient. I've had more meetings here than I would like. For one thing, it's too conspicuous. There are regulars who come here, and when people like that notice other people who are richer suddenly become regulars, their tongues get loose real fast with the cops. And being around Molly has left me with a chronic case of blue balls.

She smiles and is always polite, but we keep a professional distance. It doesn't mean I can't keep my mind off her. It doesn't mean I haven't caught her watching me in the bar mirror as I walk past. It doesn't mean we haven't chatted and gotten to know a little more about each other. None of the video footage shows her going down the hallway again. I haven't invited her, and she hasn't snooped. That makes me suspicious. Most employees try at least once to get into the storerooms. It's been a long arse time since someone has been stupid enough to jiggle the office doorknob. That gets them more than fired. If it's a bouncer, that gets one of us in the alley with them out back. If it's a woman, she gets banned from working anywhere we own. Once that gets around to the other syndicates, both have to find another line of work. And it gets around. We have spies everywhere.

And it's a spy that's got me here again today. Either we have an outsider or a leak. Either way, I need to find them. We've had a few new people start in the past month, so not just Molly. We found out someone's planning an article about us. The information isn't stuff a staff member overheard, then squealed. It was stuff they had to know before the past month and then put together with the new information. 4Play's not open yet, so I have a team of our guys in here sweeping the entire place. Under the furniture, along the baseboards, in the ceiling panels, the DJ booth, the kitchen, and the storerooms. Shane's doing the office. Nothing is turning up other than our own devices. So, no one broke in to plant bugs. That means it's a person either sent in by another syndicate, or it's one of our people selling secrets to a journalist.

I'm in a storeroom with Sean since they're pretty much soundproof. We'd be in the office if Shane wasn't going through it with a fine-tooth comb. It's the least likely place that someone could get into, but it would be the best place to bug. I run my hands through my hair for at least the tenth time in the past five minutes. It has to be sticking up.

"You're the super sleuth. I don't know how I know, but I know. You need to find out what the feck is going on."

"I have a degree in national security and computer science. I'm not fecking Sherlock Holmes."

We might say fuck about other people, and I know we all think it. But our parents would skelp our arses if they heard us use that word toward each other maliciously, and they'd ring our fecking necks if we used that language in front of a woman. So, feck it is half the time.

"Consider this a breech in national security. The info I'm getting from our source at the newspaper said it isn't enough to get the feds coming for something specific, but it's pretty fecking damning. This isn't some Page Six shite about who some paparazzo saw at one of our clubs. It lists the syndicates seen here and the number of times we've met with them in the past three months. It calls into question our clientele without specifically accusing us of anything. It just opens everything up to speculation and investigation."

"I read your fecking text. I know what you said. We've all watched the security footage from each of our places, not just here. I've searched for any online security breaches. Nothing's coming up right now. I've been hacking everyone else's shite, and none of the other families are doing more than usual to sabotage us. I'm going to have extra security assigned to watch the back doors of all the clubs, and I have more guys mingling in the crowds in all the clubs."

The other families. Yeah, those fuckers— Mancinellis, Kutsenkos, and Diazes —are the most likely culprits, but if Sean says he's finding nothing, then I believe him. But it also means he needs to dig more. It's like an iceberg. What you see on the surface is a tiny fraction of what's lurking beneath the water.

And to give credit where credit is due, Sean is good at what he does. His degrees in national security and computer science help us keep a lot more shite secret than anyone realizes. For all the shite the other families have found on us, it's just a hint of all the things we're into. He's better than anyone else at knowing how to hide shite. If he knows how countries hide their nuclear development programs, then he knows how to keep our private family business private.

It's only when one or two of us think we can handle things on our own that it blows the fuck up. We all know better. Nothing is stronger than family. And we're all finally at an age and been in this long enough to know nothing goes well when we act on our own. Whether I sanction it or not, "projects" we don't all work on together go to hell. And that's why we're all working on finding the spy or the leak.

"This has to remain a priority. That article isn't going to materialize out of nowhere. This person either already knows more or is actively seeking more. We don't need the attention. It's obvious this isn't about sensationalizing us. It's about ruining us."

"Dillan, you aren't saying anything we don't already know.

Where are you with the deeper dives into everyone's background checks?"

"I'm working my way forwards. I've started with anyone not from our community who began working for us in the past year. We need to tighten up. We've let too many outsiders in. We stick with the families we know. No more 'it sounds Irish enough.'"

"Molly?"

I want to knock the smirk off his face. It's the same one Shane gave me the night I met Molly. Fecking Doublemint twins. It's annoying on one person. It makes me want to punch them on two. Especially when they're together. It's a good thing I love them.

"Yeah. Mairghráid MacDonnell is a great name, but she's not one of us."

"What have you learned about her?"

"Nothing yet. She's only been here three weeks. I doubt she knows enough to have given the reporter what they're supposedly going to include in the story. I won't rule her out, but I haven't gotten to her yet on my list."

"You could always ask her out. A little pillow talk to speed things up."

I shoot my cousin one of my stares where my face is completely expressionless except for my eyes. They bore into him. If it were anyone outside my family, it would make them squirm. It just turns his smirk into a full-on grin.

"Arse."

"But I'm not wrong, am I? If it's nothing, then you have someone to enjoy."

"You make her sound like a new puppy. I don't date. You don't date. None of us date. And I doubt she's the type to go to one of *those* clubs."

A BDSM club. One of our best-kept secrets is that we're

silent investors in every one in New York. Not just Manhattan, but all the boroughs. No one ties someone up or gets tied up without us knowing. It's been handy to know about various city and even state officials and their proclivities. It's great to know where all the members of the other syndicates go to fuck and what they're into. Not leverage we've obviously played, but it gives us plenty of insights. It also helps us keep track of them. Silent ownership still means we have the member lists, can view the security footage, and have dungeon masters and mistresses and bartenders on our off the record payroll.

"Ask and find out."

"No. I don't fuck employees. I don't date. And I'm not asking a random woman to let me tie her up and fuck her in the arse. Enough."

He laughs. He knows most of that is true. He also knows I wouldn't turn down— hypothetically, since there's no way it'll come to that —the chance to fuck her any way I can get her. But, like I said, I don't fuck employees, and I don't date.

"Touchy. You like her."

"How I feel is irrelevant right now. We need to figure out who this leak is."

"How you feel is irrelevant." He snorts. "That isn't a denial. Seriously, for your sake, I hope she's clean."

So do I. I can't do the hot things I want to do with her, but neither do I want to do anything to make things difficult for her. I don't want to fire her, and I don't want to make it hard for her to get any job in the city. But I will.

"Just do some more digging. Okay?"

"Sure. Let's see if Shane's found anything. If not, I'll work in the office. I'll get the trackers running on everyone's cells."

We track where our enemies are around the clock. The only time we can't track them is when they go to their "place." Each syndicate has one. It's where we take care of the unsavory parts of our business. The place where the only people who leave are us. We know exactly where the bratva, Cartel, and *Cosa Nostra* deal with things. They all turn off their GPS about five miles before they get there. They don't want to be tracked. But habits can tell you almost everything. Canvasing the five-mile radius from the entire circumference means you can pinpoint the abandoned garage the *Cosa Nostra* uses, the abandoned warehouse the bratva uses, and the out of business bodega basement the Cartel uses. None are on any city records, which makes it even easier to pinpoint when you find a building where there should be none or there should be no one coming or going.

I know they think we have a storage unit in Queens, which is where the others have their place. We all grew up in that borough. I know they think we used a storefront the bratva blew up. Nope. Never. We keep our shite to the Bronx and Staten Island. The two least likely places, and that's why they're there. Our place in the Bronx is the subterranean level of an abandoned railway station, but anything we need to keep out of sight and out of mind goes to a basement in a house on Staten Island. That includes people we need to keep alive until we can take them to the Bronx. Transporting is risky, but sometimes it's for the best.

I pull my thoughts back to the present as I continue to speak to Sean. "For this sort of shite, pay attention to Sergei and Anton. I have a feeling it's them. Carmine's a nosey little fucker, and Enzo's hacking skills are as good as the skills in any of the families. But this just feels bratva."

"And if it is?"

"We plant information all three families can find and see who confirms it. Then we follow whoever we link to them and catch them meeting with the bratva. I know it could be Jorge, Joaquin, and Javier, but I don't think it's them. They're busy fucking with the Mancinellis, and I heard their aunt has cancer. They only have the attention span for one task at a time. Dumb fuckers. When we know who it is, set a meeting that leads them back to us. I want them to come to us, not us go after them. Fucks with the mind more when you think you're getting away with it only to wind up right at your enemy's door."

"And your contingency plans?"

Because I always have them.

"If no one confirms what we're planting, then we look at who stays the furthest away from us. Finds reasons to exchange shifts, suddenly doesn't want to work on another family's construction site, won't go to any of their bars or clubs. If no one confirms it, we plant stuff straight in front of the other families and see who they go to. If we have no one to follow, then we lure the other families out. Lure Anton and Sergei out with information they want to verify. We blow something up— literally or figuratively —that makes Anton and Sergei or whichever family it is track this fucker down. One way or another, we'll flush out who did this. If we can't get the snitch to come to us, we give them a shadow long enough to be paranoid before we scoop them up. Or we raid their place in the middle of the night, drug 'em, and take 'em to Rochester and drown them in the river up there."

We have warehouses up there. We lost a few thanks to my fuck nut cousin who's no longer alive to run our syndicate. We have more, though. We always have more. I never let us buy one building without getting two more just in case. And since it's us, we usually get three for the price of one.

"What sort of thing do you want me to plant?"

This is what Sean excels at. If we weren't who we are, he could have worked for the NSA or been a spook for the State Department or CIA. But the family comes first. We need those skills. Plus, we might get people onto the NYPD or into the

FBI, DEA, and ATF, but the national security ones wouldn't let us breathe in their parking lot, let alone get any closer.

"The shite we want to do to Enzo in Chicago with the Rizzos and Grassos. Make it happen sooner. Our snitch in Chicago isn't just giving us information. You know we planted him so the bratva and *Costa Nostra* think he's working for each of them. He tells the bratva or the *Cosa Nostra* that Enrique has a guy in with the Rizzos, who's feeding all the info to the Cartel. He does."

"Do you think our guy is really our guy? Do you think he's loyal?"

"No. We don't need him to be because we'll learn even more if he isn't. Either way, we still need the Diazes squawking to the FBI just enough to get the feds off our asses for the O'Brien disappearances down in Trenton. We use our guy to set up the Diaz fucker to tell Enrique that Maks knows about the drugs Enrique wants to bring in through New Mexico. That carfentanil will kill someone from whichever syndicate is dealing. At least one less foot soldier to deal with, and when they're gone, we'll know for sure who got the shipment."

Shite gets complicated fast with four big families who run this city. Sean sorts it out aloud. "Bratva and *Cosa Nostra* find out about Enrique's guy out in Chicago. Cartel finds out the bratva knows about their interest in the carfentanil."

"Yeah. Don't stagger it, though. We put all of that out together. I want to watch who our snitch goes to first since that's all expensive info the bratva, Cartel, and *Cosa Nostra* are willing to buy. Whoever the informant goes to first is who they're actual loyal to, but they might try the others for more money."

"You gotta narrow down who you want followed here though. We don't have the resources to follow a hundred people who work for us and might be in on this."

No shite, Sherlock. That's why I remind him I'm already on top of that part. "That's why I'm working from oldest to newest at all our businesses. We assume it's anyone and everyone hired within the last couple of months. Then we weed through from that first hire to the most recent."

"That means Molly."

"So?"

"For fuck's sake, Dillan. It'll suck, but at least admit you're into her."

"What's the point?"

Sean rolls his eyes. "The point is to stop lying to me and everyone else when we all see it."

"Overactive imaginations because you obviously don't have enough to do."

"Feck off. We all have plenty to do. But we also know each other as well as we know ourselves. If you weren't into her, then one of us probably would be."

I force myself not to react with anything other than a dismissive one shoulder shrug. "Can we get on with this?"

Chapter Four

Greta

I've got full-blown paranoia. I've got the creeps like someone keeps following me. Like not just right now, so I keep checking over my shoulder. I feel like everywhere I show up, I have eyes on me. It's uncanny, and I don't have a way to explain it. I just sense it. I keep alert to take note of anyone I see in places they don't belong or over and over. But there's no one.

I've been working for the O'Rourkes for a month. The tips are better than I expected, so that makes up for a lot. It doesn't make up for some guys who get too handsy, but I know I can speak to any of the bouncers or the O'Rourkes. I also know Dillan is the one who's dealt with the customers personally. The bouncers or the O'Rourkes at the club get the guy to leave me alone for the night, but Dillan makes sure they never come back. That would freak me out if I hadn't seen a few of the guys come back and try to get in another night.

I'm a good waitress, and I know that. It's part of why some men think they can touch what's not theirs. I smile, I soften my voice, I lean forward. I'm fast and accurate. All the things. It means not only are my tips good, but Shane has given me way more shifts. But he hasn't assigned me to the mezzanine again when Dillan's there. Which fucking sucks. He's there for meetings, and from the ladies who work here, the frequency is unusual.

I've figured out who I can ask, and who I can't. A couple side eyes made me realize I needed to learn how Irish a woman's family is. Those who identify strongly are the ones I avoid. I'm pretty sure their families are way more connected than just through them. The ones who only care about St. Patrick's Day are the ones I eek info from. Like getting fucking water from a rock. And now that I've asked one person three times, I need to be careful that they don't get suspicious.

Being around Dillan is fucking torture. Workwise, it sucks to be so close and not learn more. But personally, I'm around him enough for him to be constant temptation. He's not what I thought he would be. None of the men are. I didn't expect them to be the stereotypes from the movies, but I thought they'd be rougher around the edges under their designer suits. But they're not. They're like the fucking boys next door. They're funny, and they tease one another mercilessly.

It was horrible the first few times I saw how close some women are to Dillan. I thought the first one was his girlfriend and the second his ex. But none of the women have ever dated him. They've known him since they were kids. That helped me figure out who's mob connected beyond just this job. I found out he has a strict policy about not dating any employees at any of his businesses. That's great for my jealous mind. And it shouldn't matter since I'm here to do a job. But I can't help how relieved it makes me. I didn't want to see my unrequited feelings being directed at someone else.

"Hey, Molly."

I wave to Cormac as I walk toward the dressing room where I can stash my stuff. He and Seamus were the biggest surprises. They're like fucking ox in size. You'd assume all they did was lift weights and consume like ten thousand calories a day. I know all the guys work out twice a day, but they're both gentle giants. They're the most courteous of the men, always letting the women pass first. Always careful with their size and strength. They're also wicked smart—said in the New England accent I can imitate after seven years of living in New Hampshire and four years in Boston.

"Hi. Be careful when you go out to your car. I parked next to you, and there's a strip of ice behind yours."

"Are you all right?"

"Yeah. I caught myself, but I thought I'd let you know."

"Danny! Get the salt and shovel. Deal with the parking lot... I don't care that you're eating. Go. Now."

"It's okay. It can wait."

"No, it can't. He's supposed to be keeping an eye on that. And the other girls will arrive soon. We don't need a fecking lawsuit on our hands."

It's cute how none of them will say fuck in front of us. I've also noticed it can be a noun or adjective, but usually not a verb. I've overheard the guys several times saying fuck as a verb. There are other little things too that make all the men—O'Rourke or not —a surprise. The food is fantastic, and we all get a meal with our shift. I prefer to eat early like the bouncers. Some girls don't enjoy hanging upside down with a full stomach. Understandable. But whenever I come over to a table, the guys stand, and one of them pulls out a chair for me. If I'm there first and get up, they'll stand, and someone will push it in for me. Like chivalry isn't dead.

"Is Dillan here yet? I need to speak to him."

"Yeah. Let me get him."

He must be in the office. No one has told me I can go down there except for Dillan himself, and that was once. I put my stuff away and hurry back out just as he steps into the main room. His gaze skims over me like it always does. I wish it made me feel like he wanted me. It's more like he's checking my appearance to make sure I'm up to code for the job.

"Hi. Cormac said you wanted to talk to me."

"I do." I glance around.

His question is immediate. "What happened?"

I blink a couple times rapidly, unprepared for the protectiveness in his voice.

"I keep getting the feeling someone's watching me. Like not just here. Like everywhere I go. It's like a second shadow, but I can't see them. I don't know if I'm making it up, or maybe it's one of the Albanians. Or it could be someone else from here. But I just get the strongest feeling."

"How long has this been going on?"

"Like a week and a half. Almost two."

"You haven't seen someone new show up at more than one place you go to?"

"No. That's why it's so disconcerting. I don't see anyone. I just sense it. Call it intuition. I don't know if you believe in that, but I do."

"I definitely believe in intuition."

Not surprising. It's probably why he's lived to be thirty-three. He's three years older than me. Not a bad age gap since they say men die younger than women— assuming he survives long enough to get old. Not that it should matter to me. It's not like I'm planning a life with him. Daydreaming, maybe. Planning, no.

"I've been ignoring it, but it really freaked me out this morning. It felt closer than ever. I walked out of my building to go to my car. I sensed it and looked around. The building across the street from me has a vacant unit on the third floor. I've considered moving there. The blinds were open like usual. I looked around at the cars and couldn't see anyone in any of them. There was no one unusual on the sidewalk. Just some neighbors I know. When I glanced up at the building again, there was movement at the window in the empty apartment. Like someone hurrying to hide. I know the super, so I texted him before I pulled out of my spot. I asked if the unit was still open because he knows I'm interested. He said it was. I asked if there are viewings, and he said not until next week. It isn't ready. I asked if that meant remodeling. No. The owners are on vacation, so they don't want to deal with bids yet. There shouldn't be anyone up there. I didn't say anything to the guy because I didn't want him going up there to look in case— I don't know. If there was someone, they could be dangerous. Which sounds so vain. Like I'm someone who needs to worry about being stalked."

"Molly, any woman should worry about it. Especially somewhere like New York. Not having him confront someone was a good idea. If you want, I can send one of my guys over to check out the neighborhood, check to see if anyone tampered with the lock."

"They wouldn't have a way to get in. They'd have to have someone buzz them in. Or they'd have to follow someone in."

He says nothing. He just looks at me. I'm supposed to deduce from his silence that neither of those things would be an issue. Wouldn't that basically make them guilty of the exact thing that's scaring the shit out of me— someone broke in and was watching me?

"I can see you don't love that idea. I can make sure you get home safely and see if anyone pulls up right after you. I can also make sure no one's watching you in the morning and following you."

"I don't want to put any of your guys on some boring babysitting job."

He steps closer to me, so we're nearly touching.

"I said *I* can make sure. I didn't say I'd send someone else. I told you to come to *me* if something happened. I did that for a reason. If I caused someone to bother you, then I'll make sure they don't."

"Dillan, it's probably no big—"

"Do not finish that sentence."

The command in his voice is about the sexiest fucking thing I've ever heard. What exists of my flossy g string is soaked. If I bend too far over, someone's bound to see the evidence on the inside of my thighs. Fucking hell. He does this to me any time we're in the same building. But right now. Fuck. My cunt aches for him.

"Yes, Sir."

Oh. Fuck me. And not in the begging sense either. I did *not* mean to say that. I'm not from the South. I'm not even from the Midwest. That's not in my regular speech.

He steps even closer until our shoulders touch.

"Good girl. Don't argue with me because I won't listen. I'll follow you home in my car, and I'll wait for you in my car when you're ready to leave tomorrow. You don't acknowledge I'm there. You act exactly how you normally would. Look around like you usually do, but nothing extra. You will accept my help. Do you understand?"

"Yes, Sir."

It comes out as little more than a whisper. All I want to do is beg now. He leans back and our gazes meet. His deep green eyes to my deep blue ones. Our kids would have amazing eyes. Fucking hell. Not what I need to think about right now. I just let on that I like shit kinky. I just let on that I'm submissive with him. He's seen me assertive plenty of times. He knows I have no problem saying no or disagreeing. I'm not submissive by nature except with certain dominant men— a certain dominant man. I know I wouldn't have said that to Shane, Sean, Cormac, Seamus, or Finn. I met him two weeks ago. He's Shane and Sean's older brother. He and Dillan are two peas in a pod. Best friends. But he does nothing for me. They're all alpha men, but only Dillan makes me want to get down on my knees, cross my wrists behind my back, and open my mouth to suck him off. Now I'm ready to beg fuck me. Please.

He keeps me locked in place with his piercing stare. When his gaze drops for a second, I know it's because he noticed how hard my nipples are. It's not cold enough in here to explain why they're two darts pointing straight at him. In for a penny, in for a pound. I lower my gaze to look at the floor between us.

Wait. Does he— I think he has —is he hard for me? Like I thought the first night: if that's just him limp, then he has a fucking sledgehammer in his pants. Hell. I'd like to know if it's a fucking jackhammer.

"Come to my office when you're ready to go, *cailín*."

I school my features not to react. Little girl. I don't want him to know I speak any Gaelic. Mine might be rusty at times, but I understood that just fine. His pronunciation tells me everything I need to know. I studied the O'Rourkes all the way back to Ireland. They're from County Leitrim, which was in the ancient Connacht kingdom, and they speak that dialect. A powerful clan until the seventeenth century. Not surprising they brought that sense of authority to America and now lead the mob. It's a slower, softer version than I'm used to. My family hails from County Antrim, which, once upon a time, was part of the ancient Ulster kingdom and now the province by the same name in Northern Ireland. Our pronunciation is much more clipped.

I cock an eyebrow as if to ask what that word means. Really, in my mind, I'm challenging him. I might be submissive, but does he think I'm a Little? I most definitely am not. I have friends who are. Some who are Middles. But I'm not into age play. It's not my thing. Is it Dillan's? No. I feel safe and even taken care of by him, but it's not paternal in a way where I feel like— or he thinks —I can't do things for myself. Though, I'd call him Daddy if he bent me over one of these tables and fucked me. Strong, silent type. That's why the term comes to mind. Protector. Provider. The things I guess dads are supposed to be. Not a hold my hand to cross the street or tuck me in with a storybook. Might be some people's jam, but it's not mine, and I don't get the sense it's Dillan's either.

Shit. He's expecting me to respond, and I'm in la-la land.

"Dillan, I truly don't want to inconvenience you. That wasn't part of your plans. I only mentioned it because you told me to tell you if any of the Albanians bothered me. I don't know that it's them. It could all be in my head."

He narrows his eyes at me and raises his chin. He's totally a Dom, and he thinks that's going to make me back down. If we were doing a scene, it would. But I'm not going to my place right after work tonight. I can't have him follow me. I need to dissuade him from this.

"I have other plans. I'm not going straight home."

His entire expression darkens. Now he appears angry. I know he must assume I'm going to a boyfriend's or girlfriend's place. Does that bother him?

"You're going out at four a.m.?"

"Not out. I just have other plans."

Let him simmer on that. I move to step around him, but his hand shoots out and rests on my waist. Scalds my waist.

"Tell me where I should follow you from in the afternoon. I'll only compromise on not following you since you *will not* go to an empty apartment."

Is he assuming I have an apartment? Or did he check my address?

"I'll be leaving my place in the afternoon."

I have a fucked-up sleep schedule now since I work from eight p.m. until four a.m. I sleep half the day away. I cock an eyebrow at him again and stare straight into his eyes.

"You don't need my address, do you?"

His hand tightens at my waist. Fucking presumptuous, as always, considering he thinks I'm going to someone I'm fucking.

"Don't worry. I'll find you."

From someone else, that would be ominous and stalkerish as fuck. It's exciting with him. I rest my hand on his outstretched forearm.

"Thank you. I might not think it's a big enough deal for you to watch out for me personally, but I appreciate it."

"Always."

This shift will never end. It's only one o'clock, and my feet hurt from a guy stepping on my left one and my right one slamming into a chair leg as I tried to avoid getting my other toes smashed. I had to grit my teeth and pray he didn't break any of them. He was drunk and pissed when I cut him off. He stood up and tried to push me. For colossi, I never would have imagined Sean and Cormac could move so fast. The moment the guy raised his voice and stood, they were pushing past people to get to me. Stepping on my foot was the only thing the asshole got to do. He tried to take a swing at Cormac, and he got nailed in the gut instead. Cormac and Sean escorted him out, and Dillan came to check on me. I swore up and down I was fine, so now I have to be. As much as I'd love to put my tennis shoes on, that's not an option if I want to keep blending in and making money.

I recognized a guy who came in about half an hour ago. He would never expect me to work somewhere like this, and I'm keeping my distance. But I know he's looked in my direction. Anything other than heels would stick out too much. I've kept away from the bright lights and kept my back to him as much as possible. That's most of why this night is dragging. I want him gone. I work with him at my actual job, and I don't need him recognizing me and asking questions since he thinks I moved out of state.

I'm keeping an eye on that guy, so I don't notice Dillan when I turn around. Luckily, I have no glasses on my tray because it rams into his stomach before flipping up to smack me in the chest.

"You're limping." It's more of an accusation than a statement.

"I'm fine."

"Then don't limp."

I take a long, slow inhale. My jaw clenches, and I look away for a moment.

"I'll do my best. Sir." That wasn't a slip. That wasn't deference. That was purely snide.

"I'm sorry. I just dealt with someone annoying, and I snapped at you. Are you all right? You can take your break and ice your toes if you want."

I won't cut off my nose to spite my face. "Thank you. That's a good idea. I'll grab some ice and go in the back."

"Go in the back, and I'll bring you the ice. The reason to do it is to get you off your feet, not take more steps."

I nod and put my tray on the bar as I pass it. The dressing room is noisy since there are plenty of girls rotating through their performances. I step to the side, so I'm not in the way.

Stacey and Diana are waitresses on their break. They're sitting together at a table at the far end, eating dinner. Once I get my ice, I'll join them. Maureen, one of the strippers, looks at me, and it's not friendly. She doesn't like me, and I don't know why. I'm polite, but I've barely spoken to her. I turn away when I hear a knock. When I open it, Dillan is standing, so he can't see into the mirrors.

"Take as long as you need. Even if it's more than fifteen minutes."

"I can't. The others—"

"Don't own this club. You have a nasty habit of acting like you don't need anyone or anything. Like you don't merit things you do. Take the ice, *cailín*. For once, don't argue."

I didn't argue the two times I called him Sir, and they were genuine. I didn't think I argued at all.

"Thank you, Dil— Sir."

He hands me the ice and drops his voice, so I have to lean forward to hear him.

"You let it slip the first time. It felt right the second time. And you mocked me the third time. You don't owe me your submission when I do things for you. It's not why I do it."

"I know. But I was insincere the last time, and I wish I hadn't been. You're being super nice to me. I didn't need to be a bitch. I'm sorry."

"Come to my office when you're ready to go."

"I will." I hold up the ice. "Thanks."

I step back and close the door. When I turn around, half the women are looking at me. Maureen looks like she's ready to bludgeon me with the heels she's holding. I lift the bag of ice and shake it for them to see.

"Some asshole practically broke my toes."

No one relaxes. This is awkward as fuck. I take four steps to cross the room, and Maureen steps in front of me.

"He won't fuck you, you know."

"I didn't think he would." Though I wish he would. I would say yes if he offered. But I have lines I won't cross, and sleeping with a guy to get information is one of them.

"I've seen you. You're a fucking bitch in heat around him." Maureen steps toward me, practically in my face. But I don't react. Instead, I take a step around her. Her hand flies out and grabs my hair. "Fucking cunt."

"If I'm a fucking cunt, that means I'm getting laid. I know no one's been sniffing around you. If I'm a dog in heat, and he's coming to me— I don't know what to tell you other than get your motherfucking hands off me."

I grab her wrist and try to pry her fingers from my hair. She yanks, and her nails on the other hand leave streaks down my right arm.

"Let go."

I give her to a silent count of three before I react. I twist and yank her arm up while pushing against the outside of her elbow. She releases me, and I shove her hard. She slams into the shelf table connected to the wall-length mirror. Shit goes flying.

"Don't touch me, Maureen. I don't give a fuck whether you like me. Touch me again, and I will make it hurt."

She spins and lunges for me. Good. I'm pissed, and she took the bait. I know not to do anything to her face. Nothing that'll leave bruises. If I'm the reason she can't work, I'll be the one who gets fired. She's the hottest woman here. I put both hands on her chest and shove her again. She's tall, so it's her ass that slams into the table this time. I kick off my shoes. I won't win this fight wobbling. Fucking hell, my toes hurt. I dropped the ice. Damn it.

When she lunges again, I snatch the arm I already bent the wrong way. I twist and take her down to her knees as I leverage the arm behind her back and up.

"This is a position you should be used to. I've seen those callouses on your knees."

I bend her arm so I can use it to push her forward. She's trying to fight me, but she underestimated my strength. Heidi just darted behind me to the door. Let her get a bouncer. I don't even give a shit if they all lie. My hair was up and styled. Now it's a mess. That'll tell the story.

I force her head to the floor, her face turned away from me. I kick her legs out from under her and follow her down. My right forearm goes across her neck as I keep pressing her arm in the wrong direction. My left elbow goes where her shoulder blade sticks up. I put a good portion of my weight into it.

The door flies open, but I don't look up. I don't look over. I know it's Dillan without seeing him. Two other guys are with him, but I know Dillan's in the lead.

"What the ever-loving fuck?"

He roars as he storms over to me. His hands go to my waist, and he lifts me up. I release Maureen immediately. Though the idea of kicking her is so appealing. He backs me toward the wall, his body shielding me from everyone else. He tugs my top into place. I didn't even realize I was having a Janet Jackson moment.

"She attacked me!"

Maureen's squawking like an angry goose. My gaze meets Dillan's. I'm certain he's silently telling me not to speak. He whispers to me instead.

"Are you all right? Did she hurt you?"

I whisper back to him, my lips barely moving. "I'm fine."

He looks at my hair, and I can only imagine the mess it's in now. His hand moves at his side as though he was going to lift it, but he lets it drop. Was he going to straighten it?

"Stay here. Say nothing."

I dip my chin.

"Mo, shut up. You were a whiney kid, and you're being a whiney bitch now. I've warned you about not being nice. This isn't the first fight you've picked. It's just the first one your opponent didn't back down from. I already know you started it. I have no problem that Molly finished it. Get your shite and go. You were already on probation. Now you're fired."

"But that cunt—"

Shane steps in front of her. "Finish that sentence, and not only are you fired, but I will wake your grandfather up and tell him just what you said and did."

The woman's eyes widen to saucers. She darts her gaze to me, then Dillan, then back to Shane. She nods and tries to push her hair back from her face. When Dillan steps away from me to stand next to Finn, Maureen shoots me a look that says this isn't over. Shane grabs her coat from the chair where she picked up her bag and shakes it at her.

"For that, I'm still going to visit him, but I'll wait until noon. That'll give you time to let him know why I'll be paying him a visit. Stay the hell away from Molly."

Maureen puts her coat on and pushes all her makeup and shit into her bag. When she's ready to go, she walks up to Dillan. "I may be a stripper, but she's a whore. We all know you're fucking her. You don't date your employees, and you rarely fuck them. But you pay her, and you're fucking her. Serving drinks doesn't make her any less a slut."

"Jealousy isn't a good look on you, Mo. Just because we passed you around in high school doesn't mean any of us still want you."

It's my turn to have my eyes widen. I can't believe Finn just said that. I look in the mirror to see the women at the other end of the room. Not a one looks surprised. I look at Dillan, and he's unfazed by his cousin's comment. I look at Seamus, who shifts his attention to me. He shrugs.

"Cocksucker." She hurls the word at Finn, but his cousins burst into laughter. It's Dillan who responds.

"Hardly."

Finn's gorgeous. The one who's so hot it's too good to be true. I've seen women come into the club with guys. They completely ignore the show on stage and forget the guy they're with. I've seen at least half of them approach him. I know that means nothing. But I also know he and Heidi are fuck buddies and have been for years. She's in an open throuple, so when the mood strikes, Finn and Heidi bang. I know the chick from that arrangement joins them sometimes, but the guy never does. If neither Finn nor Heidi wants it, then they don't. It's no secret.

What he does with people away from the club is anyone's guess. The women talk, and none of them know. He's the only one they even know a hint about when it comes to the O'Rourkes' sex lives. The others are a mystery. And that's why Maureen got pissed. She wants Dillan, and to think that not only does he want someone, but he might let people know, was too much for her.

"Fuck you, fuck you, fuck you, and fuck you, you cunt." She points at Shane, Finn, Dillan, and finally me.

"According to you, I don't need to. I already have someone else." I should have kept my mouth shut. I shouldn't have said anything. But she's the cunt.

Shane doesn't manhandle her, but he gets her out of the dressing room, and I know he'll make sure she leaves the property. Finn goes to talk to the other women. Each dancer has a three-song rotation. The next ones up need to get out there. Diana walks over and start straightening up the shit that went flying.

"Dee, I'll do that. Thank you though. You didn't cause the mess. I did."

"No, you didn't. Mo did. They should have made her clean

it up. She's been like this since we were kids. She never had to put anything away. Her mom always did everything for her. My mom would make me clean up after both of us."

"You've known her that long?"

"She's my cousin."

I wince. "I'm sorry."

"Don't be. I can't stand her. I got her the job here, and I've regretted it since the day I suggested her."

I lower my voice because I know Dillan can hear me otherwise. "What Finn said. Is it true? Did they all…?"

"Yeah. She's a slut. I'm all for women freely fucking whoever they want and as many people as they want. But she didn't care if any of them had girlfriends when she offered to suck their dicks. As far as I know, none of them ever cheated. But when they were single, they mingled with her. She thought she'd get one of them— Dillan mostly —to commit. Fucking joke. What guy wants to put a ring on the finger of a woman who's fucked his entire family? Besides, Dillan isn't the commitment type."

She gives me a speaking look. A friendly warning? I nod. The dressing room clears out, and I think Finn is keeping the girls coming off stage out of here. The moment we're alone, Dillan wraps his arm around me and pulls me back to his chest. We look at each other in the mirror. He pulls the clip out of my hair, and it falls down around my shoulders. I'd have to redo it, anyway. He hands it to me before his fingers skim up my arm, feathering over the scratches Maureen left.

"Tell me what happened, *cailín*. One moment I'm handing you ice. The next, Heidi's running to Finn, telling him Mo attacked you, but you were likely to break her arm off."

"That's exactly what happened. It pisses her off that you paid attention to me and did something nice. She said you'd never fuck me, but I'm a bitch in heat. I don't remember what else we said. She grabbed my hair and pulled while she scratched me. I told her to let go like twice. When she didn't, I broke her hold and shoved her. When she came back for me, I got her down on her knees, said something about them already being calloused, then got her flat on the floor until you and your cousins came. You made me let go."

He kisses my shoulder and up my neck. He pulls the hair away, so he can kiss up to behind my ear. "I thought it pissed me off when men get too handsy. If she'd been a guy... She's lucky Finn's handling it."

"I'm all right. I promise."

I lean back against him, though. He can tell how hard my nipples are again. They've gotten that way while he's held me. We can both see it in the mirror. I can feel how hard he's grown while standing behind me. I twist to turn in his arms. I rest my hands on his biceps. Even through his suit coat, I can feel the solid muscles bulging.

"Will people think we're screwing now that Maureen's said that?"

"No." He kisses my neck again. "They know I don't feck employees."

I lean back. What the hell is going on between us? Is he going to break that rule? Is he going to fire me so we can feck? I guess it can be a verb. I can't lose this job right now. And I don't want to get the information because we're fucking. I won't whore myself out that way, even if no one is telling me to.

"It won't go beyond this right now, Greta. I just want to know you're okay. I had no idea what I was going to walk in on. I couldn't get to you fast enough."

"Greta?"

"You're not a Molly. That makes me think of a young girl. Someone still living to have a good time. Someone I don't take as seriously as I do you. Margaret. Greta. It makes sense to me."

"No one has ever called me that."

"I know your real name is Mairghráid. Greta. I still think it fits."

He looked at my ID photo or my tax form. Fuck.

"*An labhraíonn tú Gàidhlig?*" Do you speak Gaelic?

Shit. I won't— can't —lie.

"*Tá.*" Yes. "But I rarely do anymore. I'm rusty with anything more than casual conversation. My granny has dementia. Sometimes she forgets English, so I have to use Gaelic for her to understand. She didn't learn English until she went to school. It's always come more naturally to her."

Why am I over sharing? Maybe to distract from the fact he now knows I've understood conversations he thought I didn't.

"*Ba chóir duit a bheith ráite liom.*" You should have told me.

He releases me. Not because he's angry. At least, he doesn't seem that way. It's because we can hear voices just outside the room. I grab the ice off the table as I speak.

"It didn't come up. I figured when you were speaking it, you didn't want people listening. So, I made sure I didn't stand too close."

He nods and heads to the door as it opens. Then he's gone.

I have the ears of a dog, so I still heard plenty. That's why I can't have him follow me tonight. It'll mess everything up.

Chapter Five

Dillan

Fecking hell.

What a fecking night. I'm in my office with a whiskey I'm nursing. My head hurts. I tilt it back and close my eyes. It took so much restraint tonight. Restraint not to beat the shite out of the guy who was about to shove Greta— God, that name suits her so much more. Restraint not to pick her up and carry her in here to take care of her toes. Restraint not to lose my shite on Maureen for touching her. Restraint not to carry her in here and take care of her scratches. Restraint not to fuck her where anyone could have walked in on us. Restraint not to ask her out. And most of all, it took restraint not to demand an explanation for why she never mentioned she speaks Gaelic when she's heard us use it plenty of times. She knows shite now.

I trusted her. I trust her. I— I don't fucking know. I pick up the glass and swirl the amber liquid. It could mean nothing at all that she overheard conversations no one outside the family should hear. Maybe she won't do a damn thing with that information. Or maybe she'll turn it over to the feds. Or maybe she's the leak that led to that upcoming newspaper article.

We've said nothing out on the floor we can't afford people understanding. Some of our dancers and bouncers speak enough Gaelic to repeat it to someone who does. That's part of the test. None of the guys who work here are privy to the important shite, so I don't fear what might get passed on.

But I can't get over seeing her that first night standing in the hallway right outside this door with her phone. Was she recording what she could hear?

All the signs lead to the bratva. Whoever our leak is, they're giving them the information. We think they're letting some of it trickle down to the Mancinellis and the Diazes, which is fine. The shite she's heard in English was what we meant for our spy or leak to share. Even the things said in Gaelic weren't shite that can take us down for good. It would just be a monumental inconvenience if she ran to the cops or feds. However, I've said incriminating things in here, thinking it was private. Nothing that could ruin us, but things that could make life complicated with the other syndicates and law enforcement.

This is why no one comes down this hallway unless they're one of my cousins, or one of us invites them. We only invite non-Gaelic speakers for this reason. I wouldn't have told her to meet me here that night or tonight if I'd known.

I chug a huge gulp that burns all the way to my belly. I was not at my finest tonight. She's becoming a distraction I can't afford. And if she's recording my conversations or just listening in, then she's becoming a liability. There's no chance I'm not following her tonight. I just pray I'm wrong.

Please, please, fucking please, don't let her be into shite that could fuck us all over.

I mull things over and over until there's a knock on the door. It's her. My relatives wouldn't knock. I take the last swig and put the glass down. I make sure the cap's on tight before I put the bottle in the desk drawer. I'll deal with Shane later when he bitches about me dipping into his good stuff. I bought the shite for him as a Christmas gift. I put my suit coat back on as I walk to the door. When I open it, she's looking straight ahead. That means she's staring at my undone tie hanging out of my lapel pocket and my shirt that's unbuttoned at the neck.

"I'm headed out now. I wanted to check in like you told me to, but I don't need anyone following me. I don't want anyone following me."

I stare at her before nodding. But it's more like my head moving back and forth, rather than my chin going up and down. I don't know what to make of her now.

"Are you pissed I didn't tell you I speak Gaelic?" She just puts it out there.

"It would have been decent to tell us since you know we speak it to keep conversations private."

"I didn't listen to them."

I narrow my eyes at her. "You might be a good liar to everyone else. You listened."

"I caught bits here and there. I speak it, but I'm not fluent."

"You speak it well enough."

"Are you going to accuse me of something, Dillan? If not, I want to go. The ice helped—thank you. But my feet still hurt, even in my sneakers."

"Did you know who we are before you came to work here?"

"Yes."

I believe her.

"But you came anyway."

"The money's too good to ignore this place. What you do on your own time is your business."

"But you made it yours when you listened to conversations you weren't meant to understand."

"Dillan, anything I heard was in passing. It's not like I stood around taking notes."

Notes. That reminds me of the video of her.

"Maybe you weren't typing them, but you might have been recording them. I saw you with your phone before you knocked the last time you waited outside my door."

I see the cords in her neck flex for a second. She's worried I know.

"I checked something on my phone, then knocked. I put it away before you answered the door, so I wouldn't be rude."

Sure.

"Something's come up. Finn's going to make sure you get wherever you need to be. I'll be at your place when you're ready to leave. What time will that be?"

She hesitates. Is she pissed I'm handing her off? I'm not. I'm definitely following her, but I don't want her to know that.

"Like six. I always leave enough time for traffic."

She lives in Harlem, but the club is in Brooklyn. She could take the subway, but I'm glad she doesn't. The women who work here know we'll always pay for a ride share or send them in one of our town cars before letting them ride the subway at four in the morning. It's not the getting here part we worry about.

"I'll be in the silver Mercedes."

She nods, then waits for me to say something. I know getting the cold shoulder from me is disconcerting her. Part of me is pissed and hurt, but part of me wants to confuse her into thinking she's pissed me off enough that I've now written her off.

"Okay. I'm going to find Finn and see if we can go. Goodnight, Dillan."

"Night, Greta."

She stares for a moment, but I do nothing more. That

confuses her again. Good. I watch her leave. I get my phone out and wait for the text. She and Finn are in their cars. I have my coat on already. I walk to the door and watch them both pull out. I hurry to my car, which I already turned on. No snow or ice to scrape tonight. I keep Finn's Mustang— sorry, Saleen —in sight. He's quick to remind me it's a special edition Mustang. Even more special than the Saleens you can buy off a Ford showroom floor.

He doesn't have any aftermarket special features the rest of us don't. My Mercedes is the same. We all get a lot of shite customized. Our headlights don't flash when we lock or unlock the door. The horn doesn't beep when we lock it. We have sensors that keep the dome light off if there's a car bomb. Bulletproof glass for every window. Reinforced undercarriage. Tires that still roll even if they're punctured. None of our personal cars are the beasts we've made our SUVs. Fortunately, we've never needed them to be. But we're not as easy targets as most would believe.

Since I told Greta I drive a silver Mercedes, I stay two cars behind Finn. I know she can't see me in her mirrors. Since Finn knows I'm following, he'll make sure I don't lose them. The streets are pretty quiet, so it's easy to keep close while staying incognito. We leave Brooklyn and head into Harlem. I don't know this area well, but it's neither bad nor good. It's safe enough. I slow down as I see her pull into a parking spot. Finn pulls up alongside her for a moment. He'll watch her go into whichever walkup she's headed to. She turns on the stoop and waves goodbye. I circle the block once to make sure she doesn't wonder why there's a car idling half a block down. I find a spot where I can watch the building.

She's only in there for fifteen minutes. I watch her get back into her car. I know where she lives, so I'll follow her once I know who's in there with her. Another fifteen minutes later, the door opens again. And that's when shite goes sideways. Motherfucking fucktastrophe.

Sergei and Anton.

It's the bratva, and she's the spy.

It's a gut punch. I knew it was possible. I knew it was even likely, despite denying it. She got the job just to get information on us. How'd she get connected with those two? I know she's not fucking either of them. They've been together since high school. That's a secret I've told no one. If either of them is going to die, it's going to be from being bratva, not from being gay. I couldn't give two shites, but I won't be the one who sends them to the grave because their old guard finds out. I'll only do it if they hurt someone in my family, or it's better for business to have them gone even if it upsets the tenuous balance the underworld has.

I'm not ready to confront them, so I lean toward the passenger seat to ensure they don't see me. They get into Sergei's car, and I should have recognized it. We drive the same fucking model, except his is midnight blue. I wait five minutes before pulling out. It's tight, but I do a three-point turn and head the wrong way on a one-way street. No one's around. I know they'll be looking for someone following them.

This tempts me to put a tracker on Greta's phone and car, but I won't. If we ever got together, I would in a heartbeat. I would insist upon it for her safety. But part of the reason none of us date is the danger it would bring to the person we care about. As much as the Mancinellis fucked shite up, my dead cousins are as much to blame for women now being targets. Women and children used to be strictly off limits. Untouchable. But my predecessors, Donovan— my mom's brother —and Declan— my mom's cousin through her dad —fucked it all up when they each went after a bratva wife. I warned them.

The other reason we don't get involved is because we have

nothing to talk about beyond the banalities. We can't even discuss our day with someone.

How did your day go?

Okay.

What did you do?

Stuff.

Like?

Silence.

I can't say, oh, ya know. Blew some shite up. Beat the snot out of someone. Turned them into acidic sludge or ash that's now in the Hudson. Embezzled a few million. Sold a few kilos. Funded some pirates to steal in international waters. Just a typical day at the office, honey.

I'm not interested in any of the girls from the block. I don't need a father-in-law telling me how to run things like they did back in his day or trying to climb the ladder because I put a ring on it. I don't need a meddling mother-in-law who wants us over for every. Single. Fecking. Sunday dinner. I've known them all my entire life. I either wasn't interested. Ever. Or I fucked them in high school and moved on. I'm not a man whore, so not that many. Even back then, I knew I'd wind up where I am now. We all knew where we'd wind up, so none of the guys in my family diddled too many girls in high school. No one wanted expectations or bitterness once we stepped into our roles.

So, besides the fact Greta *worked* for me and turned out to be a spy, I can't bring her into this life. She might know we're mobsters, or just mob affiliated at best, but that doesn't mean she needs to get sucked in further. I have to fire her. I'm not turning her into some fecking double agent. If she's loyal to the Ivankov bratva, she wouldn't switch sides, anyway. But I feel played. Like a fecking idiot.

It doesn't take me long to get to her place since it's in Harlem too. My windows are tinted, and I rotate my tags. Most of the time, I make sure I do nothing to draw attention from the cops. I don't need them running my plates. But it keeps it harder for the other syndicates to recognize my car. I also have three other ones I drive to make me less obvious. When I get to the street corner, I look toward her place. It was one of my guys she saw in the window yesterday. I need to deal with him and his lack of skills.

I see two bratva cars. One near me, and one at the other end of the block. I don't know if they're always there, or if it's just because she had a meeting with Sergei and Anton. They might be making sure she got home safely, or they could be waiting for someone like me to visit. I already drove past the back of her building. There's a fence I'll have to jump. Wouldn't be my first or my last. I reverse until I can turn down another side street and park two blocks away. It's getting close to dawn, so I need to hurry before people walk their dogs.

While I waited for her to leave her meeting, I changed into jeans and a sweater. I had a regular coat in the car rather than the trench coat I wear over my suits. Not easy at my size to maneuver in the front seat, but I got it done. I slip out of my car, pull my sweater down in the back to be sure it'll hide my gun if I take my coat off, and zip it. I walk briskly, but not enough to make anyone wonder.

I'm over the fence without a sound, and it's way too easy to pick the lock to the back door. I know she has a unit facing the back, so that's convenient. None of her lights are on, and I doubt she got ready for bed that fast. Did I beat her here? I get to her door and knock. It dawns on me I don't know if she has a roommate. I don't think so, but she could. I didn't check the buzzer since I didn't come in through the front. I should have checked the mailboxes.

When no one answers, I jiggle the doorknob. Locked. I can't make too much noise, or someone will hear. I'm fucking tempted to go in and wait in the dark. Scare the fuck out of her like some thriller movie when she flips on the light. That's too much. She would never forgive me. And despite what the evidence shows, that matters to me.

She felt so fucking right in my arms tonight. I indulged and kissed her shoulder and neck. I didn't give in to my desire to kiss her mouth. But when Heidi came running for Finn, saying Mo attacked Greta, I couldn't get there fast enough. I've known Mo since we were toddlers. She was a fucking biter back then. She's vicious in a girl fight. I've seen her as recently as six months ago. She provoked that woman but didn't make the first move. She made it appear like self-defense. It wasn't.

Mo was looking to beat the shite out of the woman for stealing Mo's four best lap dance customers. She was losing a few hundred a night because of Tanya. She figured, since Tanya wasn't Irish and Mo is, we'd side with her. She wound up on probation, and Tanya asked to go to another strip club. Maureen Spinosa is not as Irish as she claims. She hasn't had family there in nearly six generations. But her mom's family remains connected, so she thinks she's a genuine member of our community. Just barely.

I don't have long to wait before I hear footsteps on the stairs. I lean against the door jamb, my arms crossed, my left ankle over my right shin. Arrogantly and patronizingly calm. She's looking down, watching where she steps, so she doesn't see me. When she looks up, she lurches backwards. I'm fast. Thank God. I grab her before she tumbles down the stairs.

"What the fuck are you doing here, Dillan?"

"By the end of our conversation, you'll be calling me Sir. And it won't be because I'm fucking you."

The way I want her is definitely fucking. Forget the niceties. She pushes against me, and I let go as soon as she's closer to her door than the edge of the landing. She stares at me.

"Let me in, Mairghráid. Or I'll let myself in. You do not want to have this chitchat out here."

"Don't call me that."

"Your name? I hate the name Margaret. No one under the age of seventy should be named Margaret. My great-aunt on my dad's side had that name, and she was hideous. Cruel. So no, I will not call you that. And I'm pretty pissed right now, so no, I won't call you Greta, either. Open the damn door."

"No. Leave. I'll call the police."

I laugh. It's quiet, but she hears me. I turn my lips down in a mocking flash of a frown while I shrug. *Go ahead.* I'm daring her. She knows it'll do no good. They might come. Then they'll take one look at me or my ID and find a reason to leave. Irish Americans still make up a huge part of the NYPD. Even if they aren't on our payroll, they know us too well to make this the hill they want to die on.

"Dillan, I'm serious. Go. I don't want to talk to you. And you shouldn't be here."

"And you shouldn't have gone straight from work to the bratva. You will explain."

"I owe you nothing. I don't have to explain a damn thing."

"You're so very wrong about that, *cailín*. You're going to explain it all." I might speak more quietly, but the command is far louder than anything I've said so far.

"Do you think this is when I'll call you Sir?" She fishes around in her purse.

"You won't mace me or pepper spray me. I'll have it out of your hand before you can do anything. But I will hurt you in the process, and that's not acceptable to me."

"Then leave."

It's my turn to reach for something. I pull the lock picking set from my back pocket. I brush past her and have her door unlocked far faster that anyone should see. I open the door and feel around for the light switch. She doesn't want to cross the threshold. I roll my eyes, step back into the hallway, wrap my arm around her waist, pick her up, step backwards into the apartment, then close and lock the door.

"You have no right—"

Our stare is intense. Then we're closing our eyes as our mouths smash together. Not the most elegant start, but neither of us cares. Her coat is a three-quarter length, so I unzip it without breaking the kiss, then slide my hands beneath it. I grab her arse and squeeze. Hard. Her hips tilt forward to press her pussy against my cock. I pin her to the door as I yank her coat down her arms. She's struggling with my coat zipper, then she's pushing it off my shoulders. We let them drop to the floor before I snag her wrists and pin them over her head with one hand as the other rests at the base of her throat. I press my left leg between hers, and she moans. She undulates her hips, and her cunt is touching me, but not the part of me I want her to ride. I let go of her throat to grab her arse again. We have to come up for air.

"That's been building since the night we met. I didn't kiss you because I expect you to explain yourself. That hasn't changed. I kissed you because I want to devour all of you. I want to fuck you into next week. I want to know every kinky fantasy you've ever had and fuck you every way you can imagine."

"And I'm not telling you a damn thing because it's none of your business. But I kissed you because you make me wet just thinking about you. Because my pussy aches every time I see you. I want to lick and suck you off until your eyes roll back into your head, and my name is the only one you know. I want to feel you inside me as I come on your cock, which I know proves size matters."

I chuckle. It's a deep and controlled sound. She rubs

against me, and I pull her tighter. Then I pick her up, and she wraps her legs around me. I'm careful that she keeps them low enough over my arse not to touch my gun. I walk with her to the sofa and sit down.

"Those men you met with are dangerous, Greta. They won't harm you, and their men won't either. That's the only thing I can say for them. But whatever you're into is inviting trouble you can't imagine. It's risking your life for something that can't possibly be worth it."

"And I don't believe you'll hurt me or let any of your men do it, either. I know you have the power to decide. But it's none of your business, and I won't give in to your coercion. No matter how tempting you make it."

"I told you I didn't kiss you to make you explain. That's why we're sitting and talking."

"I'm sitting on your lap with my pussy pressed against your dick."

"Do you want to get off?"

I cock an eyebrow, meaning the double entendre. She narrows her eyes at me. We both know the answer is no to only one interpretation.

"Dillan, I want you. You've known that all along, and I proved it just now. Thank you for the kiss. Now you should go."

She says that, but she doesn't get up. My hands on her hips tug her closer until she leans forward. Then we're kissing again. I shouldn't be doing this. If she's selling our secrets, I shouldn't be touching her. Enjoying her. I shouldn't be telling myself this is okay, even if she's betrayed my family and me. I'm not reasoning that it's okay because I'll eventually get info from her. I'm praying I don't. I don't want to give this up now that I know how she feels, how she tastes. My hands slide down her yoga pants until I can cup her bare skin. I groan. I can't help it. Her curves are generous, and I love it. There's plenty for me to hold and touch. My hands skim over all of her arse and hips. Then I dig into her flesh and guide her to dry hump me.

I pull one hand free and snag her wrist. I move it behind her back, and the other follows on its own. My hand slides up her back and tugs the string to her bikini top loose. When I cup her tits, moving my hand from side to side, I nearly come.

"Fuck, Greta. Why do you have to feel so good?"

I shouldn't have said that out loud. It's a rhetorical, tragic question. She's the definition of the forbidden fruit. When she whips her sweatshirt over her head, pulls the string loose around her neck, and puts her hands behind her back, I dive in. I knead one breast while I suck the other. She moves her hips in a way that makes me think she could be one of the dancers. But I'd fucking massacre our customers if any of them saw her doing this.

"Why do you feel so perfect, Sir?"

Neither of us pauses when she says that. Just the opposite. I fist her hair and dig my fingers into her ample arse. I'll leave marks, and that's exactly what I want. When she looks in the mirror, she'll know she was mine for at least tonight. But I let go before I can make them deep bruises. Instead, I slide my hand around her waist and down the front of her thong.

"Fuck, Dillan... Yes."

My fingers slide between her pussy lips, but the moment she consents, I press three into her. She's riding them and my jeans covered cock. I want her naked and wet against my bare dick. I want to feel with more than just my hand how wet I make her. My thumb finds her clit, and I rub slow circles.

I don't just fuck anyone at my BDSM club. I don't have any monogamous arrangements with a sub. I have four women I've been with during my membership. Two are now in committed relationships. One's married to her Dom, and the other has a contract with hers. I see the other two pretty much weekly, but if I don't show, I don't show. I've been with other women— Mo, obviously —so I may not be a man whore, but I know what I'm doing to get Greta off.

"Dillan, please."

"Please what?"

"Please, Sir."

"What do you want, *cailín*?"

"Harder, Sir."

I oblige, but I move even slower. She whimpers and tries to rock her hips faster. I don't move. Her whimper is louder, more frustrated. She clutches my sweater at my shoulders, and her head falls forward.

"Who decides?"

"You, Sir. But please. Seriously, Dillan. I ache so much it's a burn. I need this. I need you."

"Shh, *mo cailín*." My little girl.

Those aren't two words I just fling around. I've never called any woman little girl before, and definitely not with any sense of possession. I stroke the inside of her pussy, finding her g spot as I rub her clit. My thumb moves harder and faster. She's rocking against me until she's not. Her inner muscles contract around my fingers as she rises on her knees. She grabs my wrist to stop me.

"Greta?"

"I've never had that sensation before. I think I was about to squirt. This isn't the time or place for that."

"Have you done that before?"

"No."

I stand and carry her through the kitchen to the bedroom. As we walk past the stove, I grab the hand towel. When we get to the bed, I lie her down. I tug off her sneakers and socks, then pull down her pants and panties. She doesn't fight me when I press her feet onto the mattress. She lifts her hips so I can put the towel beneath her. Then I'm kneeling between her legs. I kiss along the smooth skin of her inner thigh. I can't get enough of them. I love that they're not skinny. I love that there's plenty for me to kiss, nip, lick, touch. All of it.

Then I lick her cunt. She grabs handfuls of the comforter. She tries to lift her hips to me, but I press down on her lower belly. I slide the three fingers back into her, back to the spot they were before. I suck her clit as I work her g spot and press against it from the outside.

"Fuck, Dillan. It's— it's —intense. Like— Oh!"

I lean back. The hand on her belly lifts the towel while the one inside her keeps working her. I've never made a woman squirt before. I've been curious and tried. When it stops, I latch onto her clit again and flick it with my tongue. Over and over and over. My thumb rubs the spot just below it. She squirms, and her hips rock again. Her thighs tighten against my ears as she strains for more. I rub everything harder and faster as I draw her clit as deep into my mouth as I can.

"May I come, Sir?"

I make a sound of approval, not letting go of her.

"Dillan!"

It's more a sob than a cry of ecstasy. I don't pull my fingers out, but I stand and lean over her. I slide my free hand under her back and pull her against me. I kiss along her neck as I continue to finger her.

"*Tá tú agam, a chailín.*" I have you, little girl.

"*Ná lig dul.*" Don't let go.

Her Gaelic is perfect. It's a northern accent, unlike mine. Antrim, Derry, Down, Tyrone, and two others I can't remember. One of those counties. Less than one percent of Americans speak Irish Gaelic. She sounds like a native speaker. She doesn't just use it sometimes with her granny.

"*Cad atá uait?*" What do you want?

"*Cibé rud a thabharfaidh tú dom, a dhuine uasail. Le do thoil.*" Whatever you'll give me, Sir. Please.

I'm not testing her. It's just natural to switch. Her eyes are closed as she pants. I don't know that she's even noticed we're not speaking English anymore.

I keep rubbing her clit as I kiss her. When she tries to wrap her legs around my lower back, I have the presence of mind to scoot back. I suck on her tits instead, so she wraps her legs around the middle of my back. When she comes again, her heels dig into me.

"You didn't ask."

"*Tá brón orm, a dhuine uasail.*" I'm sorry, Sir.

I switched back, but she kept going in Gaelic. The more she says, the more obvious she's fluent. She said conversationally fluent. Okay. Maybe she couldn't write a dissertation in it, but she can do more than just follow along. It's a bucket of ice on me. I stand, pulling her legs from around me. Her eyes flutter open. Her cheeks are flushed, and she's trying to clear her vision. She looks thoroughly well fucked, even if it didn't get that far. She's exquisite.

And she's a spy.

I don't have it in me to go another round of my demands and her refusal. I know I could ask nicely. I could have done that from the start. But it wouldn't have gotten me any further than my more commanding approach. She's staying tightlipped. At least about her secrets. God. I want to kiss her again. As she sits up, I snag her wrists behind her back— I love them there, but I can't afford her finding my gun —then I fist her hair. My kiss is angry and possessive. Why the fuck does she have to be deceitful?

I nip at her lip, tugging it until it must hurt. Then my tongue invades her mouth. She's taking my kiss. She's not leading. She's not even holding her own. But when she sucks my tongue, it takes all my resolve not to strip naked and fuck her until she can't think of anything but my name as she begs for more. Fuck her until she's sore for the next week. Each step reminding her she's mine.

And that's what she should be. But she can't because she's a fecking spy.

Chapter Six

Greta

"You're fired. Don't come back."

My brow furrows. What? After what we just did, that's what he says to me. Not you're fired and now we can fuck. The tone definitely doesn't invite more of this.

"Dillan?"

"Your Irish is too good to just speak it once in a while with your grandmother. You met with two Russians basically in the middle of the night. You won't tell me why when you know who I am. I want you more than any woman I've ever met. Ever seen. But I don't trust you. That means I want you nowhere near my family or my businesses. Don't come back, Greta."

I can't stop staring. I shiver as all the heat we generated seeps from my body. He definitely didn't do that to coerce information from me. He's not giving me ultimatums. As he straightens his sweater and runs his hand through his hair, I don't think he's waiting for me to volunteer or beg. He's done.

I can't move as he watches me. He curls his lip in disgust

and turns around. His long stride carries him back to the living room. I'm freezing after feeling like I was sweltering. Do I go after him? I can apologize, but for what? I'm sorry I fell for him? I'm sorry I'm not who he expects? I'm sorry this can't go anywhere? Those are things I can and would apologize for. But he wants me to apologize for keeping secrets. I won't do that because I'm not sorry. When he gets to the living room, he looks back at me. He picks up my sweatshirt and bikini top and puts them on the sofa.

I grab my robe and wrap it around me. I follow him as he gets to the door. He picks up my coat and hangs it on the rack. He slips his on with his back to me. He opens the door and half steps through. He turns to look at me, and the anguish is practically palpable. I can't stop the tears that stream down my cheeks. Even if I would tell him what I'm doing, this has no future. It's a happy memory that turns sour at the end. He locks the doorknob— still protecting me —before he pulls the door shut. I hurry to it and look through the spyhole as I flip the deadbolt and slide the chain. He's still outside my door, but the moment he hears the lock, he walks to the stairs. Then he's gone.

I cried myself to sleep last night. No sobs. I was too numb. Just a constant trail of tears. I had to put in twice as many antihistamine drops as I should to stop my eyes from looking so bloodshot. Ice under each eye got rid of the puffiness. I pulled my shit together for my first day back in the office. I dump my stuff at my desk and go straight to my editor's door. It's open, so I don't have to knock.

"Molly, I didn't expect you back so soon. You got everything already? You told me you'd need at least two months."

"I got caught. None of them knows what I know or where I work. But one of them followed me last night and saw me come out of a meeting with my CIs."

When I pitched the story to the editor-in-chief of the biggest newspaper in New York, he turned his nose up at a story about the mob. He said people have been over them since the 90s. I reminded him, if it bleeds, it leads. He still wasn't convinced. I went down the ladder to the National Desk editor. My direct supervisor. I got further into my proposal than I did with the big boss. I told him I had two reliable CIs.

Of course, he asked who my confidential informants are. Of course, I refused to tell. But I promised him they were in a position to not only know shit— not the word I actually used —but were motivated to tell. I told him the truth. They approached me. When I pitched the story, I explained I would get a job as a waitress at a strip club since that's where the least reputable people meet to do business. I wasn't wrong. He wanted me to come to work every day like normal. I had to point out there was no way I would work eight to five every day for the newspaper, then work eight to four a.m. every night at the club. Three hours off. When and where would I sleep?

He agreed to me infiltrating for three months as long as I regularly reported back with something new each time. I have. He cleared me for another two months, but that went down the shitter.

"Are you safe?"

I appreciate that's his first question. He's a task master if ever there was one. But he's kind.

"Yeah. They don't know how much I know. And they don't know why I was there. They just know I wasn't there for an honest night's work."

"And you don't believe they'll go after you?"

"No. I'm certain I'm safe from them."

What more could happen? I get injured. I wind up dead. Definite possibilities. But what hurts way more is that I broke my own heart by letting myself fall for Dillan. The look on his face when he left. That will haunt me.

"Do you have enough for your first feature article?"

"Yeah. I'm going to get started now. I wanted to check in and let you know I'm back."

"Do you have enough for the series you wanted to run?"

"I think so. At least enough for two. I can get more through my CIs, since I can't get anything first-hand."

"Go get 'em, cookie."

He calls all his reporters "cookie." I don't know how it started because it was probably before I was born. You know you have job security when you progress from your name to the nickname. It's a rite of passage. If it doesn't happen within six months, there's a good chance you'll be out on your ass. He started calling me that after two months. I've been here almost two years.

"Oh. One thing." It just came to me. "When this runs, I don't want my name in the byline."

"You said you were safe."

"I am. But I don't want anything happening to my CIs once the O'Rourkes put two and two together. Seeing my name will only speed that up."

"All right. We'll use a staff byline."

"Thanks. I need to get my notes in order, and I'll get something preliminary to you by the end of the day."

I head back to my desk and hang my coat over the back of my chair. I lock my purse inside my desk drawer and click my laptop onto the secured docking station. As my computer turns on, I glance at the family photo beside the front wall of my cubicle. My mom, my dad, my granny, and my grandda when I was five. They killed him that day. We left Northern Ireland a month later.

I've had a good life in America. I've benefited from opportunities I likely wouldn't have had if we'd remained in Northern Ireland. But nothing so great has happened here that it makes up for the O'Rourkes murdering my grandda right in front of me.

I lean back over my chair, stretching and enjoying the sound of my spine popping. The tension releases as I sit up and tilt my head from side to side, my neck popping too. I've been at my desk for six hours without getting up. My friend Anna grabbed me lunch, which is half-eaten beside me. I dive into the sandwich as I reread what I've written. It took me several hours to sort through my notes, type them up, fact check several things, then write the two articles. The writing was the easiest part. Until now.

I close my eyes as I chew. There's so much more I could put in here. I don't want to dump everything into the first article, so I drafted two. I want to tantalize the readers enough to come back to me for more. But it's not just that. I found it really hard to include specifics I know would endanger Dillan and his family. If they'd been the monsters I'd assumed, this would have been as easy as I expected. But they aren't. Far from it. They're so fucking normal we may as well all have worked in Mayberry. A Rated X Mayberry, but idyllic, nonetheless. A place where family is everything. No one takes anything too seriously. And it's a pleasant place to be. Even if it was a strip club.

When I first started poking around, wanting to find out the deal with the O'Rourkes, I stumbled upon the bratva. I happened to pick the same place to watch Sean and Shane as Anton. When it became obvious we were there to do the same thing, we started asking each other veiled questions. When I wound up doing the same thing with Sergei, we gave away a little more. I haven't revealed all my plans, and they sure as shit didn't tell me even a thimbleful of theirs. But we agreed to swap info as we got it. They also promised to provide me protection. From the O'Rourkes.

They said nothing about anyone else, and when I hinted at it, they made it clear I was on my own. I know they had guys watching my place to make sure I got home safely every morning. But that was it as far as safety. It wouldn't surprise me if they didn't have someone watching me to make sure I didn't double-cross them or whatever the syndicates call it. Narc, I suppose. I didn't mention to Dillan that I texted Sergei to ask if they had someone across the street watching me. He said no. That's what freaked me out enough to tell Dillan. Not just because it scared me, but also because I didn't need someone interfering.

"Molly, you ready to go? You're still eating your lunch? I thought we were doing dinner."

I look up at Anna and Mackenzie as they stand beside the side partition. I quickly save my work and exit out of the program. I'm done rereading the rough drafts of the two articles, but I don't want anyone else reading this. I don't want someone snagging the story out from under me. I don't want it leaking. I don't want to answer any fucking questions. *I don't want to break this story after all.*

That's shocking. But, as I look at my laptop, I know it's true. I feel better having things written down. Catharsis. I think, even though it's still rough, it's among my best work. And that's the reason I suddenly have a consuming need not to go through with it.

"I waited so long to finish my sandwich that I'm starving. This won't cut it. I'm ready."

I unlock my laptop and drop it in my bag before retrieving my purse from my desk drawer. I put on my coat as we walk to the elevator. When we step outside, an arctic blast hits us. I turn my head away from the wind as I pull my scarf higher over my nose. There's a guy at the end of the building, looking down at his phone like he's texting. From here, it looks like Tommy. He's a bouncer at 4Play. Why would he be over here in Midtown right now?

It probably isn't him. But he doesn't start work until ten. It's five-thirty now. Who knows? Mackenzie, Anna, and I head to the subway. As I turn the corner, I notice the guy coming down the stairs, but he has a beanie on and is looking down. I can't tell if it's Tommy. But it sure as fuck looks like him from here. He blends in, so I can't see him as he waits for a car that'll stop a few down from where I'm standing with my friends. It fucking unnerves me when the guy gets off at the same stop as us and heads up to the street, using the same steps as us. I say nothing, acting like nothing is out of the ordinary.

When we get to the restaurant, I duck into the restroom. I genuinely want to wash my hands, but I grab my phone and pull up Dillan's number. Shane gave it to me along with all the others once Dillan got worried about the Albanians.

ME

Get Tommy to stop following me

I don't expect an immediate response, but it comes through. He must have already been on his phone.

DILLAN

He's not.

ME

Then why's he following me?

DILLAN

I don't know I didn't tell him to

ME

Tell him to stop. My friends didn't notice but they will I don't want to have to explain that to them

DILLAN

If he's there then you tell him

ME

WTF???

DILLAN

He won't do anything to you whatever his reason is he's not stupid he won't touch you

ME

Why? Because everyone thinks we're fucking

DILLAN

Sure

ME

I get you're pissed at me but how do you go from overprotective to couldn't give a fuck if I die? Is that really how low you think of me? That your guy can follow me scare the shit out of me and I can just deal with it myself

DILLAN

He won't touch you.

ME

So he volunteered to follow me and report back to you?

DILLAN

I told you I don't know why he's following
you.

ME

Fine. Whatever. Goodnight.

DILLAN

Goodnight, Márgrég Mac Dhòmhnaill.

I just stare at my phone. How does he know my true first name? The only place it appears is on my birth certificate and the passport I had before I became an American citizen. My parents changed it to Mairghráid when they could. I go by Margaret because it's so much easier. Sometime around first grade, kids started calling me Molly. Mac Dhòmhnaill is the original Gaelic spelling of McDonnell. That was never my last name, but it fits since my parents gave me such an Irish first name.

Half the time I leave the fada— the accent over the a —off Mairghráid since people never remember. Two accents people don't know how to use was too much for my parents when they realized my name would always get butchered. It's easy to pronounce if you know. Márgrég is Maregreed. Mairghráid is Maregraid. Almost the same, but the latter is marginally easier for Americans to figure out phonetically. Molly just makes people ask far fewer questions.

He sent that last text to stick the knife in. The next one twists.

DILLAN

Thanks for doing 23andMe. Super helpful.
Born in Ballycastle, County Antrim, Northern
Ireland

ME

An bhfuil muid fiú ansin

Are we even then?

DILLAN

Ní fiú gar cailín

Not even close little girl.

That shouldn't affect me the way it does. I was supposed to have exorcised him from my system last night. Writing these initial articles were supposed to remind me— it did remind me, but apparently, I have a short memory —of how wrong he is for me.

ME

Call off your henchman Dillan or I will make a scene about him following me

DILLAN

Go ahead. He's working on his own time it'll teach him to be better at hiding

ME

You are seriously too much

DILLAN

Aren't you the pot calling the kettle black?

I can't anymore. My friends are going to be wondering what the fuck happened to me. I head out of the bathroom and drop my phone in my purse. If I'm going to deal with Dillan, I'm going to do it later. On my time. Let him wonder why I didn't answer. Hell, let him think he got the better of me.

Anna slides down the booth and looks at me as I put my purse down beside Mackenzie.

"Was the line crazy?"

"No. Sorry. I got a text about some family stuff. Nothing important, but I got distracted. Did you order yet?"

Mackenzie nods since I don't see the menus anymore. She fills me in.

"We got you a bay breeze, the house salad, and the shepherd's pie."

"Thanks."

For fuck's sake. I mention one time that I like the dish. Now they both assume because I'm Irish, that's my go-to dish everywhere. When I first started working at the paper, it came out in a meeting that I was born in Northern Ireland. I mentioned something, and a guy picked up on it. He asked what kind of Irish I was. I just stared blankly. He clarified he meant Irish from Ireland or Irish American. I said the former. Then he asked if I was from Northern Ireland or real Ireland. I just replied I'm Irish. He tried to push me, but I changed the subject. I'm not getting into that. I don't need to give anyone lessons on geopolitics and history.

Mackenzie smiles at me. She's super nice, but a little self-involved. She'll ask how someone's doing as a pro forma nicety. Then she launches into herself. But she means well, so I like her.

"You were undercover for so long, I never got to ask you how your Christmas went."

"It was really nice. My parents and I spent it with my grandmother at her memory care center. She was pretty clear for most of the day. She still has a beautiful voice, so it was nice singing carols with her like I did as a kid."

"That's sweet. My parents dragged James and me to Mass again this year. It's so long and boring. And the incense. It's like having hay fever. You know how that goes, Molly. Catholic Masses last forever."

"Mmm."

I sip my drink that just arrived. Because I'm Irish, everyone assumes I'm Catholic. I'm not. I'm a Protestant from Northern Ireland. Church of Ireland to be exact. Which is basically kissing cousins to Church of England. Episcopalians in America, and Anglicans pretty much everywhere else. It's always stuck with me that Robin Williams once said, "I'm an Episcopal. That's Catholic Lite. Same religion. Half the guilt." That's the simplest way to explain it.

Again. I'm not giving lessons in history or geopolitics. It's easier to just sidestep the topic. Not the hill I want to die on. At least, not with them. I'm willing to plant my flag and take a stand somewhere else. That reminds me. I need to read through what I wrote when I get home. Too much alcohol, and I'll get heavy head. I need to finish it if I want it to run by the end of the week.

Liar. You don't want to run it at all.

The conversation goes on around me, and I keep track of it, adding my two cents here and there. Tommy's at the bar, and now he has two buddies with him. Maybe it's a coincidence. But I know the other guys too. They work at 4Play just like Tommy. Alex and Smitty. Tommy was okay, but Alex and Smitty always made me uncomfortable. Shane had to tell them to back off a couple times when they kept trying to corner me. I know they're with some of the other women from time to time, so they thought I might be down to fuck, too. I am not.

We finish dinner and head out to the subway. We live in different directions, so we're catching different trains. We say goodnight, and I walk another three blocks to the stop I need. It's still blustery as fuck. I have my hat pulled down, my scarf pulled up, my gloved hands in my pockets. It's early enough that the sidewalks are still pretty crowded. I squeeze between people until I get to the steps down to the stop. Blessed reprieve from the wind. Still cold as fuck, though. I swipe my pass and go down to the platform.

I have three fucking shadows now. All three live on Staten Island. I live in Harlem. They are *not* headed the right way to go home or to work. I move down the platforms to put me two cars from where I was. I can't go any farther, and they just stopped at the second door to the same car as I'll get in. When it arrives, I step forward, watching the three of them get on. But I move to the side just as the doors close. I bolt for the stairs as I dig for my phone. I look back, but they're on the train. I see them through the window. All three. I literally counted.

"Dillan, stop. This isn't cool."

I don't even wait for him to say hello.

"What are you talking about?"

"Tommy, Smitty, and Alex. You know Smitty and Alex make me super uncomfortable. Make them stop."

"Where are you? How close to you are they?"

"They tried to follow me onto the subway. I looked like I was getting into the same car as them. They got that close. But I stepped aside. Once the doors were closing, I ran for the stairs. They're stuck heading toward Harlem. I'm on the street right now. I was at the station near 50th St and 8th Ave. There's a coffee shop on the corner of 49th and 9th. I'm going there to be sure they don't come back. I'm going to my parents once I'm sure they aren't still following me."

"No. Stay there, *cailín*. I'm coming to you. I'm in Midtown East. I'll be there in a few minutes. I have a driver, and I'll be in a black town car. Stay in the coffee shop until I come and get you. Understand?"

"Yes."

"I'll be there as soon as I can. I promise."

"I know."

We hang up, and I walk into the place. It's not crowded, so

I can see everywhere. But there are enough people that I think I can blend in. I order a chai and sit where I can see the door and out the window, but not too close. It could take him anywhere from fifteen to thirty minutes even if it's not that far. I don't know if there's any road work going on in the streets between us or what the traffic's like. I sip my drink. It's still nearly scalding when I see him pull up. He's out of the backseat, buttoning his suit coat before the car comes all the way to a stop. Finn's getting out of the front passenger seat, and a guy I don't know rolls down the driver's window.

I'm out of my seat and across the restaurant as he pushes open the door. Then I'm in his arms. Someone— Finn —takes the drink from my hand, so I can wrap my arms around him. I burrow against Dillan's chest and inhale his cologne. He always smells of sandalwood, even when I've seen him come straight from the gym to drop something off to Shane. I can hear his heart pounding. Even though it's rapid, it's steady. It's calming.

"I'm here now, wee one."

He whispers to me, and all I can do is nod. It's not until later that I remember what he calls me. Wee one. Really, only the Northern Irish say wee. He's calling me something I recognize. Something familiar. Something comforting.

Now that I'm safe, just how scared I was hits me. He turns us and leads me to the door, which Finn is holding open. The driver gets out and opens the door Dillan got out of. Finn hands Dillan my chai once he's next to me. The door closes, and I notice the privacy glass is up. I'm about to fasten my seatbelt when Dillan pushes it back. He tugs my arm until I move to the middle seat. He wraps an arm around my waist and hoists me onto his lap as he pulls down the center armrest and puts my drink in the cupholder. How he did that without spilling is anyone's guess.

When the car pulls away from the curb, I consider moving

back to my seat, but he holds me tight against him. I settle since I don't want to fight him on this. I know it's stupid dangerous. I know the law says a seatbelt. But I feel safer with him wrapped around me than with a seatbelt. He kisses my temple and strokes the hair down my back. I rarely wore it down at the club because it was too hot.

"Where are we going? Did you tell your driver my address or my parents'?"

"Your parents. Sit back and rest. You know it'll take a while to get to Greenwich."

I grew up in Connecticut, but not the New Englandy part. The New York City part. It'll take about an hour to get there. It's definitely the opposite direction from Harlem. I'm so comfortable with Dillan that I doze off. It was rough getting up this morning with only three hours of sleep. He nudges me awake.

"*Cailin*, we're about a mile from your parents' place. Do you know what you want to tell them? You aren't arriving in your car, and it's not the weekend."

"Hmm?... Oh. Yeah... They know I have a colleague who commutes from Stamford. I'll say he dropped me off. I'll take the train in. I'll say I need... I don't know. I barely have anything there except a few changes of clothes. It's too late to say I'm there for dinner. They'll wonder why I want to spend the night."

I feel panicky by the end. Fuck.

"Do you want to go somewhere else?"

"No. You guys drove all the way out here. By the way, why was Finn sitting up front when you got to the coffee shop?"

He goes silent and just looks at me. What am I supposed to guess from that? He wasn't driving, so it's not like he was Dillan's chauffeur. They're cousins and best friends. Why wouldn't he sit with Dillan? Only a...

"He's your bodyguard."

He doesn't confirm or deny, but I know I'm right. That explains why he never arrives at the club alone. Sometimes another guy walks in a couple minutes later. But now that I think about it, those weren't coincidences. He's the mob boss. Of course, he doesn't go places without security. Even to a place he owns.

I think of a reason I could be out here. I think my parents and my boss will buy it, and it could be legitimately useful.

"I'll go and see my granny in the morning. I'll say I came out to do that. I'll say I worked late, so I get to come in late. Except for Christmas, I haven't seen her since before I started working for you. I rarely go that long without seeing her since I moved back to the city."

"Okay. We'll wait until you walk in. We'll circle the block a couple times, then wait around the corner for half an hour before we go. If anyone's following you or guesses where we're going, we'll see them."

"But what if they're like you, and they wait thirty-five minutes because they know you'd wait thirty? It's not that I need you to stay. It's just—"

"What?"

"Nothing."

"No. You were going to say something. I want to hear it."

I hesitate. We're pulling into my parents' driveway. I gather my stuff and slip off Dillan's lap. I open the door and stick one leg out before I twist to look at him.

"Mobsters are too predictable."

Chapter Seven

Dillan

What the fuck is that supposed to mean?

"Care to elaborate?"

I want to know why Greta thinks we're predictable. That our instinct is to react with violence? That we always want to prove we have the biggest dicks in the room? That I'll do what I have to protect her? The bratva and *Cosa Nostra* men have already proven there's no limit to what they'll do to defend their women.

But Greta isn't mine. She and I both made sure of that. She's a fucking spy, and I wrote her off. Yet, it didn't take a moment's thought to know I needed to go to her when she called me. I intend to find out exactly what those fuck nuts thought they were doing. No one outside my family knows about Greta. They have no reason to follow her unless it's to hurt her. And I definitely didn't order that. My cousins wouldn't either. As for Greta elaborating...

"No."

Her answer sure is short and to the point, even if there's nothing sweet about it. She's had enough happen tonight, so I won't fight her on this. I watch her walk to the front door and let herself in. Normally, I would have stopped her from getting out of the vehicle without my driver or bodyguard opening the door for her. I always want someone doing a sweep of the area before anyone gets out of the backseat. That's why I have a driver and bodyguard. But we pulled up next to the front door. It wasn't worth the argument that would have inevitably happened, even if I did just rescue her from three men following her.

She doesn't look back, and that hurts. I admit it.

I lower the privacy glass, and Finn looks back at me. I cock an eyebrow.

"I don't know, Dill. None of them are answering my calls or texts."

"I want to know if someone else sent them, or if they're acting on their own. I want to know before the sun's up."

"I'm already working on it. Seamus and Cormac will go to their place. Convenient they all live together."

They'll either show up to work tomorrow with broken noses and black eyes, or they'll never show up for anything else. Their choice.

I lean my head back and close my eyes. Why do I have such a visceral reaction to all things Greta? Why do I have a pet name for her? Why do I want a woman I don't trust? What the fuck is wrong with me?

I have tons of questions and no answers because it's more than my dick wanting to fuck her. I definitely want to do that. I was so close to doing that the other night. I've been jacking off to thoughts of her for a month. I tried to fuck her out of my mind a few times at my club, but I kept thinking about how much I wanted to do all that kinky ass shite to her. I've never been into the idea of true punishment for a partner. But, God, I want to spank her until I'm too tired to land another one. Then I want to fuck her over and over, but only I get off. I want to edge her until she's begging. I don't care if it's begging to stop tormenting her or to start making her come.

I would never touch her in genuine anger, but that's how I feel right now. If I ever had the chance to do anything BDSM related with Greta, I would always be monumentally careful not to overexert my strength. I'm a lot bigger than her and definitely far stronger. The idea of truly hurting her makes my chest tighten. I'm just so pissed.

"Dill, we have another problem."

"Huh?"

"I just sent you a link. Read your text."

I pull my phone out as I watch Finn scrolling something on his phone. I open his text and click the link. Motherfucking son of a cum eating whore.

NYC Underworld Run by Irish King

That's the headline of a news article on the city's largest newspaper website. A news outlet that people around the world read. Nowadays, they can slap an article up at any time of the day or night. They don't have to wait for printed additions. It makes it a fuck ton harder to keep things out of the news. I look up from scrolling the article. This is far, far, *far* more incriminating than one just listing our businesses and questionable guests.

"Who's it by? There's no name. It just says staff?"

Finn's expression is hardly reassuring when he answers.

"I don't know. I'm trying to find out. But it's leaked. This definitely wasn't meant to go out yet. There are four typos, and it doesn't read like it's been polished. But it's damning and damn good writing. How the fuck does someone know this much?"

"I don't know. This is more than a spy could get. Our history. There's shite no one knows. No one knew."

Finn points to his screen as he twists more in his seat.

"Did you see what was all bracketed off at the end? Like maybe it was the journalist's notes they planned to go back to."

"Yeah. That's where all the most damning evidence is. Who?"

I lean my head back again. Finn's right. It doesn't read like it was ready to run, but it was close enough. Whoever leaked this, maybe even the author themself, wanted to get it out more than they worried about style. The information— a fifth grader could have written it, and it wouldn't matter. It's everything it reveals. Finn confirms that, but he's ever an optimist.

"It reveals a ton, but it's not stuff the average person would understand. It's what they allude to that's the dangerous part. The feds will understand. Our business partners will squirm because we're in the news. But they won't bolt."

"I know. But the feds are not what we need right now. Not when we're trying to get them to do us a solid with Lorenzo. I want them focused on him and his fucking family, not us. Let the Mancinellis be under the spotlight for a while."

We've been doling out bribes like it's a fucking Mardi Gras parade. Beads and bribes. Our plan to fuck over the *Cosa Nostra* has been in the works too long to let this article fuck it all up.

Finn sounds more confident than I know he feels when he tries to reassure me. "They'll have to dig way more to get all they need to build a case off everything in this article. They have next to no work to do to get Salvatore through Enzo. We need to remind them of that."

The only reason he's trying to downplay this is because he

already knows shite with Greta bothers me more than just about anything ever has. I don't want to voice my fear, but I'm sure Finn's thinking it.

Greta's been spying. Has she been selling information to our leak? Is she responsible for this?

That damn article has been eating at me all night. I sleep fine no matter what's going on. I'm usually so fucking exhausted that I sleep like the dead for the four or five hours I get. But I woke up this morning to reality. Cormac and Seamus found Tommy, Smitty, and Alex. They had a little chat that resulted in two broken noses and a fractured cheekbone. That was just their faces. Several broken fingers, two dislocated shoulders, and a dislocated kneecap. Apparently, they were Camp Mo. According to their earlier testimony to the court of O'Rourke, they wanted to intimidate Greta. It came out later that they planned to assault her once they realized she was traveling home alone.

I told my cousins to let them live in agony until their injuries start to heal. Then they can take them to our place. Let them think their punishment is done. My family has fucked up in ways I never imagined possible before four years ago. Trying to fix what the last two leaders set in motion has been a shit-show that's taken me nearly three years to make right. In the process, more than one woman's gotten hurt. That violates the covenant the syndicates once had. Women and children are off limits. I can't control what the other families might do, but I sure as fuck can control what my men do. I can send a message to the others too. My predecessors might have been fine with hurting women, but I'm not.

And that's a big part of what's so fucking troublesome

about this article. It doesn't name any of the women, and it doesn't name me or anyone living in my family. But it gives details about Uncle Donovan and Declan. My uncle and my first cousin once removed through my mom. Uncle Donovan inherited the position as skipper when his father, Liam— my grandfather —died in a plane crash. When rivals killed Uncle Donovan for hurting a bratva wife, Declan took over. He wasn't any smarter. He got himself killed for targeting a second bratva wife. It was their mess that landed on my shoulders, and some of it was so far into execution that I couldn't stop it. It made me look guilty as fuck. As though I condoned it. I had little choice. It was my family or theirs, and mine will always come first. Always.

I look up as someone knocks on the front door of my Brooklyn house. I don't know which of the twins it was, but Sean and Shane let themselves in. We have keys to each other's places and an open-door policy. Since none of us bring women home, we don't worry about intruding. I shift in the overstuffed recliner in my living room and look up from the computer that's resting on my lap. I may not be old enough for a BarcaLounger, but I like my comforts at home.

I don't need to look to know Sean speaks first. I've known them since before I can remember anything.

"Did you see this?"

"The article from last night? Yeah."

"No. The one from this morning."

"What? No. What the fuck?"

Shane hands me his phone, and I skim the article before going back to read it. Fucking hell. This one is even more damning than the last. It still doesn't name names, but it doesn't have to if you're in the know about the New York underworld. The first article gave some family history that went back twenty years. This one gives a shite ton of current information. I hand the phone back to my cousin.

"It's written like the one last night. It's good, but it's not polished. It leaked. I want to know who wrote it, and I want to know who leaked it."

"Then what?" Shane drops the phone into his back pocket as he asks.

"You can guess if it's a man. If it's a woman, we get them fired and unable to work at any major news outlet in the world. Let them work for some Podunk gazette in East Bajesus for all I care. I want them out of the city and permanently put on mute."

I could bankrupt them, but then I risk making them homeless. Once they're on the streets, then they could genuinely get hurt. Like I said, I don't condone hurting women. But neither am I God. I don't forgive easily.

I need to know about Finn. "What's your brother found out? As much as I want to know who, I want to know why more."

Out of all of us, Sean's considered the quiet one. The one hardest to rile. But he's also the most stubborn. The man can be unbendable. As best I can remember, he never had tantrums when we were little. He just refused to do whatever it was he didn't want to do. He'd just sit or stand silently. It means he has the most patience because he could outlast anyone trying to coax or command him into something. He speaks up now.

"Finn's trying to flush out who could know some of this history that goes back so far. Whoever wrote this has a vendetta against us. Whoever leaked it wants either swift retribution or they intend to extort us. They'll sell their silence. My guess is the latter. Whoever got these printed did it without going through an editor."

"Find out who's shitting a brick in the newsroom. Someone

has to be freaking out about these going to publication before they were ready. I want that person in front of me by three. Today."

Sean shoots me a doubtful look. "Does Finn know that?"

"Yes. But now it's not a request like it was before I read this second piece of trash. We can't afford more articles coming out. We have people inside the paper. Get them to talk."

"Fine." Shane's our press liaison. He was into journalism when we were in high school and college. He's a nosey fucker when he wants to be. It's Sean who has the hacking skills to be our main intel gatherer. But Shane can find out just about anything. His time on school papers made him some serious connections, so he'll call in some favors. He trades secrets for times like this when we need to move the press to our side again.

Sean walks over and plops down on the sofa. Shane takes the other recliner, which he spins to see us better. Sean cracks his knuckles— a habit that drives my aunt crazy —before he speaks again.

"We're the same ages as everyone except for Salvatore and Enrique. They'd know this shite because they were around back then. We grew up with all the other guys. They could have learned shite about us at some point, or someone in those families could have told them."

Our lives are so far past fucked-up, there aren't words for it. Salvatore is the *Cosa Nostra* don, and Enrique Diaz is the Colombian Cartel *jefe*. They're both in their early fifties. Both of them have been in their positions for more than twenty years. There's a reason both are going to live to be old men. They're no fools. But that's not the fucked-up part. All four families lived in Queens when my generation was growing up. The only ones who didn't were Pablo and Juan Diaz, Enrique's nephews. But they may as well have for all the time they spent there. They're in Jersey, just outside the city, but Enrique's other nephews were in Queens.

We didn't go to elementary or middle school together, but we all went to the same high school. Gerrymandering at its best. But when we were young kids, we played peewee and little league sports together. We were all fucking friends. At least when we played on the same teams. When we were opponents, it was just a view into the future. We went from allies to enemies by season. Not so much has changed.

Our long ass family histories are why it's completely plausible it's one of the other families. The family that heads the bratva didn't come to the U.S. until they were in middle and high school. They didn't have too many opportunities for sports when they arrived. They were too busy surviving their old *pakhan*. That man was the poster boy for psychopath. He loved torturing. He got off on it. I'm sure he jacked off to people's screams. But once we were all in high school, the Kutsenkos and Andreyevs dominated all the sports teams alongside the Mancinellis and us. We literally had to play nice. There were nonaffiliated kids on the teams too, so we couldn't bring our syndicate shite to school. But outside of school... Game on, motherfuckas.

"Hello?"

"Huh?"

Shane scowls at me. He brings me back to the insiders he has in the media. "Dude, hello. Do you want me to call in favors? And how much are you willing to pay?"

"Nothing if it's a guy. Tell him it's better for his health if he helps. Ask your brother how much he's willing to pay if it's a woman."

Finn's the accountant, and he balances the books. The man is so precise the accounts have reconciled to the penny every day since he took on the job when he was twenty-one. More than a decade. I'm three months older than him. Sean and Shane are more than identical twins. They're Irish twins to Finn. Ten months younger than him. Cormac and Seamus are Irish twins, too. Seamus was premature, so they're only seven months apart. You'd never guess by his size now. They're the same age as Sean and Shane. All our parents planned to only have two per couple. Break the stereotype. It would have worked if Sean and Shane hadn't come out as a two for one. I'm not really an only. My sister, Colleen, was a year-and-a-half younger than me until she died. I... I just can't.

I swallow the lump that rises in my throat, take a deep inhale, and sigh.

"You know I trust you guys to handle it all. I have a meeting with Hollands and Watling. Cormac and Seamus filled me in on a nice little secret that's going to come in handy about Hollands."

"Oh? You gonna share?" Shane dips his chin and raises his eyebrows at me as he speaks. It's the same expression he came out of the womb with. Arrogant little shite. Good thing I love him more like a brother than a cousin. We're all more like brothers than cousins. Our parents raised us that way.

"They found out Hollands and Mason Spiegel — an agent from the ATF —are fucking. As though them being brothers-in-law isn't rich enough. Spiegel's wife is the fucking Deputy DNI."

Hollands is the director of the FBI. She's second in charge behind the Director of National Intelligence, one of the FBI's oversight organizations. Fucking nepotism got them both those jobs since the ethics are sketchy as fuck. But Cormac and Seamus put Hollands in our pocket for a rainy day by threatening to tell the guy's sister about the affair. No one in my family is old school Catholic. Fuck whoever you want. But if it's convenient for us to know, then we will.

"No fecking way!"

Shane practically crows. He's had several run-ins with Hollands. My cousin focuses on our construction division, but we're all co-owners of an import/export company, and he owns a shipping company. He's the best negotiator, so he's struck some agreements that have kept our guys out of prison when they should be in for life times ten.

"Oh, I can't wait to talk to him again. That shite's going to be good until he retires."

"The meeting's in two hours, so I need to finish reviewing these briefs. I want to know the precedence before Cormac and I walk in there."

Cormac, Seamus, and I are all attorneys. Cormac specializes in criminal law while Seamus handles our corporate entities. I only got to practice for a couple years before giving it up to assume the mantle of mob boss. I'd just finished my LLM in corporate law, and Seamus and I were in the middle of a massive acquisition that got ugly. I'd been advising Uncle Donovan for years, but he ignored me. During the negotiations, he fucked around and found out. Thank all the saints Declan only led for a month. Fucking useless piece of shite, but he was older than me, so he refused to listen to my advice. Uncle Donovan was the head of our family for nearly a decade because he listened to me. Declan never would.

They ended a career I really enjoyed. I don't have time to work on these things, so now Seamus takes care of it. But no one can take my knowledge from me. I might have specialized in corporate in school, but I know the criminal codes like they were tatted on my brain.

I look at Shane before glancing at my sleeping screen. "Do you have time to come with us? If Hollands pushes back, Cormac and I have the secret. Now you do too. You can lead the negotiations."

"Where are you meeting?"

"Kittens."

Another one of our strip clubs. Kittens... cats... pussies. Not too many leaps to get to that. Neither Hollands nor Watling want to be seen meeting with us if it isn't with us handcuffed in an interrogation room.

I watch Sean and Shane both flex their left hand. It's a tell they never show outside the family. They enjoy strip clubs about as much as I do. Necessary evil in our line of work. Shane only goes when he has to run payroll, do inventory, or attend a meeting. He does the first two on the same day. There's something else going on, though.

"What now?"

Sean looks at me, and it's his turn for the deep inhale and sigh.

"What about Molly?"

Chapter Eight

Greta

I'm— I'm —Imma fucking murder someone!

This cannot be happening. Fuck me. Fuck me. Fuck me up the ass with a pogo stick. The pathos— the irony —the whatever is not lost on me. The entire reason I've undergone this ruse is to write an exposé on the O'Rourkes because of what their family took from me. The person they murdered. And now I'm ready to do bloody murder. Bludgeon someone to death.

"Gary, what the hell? Who posted this? I didn't submit my articles."

I'm standing inside my editor's office with the door closed. I'm not screaming, but I thought it might be a good idea in case I do. I've never felt rage like this before. I was too young to feel it when the IRA killed my grandfather with a bomb Peter Doyle built for them. Oh, I know his connections to the bratva, and I know what his own brother had to do to him. It's that connection that brought Sergei and Anton knocking on my door after running into both of them.

Peter was Laura— née Doyle —Kutsenko's paternal uncle. Her family has had connections to the mob for generations. Her grandparents tried to keep their sons out. One— Laura's father —lived by their wishes. The other— Peter —didn't. He wound up in Ireland because of shite he did here. He lived in Ireland but ran guns and explosives to Northern Ireland. Made a shit ton of money and killed a sweet grandda who used to take me to catch tadpoles and let me feed his koi carp. Those aren't even my memories because I was too young. My parents and granny told me.

"Molly, I don't know. It was as much a surprise to me as it was for you. I woke up to Chuck screaming in my ear at four a.m. He didn't want you to do the articles, and I hadn't told him about it. We're both lucky they didn't bar us from getting into the building."

"That's not good enough. I had notes at the end of those articles that weren't for public consumption. It puts a ton of shit out of context."

Gary watches me for a moment before he leans back in his chair. Whatever he heard in those words or sees on my face, I'm not going to like it.

"I don't think this has to do with the articles going out without a line edit. This isn't about it not being your best quality. You regret it."

"I regret that they throw my journalistic integrity into question because they're not accurate the way they are. I didn't submit them to you or a line editor for a reason. They weren't ready. I want to know who hacked us and got those drafts. I want to know what else they accessed. Did they get into my notes? My emails?"

I'm going to ask Sergei and Anton to look into it since I don't trust IT here or the brass to care enough to dig deep into this. I also need to know if this person went through my personal stuff, too. After being followed last night, I'm super freaked out. The worst part is, unlike yesterday, I positively can't call Dillan. I can't ask him to protect me. Fucking hell. I'm keeping it together in front of my boss, but I feel like my world imploded then exploded. It crushed me, then blew me to smithereens.

I came in late since I was in Connecticut this morning. I went to see my grandmother, so I didn't lie to my parents or Gary. If I'd been late for any other reason, he would have cared. But family is everything to him. He lost his wife and son in a car accident, then his daughter to cancer. If we have some type of family commitment, he's adamant work never comes ahead of it. Seeing Granny helped. It wasn't one of her good days, but she still smells like pressed powder and Oil of Olay moisturizer. She told me stories about me as a little girl, but she didn't know who she was telling them to. I was a stranger. But any time with her, I'll take while I can. I went to her house every day after school until one of my parents could pick me up. She raised me as much as my parents did.

"Gary, I know I was late coming in, but I need to see my CIs if they're available. This won't land well with them."

Unless... Did they do this?

"How's it going to land with the O'Rourkes? You said they made you. If they know you were spying, will they assume this was you?"

"They may think I'm the one who supplied the current info, but they can't know how I came by all the history. They'll think I fed the recent stuff to someone."

"All the more reason to worry. Won't they come after you to find out who you told?"

"No matter what happens, I am safe with the O'Rourkes. They will never forgive me, but I'm not in danger from them. I'm more scared of who did this. Was it someone here?"

"I truly don't know. IT is working on figuring out how they got into your cloud, then how they hacked our system to post the article."

"Neither of those should be that hard for them to figure out. I may not know how to do it, but IT should know how to search for hackers. A paper this big must have among the world's best tech support."

One can hope.

"Can your CIs keep an eye out for you? Would they protect you?"

"Yes. But I don't want it to come to that. I want this fixed, Gary. By close of business."

I don't wait for him to say anything. I yank the door open and stalk down to my cubicle. I keep my gaze straight ahead, but I know people are watching me. Gary wasn't the only one who woke up early with the news. Mackenzie is an early riser and goes to the gym at four-thirty. She spotted them and called me until I woke up. I didn't know what she was talking about at first until she made it clear: Look at our website. It's on the landing page. I dropped the phone, ran to the bathroom, and puked. I didn't drink that much last night, but it all came up.

ME

Who did this?

Sergei or Anton will get back to me soon. They're never far from their phones. It's only three minutes later when I get a response.

S

We're working on it. It came as a surprise to us too.

ME

Has he done anything about it yet?

I don't have either of their names in my phone. Only the first initial of their first names. We don't use anyone's names in our texts. Sergei knows who I'm talking about.

S

No. He's searching though.

ME

He'll figure out it's me then what?

S

Come to us if you're in danger.

I knew he would make the offer, and I know I can. But he and his family aren't who my gut says I should go to. It's still Dillan. He's the one I want to go to, even though I'm the one who caused all of this.

ME

Thx

There's nothing else to say, so that's the last message for now. I'm at my desk wondering what the fuck do I do now?

I still feel like I have a shadow. Except after being followed by those three guys, it feels way more ominous. When I first sensed it, I just felt watched. It scared me, so I went to Dillan about it. This feels way different. I can't explain why. It's intuition. It's like this invisible presence keeps creeping closer and closer. It's been three days since the articles leaked, and every time I leave my place or leave work, I get a chill up my spine that has nothing to do with the weather. It's— I don't know. Something's just lurking. Watching me. Waiting to pounce. I saw Sergei and Anton last night and told them about it. They weren't pleased. They pointed out I could have and should have told them immediately. They're personally taking turns watching out for me.

A black sedan is exactly where Anton said it would be. He's there. I'm not riding the subway these days. It's racking up the costs, but I'm Ubering or using Lyft. The sedan is on the corner where I'll meet my driver. Anton and Sergei do that, so they can see me clearly from the minute I walk out till the minute I get in the ride share. Then they follow me to my place.

I'm utterly unprepared to see Dillan step out of the black sedan and button his suit coat. He's staring at me, and I start to slip because I kept my eyes on him rather than looking down at the sidewalk. I don't know how he does it, but he's catching me without slipping himself. He pulls me against him, and my cheek goes to his chest. He hesitates a moment, then he wraps his arms around him.

I can barely eek out more than a whisper. "Thank you."

"You're all right now, *cailín*."

But I'm not. I'm so fucking far from all right. When I step back, I meet his gaze, and the dam breaks. Tears stream down my cheeks as I sob. That couple of moments he held me were the only reprieve I've had since the night he left my apartment pissed and hurt. Now it's gone, and I'm back to standing on my own. That means figuring this shit out without Dillan because I've done more than just listen in on some conversations.

"Greta?"

It's only been four days since he called me that, but it feels like an eternity. I sob even harder, my throat burning. I don't know where to look or what to do. The one place I wish to seek solace— back in Dillan's arms —is the one place I can't go.

"Greta, we're going to talk. But did something happen today?"

I nod as I shrug. I don't know what emotion to feel. I hear a horn beep, and I look up to realize it's my Lyft driver.

"I have to go, Dillan. That's the ride I ordered."

"No." He looks over his shoulder. "Jake, deal with it."

I watch a guy I don't know get out of the driver's seat. I watch him walk over to the ride share guy and stick out a single bill. The wind pushes it up, and it flaps. It's a hundred dollars. The guy practically snatches it from Jake.

"He doesn't have to pay for my ride. That's not right."

"He isn't."

"But—"

"Greta, let's go."

He grasps my arm just above the elbow and presses me forward until I get to the open car door. Until this moment, I was certain Dillan would never physically harm me. But I have a moment of panic. Before I can act on it, he turns me and kisses me.

My response is immediate. I need this more than my next breath. I need this to feel like I can make it through another day. I'm not scared right now. I just feel wanted and cared for. I feel desirable, and I'm hungry for the meal I never got to finish. It's frigid out here, but the way he holds me makes me feel like it could be the sunniest and hottest day in summer.

"Daddy." I mumble the word, then freeze. Dillan doesn't drop a beat when he answers.

"That's right, *cailín.*"

"Dillan, I—"

"Get in the car. We're going to my place in Brooklyn. We'll talk when we get there. This isn't the place to do it. We've already stood around long enough."

That makes me dart my gaze around, trying to see anything that might be out of the ordinary.

"Little one, you wouldn't see it. We need to go."

I let him guide me into the car before he climbs in after me and shuts the door. It's barely closed before the driver pulls away from the curb. The last time I was in a car with him, I sat on his lap. I don't see that happening again. He knows. I'm sure of it. That's why he's here. That's why we have to talk. Accepting that turns the water works back on. I look out my window as I cry. I do my best not to make a sound, to just look like I'm watching as a passerby. I gasp when I feel the belt go lax, then his hands go around me before he lifts me onto his lap. He presses my head to his chest.

"You are going to tell me the truth, Greta. All of it. I will punish you, and you will not enjoy it, though we'll both feel better once it's done. Then we're moving forward."

I don't want to fight any of it. I'm into BDSM. Whatever he's going to do is likely the same shit we've both gotten into at our clubs. I know he belongs to one. I've never been in a domestic discipline relationship, and we're hardly in one now. But I have been a sub. I know what punishment means. I had a Dom while I lived in Boston. It wasn't romantic, but it was still hard to leave when I got the job down here. I applied because I knew I was free to go if I chose to.

If Dillan says we'll both feel better for it, then he believes I'll release my guilt, and he'll be able to forgive me. I think only one of those two things is possible. I doubt either will happen. For now, I lean against him as I continue to cry. His left hand cups my ass while his right hand strokes my hair. When he kisses my forehead, I sob. Why is he being kind?

"Is this part of the punishment?"

"What?" He tenses. "No. Why do you think that?"

"Because if you know enough that you believe I need punishing, then I can't understand how you can show me an ounce of affection. You're doing this to start the punishment.

You're making me think you can care about me to fuck with me."

I yelp when he fists my hair and pulls my head back until our gazes meet. Then his mouth is on me again. This kiss is an amped up version of any of our previous ones. It's aggressive in a way no man has ever been before. He holds my head in place, pressing it to his face. His free hand fumbles to unfasten the buttons to my peacoat. He gets one, but then gets frustrated with the next one. I reach to do it, but both of his hands snatch my wrists and press them against my lower back. Then he grabs each lapel and yanks. The last four buttons go flying. I love this coat, but I'm not even mad.

He shoves my coat down my arms and tosses it on the floor before lifting me to straddle him. All the while, we're kissing again. He's calmer when he undoes the button on my pants and pulls down the zipper. His fingers slide between my pants and my thong until he can press his fingertips into me.

"You're wet, Greta. You want this as much as I do. I know you can feel how hard I am because you're already riding my cock."

"Yes, Daddy."

It feels incredibly natural to say that. I've never called a Dom that before. I refuse to use the term Master, so it's always been Sir. He nips my lower lip, his teeth grazing the inside. I feel him shift, so he can reach into his pocket. Then I'm twisting in the air until my back is against the car seat. He sheds his suit coat, then I watch him unbutton his pants. I do nothing as he unzips and pushes them down his hips to reveal his boxer briefs.

"I'm going to fuck you, Greta. I'm putting on this condom, but I'm taking it off right before I come. You're going to feel my cum on your thighs and clit. You're going to know that you are mine."

He waits a moment. I know he's letting me reject him, but I don't. Instead, I pluck the condom from his fingers and tear the wrapper. He pushes his boxer briefs down, and I roll the condom over the biggest cock I've ever touched. Before I can suggest sucking him off first, he's pushing my left leg up until I wrap my arm around my shin. Then he's inside me. I'm so fucking wet there's no friction. But the incredible sense of being full. We both groan.

"I'm going to make you come on my cock, little girl. Do you know why?"

I shake my head.

"Because your pussy along with the rest of you is mine. Mine to pleasure. Mine to deny. Mine to protect." He looks like he's about to say something else but catches himself.

"Yes, Daddy."

"You are going to come as many times as you can between here and my place. Jake won't open the door until I tap on the window. I decide when we're done fucking, and no, I don't mean this time. When we go inside, I am still going to punish you. You know as well as I do, that means no pleasure for you. I will not have the first time we are truly, fully intimate be one that is only a memory of pain and regret. The first memory of us fucking is you knowing I've never wanted a woman more than you. I'm inside you right where I belong. We will figure this shite out."

"Daddy."

He's been moving, his cock rubbing my pubic bone. Between that and the things he's saying, I'm so damn close.

"Yes, *cailín*."

"May I come?"

"Already?" He smirks at me.

"Please, Daddy."

"Come."

I grip his ass and undulate my hips until I get just what I need. "Fuck... Fuck... Harder, Dillan."

"I won't hurt you."

"I know you won't. I get what you mean. But I want more. I need it. You say you want me more than any other woman. Right now, things are so fucking fucked-up. I need you to show me. I'm sorry. That's needy as fuck. But it's where I'm at."

He grasps my hips and slams into me. Fuck. It's painful, and I revel in it. Each thrust feels almost deeper than I can bear. I reach up and unbutton his shirt. I want to see more of him. I know how in shape he is, but he's even more cut than I expected from this angle. His abs flex over and over as his pecs strain. I explode. I scream. I may have glimpsed heaven. He slows for a moment, and I don't think it's to let me recover. I think he's close to coming, and he doesn't want to be done yet. He pulls out and slaps his cock against my clit four times before thrusting back in.

"Put your hands over your head. Don't move them. I'm fucking you, not the other way around."

I'd grabbed his ass just before I came. Granite under my fingers. I tried to press, but nothing happened. His ass is too muscular.

"Yes, Sir."

"I am not your fecking Dom, Greta. That's not what you call me. It's Dillan or Daddy. You will never be my sub."

That's a bucket of cold water. Fucking freezing water from the fucking Long Island Sound. I stop moving against him. I don't want this to be over, but it's not the same as a moment ago. It feels good, but I want to cry yet again. He notices immediately. He lowers himself onto his forearms, which rest beside my ears. We're chest to chest. He kisses my neck, then my cheek.

"What just changed, wee one?"

"You said I'll never be your sub, but before—You made it sound like..." I feel like such a fool.

"You won't be my sub. I don't have one right now, and I know you don't have a Dom right now. But we are going to fuck a lot because after today, I won't be able to keep my hands off you."

"Fuck buddies?"

"No."

I puff out a breath through my nose. What does that mean?

"It means— I can hear you thinking, Greta —that we will sort this out when your punishment is done. But I'm not fucking you to punish you. I'm not fucking you to get back at you. I'm fucking you because— I know I've said this already at least twice —you're mine."

This kiss isn't quite as savage, but he's still thrusting into me with the steady rhythm and force of one of those dildo machines. I almost smile thinking that he could be my personal sex machine. Instead, I splay my fingers when I feel his cover mine. We lace them together and keep going until we feel the car slow to a stop. I've already come three more times when we know Jake puts the car in park.

"Dillan!"

He jerks back onto his knees and rips off the condom. I wrap my hand around him, and he covers it with his as we stroke until his cum splatters the inside of my thighs, my clit, and my pussy lips. He lets a drop land on my belly. He runs his palm over the tip before sliding back into me. I have an IUD, so I'm not worried. He scoops me up until he's sitting, and I'm straddling him again. I flop forward, breathless as I wrap my arms around his neck. My cheek rests on my left upper arm.

What just happened?

Chapter Nine

Dillan

What just happened?

I keep asking myself that. That was all over the place. It started as me wanting to prove something to her— to me —I don't fucking know. I had a surge of possessiveness that was utterly foreign to me. I've shared everything my entire life with five other guys and my sister. Then I was angry when I remembered why we're in the car in the first place. Then I wanted to comfort her, which was why I originally pulled her onto my lap. Then I wanted to— I don't know —give her my soul. I have no fucking clue beyond the fact that was more than just fucking. It wasn't making love, even in a rough sense. We're not there yet and may never be. But it was more than scratching an itch.

She's helping me button my shirt as I zip her pants up. She could get off my lap, and we could deal with our own clothes. But neither of us has moved her. When I'm dressed enough, I snag her hands and put them over my heart.

"Greta, I showed up and told you, you were coming with me. I initiated this. I was demanding. I've been in control until now. We're at my place. If this isn't what you want, if you don't want what I said, then tell me. I'll take you somewhere safe. I won't force you to agree to anything you don't want by your own volition.

"A lot of shit has happened in the past four days. Fuck in the past six weeks. This was the first time I've felt in control of anything, and that's because I let you have all the control. Not someone else fucking with me. Not my job. Not your— position. You. I still need you. I need that. If you've changed your mind, then I'll deal. But I want what you told me is going to happen. I've never called another man Daddy. Not even my own. It's always been Da. I can only think I did it because I feel protected when I'm with you. That you'll take care of me. That you're solid and reliable. The things I guess a dad is supposed to be. But I am not a Little."

"I never once imagined you were. That's not my thing. We wouldn't be here if you were. I have friends who are Daddies and friends who are Littles or Middles. But I am not a Daddy Dom."

She nods and looks around for her coat. When she slips it on, we both remember the buttons went flying. I wince, but she laughs. She cups my cheeks and kisses me.

"No man has ever been that impatient to fuck me. It felt good to experience that."

"Impatient doesn't describe even a tenth of what I felt then. Or now. Come on."

Jake pulled into my garage that's at the back of my brownstone. The engine is off, and the garage door is closed. It's safe to get out. Standard practice. Don't turn off the engine until the door is so close to touching the ground that not even a bullet could fit under it. You don't get out until the door doesn't move.

I help her out of the car and take her through the mud room into the house. Jake's walking back and nods. He did a sweep of the house. I know something is going on with Greta that's beyond her control. But I don't know what yet. Anyone could have seen her getting into the car with me. And after the articles, anyone could be pissed enough to come for me. I don't always have someone search my home before I go in, but I'm doubly cautious right now.

I lead Greta into my living room as I hear the front door close. I offer her the sofa, and I sit in my recliner. I lean forward and reach for her hands.

"*Cailín*, you need to tell me what's going on. Who did you tell?"

She freezes for a moment. Less than the time it takes for a breath. She's deciding how much of the truth to tell me. That means there's shite I really don't know, and I've already done a deeper search into her past. I found something.

"Dillan, you found out my real name. What else did you find out about my family?"

"You immigrated to the States when you were a kid. It was your parents, your grandmother, and you. Your family settled in Connecticut where your mom's a teacher, and your dad's a VP of sales for a pharmaceutical company. You grew up there but went to Dartmouth before moving to Boston. You worked at the newspaper there before getting a job down here."

That's what I found. She already has connections, and one of them did this.

"Do you know why we moved here?"

Where is this going? There's a reason she's asking, and I'm certain I won't like the answer. It'll be the reason she spied. I need to know this as much as I need to know who she told. She

— Holy Mother.

"You didn't tell a colleague. You wrote the articles, didn't you?"

When Shane ran her background check before offering her the job, he looked for criminal records and any hint of syndicate affiliation. I read her application. She said nothing about working at any newspapers. I only learned about that when I dug deeper. I wound up sending Cormac and Shane to the meeting without me. I got sidetracked with this. I had a sinking feeling when I learned she was a journalist, but now I'm certain. I didn't want to be, but I am. I've been mulling this over because I couldn't confront her that day. I should have put it completely together, not just a piece of it. More fool am I.

"Yes."

"Why?" I could have barked the word, but I'm deceptively quiet. Or maybe not. She flinches and tries to pull away from me. I only let go of one hand.

"Do you know what happened to my grandfather?"

"Yes. He died when you were five."

"Do you know how?"

"The IRA. He wasn't involved. He was at the wrong place at the wrong time."

"Do you know who made that bomb? Who placed it? Who planned the entire damn thing?" She doesn't raise her voice, but her anger comes through with each question.

"No, but you do. Tell me."

"Peter Doyle."

She yanks her other hand free and sits back. Jesus, Mary, and Joseph.

"He's dead, Greta. I can't do anything to avenge your grandfather."

Her brow furrows, and she looks at me as though I've sprouted a second head.

"I don't need or want you to avenge my grandfather. I want your family to pay for what they took from mine."

She blurts her response, then closes her eyes, and seems to sink into herself. She shakes her head. I say nothing. If I remain quiet, she'll tell me more than if I bombard her with a barrage of questions.

"Why couldn't you be the monster you were supposed to be? Why are you so fucking normal, Dillan? Why are you so fucking kind?"

"Because, unlike Peter deciding to join the mob, I didn't have a say in becoming who I am as the boss. But that's the very reason I'm damn sure of who I want to be as a man."

"And everything that's happened with the other families since you became boss?"

"Was shite set in motion by the two men before me. Shite that got them killed. Shite I couldn't get out of without doing more harm than good to my family. I regret everything that's happened. I regret the roles we've played, but I do not and never will regret doing anything to protect my family. Nothing and no one outside my family comes before them. Ever."

"Why am I here? It makes no sense. You said you'd punish me to make us both feel better, then we'd figure things out together. If I were a man, I'd be dead. Why aren't I? Is it just because I'm a woman?"

"You are here because I can't stop thinking about you all fecking day and during every fecking dream I have. Granted, they've been nightmares since those fecking articles came out. Because I knew there had to be a sound reason for your involvement. But it— I don't even know what to do about you being the author. I— feck me."

I try to remember the manners drilled into me about swearing in front of women, but I finish with frustration unlike anything I've felt since I became the fucking skipper. I hate that motherfucking title. How the hell am I supposed to get the guys on board with this? No pun intended. It was one thing when I thought maybe someone coerced her. But she did this on her own.

"Am I alive because I'm a woman? Answer me, Dillan."

"If you were a man, I wouldn't be so damn attracted to you that I can't think straight. I wouldn't have a reason to want to spare you. So yeah, in part it's because you're a woman. But it's not that fecking simple."

She remains quiet. She's doing what I did earlier. She thinks if she stays quiet, she can wait me out. She's right.

"Greta, why? Have you been plotting your revenge since you were a child? Why now? Did you become a journalist with the plan to expose us?"

"I knew it was the IRA who killed my grandfather. Wrong place, wrong time. He was collateral damage. About three months ago, on one of my granny's worst days, she got agitated and thought she was back there that day. I was with her when it happened in Ballycastle. My parents were, too. I saw the explosion. She started yelling about what happened back then. She was more coherent in her speech than she often is, but she had no idea we were in America and that it's been more than two decades since it happened. She told me about Peter Doyle. She told me how she found out about his involvement. She told me about how angry she'd been that she could do nothing to repay Peter for the pain he caused my entire family. He may be dead now, but your family profited from the guns and drugs he ran in both directions. You still have ties in Ireland you got through him. I never wanted any of you dead. That's not what I wanted to take from you. Peter profited from other people's pain. So does your family. I wanted that profit gone."

"'Wanted,' Greta. Past tense."

"I don't know what the fuck I want now, other than to be safe."

I can't blame her for that. But I need to know where we stand. Not romantically or sexually at this point. I need to know how much more damage she intends to wreak on my family.

"Is there another article?"

She looks me in the eye. "No."

"But there could be. You have enough for more, don't you?"

"Yes. There's a reason I didn't submit those for edits." She puts her face in her hands, her elbows resting just above her knees. "I wasn't going to go through with it. I wrote them because I committed to them as my job. I wrote them because they were cathartic. But even before I saw you that night, before someone followed me, I knew I was going to back out. I was going to find a way to tell my editor I couldn't. The Editor-In-Chief was opposed to them, so I didn't have his go-ahead. But my direct supervisor gave me permission. Only he knew what I was doing. He didn't even know where I was spying. But someone wanted to hurt you even more than I did."

"The Editor-In-Chief was opposed because he takes bribes from every syndicate family to keep shite out of the paper. He couldn't tell you that, but I'm surprised your news desk editor didn't." I run my hand through my hair. "Greta, I know you met with Sergei and Anton, so I know they're involved. They're not the leak."

"I know."

"But we came by that knowledge in very different ways."

"Are— are they okay?"

"Of course. They are the *pakhan's* cousins. They're untouchable unless we want all four families in a street war. The wives should have been, too. As far as my family is concerned, they are now."

"Then how did you know?"

"I can't answer that."

"But you want me to tell you everything."

"Yes, and it blows because it makes me a hypocrite. But the difference is, me telling you risks your life and plenty of other people's. There are things I will never tell you. They aren't safe for you to know, and they aren't safe for other people if I tell."

"You speak as though there's a future."

"I want there to be." I move over to the sofa and take her hands again.

"I don't understand, Daddy." She whispers, and it nearly breaks my heart. This is the most vulnerable she's ever sounded. I hate it.

"*Cailín*, my family's weathered far worse than this story. And if any family understands revenge... Mine won't be pleased to find out you were behind this. But they will understand your reason. What you wrote was bad. It's going to cost us a lot to fix it, but we've survived far worse. But what you wrote is also endangering you. Not from my family. Someone else. I don't know who yet, but someone hacked you to hurt you as much as to hurt us. Do you have any rivals?"

"Yeah. Of course. Some of my colleagues would sell their mother for a chance to get an exposé like I did. They'd sell their own kidney to get placement like those articles did. But none of them would do it and risk your family coming after them."

"Then someone is very secure in their position to believe they're untouchable from us."

"Apparently."

She closes her eyes and tilts her head. Her brow's furrowed. I don't think she realizes how tightly she's squeezing my hands. Her expression changes. It's sadness, even if her eyes are still closed. When she looks at me, I remain quiet again.

"You pointed out that I said 'wanted.' That my need to

retaliate is in the past. But you still haven't told me why you made it sound like there's a future."

"Because there is one if you want it."

"How? Maybe your family will understand. That doesn't mean they'll forgive me. How have you forgiven me?"

"Because I don't think you faked the way you feel about me. I don't think you would have done any of this if not for a sense of duty to your family. Anger, yes. Hatred, yes. But those only festered because you believe in family. We're not so different there. We're both loyal. To our core. That's what matters most to us. Family, honor, duty, and loyalty. You work hard. You're diplomatic and tactful when you need to be. But you take no shite and will put up a fight when you need to. You're also fecking hot as feck. That's not the main reason I'm attracted to you, but my cock definitely won't let me forget. I want you, Greta. Not just in my bed. I want you in my life. It felt like the worst kind of betrayal to realize you were spying on us. It was a fecking punch in the balls to realize you wrote those articles. If I weren't part of this world, I would walk away. I wouldn't be able to forgive and forget. But the thing is, I get it. The world believes we're devoid of all morals. Those of us who exist in it know it's just the opposite. We have strict morals and ethics. That's why there's retribution. Now that you explained I trust you. I understand. I can accept we aren't that different. In your position, I would have done the same thing."

"So just like that you forgive and forget and trust me again?"

"Do you intend to hurt me again?"

"No." Her response is swift. I can spot a liar. I spend enough time coercing the truth from people to know. She's genuine.

"What do you want, *cailín*?"

"You."

I pick her up as much as she leans into me. I love holding her on my lap. I still don't think of her as a Little. I enjoy having the closeness. Physically, and it brings an emotional closeness, too.

"Dillan, what does this mean?"

"I'm not sure yet. But it means we figure it out together."

"I told you I felt like I was being watched. I—"

"Those were my men across the street from your place. They were mine on your street. I knew something was off once I discovered you met with Anton and Sergei. My guess is you wanted to do this piece, and they were the encouragement you needed to go through with it. You swap intel."

"Yes." She waits for my reaction.

"Wee one, I've been facing off against those two since we were teenagers. They won't hurt you. But whoever leaked your pieces may hurt you because of your association with me or the bratva. This threat could hurt you because they don't approve of what you wrote. They could intimidate you into giving them whatever you haven't written."

"No one is intimidating me into anything, Dillan."

"It won't surprise me if they threaten your life and safety."

"If you truly mean you want to see what the future holds as an 'us,' then this person seriously underestimates my resolve. I fucking infiltrated your organization, worked with the bratva, and wrote articles once intended for the entire world to see. The entire world has seen them. If they think I'm a pushover after having the balls to do all that, they will be sorely disappointed."

"And your lack of cooperation puts you most at danger."

"I'm not wishy-washy. I'm not a fair-weather friend. I don't change sides with the wind. I already swore I wouldn't have gone through with the exposé. If that means you can trust me and you can forgive me, then there is no other choice but for me to take your side. You said family, loyalty, honor, and duty are important to me. They are. Do we have shit we still need to work though? Probably. But I'm not interested in waging a vendetta against you or your family anymore. I can't bring my grandfather back. I can't bring Peter Doyle back to punish him. In the grand scheme of things, my two articles are likely pebbles thrown that you don't even feel."

She's right. These are a serious nuisance right now, but they won't bring us down. I don't think she wrote them on a whim, but I also think she has perspective now that she didn't when this started. Is she pragmatic enough to realize plans and emotions change drastically and unexpectedly? Yes, and I need that in a life partner.

"I believe you. I'm still scared for your safety. Smitty, Alex, and Tommy followed you because they were pissed about Maureen. They blamed you. They were going to corner you and assault you. But they acted on their own. I know you've been anxious about someone else watching you. I saw it the moment I said you wouldn't be able to see anyone lurking. It was new fear that was even greater than the last two times you've worried about being followed. What's going on?"

"I don't know. It's intuition. It screams something way more — dangerous — sinister —foreboding. I don't know. It's just an intense feeling someone is way closer than your men ever got."

"I want you to accept a security detail. For right now, I don't want you going anywhere without me or a man in my family along with another guard I choose."

"What? Your family will hate that. They won't be as forgiving as you are."

"I couldn't give two shites who does or doesn't like it. They don't run this family. I do. But they won't object. They know I went to meet you and that I'm here with you. They know there's something between us. I've heard all of them say shite to me about growing a pair and asking you out. Dating isn't that simple for any of us. They didn't object when I told them I wanted to see if you and I have a future. Even if we weren't contending with all this, you'd still need a detail if we're together. Greta, there are inherent risks being with me."

"That goes without saying. What do I do if we're together and something happens? Like you get arrested or shot?"

Ever blunt when diplomacy isn't needed.

"You get away from me as fast as you can. You run. You hail a cab. You hide. I don't care if you think I'm about to bleed to death or that you can explain things to the cops. You *do not* stay with me, Greta. My family knows what to do for me, and they will get to you. I want you to wear a tracker, too. I won't monitor your comings and goings. But if something happens to you, or you're with me when something happens, I want you to have an alert you can trigger."

"Do you wear one?"

"Yes."

I show her my watch. It looks like there's an extra knob to set the date. The bigger one looks like it sets the time. The smaller knob does that. If I press the bigger one, it sends out a distress message to my cousins. They can track me on their phones.

"And all your cousins have them, too?"

"As do our parents. Greta, I'm controlling in a lot of ways. I have to be. There are things you will discover I'm utterly unbending about. I won't even consider having a conversation with you about them. I won't dictate where you can and can't go or who you can and can't see unless it's for your safety. That's what matters most to me. I want you protected. The men in my family are the only ones I believe are good enough to guard you. I can trust my men to go with you for regular daily things like to and from work. However, if you're deviating from a routine or schedule I know, then I want a family member with you. I know I can't be with you 24/7. It's not possible and not healthy. But I will make sure I always take care of you."

She stares into my eyes, and I hope she reads the earnestness in them. She cups my jaw with her left hand and strokes her thumb over my cheekbone.

"How do I take care of you, Dillan? I don't want this to be one-sided. I don't want to ask for your forgiveness, then take even more. What do you need?"

I can't remember the last time someone asked me that besides before a meal or a job assignment. It makes my heart ache.

"I just need you."

"Can I have my punishment now, please?"

I stare at her for a long moment. I'm uncertain I want to carry this out. She must see my doubt.

"Daddy, you were right. We will both feel better if we do this. I want it to clear my conscience."

"Come then."

I lead her upstairs and down the hall to a guest bedroom. I planned to bring her here all along, so there are some things waiting for us. I ran an errand before I went to her office. I took a cab— a rarity, but I didn't need anyone knowing where I was headed —and did a little shopping before I came back to my place to have Jake take me to her. There's a bag filled with things I want to use with her and only her. She looks around the room, then up at me. She doesn't know what awaits her. Her gaze darts toward the door, and I can guess what she's looking at. What she's wondering.

"I want you in my bed tonight. I want you in it all the time. That's why I don't want to associate this punishment with a place I hope only brings us both pleasure."

She turns toward me and slides her arms around my waist. She rests her head on my chest, and I feel her sigh. "You truly want this, don't you? Want *us*."

"I've told you several times. Why do you doubt me?"

"Maybe once the punishment is over, I won't have the doubts. It's just hard to believe you can forgive me so easily. You aren't playing me for a fool, are you?"

She doesn't let go or lean back to look at me. I reach between us and unfasten her pants. I push them down her hips enough for me to slide my hand down the front of her panties.

"I don't need to string you along to get laid. I don't need to string you along to have a BDSM partner. I don't need to string you along to feel like I'm getting revenge. I don't want revenge. I want to see if we have a future. You spied on my family for more than just work. You did it because of your family. I told you, I can understand retribution. I can even respect it because your motivation wasn't just to harm us. It was to honor people you love. Fecked-up as that is, there are few people in this world who would understand that better than me. You asked me what I want— I want someone who is that devoted to family to be on my side."

I've been sweeping my fingers back and forth between her pussy lips. Now I thrust my fingers. I wedge three inside her, and I'm rubbing the silky skin that lines her cunt.

"Strip."

"Yes, Daddy." She hurries to shimmy out of her pants and thong, then she yanks off her shirt and bra.

"Do not wear panties again. I will spank you if you do. When I want your pussy, I will have it. Do you know why?"

"Because it's your pussy, Daddy."

She falls straight into this roleplay. This dynamic we both want. She could call me Sir as easily as she could Daddy. But I'm not her Dom. I have romantic feelings for her, which would creep some people out if they knew she called me Daddy. But it's about her trust in me. She knows I could retaliate. She knows I could destroy her. But she's trusting me to do nothing to harm her. That trust goes a long way to repair mine.

"And what does that mean?"

"That you can do whatever you want to it."

"That's right." I pull my hand free. "Greta, I'm not interested in domestic discipline. You can say what you want and do what you want. You don't have to defer to me. I want to support your emotional needs, but I know you don't need me to look after you like you're younger than you are. But I am in control. I think you understand why I need that. Part of that control is knowing I can please you whenever I think you need an escape or you need to feel taken care of. Part of it is that I want to fuck you every single second of every single day. I want your pussy available for a good fuck whenever I want."

I grin and waggle my eyebrows at her. I told the truth, but I can do it with some humor.

"And if I want your cock available to me whenever I want?"

"Unzip my pants and take me out whenever you want. I won't turn you down."

"Then no underwear for you either. I want what I want when I want it. I'm an only child, after all."

"I'd happily give in to that, but unlike your pants, mine won't hide that you make me horny as hell. My pants will show my constant hard on. The moment I think of you, I'm hard. It's fecking inconvenient at times, and it's already hard— difficult —to hide that. No boxer briefs to keep things from flopping around would ensure everyone knows I'm thinking about your sweet little cunt. It'll make them think about your sweet little cunt. And then I'd have to beat them." *To death.*

I catch myself. That might be how I feel, but I doubt that's a sentiment I should share with her.

"And I'd fucking bludgeon any woman checking out your cock like that. I won't share you, Dillan. If this is what we're doing, then it's only us. I don't want to know, or worse, wonder, who else you're with. If my pussy belongs to you, then your dick belongs to me."

I don't want to freak her out, but she needs to understand what I mean when I say "us."

"I haven't dated in over a decade. I didn't have many girl-friends in high school, and the ones I did were from mob fami-lies. That wasn't an easy option in college, so I kept things casual. I haven't been in a committed relationship since college. The fact I want one now, especially in my position, is some-thing extremely new to me. I can't easily bring someone into my life. I'll admit I'm scared to bring you closer, and not because of what we're working through right now. I'm scared because of the dangers. I'm scared you'll resent the things I can't tell you. The secrets I'll keep. The lies— outright and by omission —I'll have to tell you to keep you and others safe. I'm scared to ask you to sacrifice to be with me. But I want you for more than a few quick tumbles. I want you for more than a few weeks, a few months, or even just a few years."

She listens to me, and I can't tell what she's thinking. That's pretty rare. I can usually guess, if not know with certainty, what's on someone's mind.

"Dillan, if I'm going to enter this world, then it has to be for the long haul. I won't do this if you're going to walk away. I won't do this if you're emotionally shut off beyond what's a necessity. If I'm all in, then you have to be, too. I won't accept it any other way."

"Can you see an indefinite future with me?"

"No."

I flinch. I didn't intend to, but her response was so swift and emphatic.

"Dillan, I refuse to consider something indefinite. This is too much to do without certainty. I want to see a definite future with you. At least, I want to work toward that."

I didn't realize how my heart started pounding before she explained. We've jumped a long fucking way in the past two hours. I knew from the get-go I would give her the benefit of the doubt. That's why I went to get her and why I brought her here. I knew I would listen to her explanation, and I prayed it was one I could accept. I'd already made up my mind that if I could find any way around this to understand and forgive, I would. She draws me like a moth to the flame. I just hope I don't wind up scorched.

Chapter Ten

Greta

My head is spinning. Like dazed and confused, or I need an exorcism. I'm uncertain. I don't know if I've processed this enough to think this is a good idea. Or if Dillan's charisma has lured me in. Maybe this is the best decision I'll ever make. I hope it is. But it's still a lot to take in. Two hours ago, I was still freaking the fuck out about the articles leaking. Then I was terrified when I saw Dillan get out of the car. The next thing I know after that we're having sex in his town car. An intense conversation followed, and somehow that resolved most things. Now I'm waiting for him to punish me.

And I have resisted none of this. It feels so fucking natural that it's fucking bizarre. Paging Dr. Freud. Paging Dr. Jung. Paging Dr. Adler. I don't know that three of them could figure me the fuck out. They'd have had a field day with me. I don't want to fuck my father, but Freud probably would say there is some latent issue with abandonment or what not. My father has always been perfectly present. Dr. Jung would probably say this— relationship —is the manifestation of some dream I never realized. And Dr. Adler would simply say I want to belong to a family of like-minded people. But how would he explain my sudden willingness to attach myself to the family whose member killed my grandfather?

"Greta?"

"Yes, Daddy. Sorry. Just thinking."

"We can take things slowly."

I watch him, and I think he might be just as befuddled by how things have played out as I am. But we both seem awfully certain for how confusing all of this is. I move to kneel, but he catches my arms and holds me up.

"*Cailín*, I'm not your Dom. You don't kneel for me and wait submissively for me to give my next command. And while I'd love a blow job any time you're inclined to give one, I never want you to think you have to service me or pleasure me for us to reconcile. My forgiveness and my caring are unconditional."

"May I kiss you as equals before we start?"

"Any time, *mo stór*." My darling.

That makes my toes curl. Calling me little girl and wee one are already special endearments to me. And they define our dynamic— he's in control, and I like it. But this is genuine affection, and I crave it from him. I step into his embrace and press my lips to his. I start slowly, but I eventually open to him. My tongue flicks his, inviting him into my mouth. I suck lightly before pressing my body to his as tightly as I can.

"*Diolun, cha robh dithis riamh a' fadadh teine nach do las eatarra.*" Dillan, two never kindled a fire, but it lit between them.

It's a traditional Irish phrase. I don't know how many people know it these days, but I think it's true for us. Attraction — maybe even love one day —comes naturally for people who were meant to be together.

"Márgrég, is *tú mo rogha.*" Mairghráid, you are my chosen one.

"I don't use Gaelic that often with my parents anymore, and I only use it with Granny when she forgets her English. She's spoken English nearly as long as she has Gaelic. It was more a family tradition to keep teaching it than a necessity. I'm glad I can speak it with you."

"Same."

"Even though it meant I could understand conversations you didn't intend me to get?"

"Yes. There will be times when I may need to tell you something in public I don't want anyone else to understand. Something about the people we're around who are from other syndicates. Something about a danger I want you to avoid. Something about how much I want to drive my cock into any part of you I desire."

"Such a romantic."

He cocks an unapologetic eyebrow, and I grin. I back away from him, my hands behind my back. I won't kneel, and I won't dip my head. But I can signal I'm ready for whatever comes next.

"Greta, what's your safe word?"

"I've used *stad* in the past."

It's stop in Gaelic. Easy for a partner to understand and remember. Easy to say when you're at your limit. But I don't want to use that with Dillan. I don't want to recycle something when we've just declared our intentions and at least some of our feelings. If not in English, we sure did in Irish with two traditional phrases.

I try to think of other things I can use. *En iomarca* means too much, but I could say that out of desperation but not really want to stop. *Go leor* is enough, but that is also something I might say in a context that I don't mean stop. *Rua* is red, and I know plenty of people use colors in English. But that feels too generic for what I want us to share. I suppose I could pick an English word, but Gaelic feels intimate between us.

"*Croiméal.*"

"Moustache?" He laughs, his brow furrowing.

"Yeah. I'm standing here, trying to come up with something, and watching you. The other day I thought about how you could probably grow a moustache pretty easily since you already had a five o'clock shadow. Then I thought about how much I would dislike facial hair on you since I enjoy seeing your entire face. You're rather handsome. It came back to me."

"All right. *Croiméal* it is. Go climb on the bed. Hands and knees."

I follow his instructions, making sure I stick my ass up. I'll take whatever the punishment is, and I'm certain spanking will be part of it. He walks to the foot of the bed where I spied a bag I'm guessing has a few gadgets to torture or pleasure me. It all depends on how generous he's feeling, and I don't think merciful is in the cards for me. As he opens it, he talks to me, helping me to prepare.

"What's your pain tolerance, Greta?"

"Pretty high, I think."

"Do you have any hard limits for impact play?"

"None."

"Do you know this from experience? Or are you assuming?"

"Experience. I can take birching, Daddy."

I hear him stop moving, then he comes to where he can see my face. He helps me up until I'm kneeling.

"I don't like the idea of birching you. This won't be pleasant, and I pray it's the most stringent punishment— the only punishment —I ever give you. I don't want to see lasting welts on you for days or a week. But is birching something you enjoy?"

"I have, but I don't need it. If you wouldn't enjoy it, then we don't need to do it."

"*Mo stór*, I've birched other women. I had no problem with it. It's you I don't want to birch. I need you to know there's a difference." He watches me, and my heart melts a little.

"Yes, Daddy. I can tell."

I lean forward, once more on my forearms. I hear him ripping open packaging. I gotta admit I'm happy everything he's using with me is new. Not just from a jealousy standpoint, but hygiene. I know there are plenty of different ways to sanitize toys, but ew. I don't want something that's been in another woman's hoo-ha up mine. And I don't want to think about him using any of these things on a woman in his past. I want to only think about us in the now and us in the future.

He walks back around to where I can see him, and I notice what's in his hands. Oh, fucking hell!

"I can see you're already nervous, and this didn't help."

"I've never tried figging before."

"Does the ginger scare you?"

"No. I just know it's going to burn."

"Yes, it will. That will come at the end. Does anything else here bother you?"

I shake my head.

"Answer me out loud."

"No, Daddy."

"Good."

He reaches beneath me and attaches two nipple clamps, then he passes the chain from one hand to the other as he moves to attach the third clamp to my clit. It's a kind of pain I enjoy, but in this case, I know it will turn me on and leave me frustrated.

"Why are you being punished, Greta?"

"I betrayed your trust. I lied about why I worked for you. I sneaked around and listened to conversations I wasn't supposed to hear. I wrote articles intentionally meant to hurt you and your family. I—"

"That hurts, but I'm not punishing you for that. You did what you did with the articles for your family. It's the infiltrating my family, my life, only to abuse my faith in you. That's what I'm punishing you for. You betrayed me. Period. Not just my trust. Not just my feelings for you. You aimed to hurt me by playing me for a fool. You could have stopped before I caught you. You could have told me."

"I know, Daddy. But once I was up to my eyeballs, there didn't seem to be a way to tell you."

"I get it scared you. I—"

"It wasn't just being scared. I regretted it, and I was too ashamed to tell you."

"You had my trust, but I didn't have yours. That's a betrayal in and of itself, too. You knew how I felt, and you manipulated me. That's what I meant when I said you aimed to hurt me and make a fool of me."

"I know, Daddy." What else am I supposed to say, even if I am repeating myself? It's true.

"Since this is a true punishment, I will not warm you up. We will begin with my hand, and it will hurt. Then we will move to the paddle. I wish to do more, but I don't know if you can tolerate that much to begin with."

"I can. I know it."

"Kick, cry, whatever you need. But do not put your hands back there. If I catch them by accident, it will hurt a shite ton more than your arse. If I hurt you, I won't be pleased."

"Can I sit up again, please?"

"Yes. You don't have to ask. I know our dynamic is— weird.

You submit to me, but you aren't my submissive. You don't have to ask permission to speak to me as an equal. You can always do that."

"I didn't trust you when it came to my family. I could have confronted you, but I chose to continue to be deceptive. But I have trusted you. Over and over. I trusted you to protect me from the Albanians and the men in your club. I trusted you to protect me from Tommy and the others. I trust you to protect me from whomever is after me now. I trust you to know how much I can take and to administer this punishment safely. You have my trust in a lot of big things, Dillan. I fucked up by lying and by targeting your family. But I haven't lied about how I feel about you, and I have always trusted you with my life. I can trust you to spank me."

I settle back onto my forearms, and I'm barely in position before his hand crashes onto my ass.

"OW!"

Mother of God! That fucking hurts!

I squeeze my eyes shut and clutch the comforter in both fists. I fight not to scream again. I fight not to kick my feet. I fight not to cry as one after another lands across my horizontal crack. I won't sit for days, and this is just the beginning. My head hangs down as I pant. He alternates sides, sometimes doubling and tripling up on one cheek before moving to the other. Sometimes he lands them across both halves. Over and over until he gets to fifty. He squeezes, then rubs. It takes some of the burn away.

"Are you okay?"

"Yes, Daddy. It hurts so much."

"I'm sure it does."

He picks up the paddle he laid on the bedside table with the ginger root. He puts it in front of me, so I can examine it. It has holes in it. Fucking hell. The holes allow it to move faster through the air, so it'll land much harder than a solid paddle when the same amount of force is applied to the spank.

"I see you understand just how much this is going to hurt. What do you say if it's too much, *cailín?*"

"*Croiméal.*"

"If you need to say it in English, you can. I'll respect it. If you can't get out words, then snap. I'll respect that too."

I barely nod before the paddle lands across my ass. I know it makes my ass bounce. It's my least favorite feature, but he always seems to like it. I've accepted I'm not slim. Most would consider me chunky or chubby. 4Play caters to men who like plus size women with the strength and agility to twirl on a pole. They like asses on waitresses they could pat— squeeze —even though they aren't supposed to. They like tits practically falling out of the bikini tops we wore. They even like soft bellies. I definitely have that, and thighs much thicker than you would see on waitresses or dancers at any other club. I never saw Dillan checking out his employees, but I know he used to fuck Maureen, and she's built similar to me. It must have been his thing even back then, unless she was thinner in high school.

I pull myself back into the present when a spank lands particularly hard across the top of my ass, nearly at my lower back. There's little padding there to absorb the impact.

"Pay attention, Greta. No slipping off into your mind to forget about the pain. Count for me. I'm giving you twenty more."

"Yes, Daddy." I didn't mean to let my mind wander, but it helped me cope. Now I'm going to be fully aware of everything.

"Rest your shoulder on the bed and spread your arse cheeks for me."

I do as I'm told.

"I am going to fuck your arse in the morning. I'm going to leave my cum in you, and you're going to hold it in there until your muscles are too tired to keep squeezing. Then you're going to feel it dribble down your leg. It's going to dry and be sticky until I wash it away tomorrow night. You will remember you belong to me."

"Yes, Daddy." I'm breathless. Not from the spanking. I'm breathless from the prospect I might spend the night, so he can fill my ass in the morning. That he'll want to see me again tomorrow night.

He trails a finger along my ass as he reaches for the ginger. Oh, hell!

"I took a cab to the store to get these— tools." His grin makes my pussy ache. "And I carved the ginger on the ride back here. I made sure it was perfectly ready to go before Jake took me to your office. Hold still, wee one."

I love that he has different ways of reminding me I'm smaller than him. I'm a lot smaller in height and breadth of my frame. His finger taps my asshole before pressing against it. He doesn't dip his finger into me, but he covers my hands with his and pulls my ass cheeks apart harder.

"I might be looking at this pretty little star, but I see a juicy pussy. You liked your spanking so far. As much as it hurt, you enjoyed the pain."

"I didn't realize. I can't tell."

I try to shift to rub my thighs together, but his hand reins down on my ass. He slides the carved ginger into my hole, and I clench. I force myself to relax. Clenching will only make it worse. I already know from reading domestic discipline romances. But I can't stop myself when the paddle lands.

"One, Daddy. I'm sorry."

Spank.

"Two, Daddy. I won't betray you again."

Spank.

"Three, Daddy. If I have a problem with you or your family or whatever, I will come to you."

He's remaining silent through it all. I adjust my position to catch a peek at his face. He's not enjoying this. Once he's sure he's aligned with my ass, he looks away every time the paddle connects to my ass. Shit. This is punishing him as much as it is me. That breaks my heart.

The spanking keeps going as I count. I can't stop from kicking the mattress as my ass burns from the inside out. I tried to relax myself and not flinch. But when the paddle lands, my instinct is to clench as I brace for it. Clenching only presses the ginger tighter against the sensitive skin inside my asshole. It makes my skin absorb the oils faster.

"Ahhhh-haaaaa! Ahhhh-haaaaa!"

I can't stop the sobs that now pour forth. I'm crying for the pain, the shame, the guilt, the need for forgiveness. I don't even realize the spanking stopped because I'm shaking too hard. I feel Dillan ease the ginger from my ass, then he's cradling me in his arms, rolling me toward him as he sits on the edge of the bed. He opens his thighs, so my ass fits between them. He releases the nipple and clit clamps, which I'd forgotten about since the pain in my backside stole my attention. Now the blood rushes back into all three, and I writhe. It's a fresh wave of unholy pain. I need him to lick or suck away the pulsing ache, but he's just looking down at me.

"Dillan, I am so sorry. So, so sorry."

"I know you are. But it's done. It's forgiven. We exorcised it from our relationship. Now we move forward together."

"Is it really that simple? How can it be?"

"No. It's not that simple, but that's how I see it. I don't want to dwell on this, or it will break us apart. We agreed to move forward together. If we live in that part of our past, we have no chance to make this work."

"Have you always been this philosophical?"

"I think it's just pragmatism."

He wipes my tears as he kisses my forehead, my nose, my cheek. He tilts my head up and presses the tenderest kiss to my lips I've ever received. I can imagine it one day being filled with love. I return it, and I hope he gets the same feelings in return.

"Is my punishment done? Or should I stand in the corner?"

I'm genuinely wondering. I read DDLG romances sometimes, and I have a friend at my club who's a Middle. She has to stand in the corner when she's been punished.

"No. You aren't a child, nor do either of us want you to feel like one. Let me hold you unless you're too uncomfortable. Do you want to lie down?"

"Maybe in a little bit. Right now, I need you to keep holding me. I need this aftercare, Daddy."

"Whatever you need."

Calling him Daddy right after he tells me I'm not a child nor feel like one to either of us may seem completely counterintuitive, but as I sit here, I'm thinking about why the term fits. He's a protector. He's a provider— not of a roof over my head or food on my table, but for my emotional needs. He's strong and steady, dependable. He's forgiving and kind, but stern when needed. He makes me feel special. Aren't those all the things a Daddy is supposed to be? I also think it's kinky as fuck. So, there's that.

I nestle against his chest and let my heartbeat slow. The perspiration on my brow dries. And I suddenly feel so sleepy. It's sub-drop. I haven't experienced it since I first started getting into BDSM. For many, it starts hours or even days after the scene. I recognize the feeling. It's not just exhaustion from the physical exertion. It's the sudden surge of weepiness that's different from the crying in pain or guilt. I squeeze my eyes shut.

"Greta, talk to me. What's going on?"

I hear the worry. My face is buried against his chest, so I don't think he can see my eyes. But that alone is a pretty clear sign I'm hiding from what's happening to me. Or trying to run from it. I shake my head. I can't speak. I want to. I think I open my mouth to, but nothing comes out. When he stands, I fear he's going to put me down. I scramble to cling to him.

"Shh, wee one. I'm kicking off my shoes, so I can climb onto the bed. All that adrenalin and endorphins just vanished, didn't they?"

The best I can do is nod. He climbs onto the bed, and I feel him unbuttoning his shirt. He moves around and slips it off, then he's helping me put it on. I don't realize what I'm doing until much later, but I pull the shirt to my nose and inhale his cologne and detergent scents. He strokes my head, my back, my tender ass.

"Rest, Greta. I'll hold you until you tell me to let go. Sleep, and I'll still be here when you wake."

"You're going to get bored."

"No, I won't. Nothing about being near you is ever boring."

"Your arms will get tired."

"I can carry Seamus's and Cormac's heavy asses up and down stairs. I can sit here and hold my little girl."

"You'll get cold."

"Greta, I'm not letting go. I'm not going anywhere, and neither are you. You're staying here tonight. In the morning, I'll take you to work with my cum in your arse. No, I didn't forget about that. Then I will pick you up. We'll go to your place, and you'll get whatever you need to spend the next few days here with me. I told you. I want you in my bed."

I tilt my head back and look up at him. God, I hope he means for forever.

Chapter Eleven

Dillan

I'd say forever if I didn't fear freaking her out. She's drifting off in my arms, and I can't think of anything better than holding her. But I need the quiet to work through everything in my mind. I'm one of the least forgiving people alive unless it's toward someone in my family. I can hold a grudge with the best of them. I can exact revenge with a precision that makes the old Soviets in the movies look like pussycats. I could have followed through with my threat to destroy a woman responsible for what's happening.

But I can't do anything like that to Greta.

I think back to the days when Peter Doyle was still floating around. The man betrayed his family. Oh, he claimed it was a righteous cause. Family honor. But unlike Greta, it was entirely self-serving. His father made his two sons swear to stay away from us. The O'Rourkes had mostly let the Doyles out, which isn't entirely unheard of, but rare. Killian and Peter Doyle were free and clear. Killian obeyed his parents' last wish and stayed far, far away from us until he had no choice thanks to his brother.

Never did any of us imagine Killian's daughter, Laura, would wind up married to the head of the bratva. Uncle Donovan took issue with Laura picking the bratva over us. But she had no idea her family ever had mob ties. When Peter got involved, Killian couldn't— wouldn't —forgive him, so he paid the price.

He'd fled to Dublin, then Galway after their parents died in an explosion arranged by the then-leader of the bratva. Maksim's predecessor. It wasn't entirely unprovoked retaliation. My family fucked with Vlad Lushak to the tune of two bullets that couldn't be removed from his leg, so he got pissed. Supposedly, Peter was in the car when it exploded. It was an excuse my grandfather created so Peter could flee. I was super young and have no memory of this part. Once he was in Ireland, Peter helped us run drugs, guns, gambling rings, and a few other ventures there. We lost several contacts in Ireland when he died.

It was news to me he was involved in Greta's grandfather's death, but it wasn't news to me he was arming the IRA. The man had no moral or political ties to the cause. He had ties to making money, so those were unaffiliated jobs.

Peter could have stayed out of all of it, but he wanted in. He wanted this life because he believed his father and brother were cowards. He believed he defended the Doyle name by becoming a member. My grandfather didn't want him. It's why he concocted the story that Peter died alongside his parents, so he could ship Peter off to Ireland. The most he had to deal with back then were periodic phone calls. Uncle Donovan would get texts and emails— despite how I advised Grandda and Uncle Donovan not to use unsecure servers.

I was so pissed when I found out Uncle Donovan let Peter

get involved with the Kutsenko issue and that they'd targeted a woman that I took an uncharacteristic vacation. I left the country, so I wouldn't kill either of them. How he thought the plan would work is beyond me. Uncle Donovan started listening to my advice when I was fifteen. Even back then, I had a mind for strategy. He never admitted to anyone outside the family that he let a kid pull the strings, but he did. Shite only went to hell when he acted against my advice.

I inhale breaths so deep my chest feels like it stretches tight. I can't think about that time without rage boiling within. Donovan didn't have kids, so it was a foregone conclusion I would inherit from him. But I took that poorly timed vacation and came home to Declan in charge. He categorically refused to listen to me, despite how all the senior leaders warned him not to act against my advice. No one outside our family knows this, but he put hits on my mom and my aunts— his cousins —to ensure no one stopped him. He hired Robert Simms. The guy's a ghost. A hired mercenary who has no loyalty to anyone but the almighty dollar. No one outside the family knows it was my father and uncles who made sure Declan was at the warehouses at the docks when Bogdan Kutsenko struck back for what happened to his now-wife, Christina. My mom and her two sisters married three brothers. It's how their last names never changed. My two sides of the family haven't been related for at least ten generations, but there have been enough sons on both sides to keep the name going.

Before I could call off Simms, one of his hired guns targeted my aunt Saoirse. The hits on my mom and aunts still stood, and the woman confused Colleen for my aunt.

I close my eyes as I remember that day.

My sister was so beautiful. Not just her red hair and green eyes. If anyone thinks the Kutsenkos genetics are unreal, they should look at all of us with our red hair and green eyes. It was her smile. It was a million kilowatts when she looked at you. She had one of those laughs that you had to be broken if you didn't laugh along. She was the absolute ringleader with six boys following her commands since we were toddlers. She was younger than me, but she could get me to do anything. Even when I knew I'd wind up in more trouble than anyone else because I'm the oldest. She had the kindest heart of anyone I've ever met. She was a veterinarian who specialized in treating rescued animals from puppy mills and ones the ASPCA brought in. We're talking the dogs in the Sarah McLaughlin ASPCA commercials.

The bratva believe they lost a lot because of Donovan and Declan, but all their women are still alive.

I gaze down at Greta, and protectiveness surges through me. Colleen was my sister. Greta is mine. That thought wraps me back around to where I started. Peter claimed his actions were all in the name of family. To avenge his parents. But they never wanted that. I doubt Greta's grandparents would have wanted her to risk as much as she did coming near my family and me. But she wasn't willing to kill. She wanted to expose us and make us lose money. She doesn't understand that she might not pull the trigger, but exposing as much as she likely could have might have gotten at least one of us killed if we didn't prepare for shite like this. I won't pour salt in the wound for either of us, but I will have to explain that at some point. The difference in intention is why I can accept Greta.

My phone vibrates in my pocket, and I fish in it to pull it out. It's difficult with Greta still sleeping in my arms. I look at the screen. I sigh. Speaking Gaelic won't make this private if Greta wakes.

"Hey, Finn."

"You alone?"

"No."

"Does she speak Spanish?"

"I don't know."

"*Esperemos que no.*" Let's hope not.

"*¿Qué pasó?*" What happened?

It's New York City, and the Colombians are one of our chief rivals. It should surprise no one that we speak Spanish. We all speak far more Italian than the Mancinellis know, and we've learned a shite ton of Russian too. I insisted upon it when we were in high school and college. The other families may not know what we're talking about when we switch languages, but we know almost everything they're saying. What one of us doesn't understand, someone else is bound to. Let them think we're ignorant potato farmers. Works for us.

Finn and I continue in Spanish as he explains. "Misha and Pasha took three of our shipments."

"Which ones?"

My cousin needs to narrow it down. We have shite coming and going. The *Cosa Nostra* control as much of the docks as we do. Neither the bratva nor the Cartel get anything in through the New York harbor without going through us or the Italians.

"All the whiskey for starters."

It's not anything good, but we have guys who hustle street corners with regular customers. We also sell it farther afield to places where we know alcoholism runs rampant. We provide a good and a service. What people do once they walk away isn't our problem. We all make choices.

"What else?"

"The Italian ceramics."

"They went for that? Not Salvatore? He's been pissing vinegar for months about us doing business with the companies in Umbria."

"I know. I think Misha and Pasha did it to piss off Enzo."

"What'd he do to them? He's the one with the cleanest nose

in the family." Doesn't mean we aren't planning our own shite against him. I don't tolerate any interruptions to my plans.

"He hacked their accounting software, inflated their Bear Enterprises tax liability, then drained the escrow account."

I snort. The Kutsenkos and Andreyevs will have no problems paying their quarterly taxes. It's the fact that Pasha is the family accountant that makes it funny. He and Enzo have been going back and forth for years, fucking each other over, hoping the IRS will step in. No one in the IRS is fucking stepping between those two. They'd love to nail all four families, but they won't get caught between two.

"So, they swept in, stole ceramics presumably the Mancinellis planned to steal from us, and sold them. What's the third shipment?"

"Oh, just the two thousand cars we had on that cargo ship."

"*Malparido*." Badly born.

It loses something in the translation. Basically, motherfucker. It's one of the harder hitting curses. It fits. They stole legal cargo from each shipment, but they know we can't go to the authorities. They'll then sell them legally to keep themselves looking legit. The very thing we do. We all do. But usually, we keep our hands to ourselves when it comes to such large shipments coming through customs. They'll have already forged manifests and the whole nine. Motherfucking pieces of shite sons of bitches. Except Alina and Svetlana are two of the nicest women, considering they're married to and spawned pieces of shite bratva. They used to bring these amazing sugar cookies to our soccer games.

Yeah. That's right. My cousins and I played club soccer against and with the Kutsenkos and Andreyevs in middle school. Not only that, but we also played on the same teams and as rivals to the Diazes and Mancinellis. Picture it— not Sicily 1920, just Queens early 2000s —a bunch of five-, six-, and seven-year-olds running around soccer fields, high fiving and shoulder checking each other. Only the latter is left. A mere five, six, seven years later, we were all carrying knives to school in case someone shanked us on the way home.

And yes, that happened. We all did it. I got Maks one day during junior year. I came out of a bodega near our high school, and he was standing there with the bitch he was dating, Nadia. I feel no guilt calling her that because she was. I don't even feel like I'm slut shaming her to call her one. What else do you call someone who sleeps with every bratva man under the age of eighty by the time she was twenty? She questioned my manhood. Maks laughed. I stabbed him.

"Dillan?"

"Yeah. I'm thinking. They expect us to go for the cars since they're worth the most. And they want us to go for the whiskey since we're Irish. Fuckers."

I look down as Greta shifts in my arms, but her eyes remain closed, and her breathing doesn't change.

"Get the ceramics. They're worth the least. Destroy them. Leave the dust for them outside their warehouse. Torch everything in it. If you can't do that, they have that freight coming from an Illinois factory. Get the tractors and mining trucks before they get to the Port of Houston. We sell them in Mexico instead of them. If that can't happen, then smash the vodka in their new cargo container that arrived last night. That's the least valuable, but it'll stick it to them for being fucking Russian."

"Causing an international incident. Really?"

"The shite is made in America. They went for our Irish whiskey made in Ireland."

"And if all that fails?"

"It better not. At least one of those three better succeed.

But if we screw the pooch on all of them, then take out a dozen *bratoks*." Soldiers. Worker bees. Disposable.

"Who do you want to oversee all of this?"

"Send Cormac to the whiskey, Seamus to the ceramics, and the twins to the heavy machinery, and I want you to deal with the cars. Let's get those back after we do everything else. Let them think we're satisfied with the petty stuff before we get back what we really want. Let them think we believe we can't. They can pay all the excise taxes before we take what's ours."

"And you?"

"I'll check in tonight. I need to meet with all of you. We need to talk about this situation."

Finn knows Greta is the situation. I can only imagine what he thinks I'm going to say.

"Dillan, we know."

That makes me freeze as I watch Greta. Her face is so relaxed. She looks so at peace, and I hate the idea that anything might disturb her. That anything might bring fear back into her eyes or the visceral anger I heard when she told me what she'd planned.

"What is it you think you know, Finn?" My voice is more patronizing than it needs to be. Finn's my closest friend, even though we're all more like brothers than cousins. We were all raised that way.

"We know she's not the leak, but the source."

I keep my voice neutral when I respond, but my heart is racing. "And?"

"And what? We can't convince you to break up with her, so we're not even going to try. But you owe us an explanation."

"And I'll give you one. That's why we need to talk."

"When and where?"

"Here. We can go in my office. Nine o'clock." That'll give

everyone enough time to get shite done, or at least, set things in motion.

"She's there, isn't she?"

"Yes and will be."

That makes Finn pause before he says more as we continue in Spanish. "Will she be at the meeting?"

"Not unless you guys have questions I can't answer."

"And if we have things to say you don't want to hear?"

I mentally roll my eyes. "How is that anything but typical?"

"Don't be a douche. Don't answer a question with a question."

"Do it respectfully, but it's fair for all of you to ask what you want to know."

"And if she refuses to answer?" He keeps pressing, and it's annoying.

"Then I have yet another problem to handle, but I'm not giving her up, Finn. Tell the others that."

"You'd pick her over the family."

It's not a question, but I still know the answer.

"If she'll agree, she will be family."

"You can't be serious!"

"We'll talk about all of this tonight. I'm not saying more over the phone."

"She's still with you?"

"She's sleeping."

"Dillan." I hear the exasperation. "You couldn't slip into your office?"

"This isn't something I'm explaining. What happens between us in my home is no one else's business. Ever."

"Fine. I'll check back with you when things are in motion."

"Thanks." I hang up the call and wonder how the fuck this conversation is going to go.

"Daddy?"

Greta's eyes flutter open. She's been asleep for another half an hour since I hung up with Finn. She slept like the dead. I eased her onto her side and spooned her when my arm went to sleep. She rolls to face me now.

"Yes, *cailín*."

"I must have slept for ages."

"About an hour-and-a-half."

"I never nap."

"It's been a heavy day."

I brush hair back from her shoulder and lean forward to kiss her neck. She lifts her chin, allowing me more space to work my way up to her ear. I kiss behind it before rolling her onto her back. I sit up and strip faster than I would if my clothes were on fire. I've already put my gun in the bedside table drawer. Then I lower myself over her. She opens her arms and legs for me. The tip of my cock brushes her pussy, and I can feel she's still wet from earlier. I ease into her as our gazes lock. Neither of us looks away or even blinks. I move slowly, in no rush to get either of us off yet.

She lifts her hands over her head and crosses her wrists as she watches me. The sight she makes as her back arches, pushing her tits up. I could look at this every day for the rest of my life. I love every curve she has. I've never had a type before, but Greta is everything I desire and more. I love the way her thighs wrap around me with plenty for me to hold. I love how soft she is everywhere. It's the ultimate in femininity no matter what she's doing. I can't get enough as my hands roam over her. I slide one beneath her and squeeze her arse. There's plenty for me to grab while I know I'm leaving fingerprints. I'm going to fuck her from behind tonight, and I'm going to enjoy every second of seeing her juicy arse bounce as I drive my cock into her until I make her scream. Hell, until I make myself scream.

But for now, this is gentler than anything we've done before. The calm after the storm that was punishing her. We both need this as part of the reconciliation. I need her to know we're good. That I still care about her. That I'm falling in love with her.

That's the only way I can justify why I can forgive her. Why I still want her. This is a big speed bump in our relationship, but there's so much I admire about her. It goes so far beyond the physical. It's like her soul calls to mine, and I can't help but answer.

We move together as we kiss, and I pour all my feelings into this, feelings I'm not ready to say. I think she understands because she brings her hands down and buries her fingers in my hair. My gentleness is spurring her on to be more demanding. I brace myself on my left forearm as my right hand goes to her throat. I don't squeeze, but I let it rest heavy there. She opens her eyes as I pull back.

"Daddy, I need more. I know we're not fucking just to get off, but I want you too much and feel too demanding."

She smiles at the end, and I tighten my hold.

"But who decides how I pleasure you?"

"You do. Always. I'm just letting you know what kind of pleasure I want."

"Is that so?"

I thrust hard into her, and she moans. I don't increase my speed. I refuse to. But I surge into her, increasing my force until it must be painful for her.

"Daddy, I won't break. Please."

"You'll be too sore in the morning."

"That's what I'm hoping. I don't just want your cum in my

ass to remind me I belong to you. I want every step I take to tell me you've claimed all of me."

"You'll also know when you look in the mirror."

"Did you mark me?"

"Yes."

"Good." Her left hand presses on the back of my head until I bring my ear close to her lips. "Can I tell you a fantasy I have with you?"

"Of course." I can only imagine what she's going to say.

"I can guess what you do for work, so if this reminds you of it too much, I'll stop as soon as you tell me to."

Fuck. What the hell is she going to say?

"I want you to tie me to this bed. I want you to leave me so long I'm nearly out of my mind needing you, worrying when you'll come back, scared you won't. I want you to gag and blindfold me, so I can't call to you, and I have no sense of time. I want you to come back whenever you want and do whatever you want."

Jesus, Mary, and Joseph. I might come right this second. Tying someone up and doing what I want does sound like what I do at work. But not when I picture her naked in my bed with no way to stop me slaking my lust. Knowing, by doing so, I'm bringing her pleasure.

"You want me to treat you like a sex slave? A fuck doll?"

"I want to show you I belong to you. Not as a slave, so much as someone committed to you and your happiness. And I just find the idea of being at your mercy hot as fuck. I'm in control because I'm letting you do it. But I'm also giving up all control to show you just how much I trust you."

I snag her mouth in a kiss that's brutal. My hand tightens around her throat enough to be considered breath play. I watch her, making sure I'm not doing anything she doesn't want. She lifts her chin like she did earlier when I kissed her neck. I'm careful that this isn't somewhere I'll leave marks.

"You're going to come when I say so, little girl. Five... Four... Three... Two... One. Come for me."

I punctuated each number by ramming into her and grinding my pubic bone against her clit. The moment she tenses, and I feel her inner muscles squeeze my dick, I release her throat. I come with her, and it's about the best orgasm I've ever had. The two I've had with her are the best. My past pales in comparison.

I don't stop moving since I'm going to keep making her come until she begs me to stop. Though I doubt she will. I'll keep going until I can't keep from coming again. We go around and around as she comes with my hand around her throat. I pull out to keep myself from jizzing, then I make her come, then pull out. We do this four times until she's getting red in the face enough that I don't want to push it. I'm careful that I never squeeze hard enough for her to pass out. It's a tenuous balance.

I lower my chest to hers as I spill deep inside her a second time. I can't remember ever being able to go for round two immediately with any woman from my past. Not even when I was a horny teenager. As we watch each other, for the first time in my entire sex life, I want my sperm to swim as far as possible. For the first time, I'm not worried about birth control failing. That's as disconcerting as it comes. Poor pun not intended. I've practically double bagged it since the first time I fucked Maureen. Yeah. I lost my virginity to her. Can't say the same for her.

Our kisses are gentler. More like affectionate pecks as she runs her hands up and down my back. They come to rest on my arse.

"You have the most chiseled ass I've ever felt. It's like a marble statue."

I don't want to know how many arses she's touched to compare. But I'll take the compliment. I roll us, so now it's my hands that are resting on her arse. She tries not to wince, but I know she's sore from the punishment and the way we just fucked. I ease the pressure not wanting to hurt her.

"I like all of your body too much to ever have a favorite part, but your arse is at the top of the list."

I slide my right hand up her waist until I can massage her breast. I roll us again, so we're on our sides. I inch down the bed enough that I can practically swallow her nipple. I suck as hard as I dare while my free hand caresses every part of her I can reach. Shoulder, tits, belly, hip, thigh, arse, neck. I can't get enough as I flick my tongue over her nipple before opening my mouth wider and taking as much in as I can. I switch to the other and feast upon it. I go back and forth for at least fifteen minutes. She strokes my hair, and it's so soothing, I can understand why babies fall asleep nursing. I've scrolled enough porn to know there is such a thing as adult breastfeeding. I wonder if I would be into that with her. I definitely never fantasized about it with any women in my past.

I come up for air and move back to rest my head on my pillow as I cup her jaw and press a soft kiss to her lips. Then we just watch each other. I don't know how long we lie like that. Just our arms wrapped around each other's waist.

"Greta, I want to make this work. I want you in my bed when you're sleeping. I want to hold you like I did. I want to fuck you any time the mood strikes us."

"And if I want you in my bed?"

"Then just tell me when to come over."

She looks contemplative before she nods. I wonder if she's envisioning a future that doesn't involve us shuffling from one place to the other. I can't tell her that. It would freak her out. It's way, way, *way* too soon to say that aloud. I make what most people would call snap decisions all the time. I don't. I just have the ability to assess situations quickly and come up with decisions faster than most. A lot of times, it's intuition. But more often than most people would believe, I've thought things through and come up with at least three contingency plans.

Considering I've been thinking about— wanting —Greta since the night I met her, I've mulled this over a lot. Today's discovery made me hesitate even after I decided I would offer a punishment and absolution. I thought for a moment the truth would be insurmountable. But her explanation was just that. She didn't make excuses. She told me what happened and why. I accepted it.

I draw her to rest her head on my shoulder when I move onto my back. I draw one of her legs between mine before draping her arm around my waist.

"Are you comfy, *cailín*?"

"Incredibly. I can't believe how well I slept. I didn't even feel you put me down earlier, and I could completely doze off again right now. Having your arms around me makes it feel like I'm completely sheltered from the world. That you could be like my invisibility cloak or something."

"That's exactly how I want you to feel. You're mine to protect as much as you are mine to pleasure."

"You always tell me the things you want to do to or for me. But what about what you want and need for yourself?"

"Making you—"

"No, Dillan. Don't give me that altruism. You might mean it, and I believe you do. But it means you give, and I take. No reciprocation, and I'm not okay with that. I want to know the things I can do to make you happy."

Never betray me again.

"I won't betray you again. Don't look so shocked that I said that. You didn't have to say anything out loud for me to read your expression."

"All right. I want to see you at the end of the day, and just be Dillan. Not someone's boss. Not someone responsible for a thousand people's livelihood."

Her eyes widen. Yeah. I have that many people and more on the company payroll.

"We own four casinos in Atlantic City, plus smaller ventures. Then there's the other stuff. A lot of people depend upon me, and that's fine. I'm proud that I provide for them. But I don't want to think about it when I come home. I want someone completely unrelated to that world meeting me for dinner and sleeping beside me. I want to do mundane things like cook, set the table, and do dishes with my partner— with you —just like any other typical couple."

"How often do you want to see me?"

"As often as you'll let me."

She watches me before she responds. "I would like those things every night."

I kiss her cheek. I still don't want to freak her out by suggesting we move in together this soon. But at least she's hinting that's what she wants. But we have to get through my family first.

"Let's have dinner. The others will be here soon."

Chapter Twelve

Greta

"The others?"

Fuck. His family knows. The Spanish Inquisition will look like a tea party by the time they're done with me.

I picture his house and where his family might confront me. His home is spacious for a bachelor, and it makes me wonder why he has such a large home.

"Have you been married before?" I blurt the question before I can think better of it. None of my research shows he has been. Maybe children?

"No. You?" He looks at me funny as we enter the kitchen.

"Not even close. Kids?"

"No. You?"

"There was never anyone I would consider having them with, and my career was way too new to consider taking maternity leave."

Does he hear the past tense? The part about there was

never anyone. The way he's looking at me makes me think he understands, and he's even considering it.

"You have a large house for someone who lives alone."

"You've never seen the six of us crowded into one room. Plus, our six parents too. It gets noisy and tight fast."

"Do you have them over often?"

"Yeah. Everyone takes turns hosting Sunday dinner. I'm next, and I'd like you to be here for it."

I stare. That's in three days. I'm going to meet his parents and aunts and uncles in three days. We haven't even had a proper first date. And what happens when he has to rescind the offer because no one in his family wants me there?

"I can hear your thoughts. You may as well scream them. I'm going to talk to the guys tonight. Once I have them on board, I'll talk to my parents, then my aunts and uncles."

"How can you possibly imagine any of them will accept me when I was bent on destroying your family until a couple days ago?"

"It wasn't until a couple days ago. I think you questioned what you were doing when we started falling for each other. You wrote the articles out of duty, and like you said, it was cathartic."

"That's not how anyone is going to see it. They're going to see me as a threat. Someone disloyal. Someone you should enjoy fucking for a while, then leave the moment it stops being fun."

"If they trust my judgment to lead our family and our organization, then they'll trust my judgment about this."

"Or this could be what calls that judgment into question and brings you down."

"I hear everything you're saying, and it would make sense if we were a normal family. We are hardly that."

I shake my head. If that were true I could have gone

through with the articles without hesitation or regret. "Dillan, you and your cousins are so damn normal that it's like the fucking Twilight Zone."

"Thank you, I suppose."

"And a normal family wouldn't be so forgiving."

"You tell me you trust me, and I know you do with a lot of heavy shite. If you can trust me not to harm you during breath play, can you trust me to know my family?"

Tears well in my eyes. "You don't get it. I'm not worried about me. I'm worried about causing a rift that endangers you or ruins things with your family. I'm worried that once things end, you won't be able to put it all back together again."

I scream as I'm suddenly lifted over him and rolled onto my back. He doesn't even sit up to do it. He's above me, and his stare is so intense I flinch.

"What the feck do you mean when things end?"

"When things don't work out because you realize your family is right. When things don't work out because you don't want me anymore."

"We need to take you to an ENT."

"What?"

"A fucking ear, nose, and throat. You apparently don't hear very well."

I stare at him. Still shocked how he lifted me as though I weighed as little as a child. He could have just rolled forward to have me beneath him. No. He moved me that way to remind he's in control. That he leads, and I follow. I have no objection because if I pointed out a different direction or said I want to stop, he would immediately.

"*Cailín*, maybe I haven't been clear. I'm going to discuss my future with you with my family. I'm going to make sure they understand what motivated you and where things stand now. If I didn't want you in my life permanently, then why would I bother? If I'm moving too fast for you, then say so. Otherwise, I expect us to spend every night together that we can. I don't give a feck if it's here or your place. But both beds are now ours, not yours or mine."

He speaks with such command— even if he's back to not truly swearing —that I can only imagine what he must sound like when he's doling out orders to his men or threats to his enemies. But he knows I said I want a definite future with him. I've told him I want to be with him every night. He's reminding me of what I've already said, already agreed to.

"Yes, Daddy. I'm still scared, but I know you'll protect me the best you can. I don't want them to hate me or question you. I don't want you in a position where you have to choose. I will walk away before it comes to that."

"You truly don't get this. If you walk away, it's because you don't want me or us. It is *not* because of anyone else. I have never ruled my family with an iron fist because I still defer to my parents, aunts, and uncles about a lot of shite. But I won't on this. I have brought *no one* into my life this way. I've allowed no woman this close to my family. If I didn't want you to help run this family beside me, then you wouldn't be here."

"Run the family?"

"Yes. Finn, Seamus, Cormac, Sean, and Shane are my most trusted advisors and partners in many of my legit business ventures. They're my brothers by choice, even if not by blood. They are all equals, and in my mind, only a hair's breadth beneath me. But if I'm pushed, I will show them they can't make me bend. They wanted me in this position, so they will accept all that means. I want them on board with you because it's not going to be easy for you to join this world. If they're okay with you, and you still want that future once you've met everyone, then I have a lot more to explain. You might not want it so much once you know what life with me means."

I feel like a beached whale just staring at him. I could flap my arms like fins, but it wouldn't get me back into calm waters. I'm overwhelmed by what he's saying. I've already thought about what it would mean to be with the mob boss, but I really thought mostly about the danger of him getting killed or going to jail. The probable threats against my life. I never imagined I would have a role.

I push against his chest and sit up when he moves. He looks uncertain as he shifts to sit beside me. I move onto my knees, then straddle his lap. I know he held me for an hour earlier, and he moved me like a rag doll a few minutes ago, but I'm suddenly self-conscious about being too heavy to sit on his lap. It's a sign of my vulnerability playing out through my insecurity. But he grabs my ass and tugs me closer. He rocks my hips until he gets hard again. Fucking Energizer Bunny. It takes a few minutes, but we move in silence until he lifts me and lowers me onto his cock. His fingers dig into my ass, keeping me in place.

"Dillan, I think you better explain this to me before your family gets here. It might be moot by the time they show up."

I hate saying that, but it's true. I might hear things that are a hard no for me. As we watch each other, I revel of the feel of him filling my pussy. We're not fucking. Neither of us wants or needs that. It's totally different. We want the emotional closeness this physical closeness brings us. It's a metaphor if ever there were one. Our bodies are one right now. No end and no beginning.

He slides his hands down my thighs and pulls my legs farther forward, so I truly rest my weight on him. It also allows me to sink farther onto his cock. I can't help but moan as my head falls forward. He engulfs me in his arms as I cling to him. His right arm crosses my back and cups my ass. His left hand cradles my head to his shoulder.

"Greta, I've already told you I want a security detail for you. I already told you if something happens to me, you get as far away as you possibly can. There will always be danger connected to me, and that may spill over to you. At the very least, you'll always know there's a risk you could lose me to prison or death. But there are also some practical things for you to understand. Our way of life is different than the old mobster movies. Wives don't wait around for their philandering husbands to remember to come home while the women take care of a passel of children because we're stereotypical Catholics who breed like rabbits. But some stuff is still true. There are still some gender roles. I'd like you to attend functions with me. Partly because I'll have the most stunning woman in any ballroom on my arm, and I admit I want to show you off to make every man there know you accepted me. That no one else can ever have you. I get I may as well beat my bare chest and haul you off to a cave. But mostly because I want your company when I have to go out and be sociable when I'd really rather be home, watching a movie or cooking together. I also want your perspective and advice. I want that about anything I can tell you. You'd also lead the women. My mom and aunts pretty much do that now, and they'd teach you. But women would come to you if they need something. That could be a husband who isn't treating them right. A father who's abusing his kids. Families who mismanage money or hit hard times and can't support their kids. It wouldn't be your responsibility to fix these things. You'd tell me. But they'll always feel more comfortable approaching a woman than coming to me or my cousins. You'd stand in the front pew with me at baptisms, weddings, and funerals. You'd console the grieving and congratulate the celebrators."

I listen to all this, and it sounds like something out of *The Godfather*, but neither of us is Italian. I'd be mob, not mafia.

"I'm not Catholic." That's the first thing that spills out of my mouth. The second is just as surprising. "And I'm not converting."

Why is that what I'm thinking about?

"Then we have a wedding or baptize our kids in the Church of Ireland or an Episcopalian one since I don't even know if C of I exists here."

"They would accept you as a Catholic, but the Catholic church wouldn't accept me."

"Greta, I have as complicated a relationship with God as I do with anything else in my life. I was raised Catholic. I believe in the church's teachings on how to be a good person and to live a just and generous life. I just can't live by all the tenets. It doesn't mean I don't want to. I was an altar server until I was fifteen. When I got into a fight with Maks and stabbed him, I realized I couldn't justify sinning and believing a simple confession would absolve me when I had every intention of committing the same sin over again with no hesitation. If your faith is important to you, then I will convert."

I can only sit there agog. We have some really fucking intense conversations for a couple that hasn't even gone on a date yet. But that's what we are. A couple. And we aren't— nor will we ever be —conventional. We're not putting the cart before the horse. It's just the horse— our feeling —is already two blocks down the road, and our relationship status— the cart —is trying to catch up.

"An Irish Protestant doesn't quite scream mob. It definitely doesn't scream one from County Leitrim."

"If someone thinks I'm less Irish or less of a leader because I can accept divorce, women priests, and a woman's right to choose, then they can feck all the way off. That has nothing to do with me not being Catholic. That's on them for living in the Dark Ages."

"You know there're a few more theological differences."

"So what if I can live with the possibility of converting for the sake of marrying you one day and baptizing our kids? Does that mean you can accept any boys we have will likely follow in my footsteps? I wish I could say our family's ties end with my generation, but I don't know that they can. If I stepped down, Finn would take over. If he refused, or he abdicated, then it would pass through my other cousins. If we all refused, then we'd be at the mercy of whichever family takes over. And we've done a lot of shite over the last four generations to get where we are. It wouldn't be safe for anyone."

"And if we had girls? Would you arrange marriages for them or something?"

"No. Never. That doesn't mean it'll be easy for them to date or marry. They would have to be just as careful as my cousins and me to bring someone into this world and into this family. But neither do I want to limit any children I might have to only mob affiliated families."

He watches me as he speaks, and all I can do is stare. He just told me he'd leave the Catholic faith to become a Protestant, so we could marry. He said he'd have our— OUR —kids baptized in the Episcopal Church rather than the Roman Catholic one. That's no small thing. Not the faith part, nor the talking about getting married and having a family together. Holy. Fucking. Shit.

I'll have to come back to the religion part because it's too much to comprehend right now.

"If you were arrested, they could compel me to testify against you if we're not married. But say one day we did get married, and Finn or one of the others gets arrested, they could still compel me to testify. Could I face indictment as an accessory after the fact or for aiding and abetting or something?"

"Yes. At least in theory. As long as you aren't doing anything illegal, the authorities will leave you alone."

"But I could wind up in prison." I want him to admit it. I need to hear him acknowledge this part of the danger I'll face.

"Yes. But as my wife, you would be protected no matter where you went."

"I'd think, as your wife, it would make me the biggest target."

"It would. But there will be more people willing to protect you than there will be women looking to attack you."

"And the prison guards?"

"Paid off to make your stay as comfy as a country club."

"And if it's not working, and I want to leave? The relationship, not prison."

"Then you go. You will always have my support if and as much as you want. Whether that's alimony and child support or just a friend. Whether it's a security detail for life or never talking to me again. I will never trap you, Greta. That's the last thing I want. That's why we're discussing this. I want you to know as much as you can before you agree to this for real."

"And if you want to leave me?"

He stares at me as though I've lost my mind. But it's a legit question. We've been moving just enough to remain aroused, keeping him hard and me wet. But now he's really guiding my hips and flexing his. I'd leaned away as we talked, but now he brings us back to our chests pressing together. He whispers in my ear.

"There won't be any swimming with the fish bullshit. No wearing concrete shoes or being buried in the Staten Island trash dump. I can't perfectly predict what the future holds, but I can promise you, at least for now, the only way this ends is you walking away. I won't give you up because life is hard, or people disapprove. You are mine. Mine to have and to hold.

Mine to pleasure. Mine to protect. I've never been possessive by nature, but I am stubborn. I am unrelenting. And I am protective. I never want you to stop being you just to be with me. But I'm unbending with your safety. I need you to truly understand that. I need you to understand what I'm willing to do to protect you. You have to be okay with it being more than just the hunch you have about what I do when I'm not with you. I will never tell you specifics, but I know you've already guessed. I'll keep you as far removed as I can. But those things you guessed— they will pale compared to what I'd do to anyone who tried to harm you or any kids we have. You will never dissuade me. Can you live with knowing the extremes I will go to, to protect and defend you?"

That's fucking intense. As though everything leading up to this hasn't been. How do you tell someone you'll torture and kill on their behalf without telling them you'll torture and kill on their behalf? You say just what Dillan did.

"I never planned to do any of your family physical harm. I wanted to take from you, but not anyone's life. I can guess what I've done probably endangered several of you. I can see that now. But if I'd truly wanted revenge, if I'd truly believed in an eye for an eye and a death for a death, I would have found a way. If anyone threatens you or our family, nuclear or extended, you need to understand just how alike we are. I might not have your skills to punish them, but do not for a moment think I'm not capable."

"You say that now, but—"

"Don't do that, Dillan. Don't tell me it's harder to kill than I think. I'm not taking for granted the gravity of taking another person's life. But if it's a choice between someone I— care about —and someone I don't, I have no limits. And don't tell me I might think I don't, but I really do. Don't patronize me. Test me, but don't patronize me."

"I'm not. It's just not as easy to pull the trigger as you think."

My gaze locks with him with an intensity he's not accustomed to.

"I may have wanted to destroy your businesses and livelihoods, but I knew the danger that could put me in. I still went through with spying on you. I didn't chicken out. I pushed forward. When I started this, I couldn't guarantee you wouldn't kill me. I didn't plan to just accept that. I would have fought back. I went to you when I was scared because I knew I could. But if I'd had to stand my ground, I would have.

I get up and climb off the bed even though he reaches for me. I walk over to where I see his robe hanging over a clothes horse.

"Can you give me a minute to get my purse?"

He just nods. I dart down the hallway and down the stairs. I grab my stuff and bolt back up the stairs and into the guestroom. I walk to the bed where he's sitting with a glistening cock. How very tempting. But I open my purse instead. I watch him as I fish out the first item.

I see the surprise as I withdraw and flick open a wickedly sharp knife. I step back from the bed, taking a defensive stance. I move into an offensive stance. Dillan comes to join me. I snap the knife closed, but I don't change my stance. I don't change how I hold the knife. He lunges for me, and I react just as I would if the blade were out.

I change my position, tapping his ribs with the sheathed blade before stepping away. I turn my back to him, waiting. I close my eyes, and he can see I did in the mirror. I easily get myself out of the hold with what would be me impaling his ribs. We probably look like some ridiculous version of a Greco-Roman wrestling match.

I must satisfy him because he nods and goes back to the

bed. He looks at my purse, and I can see the speculation in his gaze. I return my knife to my purse. I shift to turn most of my back to him as I pull out a gun. I make sure the safety is on before I aim at the far wall. He can see my skill level from the way I hold it. My stance, my arm height, my steady hands, my blank expression. I relax and drop the clip. Then I check the chamber before I disassemble and reassemble it like an expert marksman. I pull out my wallet and show him my New York Pistol License.

"I started carrying this when the sense I was being followed got really— malevolent. I had a college boyfriend from New England. He used to hunt during deer season, but the rest of the year, he shot clay. I know my way around a gun, Dillan. I know shooting an animal is different from a human, but I've done it. Not for sport, but for food. I had a boyfriend in high school who was into martial arts. He taught me how to fight with weapons. About a week after I moved to New York, a guy followed me from the subway toward my place. I ran, but he was faster. He didn't know I carried a knife. It was a dark street that I was stupid to be on, but I'd changed directions, not wanting him to see where I live. He grabbed me and wrapped his arms around me. He didn't see me pull my knife from my purse while I ran because I had it in front of me. Only I walked away. And I did it without a backward glance. I watched the police blotter for the next week. It took two hours for someone to notice his body, which was behind a dumpster. He'd dragged me to it in the time it took me to flip the blade open and get into a position where I could control what was happening. He was barely breathing when the ambulance got to him, so don't tell me it'll be too hard for me to kill. I already came damn near close once. If it's my life or yours versus someone else's, don't doubt who I will choose. I could have reported the attack. I could have gone to the police or called them. But I didn't. I took my chances that no CCTV camera picked me up. I got away with it, and I would do it all over again if I had to."

We are fucked-up. I apparently have no conscience. Not really. I've come close to killing without remorse, and I can accept that he does the same thing. Maybe that's why I fell for him. I'm just as morally gray as he is. Though, I can say, I've always been terrified I'll get caught and spend life in prison. Police sirens make me jump. Turning around and spotting cops behind me makes me break out in a cold sweat. Having a cop watch me walk by makes my heart race. I'm not impervious to what I did. But I don't feel guilty because I don't doubt the man would have hurt me.

Dillan draws me in for a hug, and I feel his heart racing in a way it wasn't even after we danced around with a closed knife between us. I keep my cheek against his chest as my left arm wraps around him and my right hand rests beside my face.

"Daddy?"

"Shh, *cailín*. I need a moment."

"What's wrong?" Of course, I don't stay quiet.

"Knowing someone threatened you brings up a rage I'm not used to. It likely makes me a sociopath, but I'm usually not driven by emotion when I do what I do. This is so different. It makes me want to find him, do things that make me a monster, then leave him in ash just for looking in your direction."

"Shh, Daddy. I'm all right. I know I got lucky, but I survived to tell the tale. And I'm here with you now. I know you'll keep me safe. And you're not a monster. You were born into a world you didn't ask to join. You're part of a family that lives its credo of family first. If that means you have to do shit most people condemn because it protects the ones you love or the ones who depend upon you, then I have no issue with that. You might not operate within the laws the larger society has passed, but you live by the laws of the world in which you belong. I can accept that because of the man I've seen you be. The man you are with me, and the man you are with your family."

He gazes down at me as I look up at him. I can't read the look in his eyes for sure. But I get the sense it's a mixture of surprise, relief, and appreciation. I go up on my toes to give him a peck, but he doesn't let me go. We've had rough and passionate, and then we had tender today. The time we spent with me basically warming his cock, and now standing together confirms this is more than just physical attraction complicated by life. This is the foundation for a relationship based on more than just being in lust.

"Let's have dinner, wee one. We probably have time for at least most of a movie before the others get here."

Just a normal night in for a couple. Except I'm about to face the mob's firing squad when his family arrives.

Chapter Thirteen

Dillan

We are such a fucked-up couple, and we've barely gotten together. I shouldn't be so relieved that she's stabbed someone before. I loathe knowing she had to. Now that I know she's been in danger before she even met me only amplifies the need to ensure she's safe. But she defended herself, and she's kept going with her life. I wish it never happened to her.

However, thanks to Donovan and Declan, women are now targets when they never used to be. I can't shirk my culpability in what happened once I took over. And now I have a woman I'm rapidly falling in love with, and I admit I have a newfound respect for the Kutsenkos and what they endured because of my family. How we only lost material things— some irreplaceable family heirlooms that still hurt —but not one of my family is a miracle. I don't know that I could have their restraint.

What's even more fucked-up— if that's possible —is that my family will respect her more for knowing she isn't the squeamish or morally superior type. But they will worry more that she might put a knife through my back. I have no such fears. I still can't articulate— even to myself —why she's a magnet to me. Maybe it's Divine Intervention. I served as an altar boy for nine years before I finally couldn't accept the consuming guilt of going to church to confess sins I knew I didn't regret. But my lack of attendance except for Christmas and Easter doesn't mean I believe any less. I think it must be the hand of God working right now. How else do I explain it besides fate? And that might just be God without the glowing light behind Him and white gown. Who the fuck knows?

We dress and head downstairs to my kitchen. I point things out, and we cook together. It's so natural for us. We find a rhythm as I chop the veggies to be grilled and to go into the salad. She takes care of the pork chops.

"Can you make shepherd's pie?"

I look over at her when she asks the unexpected question. "Yeah. Can you?"

"Nope. What about corned beef? Do you have your granny's recipe?"

"Nope. She refused to give it to anyone but my mom and aunts. That was on her deathbed. They've sworn they won't pass it along until they're about to take their last breath. How about you?"

"Of course. I'm a proper self-respecting Irish woman. I can make any type of potato, too."

She rolls her eyes before flipping the chops. I swat her backside as I walk past with the bowl I'll put the salad in. "I expect cabbage with those potatoes and corned beef."

"Yuck. You're on your own with that. I hate the smell and don't care for the taste either."

"Sacrilege!" I step back and wrap my arm around her waist,

tugging her toward me. I kiss her cheek. Just as I'm about to let her go, she turns in my arms. The smile she graces me with makes me want to run away with her to a place where no one has ever heard of the mob. A place where I can see her smile like this all day, every day.

"The chops are going to burn."

She goes onto her tiptoes, kisses my cheek, then playfully pushes me away. She returns to cooking, but steps out of the way, so I can stick the tray with the veggies into the oven. I open a bottle of wine and set the table as she finishes the meat. The rest of the food is ready a couple minutes later.

"Dillan, what should I expect when the guys get here? Should I get out of the way? Do they plan to talk to me?"

"They want to talk to you, but I warned Finn they must be respectful to you."

"You can't get angry with them if they're angry with me. I can't blame them if they are."

"They can be as angry as they want. But that doesn't mean I'll accept anyone being rude to you."

"And I already told you I can't accept causing a rift in your family."

"All the more reason they better be civil. If they say shite that makes you feel you have to leave, I won't be pleased."

She reaches across the table to me and wraps her hand around my wrist.

"Daddy, I can explain myself, and I can defend myself. You have to let them say what they feel they need to say, however they need to say it. You cannot begrudge them that."

Her expression is still relaxed, but her voice is resolute. She won't budge on this. I'll make sure the guys know she stood up for them before she even knew what they had to say. We chat about movies and TV shows while we finish eating, then we move on to places we'd like to travel while we clean up. We're just about to go into the living room when I hear a single knock before a key in the door unlocks it.

"Dill—"

Cormac's walking through the door, ready to call out to me when he sees us. He looks at Greta, who's back in her work clothes. But I'm in a pair of jeans and a T shirt. We need to bring some of her stuff over here, so she can spend the night without worrying about getting comfortable or having to go back to her place in the morning.

"Hi, Molly." He sounds cordial, and he offers her a smile most people would think is sincere. But I know him as well as I know myself. He's sizing her up, and he isn't certain whether he likes what he sees.

"Hi." She offers him a smile, but I can feel her arm stiffen since I'm holding her hand.

"You're early."

"I know. I need to talk to you about the stuff."

The stuff. His mission.

"I should check my email and voicemails. I'm certain my boss has contacted me by now."

Cormac's right eye narrows infinitesimally, but I see it. I shoot him a warning glare, but Greta slips into the living room as she pulls her phone out of her pocket. I lead the way to my office, which is part of the converted servants' quarters. My home is over a hundred years old, but Shane's construction company made a lot of updates before I moved in. The bones are good, and I preserved as many original features as I could. But I also gave myself a few luxuries. I know my cousin's watching Greta as we climb the stairs.

"I don't get it."

"What don't you get, Cor?"

He looks at me for a moment before he responds. He

doesn't appreciate my patronizing tone, but I don't appreciate him launching into his accusations about her before the others arrive. I don't want to have this conversation more than once.

"I don't get why Misha and Pasha went for these shipments when we had way more valuable goods come in three weeks ago. Why did they wait? No one shites without the other families knowing. They didn't just stumble upon the info that got them into our cargo. They wanted these specifically."

Now I feel like an arse. Whoops.

"I don't know. My guess is they want to smuggle something with the vehicles. It wouldn't surprise me if they didn't fill the spare tires with coke or pot. No one checks whether they're filled with air or something else. They might even have them tape shite to the chassis for all we know. No one crawls around to check underneath vehicles. There are places to hide shite not easily seen in the mirrors. It wouldn't even surprise me if they stole them to plant shite in them then frame us for it. Nothing surprises me about them."

"But there's a pretty little red head downstairs who did."

Here we go. I shoot him a look that says back off. One he knows so well he ignores it.

"She seemed like a nice girl, but what the fuck, Dill?"

"I'm not doing this right now. You can wait your turn when the guys get here. I won't explain myself more than once."

"Easy for you to say. You're going to be explaining yourself several times over by the time you're done with us and the rest of the family."

"Maybe—"

We hear voices downstairs, so I know Sean and Shane are here. They must have let themselves in, too. I'm going to have to change the open-door policy to my house. Greta could have still been wearing only my robe.

"We're upstairs." I call out to the twins, and I soon hear

them on the stairs. They pass through my door with their matching speculative gazes. My aunt never dressed them in anything matching except for family photos, then Finn wore the same thing, too. She let them pick out their own clothes as soon as they were old enough to express their opinion. She and my uncle always encouraged them to be their own people, separate of each other. But only identical twins could behave so similarly. Sometimes it's hilarious. Right now, it's annoying having mirror image scowls directed at me.

"Fucking wait until Seamus and Finn get here before you lay into me."

As though I conjured the devil, the door bangs shut.

"They're in his office."

I hear Greta's voice carry upstairs, then my last two cousins are staring at me. Seamus closes the door behind him, and the guys take their favorite seats. I knocked out walls to make most of the servants quarters into one spacious room. I have six armchairs, a sofa, and a loveseat in here, plus my desk and chair. I take my usual spot in the armchair closest to my desk. The rest aren't in a circle, but they're roughly grouped to make one.

I wait.

They wait.

I wait longer.

"Damn it, Dillan. What are you doing with her?" Shane isn't the impatient one, but he also doesn't like his time wasted.

"I'm dating her." I grip the armrests when Sean speaks next.

"Fucking her."

"That reminds me. From now on, you knock and wait for me to answer the door." That just earns me annoyed expressions, but I don't care. "Look, do you want me to explain, or do you want to hear it from Greta?"

Finn speaks up before the others can. "I want to know why you call her that."

"Because I want to."

Finn's not having it, and he lets me know. "Don't be daft. Why the nickname? It doesn't even make sense."

"Of course, it does. I gave her the nickname because it came to mind and stuck. I—"

"You want something that shows the world she's only yours."

"If you know the answer to your own question, Finn, don't waste our time by asking it." I've eased the hold on the armrest since I know they all saw how I gripped it. Normally, I don't let an emotional tell slip like that. Now my hands rest loosely on the chair's arms.

Seamus has been watching me the most intensely. I'm certain I'm going to like what he has to say the least. "You're going to ignore everything she did because you love her."

I refuse to agree with that until I speak to Greta. I will not admit my feelings to anyone before I do her.

"I am not ignoring everything. We've spent most of the afternoon and evening talking."

"Most. Not all." Seamus presses, and I want to punch him.

"We had dinner and talked about places we'd like to travel. What do you all know? Did you find out Peter Doyle killed her grandda?"

That shocks them into silence.

"He made the bomb that blew her grandda up right in front of her."

That makes eyes widen and mouths drop open.

"Did you know her granny has Alzheimer's, and during a bad day, her granny told her all about Peter and how much she missed her husband? How angry she'd been for years that Peter didn't pay for what he did?"

"But he wasn't—"

"She didn't know that. She knew our family profits off the pain other families suffer. But she didn't want to kill any of us. She wanted us to lose money. She—"

"Dillan!"

I'm out of my seat in a flash. It's Greta screaming my name. I race across the room and fling open the door so hard it hits the wall. She's running up the stairs to me.

"Dillan!"

"What happened?" I meet her halfway down. She shoves her phone at me.

"I don't know who they are. Are they going to hurt her?"

I'm looking at the back of two large men in polo shirts and khakis standing in front of an old woman in a chair with a walker next to it. They're standing far enough apart on purpose, so I can see the woman's face, but I can't make out anything about them. They're not touching her, but Greta's grandmother looks petrified.

"No. They did this to scare you. They're working on the assumption your granny won't understand what's happening enough to call for help, and no one will believe her if she tells someone." I look over my shoulder. "Cormac, Seamus, go down there. Take care of this."

Out of all of us who stand over six feet tall, these two brothers are the largest. They look like complete meatheads. Handsome Neanderthals, I think I heard them called once. No. It was hot Neanderthals. You'd never guess they're both lawyers unless they're in their suits. Right now, they're in tight T shirts and jeans.

"Wait. Do you even know where to go?"

Greta leans around me to see them as they get up. It's Seamus who answers.

"No."

She gives them the address in Connecticut, and Seamus reassures her. It gives me pause to wonder why there is so much about Greta we don't know. Finn ran her background check, but there's so much missing. That or he thought she was innocent enough not to dig that deep. Truthfully, we rarely dig that much into the women who work at the bars and clubs. Maybe we should start to.

"We'll get in there and check on your grandmother. Once we're sure she's all right, we'll wait around to make sure no one else visits."

"How will—"

She snaps her mouth shut as she looks up at me. She shakes her head and looks down at the floor, tears filling her eyes.

"I shouldn't ask. I'm sorry."

I engulf her in my arms, and she goes limp against me. I whisper to her, even though I say nothing the others shouldn't hear.

"It's all right. You can always ask. They won't hurt anyone unless they have to. They'll check on her, then they'll walk the grounds and wait in the parking lot. I don't know how they'll get in, but they'll find a way. For how big they are, they can be fecking sneaky as shite. They never got in trouble when the rest of us did."

It's true. Nothing would stick to them. The rest of us would be up to our eyeballs in the shite when our parents caught us doing whatever we shouldn't, but Cormac and Seamus always managed to look like angels. The rest of us could have told on them. It sure as fuck tempted me, but even as preschoolers, we knew never to give each other up. To always cover for each other. Our parents might not have known enough to warrant punishing them, but Colleen did. She'd make sure they got their fair share of our consequences once we were alone, even when she was the reason we all got in trouble to begin with. Fucking hell. I miss my sister.

"Read the text." She whispers the next word so quietly I wouldn't know she said it if I didn't feel the air against my neck. "Daddy."

UNKNOWN NUMBER

We'll see what she remembers.

The photo is below that message.

UNKNOWN NUMBER

Is it a good day or a bad day? Let's find out.

UNKNOWN NUMBER

Such a shame. Not a good day. We'll just have to come back.

"Do I respond? I don't know when this was taken. It could have been five minutes ago or five hours ago or five days ago for all I know."

"Let me, *cailín*."

I don't care right now who hears me call her little girl. I take the phone from her and try to enlarge the photo. But there's nothing in the frame that helps me know when the shitbags took it. No clock, and I can't see out of a window to get a sense of time from the sunlight. My heart aches because the fear is so clear on Greta's grandmother's face. The men are looming over her, and I can only imagine what they said to her. I do a reverse search of the phone number, but I get nothing more than it's from New York but not the city.

"Do you know them, Dillan? Tell me the truth."

"I don't, *mo stór*. I swear I would tell you if I did." I don't want to tell her they look like law enforcement. Feds in particular.

Cormac stops beside us, and Greta looks up at him. His tone is gentler than it was when he asked his questions earlier.

"Molly—"

"I truly hate that name. You speak Gaelic. Márgrég, please."

I didn't know that. When I said it earlier, it was because we spoke Gaelic, and that's the pronunciation.

"Márgrég, we'll make sure Granny is safe. Dill, I'll call you when we know something."

He hesitates, then awkwardly pats her shoulder before he and Seamus leave. My left arm is still around her as I pass her phone to Shane. She watches me, but she says nothing. I know she realizes my cousins or I could go through everything on her phone if we wanted. She still handed it over. When I meet Finn's and the twins' gazes, I know they realize that too. It's a monumental sign of trust considering we all know she wrote the articles, and she shared info with Anton and Sergei. Some of it is likely still on her phone.

She must read my mind.

"You'll see contacts just named S and A. Sergei and Anton. None of my passwords are saved on there in case someone steals my phone. But I'll give you whatever you need. I have confidential shit on my cloud for work, but if you want to see what I have saved on your family, then you'll be able to see everything else, too. Just tell me when you want the passwords."

When she leans back to look up at me, I see the remaining fear in her eyes. I don't know if it's purely worry for her grandmother or if she's not feeling as confident as she sounded when she gave my cousins permission to snoop through her phone. She looks exhausted and so young, despite being only a few years younger than me. I walk her over to the window, and I can shield her from the others where we stand. I want her to feel like she can be open with me without prying eyes or ears. When she speaks, it's obvious she needs this.

"Daddy, how could they get in there? Even with federal badges or whatever, how did they get by the staff? And yes, I guessed they're feds from their clothes, hair, and build. Everyone who lives in that place is there for the memory care. The staff knows she isn't likely to understand what they want, even if they have a warrant or something. They know this sort of thing would upset her. Why would they abandon her to them?"

"I don't know, but I'm going to find out. Cormac and Seamus are good at surveillance and info gathering. They're a lot like Sergei and Anton. People don't expect any of them to be intelligent because they look like they live at the gym. They might not have the Ivy League educations Sergei and Anton do, but they're just as smart."

She shifts restlessly from one foot to the other as she looks out the window after opening the blinds. It's took dark to see much, but I can see her reflection. She's sucked her lips in between her teeth, and she's fighting not to cry in earnest. She pulled away from me already, so I don't want to crowd her. But I long to wrap myself around her like that invisibility cloak she mentioned earlier, so the world can't touch her. I hate not knowing every detail of what's going on. It means I'm not in control. And that means I can't protect her. It makes my skin crawl.

"Wee one, what do you need right now?" That makes the tears finally fall. Fuck. I made it worse.

"You're going to think I'm so fucked-up."

"No, I won't. What do you need?"

She shakes her head and looks down at the windowsill. If I

press too hard, she'll retreat. But I want to demand she tell me how I can solve some of this. If I can make some of this better, then maybe she'll realize just how serious I am about always taking care of her. She finally meets my gaze, but she looks around me at Finn and the twins for a moment. She motions for me to lean forward, so she can whisper to me.

"I want how we were earlier when we were talking. I don't want to fuck. That's not what I'm thinking about instead of my family. But I want how safe I felt when you were inside me. I want to sit like that in your arms. I need that closeness with you. You're the only person I want near me right now."

That makes my dick ache. I don't want to fuck her right this minute— well, I do. But that's because I always want to fuck her. I don't want to focus on getting either of us off. I'd love to have that closeness, too. Hugging her isn't enough. It doesn't give us the full physical contact, and it doesn't make me feel as connected to her emotionally as it did when our bodies were one.

"I need to talk to Greta alone for a little bit. We'll be down the hall, but I want this to stay private. Call or text me if you need us."

Hopefully, they don't think we're off to bang. We're not. I take her hand, and I lead her to my bedroom— our bedroom now. There's not a chance in fuck she's spending a night away from me until we know what the fuck is going on. This is so unexpected. Even more than finding out who Greta really is. It's either the worst coincidence or someone is fucking with us more than I want to admit. I'm leaning toward the latter. Her articles leaked, and now someone's intimidated the most vulnerable member of her family.

I lock the door behind us before leading her over to the loveseat. I have a king size bed with the comfiest mattress I've ever felt. There's a TV mounted on the wall with the door. And across the room, in the corner, between two windows are perpendicular bookshelves built into the wall. The loveseat faces them with an ottoman in front of it. My favorite books line the shelves. You'd expect all my law books to be in my office, but the ones I use most are actually in here. If I have to study such dry text, then I want to be comfy.

"Strip, wee one, then come sit on Daddy's lap."

I unbutton my jeans first, then I pull off my shirt. I drop the shirt on the arm of the loveseat before taking off my jeans and boxer briefs. I'm already barefoot. She's doing what she's told as I watch her. I sit, and she climbs onto my lap, facing me. My hand lands hard on her arse, and her hips press forward against my chest. I spank the other side even harder, and the sound of my hand hitting flesh fills the room. The third time, I spank both cheeks at the same time before easing her onto my cock. I guide her to lean her head on my shoulder as we sit together.

I spank her five more times on the right arse cheek. She relaxes more each time my palm lands on her soft flesh. She pulls her knees up and tucks her arms between us. When her breathing slows so much I think she's asleep, I run my hand over the pinkened flesh.

"Do you know why I spanked you, *cailín*?"

She whispers her answer. "No."

"Do you think it was a punishment for something I didn't tell you you'd done wrong?"

She shakes her head as best she can without lifting it.

"It wasn't because you did something wrong. I told you. I'm not interested in domestic discipline. But I will remind you I'm in control. I don't know everything that's happening right now, but I am in control of this situation. I spanked you, so you know you can let go for a bit and let me take care of you."

"Daddy, I don't know what I'm feeling right now, but I

think I'm falling in love with you. Please let this be real. Please don't use my feelings to get revenge for what I did."

I know it's fear talking. If it weren't, I'd be insulted and hurt. But I get it.

"Greta, this is so real that I want you to live with me. I'm saying this right now because of this threat. But I've been thinking about it since you got in the car with me this afternoon."

"God. That feels like a week ago, not a few hours ago. How can you be sure so fast?"

"Because I make life-changing, life-threatening decisions in the matter of seconds. Having hours to consider this is like a luxury. Like having years to think it over. I told you what your role would be if we ever married, but we never talked about whether you can accept it."

"I would have left earlier if I couldn't. I wouldn't be telling you how deeply I feel for you if I couldn't. I wouldn't let you come inside me without a condom if I didn't see my future with you. I have all along. Or at least, I've prayed it could be. I'm still uncertain how you've forgiven me or how you can overlook— shh, Daddy. I know — how you can accept —what I did. But you can."

She knew I was about to interrupt her to reassure her again. As she said condom, she took my hand and rested it on her belly. I've been so fucking careful to never get a woman pregnant. Besides my parents killing me if I did, there's been no one I would risk being part of my life because of a child we'd share.

Now, with my hand on her soft skin, I can't help thinking about coming inside her and making a baby one day. Knowing it's my sperm that's inside her. That it's our— mine as much as it is hers —child growing within her. It's a powerful emotion that makes me possessive. Not the kind that would keep her from friends and family. Not the kind that would emotionally abuse her. It's the kind that makes me want to ensure she's happy every day for the rest of her life. The kind that wants to see us have a family together, which means I'll go to the ends of the Earth to protect them.

She creates one disconcerting thought and feeling after another. She makes my head spin. But holding her makes me happy. It's the only time when I feel calm. Even when I'm so aroused I can barely keep my dick from exploding. She brings me a sense of peace no one else ever has, even when we have unresolved shite between us.

"Greta, I know I'm falling in love with you. I have the same fears as you. Please let this be real. If this is another way to hurt my family, find something else. It'll crush my soul if you're just manipulating me."

"Do you think I manufactured this?" Her voice is quiet, but it's an unwavering demand.

"No. That's why I pray I'm not wrong."

"You're not. I wish I could wipe away everything but how I feel about you and start over. I wish I could have met you in an honest way. I wish I could have gotten to know you at the club as genuinely just a waitress. I wish I never made you doubt me. I wish I'd never put myself in such a shitty position. But I can't take it all back. I can only keep moving forward. Daddy, can you keep spanking me, please? It stings like a motherfucker, but it's soothing, too."

My hand cracks down on her, and it shoves her hips forward. She moans with pleasure. I'm not spanking her as hard as I dare, but I'm not being entirely gentle either. But she'd tensed to the point of being rigid while we talked about this last bit. She's relaxing more and more. It's helping me too. After I land ten spanks, I know her arse must burn. I stroke it as she nestles closer, her lips pressing kisses beside my Adam's apple.

We stay like this, moving just enough to keep my dick hard, for I don't know how long. We're both practically dozing off until my phone pings. I reach for my pants and pull it out of my pocket.

FINN

It's bad.

Chapter Fourteen

Greta

I can see Finn's text. What now?

I cling to him as he suddenly stands up.

"*Cailín*, I would never drop you."

"I know. But it startles me when you move me so easily."

"Get used to it because I plan to move your sexy body all the time. I'd walk around all day with you on my cock if I could."

"You'd get tired of that."

"Of having a hot woman keeping me hard and getting me off multiple times a day? As long as my cock still works, I'm going to want you to do that."

Not just he'll want that. He'll want me to do that. It's as though marriage, a family, a long life together are now a foregone conclusion. We haven't actually said that's what's going to happen or set any dates. We haven't even figured out if we love each other. We talk and act like we do. But we've only said we're falling in love, not that we're already there. My rational mind keeps wanting to question it. But that's apparently only a sliver of my brain because the rest of it is telling me to shut the fuck up and enjoy.

He walks me around the side of the bed. He sets me down and turns me to face the mattress. He pulls my ass cheeks apart, and I'm unprepared for him to spit on my hole. Normally, I think that's so disgusting in porn. But I know what it means right now.

"The lube is down the hall, and I'm not getting dressed to get it unless you need me to."

"No. You'd have to walk past your office, and I don't want your cousins to see you walking around with lube. And I don't want you to get called away."

"I'm going to be as gentle and as slow as I can. I would even if I had lube. I will never fuck your arse as roughly as I will your cunt. But I am going to come in it. And you are going to keep that cum in there. When I finally say you can stand up, it'll drip down your arse to your thighs."

He runs his cock along my pussy, coating it some more since I'm practically a fucking slip and slide down there. Then he's pressing the tip against my back door. This isn't my first time having anal. I relax for a moment before I move enough to make it easier for him to enter me.

"Put your hands behind your back. Cross your wrists and lay flat on the mattress. What's your safe word?"

"Yes, Daddy. *Croiméal.*"

He presses all the way until his hips touch my ass. He rocks rather than thrusts. He's squeezing and massaging my ass in a way that feels amazing. Then his hands are sliding along the inside of my thighs. He runs them over the outside before going back to the inside then around my hips to grip my ass. He does it over and over, and I can tell it excites him because his hips move faster. His breathing gets shorter and heavier. He abandons trying not to swear in front of me.

"Fuck, Greta. You are so goddamn hot. Your body... Fuck. I can't stop touching you. I'm going to come soon, and I haven't even started to get you off."

"Daddy, I don't want you to. I want you to come in my ass then leave me in here. I'll join you in a little bit. I want to stay here with your cum in me."

"You want me to fuck you and walk away?"

"Yes. I want you to get what you need from me because you can. Because I'll never deny you. I want you to know I'm not going anywhere. I belong to you, Daddy."

"But you're not my slave. You're not even my submissive."

"I know. I'm also not your Little. But I want you to know what you need is just as important to me."

He pulls back and thrusts this time. He's careful and doesn't do it as aggressively as he could. But he does it over and over until his fingers dig into my hips. He pulls almost all the way out before slamming into me. I nearly scream. It's painful, but in a way I like. His grip keeps tightening until that's painful too, but I know he's coming. He grasps my wrists and moves my hands to rest by my head. He drapes his body over mine.

His phone buzzes again, and I'm certain it's been longer than five minutes. He groans, and this time it's not from pleasure. He straightens and eases out of me. He ducks into the bathroom behind me, and I hear the water run, and I know he's cleaning himself up. I won't be doing that.

"*Mo stór*, if you want to wear one of my shirts and sweatpants you can. You'll have to roll them over at the waist a few times to make them short enough but find whatever you need.

If you prefer to stay in your clothes in front of the guys, come out when you're ready."

When he walks over, I think he might kiss my cheek. He does, but it's my left ass cheek. He pats my ass, then gets dressed. When he's done, he looks at his phone and shoots off a text. I don't know who sent the second one or whether he's replying to it. When he walks back around the bed, he stops to look at me. In silence, he turns around and gathers my clothes.

"I don't want you out of my reach, Greta. If you need a moment to clean up, fine. I won't hold you to what I said. But I won't be able to concentrate because I'll worry if you're not in the same room as me. As long as we don't know what's going on, I'm going to be agitated if I can't at least see you. My house is as secure as it gets. You didn't see it, but I have several cars parked around my block with men watching my place. My cousins are here, too. But I still won't be able to focus."

He doesn't look as calm as he did a moment ago. I stand and clench my ass. I'm not interested in getting cleaned up, but I wore pants today. I don't need a wet spot on my clothes. I sigh and nod before heading to the bathroom. I'm quick since it's always an odd sensation, and I don't want to keep him waiting. I flush and hurry to clean up. Then I'm crossing his bedroom and throwing on my clothes. I take his hand as we head back to his office.

Finn's standing near the window where Dillan and I talked, and Sean and Shane are sitting next to each other on a loveseat. I have no idea if they realize it— they probably do since they're nearly thirty —but they are sitting exactly the same. Like down to the millimeter of where their left ankle rests just above their right knee. Their hair looks like they've both run their hands through it. It's almost identically out of place. Their foreheads are furrowed, and the lines even match. It's incredible.

But it's unnerving as fuck when they look up from their phones because Finn turns around at the same time. Six piercing green eyes stare at me. It makes me want to look up at Dillan to find kindness to ease my newest level of anxiety. All six of them share the same color eyes even if their hair is varying shades of red. I glance up, and I don't find the softness in Dillan's gaze I was hoping for. He's watching Finn like a hawk, and I wonder why things changed the moment we walked through the door.

"*Caithfidh mé imeacht.*" I have to go.

I don't know why Finn's speaking Gaelic since we all understand it. Dillan squeezes my hand, and I look up at him again.

"All of us learned Irish at the same time as we did English. Until we went to school, we used the languages interchangeably and combined them. Sometimes we just lapse into it because we're all truly bilingual."

I nod before looking back at Finn, who's looking at me. Am I supposed to say something or wait for him to tell us?

"You got another text while you two were talking."

Did he just make that sound snide? Or am I imagining things? I can't keep looking up at Dillan to check how I'm supposed to react.

"Who from?"

"Your boss. He wants you in early because you haven't answered his calls, messages, or texts. We listened to those messages. You're in the shite."

"Wonderful. Anything important in those messages or just him ranting?"

"Both. Apparently, the editor-in-chief is out for blood. I took care of that. But your editor wants you to write a retraction. I took care of that, too. The rest was him complaining about you going offline when this is a 24/7 job."

"The fuck it is. They can pay better if that's what they want."

I grumble, but everyone hears me. Sean snorts, and Shane grins. Finn looks like his face might crack. We got along well at the club, but he seems like the most unforgiving.

"Finn." Dillan's voice is stern. His cousin's gaze darts to him before looking back at me. He relaxes, and I don't get it. I must look confused because Finn explains.

"I'm annoyed, but not at you. Sorry about that. I don't like how your boss speaks to you. Is it usually like this?"

He pulls my phone out of his pocket and unlocks it. How?

"You gave it to us unlocked. I changed the code to something we could remember."

"How'd you do that without knowing the old one?"

"Last four of your birthdate with year before day. I played around a bit, but that's a pretty typical one since it's easy for people to remember."

Is it? I didn't know that. Definitely changing it again when I get the phone back. He taps on the screen, then Gary's voice fills the room.

"Molly, I expect you to answer when I call. You know this is a crisis. Zebrowski is ready to shit down my throat, and you're nowhere to be found. I expect an explanation for the leak. I'm hearing whispers that it was you all along. I want to know why the hell you'd do that. What are you hoping to accomplish by throwing me under the bus? Call me back while you still have a job."

I grit my teeth. Gary's never spoken to me like that. I haven't even heard him speak to anyone else like that. It's not so much the words but the tone. It makes me want to punch him, but I'll settle for ignoring him. Finn said he'd taken care of it, and I'm happy to let him.

"Greta, is that how he talks to you all the time?"

Great. Now I have to calm down the angry viper next to me. He's ready to stick his fangs in Gary. Maybe I could play the flute or something to calm him down. He is a bit like a king cobra. Menacing when he stands up, patient before he strikes, and deadly when he does.

"No." I shake my head. "I've never heard him speak to anyone like that. He must be stressed all the way out."

"I don't care if he has an arse full of hemorrhoids. He doesn't speak to you like that."

It's my turn to snort. What a picture that paints. I cover my mouth, but I can't swallow my laugh. It sounds like I'm choking, which sets off Sean and Shane. Finn grins, but Dillan isn't amused. I shrug when I look up at him.

"He doesn't, Greta."

I slide my arms around Dillan's waist. "I know, and I appreciate you defending me. But it's still funny. I know I shouldn't laugh, but—" I snicker. "—I can't help it."

He gazes down at me for a moment before he nods. He looks over at Finn's brothers who've been pointing at things on each other's phones. They could be watching videos for all I know.

"What'd you find out?"

It's Sean who answers Dillan. "I hacked the memory care home, and I got into the visitor log. There's no one recorded. Not only no one to see your granny, but no one visiting at all during the two hours before you got the text."

"Wouldn't they record police or government officials coming?"

"They're supposed to. I checked. Anyone who isn't a resident or staff gets logged. I found the last four times you've been. The visitor gets entered on the day and time they arrive then leave, but it also saves it under the resident's name and the visitor's. So, every visit is triple recorded. There's nothing there."

"I want to see her, Dillan." I'm terrified they've upset her. I want to see with my own eyes that she's okay. Before he can answer, Shane stands up and hands me his phone. I see Seamus on the screen. I tap the play arrow, and I immediately see him with Granny. He's near the door, but Cormac's saying something, and I can see Granny laughing.

"Molly, I'm recording this so you can see your granny's just fine. We didn't find anyone here, and there's no record of her having guests. But she was in good spirits when we slipped in. We can't stay much longer, but we wanted you to know she's fine. She's telling Cor stories about you when you used to dress up in her clothes and wear her costume jewelry. She seems really lucid. All we had to do was tell her we were friends of yours and use your real name. She launched into telling us about her mother, and how you share the same name. I stepped away to make this. We'll be in the parking lot overnight. One of us will stay in the car while the other patrols. She's safe, Molly. Promise."

I suck my lips in between my teeth as my eyes water again. I realize I'm nodding as I listen. I swallow the lump in my throat. I'm so relieved she's okay, but it's more than that. I can see how much fun she's having with Cormac, and I can tell he's being a good sport. He's being kind, and that matters more to me than all the strength they have combined.

Dillan leans over to whisper in my ear. "Don't go falling in love with him. I don't share."

I hear the humor in his voice, and he's smiling when I turn my head toward him. I love the way the skin crinkles around his eyes when he laughs. The lines take a moment to fade, and it tells me he's spent a lot of his life smiling. It makes me happy to know that. It makes me happy to be the one who makes him smile.

I want to say something back like "I can't fall in love with him when I already love you." I know I do. It's been slowly creeping up on me the longer I've had to get to know him. All of this shit with the article is testing us, but I'm certain of my feelings now. I don't know why one smile makes it so clear, but it does.

"Thank you for showing that to me. I feel much better. Dillan, I still want to see her tomorrow. Is that possible?"

"I'll take you."

"I'll go, too."

Three voices chime in, and I don't know what to think. Do they want to meet Granny? Or are they offering because they want one or both of us protected?

"Thank you."

Shane answers my silent questions. "She reminds us of Nana. She died a couple years ago, but we lost her about fifteen years ago to dementia. We'd like to meet your granny, and we'd like to be sure you're both safe."

Sean stands up beside his brother and grins at me. "We like you more than him. You'll be a much better sister than he is a brother. We're glad to have another one."

Dillan goes absolutely rigid. His cousins stare at him, waiting for him to do something. I try to intervene.

"He was just joking."

Wait. Another one?

"Greta doesn't know, you arse."

Dillan's voice rasps as he steps toward Sean. I don't understand what's going on. I tug on Dillan's arm and try to step between them, since he looks like he's about to punch Sean. He picks me up and puts me behind him.

"Never get between two men who kill. Stay out of the way, Greta. I'm serious."

I look at Finn and Shane, completely bewildered and almost ready to panic.

"I'm sorry, Dill. That was thoughtless. I didn't realize. While you two were talking, we did a little more digging. We found out what Peter did. We discussed it, and we get why Márgrég did what she did. If anyone understands family, duty, honor, and loyalty, it's us. Fecked-up as it is, we respect her for it. I just wanted you both to know we accept her as family."

I really don't understand the O'Rourkes.

It's just as Dillan promised it would be. They understand, and they can even appreciate what motivated me. But they're talking as though they already know Dillan and I want to make a go of this with a real future. How could they?

Finn steps between them, and they both back up. Dillan's a little calmer, but he's still not pleased. "We'll be downstairs. We'll take turns."

More stuff I don't understand.

"Take turns doing what? What do you mean?"

It's Dillan who explains. "They'll take turns staying up and watching the security feeds. I have a small room off the kitchen that has surveillance feeds from the roof down to the ground. I usually just record and scan the tapes in the morning if any of my men say they saw something suspicious. But the guys'll stay tonight to keep a closer watch. They know I won't sleep otherwise."

"Your men?"

"I have four cars parked on my street and three behind the house. Each one has two men in tactical gear just in case."

"In case your home becomes a war zone?"

"Yes."

I stand there, blinking like an idiot.

Finn frowns and mutters. "Now who's being the arse?"

That seems to finally shake Dillan out of the stupor he went into when Sean tried to be nice to me, but apparently failed.

"Get whatever you want out of the fridge, but try not to eat everything. Be ready to go at six-thirty. We're going to have to run over to Greta's, so she can get what she needs for work and the next week or so."

He guides me to the door, then down the hall to his bedroom. I think about what we left in the guest bedroom. "Are any of the guys going to sleep in that room? What about the stuff you used?"

He hesitates, then frowns. "I'll get it all and bring it in here. I expect you naked by the time I join you."

"Yes, Daddy."

I slip into the bedroom and strip. But I don't know what to do now. He told me I don't have to kneel like a sub. It doesn't seem right to climb into bed, whether it's to lie down or sit up. And everywhere else feels awkward. Besides, I still have things I want to know.

He walks into the room with the bag full of items he bought to use on and with me. His eyes feast on me, and he looks like he's starving. He tosses the bag on the bed and prowls toward where I stand by the bedside table. He fists my hair and kisses me as though he'd like to swallow me whole. I eagerly return his kiss, grinding against his jean-covered cock when his right fingers bite into my ass. His left hand covers my breast before he pinches my nipple hard enough to make me squirm. Except I can't because he's holding me too tightly. There's only one thing I want more right now than to fuck.

"What happened to your sister?"

Chapter Fifteen

Dillan

I knew this question was coming, and this isn't when I want to dredge up the past. I still have a lot of unresolved feelings about losing my sister. Reopening half-healed wounds during an already stressful time isn't high on my wish list. But I can't ignore Greta.

"You know how my maternal grandfather, Liam, ran the organization when your grandfather died. My mother's brother inherited it. Donovan did a good job for years once he started listening to me. I told him to leave the Kutsenkos alone, but he refused. It pissed him off that someone with indirect ties to us might marry into that family. I was so livid I went on vacation to avoid the inevitable fall out. I came home to Donovan dead and Declan claiming he's the new boss. No one wanted that, and everyone knew I was next in line. But he put a hit on his cousins. My mom and my two aunts. Before he died for his sins to the Kutsenkos, he didn't call off the man he paid in time. One mercenary thought Colleen was Auntie Saoirse. The woman shot my sister point blank between the eyes. I was standing next to Colleen and caught her as she fell. There was nothing I could do. I sat in a pool of her blood while I called my parents. We'd just picked out a puppy for her. It was one of the rescues she'd just brought in from Philly. She was a vet. She was everything I'm not. She was loved by everyone. She had the kindest soul and the gentlest hands, but she could make anyone laugh with her dirty sense of humor. She was my closest confidante."

I don't expect Greta to know what to say, and she doesn't. She listens to me with varying degrees of shock, horror, and sadness. I don't expect her to take my hand and lead me to the loveseat in silence. She tugs to get me to sit next to her. Then she does something I don't expect. She wraps her arms around me and nudges me to rest my head on her shoulder. We sit in silence as she strokes my hair. Only five minutes ago, I was comforting her. Now she's holding me as I finally do something I've refused to do since I was ten. I cry. It shocks the shite out of me.

"Shh, Daddy. I'm here, and I'm not letting go. I'm not going anywhere. Just let it out, *mo chroi*." My heart.

I don't sob. It's just a silent, steady stream of tears. All the pain of losing Colleen. All the moments of feeling lost without her. I used to tell her way more than I ever should have, but I trusted her advice more than anyone else's. Sean and Shane might be twins, but Colleen and I may as well have been. My cousins can read each other's thoughts, and their mannerisms are definitely nature, not nurture. It was the same with Colleen.

I take a shuddering breath before I lay shite bare I haven't in a long, long time. But I feel safe telling Greta. The kind of comfort I want to offer her, I'm finding in her arms.

"I believe you can have platonic soulmates, and she was

mine. When she died, my family grew closer than ever before. Never was there a better reminder that it's us against the world. Of the guys, Finn was the one I gravitated to the most. Maybe because we were both the odd ones out when it came to sets of brothers. I didn't have one, and his younger ones were a matched pair. Without Colleen, Finn stepped up. He saved my life. He kept me from sinking into despair and killing myself with a bottle of whiskey. I started doing reckless shite, picking fights with people. Taking jobs I shouldn't have given my position. Jobs that should have gotten me killed for all the risk they involved. Finn stayed beside me and always made sure I came home in one piece. I still feel guilty for the shite that could have happened to him because of me. But he helped me get through losing her."

A lot of the shite Donovan and Declan set in motion might have been stopped if I wasn't so entrenched in my grief. I admit I didn't completely care if the other families lost someone when I'd just lost my world. She was my conscience, and when she died, it went into a coma for a while.

"That's why he's so protective of you. That's why he didn't come around to me as easily as his brothers."

"No. He wasn't angry at you earlier. Truly. You can't read him like I can. He was angry on your behalf. He didn't like how Gary spoke to you, and I'm certain the guy never will again."

"He didn't do something to Gary, did he?"

She keeps stroking my hair and now her other hand strokes the outside of my arm. Her voice is soft, and her heartbeat is steady.

"No. He will have issued the editor-in-chief some promises, and the man will have wisely agreed to get Gary to back off. Your boss might still be pissed, but he won't dare be rude to you again."

"Does it always upset you to talk about Colleen? Should I avoid it?"

"No. I can talk about her. It hurts, and I try not to, but I can. I didn't want to lay something so heavy on you right now, and considering how she died, I didn't want to terrify you even more. I would have told you all of this. I just would have done it at a different time."

She kisses my forehead before rising, taking my hand. We walk to the bed, and she slides in before holding up the covers for me to join her. She arranges the pillows, then opens her arms to me.

"I'm supposed to be taking care of you, *cailín*."

"You did already. Now it's my turn. Let me, Daddy."

The way I settle puts her tits in front of my face. I latch on, and it reminds me again of the adult breastfeeding porn I've seen as I scrolled. I can say the idea of drinking her milk doesn't make me as curious as I thought it might. But there is something soothing about this. Maybe some other time. I let go and draw her closer to me, so I can kiss her neck and cheek.

She drifts off before I do, and it leaves me time to puzzle through all the people who could do this to her. Use a frail old woman to target Greta. The list is way too long.

At the top are the Mancinellis. The Irish and the Italians have a love-hate history. There are times when we've been allies and times when we've been enemies. Right now, it's somewhere between the two. Lorenzo's been causing us shite for a couple months now. He needs to find a wife to keep him occupied like his brother, cousin, and friends did. Even his sister is married. I know they're retaliating because of what I told Finn to do to Carmine and Gabriele. But I used those two fuck nuts to antagonize the Kutsenkos. It's likely that shitshow with Pasha is part of the reason Sergei and Anton helped Greta.

What a fucking tangled family orchard. Each tree has so many branches and roots that it's almost impossible to keep track now that Maksim, Aleksei, Nikolai, Bogdan, Pasha, and Misha are all married. Sergei and Anton have been together since we were all teenagers. So, there's all of them, plus their six wives and three sets of parents.

The Diazes aren't much easier, except they're down one. Enrique is my equal, but he's not married and has no kids. His nephew will inherit like I did with Donovan, after Declan fucked shite up. Pablo is in the same position as the *Cosa Nostra* heir. They're both nephews to the men who lead. Pablo's younger brother's dead, and I can't think of a better way for the shitbag to be. Alejandro is on his own, but he's Pablo's cousin. The two of them share another set of cousins. *Tres J's.* Javier, Jorge, and Joaquin. Motherfuckers are the real psychopaths in this fucked-up world.

Those're just our major rivals. Never mind the lesser syndicates. But most of them are smart enough to stay out of our way. However, the Albanians have been getting a little big for their britches lately. As long as they keep their shite to just the bratva, Cartel, and *Cosa Nostra*, then I'll gladly ignore them. The Polish are stirring trouble too, but the Mancinellis are dealing with them, and the Kutsenkos aren't getting in the way.

So much fucking politics. But I have to keep it all straight in my head, and I can't take time off to forget about it. I have no choice but to mull this over. It's why I only sleep four or five hours a night. I lie in bed and reflect on the day, then I think about what I have to get done the next day. I'm always running the worst-case scenarios through my head. Three contingency plans are a must. I can predict what people will do, but I don't read minds. I can't always pinpoint which path they'll take.

I can tell Greta's now asleep. As I look down at her, I think about how calming she has been for me since we came in here. I didn't think I could take such comfort from her when all I've wanted to do since we finished her punishment this afternoon was offer her the same. But I feel better for having told her the truth about my sister. And now I feel better for being in her arms. Maybe for once I'll get more than just five hours of sleep.

I awake to the sound of someone knocking on my door. I glance down at Greta, but she's still deeply asleep. I ease away from her and roll off the bed. I grab the same robe she wore earlier after her punishment. When I open the door a crack, I see Cormac on the other side. I wonder why he's on the other side of my door when he's supposed to be watching Greta's grandmother.

"What are you doing here?"

"Come down the hall. We need to talk, and I know you don't want to disturb her. This isn't anything she can hear, anyway."

I follow my cousin to my office, and I discover all the rest of the guys are there too. "What the fuck, Seamus? You're supposed to be at the nursing home, just like Cormac. Why are you both here when you're supposed to be on watch?"

I want explanations right now. I don't want excuses.

Seamus sits in his favorite armchair as he speaks, and I'm not sure I like what he has to say any more than hearing about Greta's involvement to begin with.

"We needed to talk to you, so Mikey and John are there. You know you can trust them as much as you trust us. But what we have to say isn't something we can send over a text or have someone else tell you. We need to discuss this together. Is she still sleeping?"

"Yeah. At least for now."

I don't want Greta waking up alone for a few reasons. I don't want her to think I abandoned her. I don't want her to be disoriented in a place where she hasn't slept before. And I don't want her wandering down the hall and possibly overhearing part of this conversation since it's obvious it's not meant for her ears.

"Tell me what's going on. I'm not feeling particularly patient since it's the middle of the night, and I'm not convinced you should be here rather than watching Greta's grandmother. If anything happens to that woman, I won't forgive you. It'll hurt Greta, and it will ruin any trust we've built between the two of us. I'm not willing to take that risk."

Seamus continues to explain while Cormac sits quietly. The rest of the guys don't look like they already know anything. It seems this is news to them too.

"You know we all thought the same thing you did. One look at the men in those photos, and it screamed feds. So, we did a little digging while we took shifts patrolling the grounds. Turns out the guys are actually ATF. They want to stir up shite to intimidate Molly, so we think they were the ones who hacked her computer."

Finn interjects. "She doesn't like the name Molly. She said she wants us to use her real name."

Cormac looks to me for clarification. "Márgrég?"

"Yeah. Since we all speak Gaelic, she'd prefer to go by her real name. I don't think she hears it often."

Seamus picks up the story again. "While I shot that video for Márgrég, Cor kept talking to her granny. She was actually really easy to understand, and she remembered the men coming to see her. She said they demanded information about Márgrég, but she had nothing to tell them. She admitted she couldn't remember anything about her granddaughter while talking to the men. It was poignant since she'd been telling us stories so clearly only moments earlier. It started to upset her because she didn't understand what those men wanted, and she could tell there were gaps in her memory. It must not have been too bad when they were there because, as scared as she looked in the photo, they apparently treated her pretty well. At least, that was the best she could recall. She didn't think they threatened her. We can't be sure. Since talking about it bothered her more than the conversation she had with them, we decided to leave well enough alone and use that as our cue to leave."

"But that isn't enough to justify leaving the place altogether and coming here. Why did you? I want solid answers because I need to be prepared to explain this to Greta when she wakes up. If it's bad enough for you to be here, then it's bad enough I can't keep it a secret from her."

Cormac grimaces and looks at his brother, who nods. Now it's Cormac's turn to explain. "We haven't figured out why the ATF is involved in this, but we got some security footage from the parking lot and saw them walking in and out. We were able to run facial recognition from our laptops, so we know who they are. We can't figure out yet why the ATF would go to her grandmother if she's in a memory care facility. I don't know what they expected to get out of her, but perhaps they figured since she's so vulnerable, they might coerce something useful out of her. My guess is they want the information Greta doesn't have stored on her cloud to make a case against us. My guess is they want to lead a bust."

"But did they really think they would get anything out of an old woman with Alzheimer's? I doubt it. They did that entirely to intimidate and coerce Greta. I won't tolerate them abusing an old woman and going after my woman."

I know how barbaric and misogynistic it sounds to claim her as my woman, but that's what she is. She's the woman I'm going to make a future with. She's mine, and I dare anyone to stand in our way. If it's the ATF or anyone else, I'll burn their fucking world down before I let them harm her or even upset her. They don't realize just how serious we are. Maybe they don't even realize we're together, though I doubt that'll come as a surprise to them if they don't already know. Whatever their reasons are, they will live a short life if they look in Greta's direction again. If they go after anyone in her family, I have no patience anymore.

"Who are they?"

"This is why we came. The one who stood on the left is Agent Mason Spiegel. The other guy is Agent Brad Jones."

I look blankly at Cormac. The names mean nothing to me, but I know they should.

"Jones is a nobody, but Spiegel's got an interesting connection. Don't you remember? He's married to the Deputy DNI, whose brother is none other than FBI Director Taylor Hollands."

Now the name comes back to me. Cormac and Seamus told me about him nearly four days ago. It was right before my meeting with FBI Director Hollands and ATF Director Watling. It's a little sus that an ATF agent is married to the Deputy Director of the Department of National Intelligence, and she happens to be the sister of the head of the FBI. DNI is one of the FBI's oversight bodies. Rather incestuous sounding. But nepotism gets us everywhere.

"Dill, the guys are banging, and she still doesn't know. We didn't need to use that card during the meeting with Watling and Hollands. We haven't told the wife. We can still hold it against Hollands or Spiegel."

Spiegel is whatever the reverse of cuckolding is to his wife. With her brother. Arseholes. But obviously it works for them because I'm sure they are trading secrets during pillow talk. I got distracted by the fucking articles, so I sent Cormac and

Shane in my place to that meeting. I hadn't thought more about it.

It makes me wonder which one of them is trying to climb the ladder faster. Hollands is already at the top with the FBI, but it wouldn't surprise me if he isn't vying for a cabinet seat or something like that. A mere agent at the ATF would love nothing better than to become a deputy director of some department. Maybe it galls him that his wife outranks him. I wonder how small that makes his balls.

I shift my gaze to Shane for a moment before I go back to talking to Cormac. "Besides finding out what she hasn't written down, what do you think they want from Greta? Do you believe they intend to haul her in for questioning? Do you think they intend to bribe her to give over any and all information she has about us? Could they try to intimidate her by having the NYPD or FBI arrest her? Where are they going with this?"

Seamus shakes his head. "We really don't know yet, but we're looking into it. We think they probably don't intend to arrest her. They'd rather scare her into confessing everything they think she knows about us. They'll probably tell her they're the only ones who can protect her. They'll say it's her duty as an upstanding American citizen who loves her country to tell them everything she knows. They'll probably feed her a ton of shite she's wise enough not to believe even if she wasn't in love with you."

My expression darkens as I scan my gaze around the room. "Enough of that. I'm not discussing my feelings or her feelings with anyone else. Leave off. This is more serious than you guys gossiping about who does and doesn't love me. I need to know more about what's going on, and so do you. If they're planning a bust, or they want to plant spies, then we need to prepare for this. Who do we have on the payroll most likely to flip? Who's most likely to narc on us? I want extra details on them, and I want them taken to the station if we can't deal with it out in the open."

Whoever crosses us will find they have a one-way ticket to the abandoned railway station in the Bronx. We use it because we can go underground, and no one can hear a fucking thing happening down there. Sometimes kids go poking around in the old station building, and once in a while someone from the city comes out to take a look. But we've made it impossible to find the way into the subterranean level if you don't know exactly where and what to look for.

Finn, Sean, and Shane have been taking in everything that's been going on. I can appreciate Finn more now than I did when we were kids. After everything I told Greta about Colleen, it's true that Finn is the person I've considered closest to me until now. Greta fills a different type of spot, but she's just as important to me as Finn. They are both the two people I want to rely on and trust the most. I already do with Finn, and I hope I can do the same with Greta.

For now, I'm going to work on the assumption I can. I'm going to work on the premise that we have reconciled. I know it doesn't mean what stood between us went away altogether, and I know it means there's still a shite ton of things that could go wrong between us and for us. But for now, I can only deal with one problem at a time until I understand where these fuckers want to take this.

It's Finn who speaks up and offers me at least a little reassurance. He doesn't agree with my assessment, and that's fine. He's second-in-command, and all the guys are my advisors because they're willing to push back when I need it.

"If we kill the agents, we're just going to draw more attention to Greta, which means us. The focus it puts on us will spill back over onto her. It would be a hell of a lot safer for all of us if we let them live for a little while. Maybe we can make them more useful to us than we are to them."

He's right. I can't act out of emotion because I'm pissed and scared for Greta. I have to go back to my detached logic and think about the three different permutations most likely to happen and how they can best suit us. I look toward the window, and my cousins know I'm thinking. They remain quiet, giving me the chance to take in everything I've just learned and move the pieces around in my mind.

I'm an excellent chess player, and that skill comes from the same strategic mind I have when I'm running the family and all our businesses. When I'm taking care of our enemies, who'd do anything to push us down. Whether it's the other syndicates or the government, they can do their best. They can shite on us all they want, but in the end, the last one laughing is always us.

"As much as they want us, the feds want the other families, too. What can we trade to get them off our backs? They'd want someone high enough to make a point out of their pursuit, but they can't go for the very top. That means Maks, Enrique, and Salvatore are off limits. If their case is a dud, then the feds'll just make them look like martyrs. They can't risk that. We could toss Luca, Pablo, and Aleks in their direction. However, I don't think they'd go for any of them either. They're still too high up. Marco would be the best target. He's the third most powerful man in the *Cosa Nostra*, if you consider the line of succession. The only person more useful is his father as Salvatore's *consigliere*. I think that's who we should target. Marco. Put them on his tail, and we can work our way through the Mancinellis that way."

I'm thinking out loud.

"What do the Mancinellis have going on right now that we could use to make Marco their target? There has to be something. Enzo's going to have that business to deal with in

Chicago. But I think we have a little while before he figures it out. We can always send the FBI snooping around for that. It'll be a pain in the arse for the Chicago *Cosa Nostra* since they want to partner with the branch in Kansas City. Fuckers think meth's the next big money maker. We can hand the Mancinellis a bone if it distracts them."

My eyes narrow as though I can see all the way to Chicago or KC. I'm still working out my logic as I talk.

"If those two families team up, it means their relationships with the Mancinellis will only be more strained now that Luca is married and Celia is, too. There're no future blood ties. The Chicago family has no reason to remain allies with Salvatore. They're more rivals than anything else. A partnership between Chicago and KC will only make Salvatore pissed. He won't allow that. Let's stir the pot there and see what we can find. We need something else for the Diazes to get involved in. We need to make them think it's the Mancinellis, not us. Those fuckers are always in the way. If we can make Salvatore and his family the targets, then we become more useful than them. We are no longer the ones the ATF or the FBI will take an interest in. At least no interest in destroying us."

Sean's been listening just like the others; now he has questions. "If we want to make Marco the scapegoat, then what are we sending them to look for? We're going to have to feed the feds something. We can't just say his name and point in his direction. Do we have anything, or do you need me to make something up?"

"What's he been up to lately? I know he was traveling back and forth to the Netherlands for a while there. But with all the shite that family's had going on in the past few months, with somebody getting married like every other day, he's been pretty much a homebody. Maybe we can use something from one of those few trips. Everyone knows he was running drugs and diamonds while he was away. Maybe we can find something through Interpol and give that to the FBI. If Hollands and Spiegel are as close as they sound, then maybe they'll put their heads together to fuck them over."

I like that. We need to do some more surveillance, but we should be on the right track.

"Cormac, Seamus, find out everything you can about those two. Sean, I want you to dig a little into Marco's schedule. Wherever he's been, who he's fucking, what he's been doing. Check out his club, too. Shane, I want you to do the same for Enzo. Figure out if he's sniffing around at anyone new at his clubs. Not just his night clubs but where he goes to play. Maybe we can get someone planted there. Neither of them will talk much while they have subs gagged and tied up, but who knows? At least one woman on our payroll fucking them could be useful."

I'm not looking to whore anyone out. I won't make any of the women sleep with someone they don't want to. I won't pay them specifically to sleep with somebody, either. But we have plenty of dancers, waitresses, employees at the casinos, and about a zillion other places who might be into kinky sex. If they are, and they happen to catch Enzo's or Marco's eye, then all the better. Just being around those Guidos might give them the opportunity to observe or hear something. We like to make sure there's a possible sub at every sex club any of the members of the other families belong to. We all have similar proclivities. We all like to tie women up, spank them, and fuck them hard.

"In the meantime, I want Spiegel and Jones followed. I don't want them anywhere near Greta and her family. I want to find out who their direct supervisors are or who works beneath them. I want details on both. Greta and her parents need protection details. I need men stationed outside that nursing home around the clock. No one gets near any of them without me knowing. I can't tell her to just stay home without raising too much suspicion for her and everyone else. I also don't want to make her a prisoner in this home, so that means she needs to have one of us with her at all times. I wish it could be me, but that doesn't work for any of our schedules, and it wouldn't be good for us to have me living up her arse all day every day."

I watch my cousins try not to snicker at that last metaphor since I'm sure they can guess exactly how much I'd like to be up her arse. I certainly enjoyed it earlier tonight. I shoot them all a disgusted look based on their earlier opinions about Greta's and my future. They already think of her like a sister because they know she is going to be in my life for good. If that's the case, they shouldn't be making any jokes or even thinking remotely about what she's doing when we're together.

"I need you guys to get started with all of that. Don't let her parents notice they have shadows. But be sure someone's always close enough to them to get between them and any agents who might feel chatty. I need to get back to bed before Greta wakes up and realizes I'm missing. I don't want her disoriented and scared because she wakes up alone, not recognizing where she is."

Finn steps next to me as the guys joke about something or other I don't even care about. I know they might be laughing now, but they're quiet as they leave the room and leave the house. I trust them implicitly. I know they'll get these jobs done. Finn looks over at me and gives me a nod and his half smile once we're alone. It's a look I've known since we were kids. He'll make sure they take care of everything while I'm with Greta. I trust him, and I should tell him that more often.

"I don't enjoy dumping this on you, Finn. Greta's my girlfriend, and I should handle this. But right now, we have a lot of shite to sort out still. And I don't want her out of reach until I'm certain she's truly safe. When I can't be with her, I need the people I trust most to be there. I don't tell you guys often enough how much I appreciate you, but I do."

"Don't go getting all weepy on me. I don't want to be wiping your snotty nose when you start bawling."

That reminds me of how Greta held me earlier. We've done nothing in the normal sense or progression. But I think of her as my girlfriend. At least, that's the only term I can think that fits. She's not my fiancée because neither of us has proposed, even if we've talked about a future together. I hate the term lover, and we're past the days of calling her my mistress. She sure as fuck isn't a side piece. I wonder if she'd agree and if she thinks of me as her boyfriend. Has she even thought about defining our relationship because at some point, we're going to meet each other's families?

"Why would I need to have you do that when I have a gorgeous woman waiting for me? I already know she's more sympathetic than you are. I told her about Colleen."

He watches me, and I'm certain he's remembering at least some of the shite I did that he saved me from. "She's going to be good for you, you know."

"She already is. I haven't dealt with my feelings about losing Colleen. Not really. I've run from them, and I've suppressed them. I opened up to her earlier, and it's like she lifted a weight off me. I know she's still scared you guys are just tolerating her and haven't forgiven her."

"Are any of us thrilled that it's our family she targeted? No. Of course not. But do we understand her rationale and motivation? Of course. There's not a single person in our family who wouldn't consider doing what she did. There's not a single person in this family who can fault her for wanting to avenge her grandfather. Even if that wasn't her reason, we can understand the anger and hurt that drove her. Fuck. Our family has carried out far worse vendettas for far less. If we weren't the fucked-up family we are, then the betrayal wouldn't be something we could get past. But seeing you together... There's just something there. It's like the bratva with their wives. You won't find anyone better for you, even if she fucked up in the beginning. If you trust her, then we will, too."

"Thanks, Finn. That means a lot to me. We've always been close, but I know how close we are now is partly the consequence of what I did when I was grieving. You've dealt with a lot and put up with a lot. I don't thank you nearly often enough, but I hope you know I know how lucky I am to have you be more of a brother than just a cousin or friend."

"Ah. I love you too, man." Finn rolls his eyes, but we embrace, slapping each other on the back.

"Seriously though. I love you, and I'm glad you're at my right side."

"And Márgrég is on your left."

"Yeah. I haven't wanted anyone there since Colleen. Greta's a lot like her, but I definitely don't look at her like a sister."

"I know. Your hard ons are going to embarrass you one of these days. Try to calm down around her."

"Fecker. Don't be looking at my dick."

"Just a friendly heads up."

"Feck off."

I push him toward the door, but there's a knock before we get to it. I shoot Finn a warning look as I open it. Greta's in one of my T shirts and sweatpants. She put her bra back on to come down here, so she knew I wasn't alone.

"I waited for you to come back, but when I heard the guys leave, and you didn't, I got worried. I didn't realize you were still meeting with Finn. Sorry. I didn't mean to interrupt."

"You didn't. I was just going. G'night."

"Night." She smiles as she speaks. As we walk to our

bedroom, we watch Finn head downstairs, but I know he isn't leaving. He'll be in the security room, watching the feeds.

"Is everything all right, Daddy?"

"It will be, *cailín*. Have you been awake long?"

"I heard you get up, then I saw Cormac outside the door. You've been in here over an hour. Was it something because of me? Something because of what I did?"

"No. We just have some things to take care of. Nothing unusual."

And it's true. What I'm ready to do to those men who visited Greta's granny isn't unusual at all. Not for me at least.

"Can we go back to bed? Or do you have stuff you need to do?"

"I'm ready to have you sleeping in my arms again. We'll deal with everything else in the morning."

"I want to see my grandmother after work."

"We will. There is something I want to ask, though."

"Oh?"

"Are you my girlfriend?"

Chapter Sixteen

Greta

"Um. I think so. That is, if you think you're my boyfriend."

I hedge. I don't know what to make of that question. Is he testing me? Is he setting me straight about a misconception? Is he asking me to be?

"Greta, I'm not tricking you. I just want to know where we stand."

I glance at the bed. I know where I'd rather we lie.

"In less than twelve hours, we've discussed some heavy shit. I've had ginger up my ass, and we've learned someone is trying to get to me by terrorizing my disabled grandmother. Plus, we've talked about a future that might include marriage and kids. I think I'd rather sit than stand."

When I put it that way, it makes me dizzy— physically, not metaphorically. I walk back to the bed and climb in. I pull the covers over me and pull my knees up. I rest my forehead against them and close my eyes. It's all too fucking much. I have to accept my forgiveness, even if I don't understand it. If I keep doubting Dillan, then I'll push him away. That's definitely not what I want. I want him as close as he can get. Fuck. I like it best when he's inside me. I have to trust the guys aren't lying to me about accepting me so easily that it's practically ridiculous.

Then again, maybe they're just being philosophical and pragmatic about it. I haven't lived in this world, so I don't know what the fuck they think about my actions. This makes me wonder about Dillan's parents. How much is he going to tell them? What the fuck do I tell my own? If we're in a relationship, then we can't keep it a secret from them. There's no way this is going to go over well with Mam and Da. They'll plotz. There's a word that sounds better than its meaning. They're going to go batshit.

"*Mo stór?*"

I look up when I hear Dillan's uncertain tone. I hold out my hand to him. As he inches closer to the bed, like he's approaching an unpredictable animal, I move my arm out to his side of the bed. It's closer to the door. I realized that because he changed sides with me sometime while I slept. I know it puts him closer to the door. He wants to guard me even when we're sleeping.

"Daddy, I'm just thinking. Not about whether I am your girlfriend or not. I was thinking about how I have to accept your forgiveness and your family's acceptance, or I'm going to push you away. If you're my boyfriend, then that's the last thing I want. Especially since at some point, we're going to have to meet each other's parents."

That makes me want to curl into a ball just thinking about it. I want his parents, aunts, and uncles to like me. But how can they? There're any number of things for them to dislike, most of all my betrayal. Dillan said he'd convert for me. Maybe his mother'll say a rosary for me rather than wishing me to purgatory.

He slips off the robe and gives his clothes I'm wearing a pointed look. I strip as he crawls into bed next to me. We move to press our bodies together.

"You said *if* I'm your boyfriend, wee one. I want nothing more than to be that. I have since the night I met you. I admit I primarily wanted to fuck you in every way we could imagine, but I also knew I wanted to do that over and over again. I knew I wanted to get to know you. I wanted you to be someone way more than a one-night stand."

"We haven't gone on a date, but we spent a lot of time talking when you think about it. You didn't get to learn as much about me as I learned about you. I saw you as a member of a tightknit family. A business owner. A mobster. You're at a disadvantage."

"No, I'm not. I watched you like a hawk. I listened to everything you said, even when you weren't talking to me. I also ran the more extensive background check, so I even know you got a speeding ticket when you were nineteen for doing forty in a twenty-five. Your mom or dad must have known someone because it was reduced to a warning."

"It was my grandmother. Her neighbor was a lawyer. He and his son loved her banana nut bread. I think they got a loaf every week for a year."

His smile makes his eyes crinkle, and I love it. I cup his cheek, but I wait. He nods, and I lean forward to kiss him. I may start it, but I keep it light, waiting for him to take control. He knows it because I open to him, but my tongue doesn't move until he touches his to mine. Then the spark fans into a blaze. He presses me backwards until he can slide down my body, smattering kisses as he goes. He plays with my clit, then slides his fingers along my pussy, teasing me until I rock my hips.

I open my legs wider for him and tilt my pussy up to him.

He thrusts three fingers in because he knows I'm ready. I want more. I can take more. I press my heels into the mattress, lifting my cunt to him. Offering it to him. He slides his pinky in while his thumb rubs my clit.

"Whose cute little cunt is this?"

"Yours, Daddy."

"And why is that?"

"Because you want it."

"I do. But why else?"

"Because you've accepted me?"

"Yes. You are mine, Greta. Mine to spoil. Mine to watch over. Mine to comfort. Mine to love."

Before I can say anything, he latches onto my clit and sucks so hard I scream. His teeth clamp down hard enough to make me writhe without causing enough pain to worry me. I feel his finger press my cervix— rather unusual sensation —then he's stroking beside it. His other fingers toy with my g spot. His free hand presses down on my belly above the fingers inside me. He continues to lick and suck until another unusual but familiar sensation begins. It's like I have to pee, but I'm sure I don't need to. I did before I went looking for him.

"Daddy, I think I'm going to squirt!"

He looks up at me. "Do you want to?"

"Not without a towel or something. I might soak your mattress."

He grins at me and keeps working my cunt. But he eases off, and the feeling subsides.

"Next time, we'll have a towel. I will make it happen. Do you remember why?"

"Because my cunt belongs to you, and you can do whatever you want with it."

"That's right, my pretty little kitten."

"You're going to make me purr, aren't you?"

His grin widens to a wolfish expression that makes me clench my ass. Fucking hell. He's so fucking hot. He's still working me, and I feel a normal orgasm creeping up on me.

"May I come?"

"Yes, wee one. You never have to ask unless I tell you to. You're not my sub."

I like that. I like how we can talk dirty, but we're still equals in this. We're doing things together. He's not just doing them to me to get me off then to get himself off. That realization alone is so fucking arousing. I can't stop, and I don't want to. I tense so stiff my entire body trembles.

"I want to make you come."

"Oh, you will. I don't doubt that, *cailín*."

He pushes up to rest his forearms near my ears. I slide my arms up between his and cross my wrists. I arch my back and lift my tits to him just like I did my pussy a couple minutes ago. I loved the way it felt when he sucked on my nipple before I fell asleep. He only toys with them now for a moment before I feel the tip of his cock pressing into me. Then he surges into me, making me scream again. God, I hope we're alone.

He sets an unrelenting pace that makes me wonder after a couple minutes if this isn't about something more than just sex. I watch him, and my brow furrows. He's watching me like a hawk. It's not that my arousal is waning, but I'm getting worried. It feels fucking amazing, but I don't understand this intensity. It's not like we had a lot of foreplay to get us wound up this much. I'm slower as I move to keep up with him. He sees the shift in me. He wraps his right hand around my throat. It's heavy but not tight. He leans down to whisper beside my right ear.

"You make me lose control to where I fear I'll hurt you. I'll never let go completely because I wouldn't forgive myself if I did. But the way I want you— need you —is unlike anything else in my life. I'm going to fill you with my cum, and you're going to take all of it. It's going to fill your pussy until it wants to drip out of you. But you won't let it. You're going to keep your legs wide open, so I can see my cum in your cunt. And you're going to stay in this bed for as long as I say. I have things to do. I'll be back whenever I need to get off inside you again. You're just going to keep taking it. You're going to be a sticky, sloppy mess by the time I'm done with you. I'm going to do this whenever I want, so never wear panties again. Do you understand me?"

"Yes, Daddy."

I can barely form the words. I'm ready to climb out of my skin with arousal. It's back with a vengeance. He just described the fantasy I told him about. He's going to give me that. I pull my knees back, letting him sink into me deeper. His pubic bone rubs my clit, and I come again. He knows it and tightens his hand around my throat until I nearly snap. I see stars, my ears ring, and my head feels fuzzy. The moment my eyes start to close, he releases me. I gasp and suck in lungfuls of air.

"I want to make you come, Dillan. I need to. Please. Tell me what to do. Tell me how to make you come."

I'm begging. I want to give him what he just gave me. Fuck. His fingers dig into my ass as he draws back, kneeling between my legs. He lifts my hips so high that basically only my shoulders and head remain on the mattress. He pistons his hips, and I wonder how he can move so fast and with such force. I'm going to be hoarse by morning. I scream again as he rips an orgasm from me that makes my fingers curl into claws, but I have nothing to sink them into.

"Greta!"

He roars my name, and I watch his shoulder and arm muscles strain as his usual six-pack turns into at least an eight-pack. He is so gorgeous, and he wants me. Only me. That's empowering in a way I never imagined. I feel like I can face the world now. Like I can deal with whatever shit awaits me outside this brownstone. Knowing a man like Dillan wants me beside him makes me feel like I can conquer the world.

He flops forward, but he catches himself before he can crush me. He holds up most of his weight, but I wrap around him like a koala and tug him to press more of his bulk onto me. We're panting and sweating, but I'm so damn happy. Something passed between us with a newfound level of intimacy. He kisses me, and it's one-eighty from how we've just been. This is so loving it makes my heart ache with fullness.

I run my hands over his hair and back. He kisses my eyelids, the tip of my nose, my lips. I watch his reluctance to pull out, but he goes into the bathroom. I hear the water run, then he comes out and grabs a pair of basketball shorts. I watch him dress before he comes to stand beside me.

"We stop this the moment you need to. If you need a break or something's wrong, tell me immediately. Safe word or not. Tell me."

"Yes, Daddy."

He drops a peck on my lips, then he leaves, shutting the door behind him. I lie on the bed and exhale deeply. When my eyes close, I can't help but drift off.

"My naughty little girl decided to sleep rather than think about how full she is with my cum."

I wake to the feel of a foam head vibrator against my clit and Dillan speaking. I don't know how long I slept, but I must have been exhausted. I didn't hear him come in, and I definitely didn't hear him tearing open the packaging I see on the bedside table. I glance toward the window, and I can see it's still dark.

I've lost all concept of time today and tonight. It feels like this night has dragged on, yet at the same time, it's rushed by between sex with Dillan how many times? And seeing his cousins and taking two quick naps.

"Don't you have anything to say to me? I didn't say you could sleep."

"I'm sorry, Daddy. I couldn't help it."

"But you will."

He's stroking himself, and part of me feels robbed that I'm not the one arousing him.

"You don't like this, do you? You want to be the one getting me hard. Let me assure you, Greta. Just thinking about you is enough to do it. That's why I'm back only half an hour later. Seeing you naked in our bed is enough to make me leak."

Our bed? When the fuck did that happen?

He climbs onto it and lifts my legs over his shoulders. He says nothing, but I'm certain he can still see his cum in me, knows I'm wet. His cock slides in with ease. Then he's fucking me again like earlier. Maybe it's momentum that enables him to move so fast and with such force. He reaches around my left thigh and pinches my nipple. Hard. I yelp, and he just twists.

"I won't let you come. That's not why you're here. You're here for me to fuck whenever I want. You're here to take my cum in your pretty little pink pussy. You're here because you're mine to do whatever I want with. Isn't that right?"

"Yes, Daddy."

I'm submitting willingly. But there's control here that others might not see. I have control of his desire. It's all for me, and that's intoxicating. If I refuse, he would never in a million years force me. He wouldn't even try to coerce me. I'm certain of that. This isn't a fluid power exchange by any stretch, but we are equals. I keep seeing that over and over, and it's sinking in.

He moves my legs to wrap around his waist. He's been

stroking the outside of them since he put them over his shoulders, but now his thumbs press along the inside of my thighs. He's leaving a trail of red skin as he does it. He leans forward and nips at my tits, his teeth grazing my nipples. Then he's giving me hickies all over them. He's marking me. With a grunt, he stills, and I know he's coming. He doesn't wait around this time. He pulls out. I expect him to get off the bed, but he leans forward instead. He leaves love bites along the inside of my thighs and the crease where my legs meet my hips.

He stands and steps close enough where my head rests on a pillow to wrap his hand around my throat and squeeze. But he also leans in to kiss my temple, then my lips. He releases me, and I turn my head to look at him.

"Are you all right, *cailín?*"

"Yes, *mo chroi.*"

His smile warms me all the way to my toes. He looks genuinely relaxed when he hears me call him my heart. He cups my right breast and massages.

"You make it so hard to leave."

I reach for him and wrap my hand around his shrinking cock, stroking it. But he catches my wrist and pulls away. I pout, then grin. When he leans forward this time, he sucks on my nipple as he squeezes my tit. My right hand tunnels into his hair while my left slides over his shoulders. I don't realize what he's doing— how he's distracting me —until I feel his fingers rubbing my clit. I moan and shift restlessly. It feels beyond good since he didn't let me come when he did. But that one sound is his signal.

He straightens and leaves without a backward glance.

We've been playing our game, around and around, for the past four hours. He left me for thirty minutes, then fifteen, then an hour, then forty-five. Around and around until I didn't bother paying attention. All I could do was wonder what would come next. He did as he said. He came in me each time until I couldn't keep the cum inside because I was too full.

He doesn't fuck me this last time. Each time he's tender with me, it's even more so than the last time. He's gentle, knowing I'm sore now. His fingertips are like feathers as he runs them over my body. His thrusts are slow but deep. This time, he asks me what I want. What position would feel best, so I ask to be on top. He holds me throughout, and I swear we're making love.

He carries me into the bathroom, still buried inside me. But even his dick has to be exhausted because we don't stay joined by the time we're in the shower. That doesn't stop him from holding me while we soak under the dual showerheads. Hmmm.

"Greta, I don't have shower sex in here. It's not his and hers. I like the hot water pounding on my back. It eases tension and relaxes me. Though now I have my *cailín* to do that in and out of the shower."

He kisses my neck and adjusts his hold on me, so he can tip my head back under the showerhead.

"Dillan, you can put me down. I know I'm getting too heavy."

He freezes, looking down at me. I don't know what to make of his expression. I insulted him. Fuck.

"I didn't mean you aren't strong, but I'm not—"

"Finish that thought with anything but a compliment about your body, and I will spank you."

"Come on, Dillan. I know you like it, but that still doesn't mean I'm light. I have to weigh almost as much as—"

He lowers me to my feet in a flash and spins me around. His hand lands across my ass. Mercilessly. It hurts nearly as much as my punishment yesterday afternoon. He rains them down on me until I'm gasping and stomping my foot.

"Don't do that. You'll slip."

"Then don't spank me so hard. I don't even get why you're spanking me in the first place. I'm not saying anything that isn't true. I'm fa— OW!"

Motherfucker. That one burns enough to bring tears to my eyes. He hears the waver in my voice and spins me back around. He caresses my ass as he kisses me. My arms wrap around him as I burrow against his chest once he pulls back.

"Greta, I don't live inside your head. I can't change the way you see yourself, but I don't want to hear you say negative things about yourself. Neither of us is perfect, but you're so fecking perfect for me I can't handle the idea of anyone— you included —putting you down. I've never had a type, so don't go asking something like whether I'm a chubby chaser. Don't ask if I prefer thick girls. What I will chase is you until I'm too old to do it. What I prefer is you. As for being able to hold you, I can carry Cormac's and Seamus's heavy asses up three flights of fecking stairs when they're fecking passed out drunk. Feckers are fecking beasts. Ask them what happened at Halloween. They'll both turn green."

Intense.

That's the only word that aptly describes Dillan most of the time, even when he's trying not to be too profane in front of me. I nod.

"Feck. I shouldn't have done that. I'm sorry, Greta. I—"

"Don't be sorry. I'm insecure about my body, but I admit working at 4Play and having men get handsy did a lot for my self-esteem, even if I didn't actually want any of them touching me. The way you look at me always makes me feel beautiful, but that also makes me think about my imperfections. Like what if you get tired of overlooking them? I guess knowing it bothers you that much that I don't hold the high opinion of myself that you do is— well —it's sweet. You're protective of me, even if it's from myself."

"I am. You know what kind of man I am. You know what I do. I will never tell you what that is, but you can guess how I would react if it were a man insulting you."

He'd kill him. I overheard him talking about Maureen after my altercation with her. He was livid and said she was lucky she was a woman. At the time, I thought he meant he was pissed about a fight happening at his club. Now I get what he really meant.

"I don't want to diminish your feelings or invalidate them. I shouldn't have spanked you for feeling the way you do. I regret that."

"Shh, Daddy. You didn't. If you'd told me I was wrong to feel the way I do, then I wouldn't have appreciated it. But you told me your expectations about how I talk about myself— not think about myself —and you told me it bothered you to hear it. You didn't say I can't talk about my thoughts. Saying negative shit about myself definitely doesn't make me feel better about myself. Besides, even though it hurt like a mother, I still liked it."

I wink at him before turning away and reaching for the shampoo. We hurry to finish our shower. So much for leaving by six-thirty. We're an hour late, but the guys are just arriving as we go downstairs. I freeze when I see Finn come out of a small room down the hall from the living room. The security cameras. He's been in there all night watching them. I shoot a panicked glance up at Dillan. I feel sick.

"It's all right. He couldn't hear anything. The room is soundproof, so whoever is watching isn't distracted. If I thought he could hear us, I wouldn't have let you scream. I will never make anything about our sex life public. If you want to go to a sex club to be watched, that's one thing. But what we do in the privacy of our room remains that way."

"Our room? You've said that before."

"Yes, our. Until we know what's going on, I don't want you sleeping alone. If that's our bed here or our bed at your place or our bed at a hotel, you sleep next to me. Once we know you're safe, we'll decide what happens next."

"His and hers?"

He stares down at me.

"No."

The answer is so resolute that my toes curl in my shoes. This is the most fucked-up, best relationship I've ever had.

"Let's go, wee one. I'm walking you into work today. It's time people realize who I am."

Chapter Seventeen

Dillan

I didn't lie about the security room being soundproof. But I did have to tell Finn to grab food and take it with him. I told him not to drink too much either. He just nodded, but I can tell he wanted to roll his eyes. My house. My girlfriend. My rules.

"Dillan." Greta hisses my name. I just raise my eyebrows. "I write a story about your family that has the feds interested, and you're going to show up as my boyfriend?"

I guide her out the front door and to a town car. She halts and refuses to get in since I haven't answered.

"Yes."

She stares at me like I've sprouted horns. She shakes her head but slides into the backseat. The privacy glass is up as always. It's only down if the person in the backseat lowers it. All our drivers know that. They also won't open the backdoors until the passenger taps on the window. In the past, it's been because we might be on a phone call. Now it might be because I'm fucking my girlfriend.

"Dillan, I'm serious. People won't understand how I went from an exposé a day ago to walking in next to you."

"You'll be walking in with my arm around you."

"Staking your claim will only make it so much more confusing for everyone."

"Let them be."

"You're being obtuse. It's going to draw more attention than I want. You'll leave, and I'll be left with stares and questions. Please don't do this."

Since becoming the boss, I haven't had to explain myself to anyone. I usually do with my cousins as a courtesy and because it's better for us when I do. But I'm going to have to get used to explaining at least some shite to Greta. I can't assume she'll understand how this world works. I have to teach her.

"I need to see who you work with. I need to see who reaches for the phone immediately. Who reaches for it but catches themselves. Who looks at their computer screen. Who watches us with too much interest. Who watches us with not enough. Who watches us with feigned disinterest. Who has a shite poker face, and who has one that's almost too good. I need to see how the men and women react to me and to us together. Not only can I learn a lot about who might be doing this, I'll convince myself it's safe to leave you there. If I don't see it with my own eyes, I won't leave without you."

She offers me a soft smile and a nod. She slides her hand into mine and rests her head on my shoulder. I dozed in my office between visits, and I know she did the same thing. But neither of us got enough sleep last night. I rest my head back and close my eyes once I wrap my arm around her shoulders. We stay that way until we get to her place. I go inside with her, and I really study the inside of her apartment this time. Our taste runs similarly, and it's obvious we both enjoy being comfortable in our homes. Our furniture is inviting, and she's decorated in warm colors like I have.

"We have the same kitchen towels."

I point to the one hanging from the fridge door handle. I keep looking around, noticing what I didn't when I was here last time. I notice a plate in the drying rack. She must have noticed we have the same set.

"How many days' worth of stuff should I bring?"

Everything.

"Let's say four or five."

She pulls out a small suitcase and fills it with what she needs. I watch from the corner as she gathers stuff from the bathroom. I gave her a toothbrush this morning. I uncharacteristically had a spare. Maybe I subconsciously wanted it to be hers because I bought the two-pack after we met. When she goes to her underwear drawer, I push away from the wall.

"Bras only."

"What? I need—"

"No, you don't. We both know that. That's why you only packed skirts. I told you already. When I want your pussy, I will have it. No pants and no panties. Understood?"

"Yes, Daddy."

She steps back and strips off what she's wearing, walking over to the hamper to drop them in. Goodbye, trousers. She goes back to the closet and bends forward, looking at her shoes. She shifts her weight from foot to foot like she's looking for things in the back of her closet. She's toying with me. Fuck. I'm rock hard. As always.

When she stops swaying her hips and looks for shite for real, I know she's discouraged that I didn't take the invitation. I prowl over to her and slide my right arm around her waist, pulling her back against me, so her pussy is at the right height for me to rub my cock against. I know she's sore, so I'm careful.

But I also know I stretched her pussy by fucking her so many times. I slide three— then all four —fingers into her.

"You offered your cunt, and now I'm going to take it."

I work her until she's begging.

"Daddy, please... Please make me come... Please... *Daddy!*"

Her hands grip my forearm as she trembles then sags. I scoop her into my arms— I love carrying her. I love not having to let go of her —and walk to the bed. I sit with her on my lap.

"Greta, was I too rough?"

"No. Fist me next time." She shocks herself at what she blurted. Her cheeks go scarlet. I don't know why this embarrasses her after she admitted she basically had a sex slave fantasy.

"Why don't you want me to know that's what you want?"

"I didn't mean to sound so demanding."

"You didn't mean to tell me that at all. Why?"

"Because now you know two of my sexual fantasies, and I don't know any of yours. Maybe you don't have any about me."

"I have so many fecking fantasies about you it's a wonder I can think about anything else. I want to fuck you in the ocean, in a pool, on a park bench. I want to fuck you on a swing and tied up with Shibari rope. I want to watch you warm my cock while I work. I want to eat your pussy while you're on the phone with whoever, trying not to scream. I want you strapped to a Saint Andrew's Cross. I want you on a spanking bench. I want to fuck you at a party where anyone could find us but don't. Believe me, little one. I have plenty."

"Oh."

She only says that, but I see the speculation in her eyes as she watches me now that I've named only a handful of things I want to do with her. She stands and hurries to dress. I grab her bag as we leave. She hasn't said a damn thing, and now I'm completely freaked out. But she takes my hand as we walk down the stairs and out to the car. It's not until we're pulling away from her building that she speaks again.

"Take your phone out, Daddy. Open your email."

"Issuing me orders?"

"Yes. Do it."

I'm curious, so I do. But I'm watching her. She rolls her eyes and pushes my hand up with my phone in it, so I can see the screen. Then she's unzipping my pants as she moves to kneel on the floor. She pulls my boxer briefs down and strokes me.

"Read your email, Daddy. Do some work."

She slides her mouth down my cock and moves slowly. She rests her cheek on my thigh and just sucks without moving her head. Fuck. It feels divine. I want to pay full attention to her, but that wasn't the fantasy I named. She wants to do this for me, so I won't ruin it. I stroke her hair as I skim two new emails. She periodically bobs her head, but mostly, she just tongues my cock. I'm reading a financial article when we pull up outside her office building. She glances up at me and starts sucking me off in earnest. So fucking tempting. But I pull my dick away and tuck myself back into my pants.

"I know I can ask you for a blowjob if I want one, or you can offer to give me one. That— That was my fantasy to a tee."

"Mmm. We'll have to act that one out a few dozen more times. I liked it too."

Once we're both completely presentable again, I tap on the window. Joey's my driver today, and I feel safest with him behind the wheel when I have Greta with me. I'm going to assign him as her driver and let the other guys know he's on call for her around the clock. He knows that's the deal with me since he's my favorite. He's also my second cousin once removed, or some shite like that on my dad's side.

I'm pleased to see the newspaper's building has ample

security. She has to show a badge and sign me in before we can get to the elevator. There are two armed guards patrolling the area between the bank of elevators. However, I don't love that her office is on the fifth floor. Then again, if I'm being honest, I don't love her being in an office building away from me. The fifth floor is too low to deter someone from using the stairs to get to her, but it's also too high for her to easily catch the elevator or go down the stairs in an emergency.

"Relax." She whispers to me as we step through the sliding doors.

Other people get on too, and she asks someone to hit the button for us. As we walk through the glass doors into the bullpen of cubicles filled with ambitious reporters, people start to notice us. Notice me. It's not like I'm so fucking famous everyone in the city knows who I am. But I am infamous. It also doesn't help that whoever leaked Greta's articles also ensured there were massive photos of my cousins and me. Both were taken at funerals. What they didn't mention in the caption was the first one they used was from Colleen's funeral. The other was from Nana's. Double fist to the junk. My sister and grandmother died within three months of each other.

They implied it was some mob funeral like out of *The Godfather* or *Goodfellas*. Except those were about the shitbag Mafia, not us. Fucking Marlon Brando and that curled lip. It makes me want to roll my eyes, but everyone thinks anyone running a syndicate must be like him. That, or because I'm Irish, I'm some dock worker with a steel pipe in my hands everywhere I go. I leave the pipes at the station for those who need the encouragement.

I scan the people as we approach. My arm is around Greta's waist, and I can tell she's nervous. But she's looking straight ahead, her head held high. I'm so fucking proud of her. She has an iron backbone, and I love that about her. She's going to need that if we're in this together.

"Molly, my office."

I turn to look at the man calling out to her. His eyes widen when he recognizes me. I squeeze her waist and steer us toward Gary. He steps backwards into his office as Greta enters, and I follow. I close the door but stay near it. Greta slides into one of the chairs. Gary's tone is much lighter now that I'm in here with them.

"I was worried about you. I called and texted, but you didn't respond. I thought something happened to you."

His gaze keeps darting from Greta to me and back again. From where I've positioned myself, I can see Greta's expression. She offers him what appears to be a sincere smile, but I can already read the looks in her eyes. It's anything but.

"I was busy."

"But—"

"Have you met my boyfriend before, Gary? This is Dillan O'Rourke." She twists to look at me. "Dillan, this is Gary Post. He's the National Desk editor."

I walk to the jackass and stick out my hand. He hesitates, then accepts, and shakes. I have a tight grip, but not one that's meant to intimidate. I don't need to shake his hand to do that.

"Boyfriend?"

"Yes." I answer for us.

Gary looks at Greta to explain, but she sits back in her seat and cants her head. After all, Gary called her into his office, not the other way around.

"Like I said, I was worried. With the leak and all, I—" He meets my gaze, and he doesn't know what to say.

"Thought I'd put a hit on her?"

Gary stares at me, completely unprepared for me to say

something so blunt. I'm a mobster, after all. How can I not be blunt?

"Uh... Molly, we still don't know who leaked the articles. Are they the way you wrote them?" He's so confused.

"They are. But they were not ready for publication, and you know it. You know why I wanted to write them, but part of the reason I didn't push for them to be published is because my relationship with Dillan didn't make it as clear cut as I thought it would be."

"Hannah said she saw you get into a town car with a man who looked like Dill— Mr. O'Rourke."

He corrects himself when I cock an eyebrow. We are not friends.

Greta nods as she responds. "Dillan picked me up and is dropping me off. It's certainly nicer than the subway."

She looks over her shoulder at me, and I know she's thinking about how her lips were around my cock ten minutes ago. Good thing my boxer briefs are tight enough to keep my dick in one place, or they'd both know what I'm thinking about. I jump in just so I don't get distracted too badly.

"Gary, what's being done to ensure Molly's safety since someone obviously had malicious intent?"

She doesn't like me calling her Molly, but that's what people know her as here. Anything else will just draw attention away from what I want to know.

"Our IT department is working to find out how our network got hacked and who did it."

"I can tell you how it got hacked. From inside."

Sean texted me early this morning, just before I joined Greta the last time. He confirmed what we suspected. Someone within the company. But he said it would take him a while to figure out who because they were good at covering their tracks. He cautioned that a skilled professional hacker could make it look like an inside job when it wasn't, so he said not to close the door on any possibility. He cleared his schedule today to spend the morning working on it.

I don't like how Gary's pupils just dilated. The fucker knows something. I lean toward him, lowering myself a couple inches until we are eye-to-eye. "What do you know?"

I sense Greta tensing, but my gaze doesn't waver.

"Nothing."

I narrow my eyes, and Gary looks like he's ready to piss himself. "Really? Because I know you threatened my girlfriend's job. I know you were rude to her in your message. And I know you won't do that again because your boss already warned you. Now if I know all that, don't you think you could share something you know?"

"I seriously don't know who leaked it, but a couple of federal agents were here when I arrived. They didn't have a warrant or anything, but they had questions."

Greta asks what I want to know. "Which agency?"

"Bureau of Alcohol, Tobacco, and Firearms."

Fucking Mason and Brad. I'm sure of it.

"Agents Spiegel and Jones?"

"Yeah. How'd—"

He cuts himself off. He doesn't want to know how I know that or that his boss already spoke to him. Greta leans forward and rests her forearm on Gary's desk."

"You said they didn't have a warrant. Did you let them look at my cubicle?"

"Yeah. They didn't find anything, though."

"Of course, they didn't. I have nothing to hide. But you let them search without probable cause. It may be legal to go through my workspace as my employer, but that doesn't make it right."

"You're dating a—"

Once again, Gary doesn't know what to say. I smirk. Go ahead. Say it, shit wad. Greta doesn't back down.

"A what, Gary?"

"An O'Rourke."

"I am. But you didn't know that until I walked through your office door. You didn't know that when the ATF arrived. What about me made you think I was tied to alcohol, tobacco, or firearms?"

"You spied on mo— fucking hell. Molly, you spied on the goddamn mob. There. I said it. You going to off me now, O'Rourke?"

"Are you asking me to?"

The color drains from his face, and I laugh. I step away from the desk and go back to leaning against the wall near the door. Greta keeps watching Gary, who's now as skittish as a day-old foal. She gets us back on track.

"What did they say to you when you arrived?"

"They showed me their badges and asked where your desk was. I walked them over, then stayed out of the way."

"Did they say why they wanted to search my space?"

"They wanted to see if there was any clue where you might be since you weren't home when they knocked on your door last night or this morning. They wanted to be sure you were safe."

"The ATF worried about my safety? That's ridiculous. NYPD. Maybe even the FBI. Those would make sense. The ATF? No."

Maybe Spiegel and Jones drove past her place last night, but they didn't get out of their car. They definitely didn't go this morning because we were there. No one even got out of a vehicle. My men would have told me. I had guys parked outside her place all night just like I have for days.

Greta's phone buzzes in her pocket, but she makes no move

to reach for it. It's a single buzz, so a text or some other notification. Not a call. However, it distracts all of us. She stands and gathers her purse and workbag.

"Molly, you came in late this morning. Again. When you were on assignment, it was fine that you didn't show up. But now—"

"Gary, you're lucky I haven't quit. For better or for worse, those articles have increased readership. The comment sections on both are clamoring for more. The last thing you need is for me to leave and go to a different publication. You know I've never made a habit of coming in late, but I've worked late plenty of times. Cut me a little slack considering someone hacked my cloud, published my unauthorized articles, has gotten federal agents interested in me, and I've been followed. Maybe I'm being a bit more cautious about my morning routine."

That gets his attention. "Someone followed you?"

"Yeah. And it wasn't for my security. So, if my boyfriend thinks I should vary my morning schedule, or he wants to walk me to my desk, then I think that's perfectly reasonable. Don't you?"

Between Greta's confident tone and me just being here, he'll likely agree to giving her a raise if she mentions it. He nods and looks out the glass walls to where work is carrying on around us. Even when I leaned over to make sure he looked me in the eye, I kept my posture nonthreatening. Not so much my expression, but, for anyone else to see, my body language wasn't as terrifying as it could be. I'm very aware of everyone around me, whether or not there's glass between us.

"Whatever you need, Molly."

"Thanks."

She steps around her chair, and I open the office door. My hand goes to the small of her back as I guide her out. I keep it there as we walk to her desk. I observe her as she checks her workspace. She doesn't act as though anything is out of place, so I assume the agents didn't take any of her stuff. Once she has her laptop placed on the docking station, she smiles up at me with a nod. I give her a peck on the lips.

"Have a good day at work, honey."

Her smile broadens as she lifts her chin to return my quick kiss. "You, too."

"You didn't grab anything for lunch. I have to head to my office, but Shane is outside in a car. I need to program all the guys' numbers into your phone."

"Shane already put them in while I still worked at 4Play because you were worried about the Albanians."

"I didn't know that, but I'm glad he did. You can text him if you decide to go out. I want him with you, Greta. If you leave this floor, he's with you."

I'm adamant about it. Finding out agents have been here is bothering me more than I was willing to let Gary see. If Greta finds out how angry I am, it'll upset her.

"Okay. Should I text you if I'm going anywhere?" She could sound snarky. She could sound oppressed. Instead, she sounds considerate.

"You don't have to report your comings and goings to me."

"But it would make you feel better, wouldn't it? You don't want me to know how angry you are right now, but I know finding out about the agents made you furious. I don't need to add to your stress."

No one outside my family would have known how I feel. I can hide my emotions to where the few women I've dated in the past wouldn't stop complaining about how devoid of them I am. I feel plenty. I just trust very few to know it. The fact Greta can read me is both disconcerting and reassuring. She gets me, and I like that.

"Text if you remember to. Otherwise, I'll see you at five. Think about what you'd like to do for dinner."

Her eyes dart to my dick before she whispers to me. "I know what I want for dinner. Do you know what you want for dessert, Daddy?"

Chapter Eighteen

Greta

I don't know if we accomplished anything during that meeting with Gary. It felt like it went around in circles. Seems like that's the theme of a lot of my conversations lately. But I get the feeling that whatever Dillan wanted from it, he got. Or maybe it was more time to watch people. I know from seeing him at the club that he can appear entirely focused on one thing—whatever's in front of him —but turn out to be fully aware of something happening practically behind his head. His peripheral vision is ridiculous. He seriously has eyes in the back of his head. It wouldn't surprise me if he could describe every person who works on this floor.

When I'm alone, I pull out my phone and look at the text that came in.

S

You're dating D

Sergei. And it's not a question.

ME

Yes

I have to wait a couple minutes for a response to appear.

S

That's not wise

ME

My choice

S

Six weeks ago you wanted us to help you destroy them. Now you're dating the boss. Make it make sense.

ME

I don't have to. It works for me

S

You're playing with fire if this isn't a legit relationship

ME

It is. Things change. Thanks for the concern.

S

When you lie down with dogs…

ME

I got awfully close to you and A. Did I get up with fleas from you?

Oh, I'm pushing my fucking luck. Antagonizing the bratva isn't a wise choice. But I don't like anyone insulting Dillan or my right to decide.

S

Don't say I didn't warn you

ME

I'll take that under advisement.

S

When it all goes to shit come to us. We will
still help you.

There's not much more to say, is there?

ME

Thanks

When he doesn't respond, I tuck my phone back into my pocket. I turn on my computer and stare at the screen. I have no idea what the fuck to do. I don't have an assignment right now. I'm not still working on the O'Rourke pieces. I really don't want to go slinking back to Gary to ask him what to do next. But I also can't just sit here, staring off into space. I nearly jump out of my skin when my desk phone rings.

"Hello."

"Ms. McDonnell, this is Agent Mason Spiegel with the ATF. Do you have a moment to talk?"

"Is there something you didn't find at my desk this morning that you'd like to ask me about now?"

He hesitates. Either he didn't expect me to know he'd been there, or he didn't expect me to be so forthright. "You've made some very dangerous friends and powerful enemies."

That makes my brow furrow. I remain quiet. If I wait long enough, he'll give in first. The line remains silent, and I know he's waiting me out. But he called me. He can steer this conversation for now. I'm not volunteering shit.

"You spent the night at Dillan O'Rourke's house in Brooklyn. You were seen entering and exiting your home with him this morning. He doesn't have your best interests at heart, Ms. McDonnell. Your articles prove you know what type of man he is. If he's forcing you, we can help."

"Why's the ATF interested?" And now I'm going to steer for a little while.

"That's not open for discussion."

"Then why'd you call?"

"A courtesy. The O'Rourkes are part of an ongoing investigation."

I force myself not to snort. Every syndicate family is part of an ongoing investigation. "You said I have dangerous friends and powerful enemies. Do you mean you're my enemy?"

"No. We can be a powerful friend to you."

"Friends give without expecting something in return. I highly doubt your protection comes for free. What do you want from me, Agent Spiegel?"

"Meet me at the corner deli during your lunch break. We'll go for a drive, and I'll explain."

"None of that is happening."

"Because Dillan is having you followed."

"He might be. But I'm not meeting a strange man anywhere, and I sure as shooting am not getting into a car with a strange man. You'll likely have your partner with you, so that's doubly no. If you wish to speak to me, you can come here, and we can use a conference room."

"That's awfully public."

"And a corner deli in Manhattan at lunch time isn't?"

"That's the kind of public that makes you inconspicuous, Ms. McDonnell." He uses my last name to try to fool me into thinking he respects me while using Dillan's first name to humanize and lessen his significance. Two can play that game.

"Mason, I'm busy right now. If you have something you

wish to know about Mr. O'Rourke, then you'd better spend your time and energy asking him directly. Any of the Mr. O'Rourkes because I know nothing."

"Ah, but you do. The Albanians."

The hell? Once more, I go silent. I haven't given them much thought in a while. Not since my first scare that I was being followed.

"They've been talking about a woman involved with the mafia."

"I'm Irish. You must have me confused."

"Don't patronize me, Ms. McDonnell."

Unlike you're doing with me, fuck nut?

"You'll have to be more specific, then. I don't think I know any Albanians."

"You met a couple at 4Play. You worked there while Dillan met with them. Since you're so close to Dillan, you must have seen him with the Albanian mafia leaders."

"Many people came in and out of that club. I wasn't there to observe the Albanians."

"You were there to observe the O'Rourkes, which means you observed several crime families."

I pull out and unlock my phone.

ME

> One of the ATF agents called me. I'm on my work landline with him. What do I do? He's asking about the Albanians

"I didn't get introductions to anyone. I served drinks and watched the O'Rourkes."

"Molly—"

"Ms. McDonnell. We are not friends."

"Ms. McDonnell, your articles prove you did a lot more than just watch. You learned quite a bit. We'd like to know what else you learned that didn't go into your articles. Now, I've invited you nicely to have a discreet conversation with me. If you refuse, I'll drag you out of your office in handcuffs."

"What federal offense are you going to charge me with? You're law enforcement, but your jurisdiction is federal crimes. If you say obstructing justice, you'll have to do better than that. I have three excellent lawyers on speed dial."

"Cormac and Seamus O'Rourke."

"That's two of them. Dillan O'Rourke is the third. Threaten me again, and I'll make sure I'm lawyered up tighter than John Gotti ever was."

ME

He wants me to meet him. I said no. Now he's threatening to arrest me. What do I do?

"Having three mobsters defending you doesn't scream innocent, Ms. McDonnell."

"It doesn't have to. It screams protected."

I'm staring at my phone, but no messages are coming in. I tap my contacts and scroll to the S names. There's just the S for Sergei. But right after that are Seamus, Sean, and Shane. I tap the last one and pull up a blank message.

ME

Spiegel's on my landline. He wants me to meet him. Something about the Albanians. I said no. Dillan's not responding. What do I do?

"What do you need protection from?"

"Apparently you. I'm not meeting you, Mason. I have nothing to say, and you found nothing at my desk. What I know was in those articles. I have nothing else to offer."

SHANE

How long have you been on the call?

ME

A few minutes. He knows I'm at my desk. He
called me here.

SHANE

It's not about tracing your call. He's recording
it. Get off the call. I'm coming. Get your stuff.
We're leaving.

That makes my mind whirl as I think about what I've said. I've been evasive, but if the call is being recorded, have I said anything they could splice and put together to incriminate Dillan, his family, or me? I admitted I'm Irish. It's no secret. I have a hint of my childhood accent still. It's not like I can hide it on legal documents. But could he use my comment to argue I admitted to being part of the Irish mob?

"I have work to do. I have nothing more to tell you. You won't show up here again because you have no federal crimes to charge me with. If you send the NYPD or some other agency to harass me, I will lawyer up."

I think about saying something about going near my grandmother, but since she hasn't come up, I'm not putting any ideas in his head. I'm lifting my laptop off the dock while I talk. I look in my drawers to see if there's anything I don't want left here after all. I have hand sanitizer, lotion, and snacks. The rest are office supplies. I have a couple framed family photos on my desk. I guess I haven't really decorated my space much. I've never felt the need to. It's work, not home. I slip the computer back into my bag.

"Ms. McDonnell, you're making a mistake. You do not want to be on the wrong side of this."

"Of what? I know nothing about the Albanians besides

they were at the club one night. I told you I wasn't observing them."

My desk faces the door, so I see Shane arrive. Thank God. He's looking for me, so I stand. He's walking casually to my desk, but he's gaining attention. The O'Rourke men have something about them. A devil-may-care ruggedness. Most would say it's cockiness, but it's hard-earned self-confidence. It doesn't hurt that they're all hot. Like the family hit the genetic lottery. Three sisters married three brothers, so the only true differences are the slight variance in hair color. The emerald-hued eyes are identical, even beyond Sean and Shane.

"Ms. McDonnell—"

"I have work to do. I have nothing else to say without a lawyer present."

"Fine. When you change your mind—"

"I won't. Not about meeting with you and not about having a lawyer present if you try to question me again. Good day." I hang up. It's rude and something I generally never do. But I need to get off the call.

"Are you all right?" Shane keeps his voice low. He's looking at my hands, and I realize they're shaking. The call unnerved me more than I realized.

"Yeah. I can't leave, though. What am I going to tell my boss?"

I look down at my bag. Leaving is impulsive. I can't walk out on my job. I will get fired one of these days. I enjoy working here. At least, I did. I enjoy being a journalist, and I don't want to stop. Then again, I don't know how this will work out if Dillan and I are together. No one will ever tell me anything if they know I have ties to the mob. Maybe my career is over. Or maybe I'll just be relegated to writing for some tabloid.

Or I could stop catastrophizing and let this play out a little.

But when I look at Shane, I know he won't be of the same opinion. His gaze is sweeping the open office space, surely remembering everyone right down to how many fillings they each have. He holds out his hand, and I realize he's offering to carry my laptop bag. I hesitate, but when he stares at me, I'm quick to concede.

"Shane, I still don't know what to tell Gary. He's watching us. He met Dillan half an hour ago. Now you're here, and I'm getting ready to leave."

"Tell him you just got a tip on something connected to the article about us. You asked me to go with you because you're not convinced it's safe to go alone."

That's actually highly plausible. At least, it's as plausible as I could come up with. I head toward the exit, which means passing Gary. I decide to take a preemptive step and knock on his door, which is open. I still do it as a courtesy.

"I just got a tip from a CI that there might be more to the articles than I realized. It'll take me in a different direction, but I think it could be good. Mr. O'Rourke is going with me because I'm not sure it's safe to go alone."

"Where are you going?"

"I don't know yet. My CI will tell me once I'm out of the office. Since that's a bit questionable, I asked Mr. O'Rourke to escort me."

"Which one are you?"

Rude much?

"The one assigned to guard Ms. McDonnell today." Shane smirks and crosses his arms. His suit coat strains across his back and his biceps. He looks like he's practically ready to go all Hulk in it. Dillan's the hottest man I've ever met, but Shane ranks toward the top. I suppose that means Sean does, too. My dirty mind goes to a threesome and whether some woman has been lucky enough to be sandwiched between them. I don't want to be her, but I apparently have sex on the brain now that Dillan and I are together.

"I need to go, Gary. I'll check in when I can."

I turn away from him because I got the sense Shane wasn't going to wait another minute. He wants me away from here. We ride down in the elevator in silence, then he holds the door open for me as we step outside. A blustery wind assails me and nearly knocks me over. I dip my head to keep my face out of it, but I'm watching the sidewalk in front of me as we hurry to the town car I spotted when we passed through the doors. I notice the spit polished Oxfords stalking toward me. I move to step out of the man's way, but arms wrap around me. I know that body and that scent in a heartbeat.

"*Cailín.*" Dillan murmurs it beside my ear as he engulfs me in a hug. It's cold out, and he's a furnace. I burrow into him. I don't know where Shane went because I can't see him.

"Daddy."

He kisses me, but it's too brief. Then he's guiding me to a different car. I notice Shane standing beside the new one.

"Dillan, what are you doing here?"

"Shane texted me, and I realized I'd missed yours. I came immediately."

"You must have been nearby."

"Close enough. We have an office building near here that we use when we need it. I was there, and that's we're headed now."

Shane opens the rear door, and I climb in. I'm reaching for my belt as the door closes behind Dillan. I don't have a chance to snap it fastened before he lifts me onto his lap. His hand slides up my thigh and under my skirt until he cups my ass. It just stays there, holding it. His other hand cups my head as we kiss. There's a desperation on his part that I've never felt before. It's not the sexual hunger we usually have or the tenderness that's grown between us so quickly. It's as though he fears I'll disappear— no, run away —if he doesn't hold on to me.

"Dillan, I'm not going anywhere just because I got scared."

His eyes widen, taken aback that I guessed what he was thinking. "You have a habit of reading me in a way no one outside my family can. It's unnerving."

"Does it bother you? Do you not like me knowing what you're thinking or feeling? Too intrusive?"

"Just the opposite. I'm surprised you can, but you already know me in a way no one else does. My family can read me so easily because they've known me my entire life. I've grown up with five other guys that I've seen practically every day since they were born. We're six peas in a pod. You can read me without having that advantage. It means you're my other half, Greta. But are you certain you don't want ou—"

"Finish that thought, Daddy, and you'll be the one with the hot ass. And not the chiseled to perfection kind."

I grin at him, and he dives in for another kiss. His hand tightens on my ass, but it goes nowhere. When we pull apart, he nuzzles my cleavage. I undo the top button. I picked the bra I'm wearing because it's a push up. I'm proportionate, so I'm fairly endowed. The blouse I have on keeps my tits from being indecent. But now, I may as well be wearing the bikini top I did at 4Play. He kisses the tops of them and dips his tongue between them. He does nothing more than that. He presses my head to his shoulder and just holds me. He's more shaken than I realized.

"Dillan, tell me the truth. I know I can be arrested and questioned because of you. I know I won't say a damned thing. But could they hurt me? Like I supposedly resisted arrest or allegedly attacked an officer, and I just so happened to get knocked around."

"If you were a guy, yes. As a woman, even if you deal with

female officers or agents, no. The only women with any other connection to me are my mom and aunts. It's obvious who you are to me. No one who wants to live is dumb enough to sanction touching you with anything but kid gloves."

No one who wants to live. He'd kill for me. He's basically said as much before. Now he's making it clear.

"Can I ask you something about— mm —work?"

"You can ask me anything. If I don't answer, it's because it's not safe for you, my family, or the people who depend on me. I won't keep secrets from you I don't have to. I will lie to you, Greta. I'll do it often and without remorse or reservation. Sometimes it will be a boldfaced lie I say right to you. Other times it will be a lie of omission. I wish it weren't that way, but it's the only way to protect everyone. If I don't have to, I won't."

He says that last part twice, so it's important to him that I hear it. I cup his cheek and kiss the opposite side.

"How often do you get hurt? Like how likely is that you'll wind up stabbed or shot or dead?"

"Oh, *mo stór*, I don't want you to fear that. It's been a long time since I've been in anything more than a fist fight."

"But I've seen and felt the scars. I know the slightly puckered ones must have been from bullets. I think the longer raised ones must have been from knives. Some seem really old, but others not so much. I want to be prepared, Dillan."

Wonderful. Just as I say that we pull up outside a glass skyscraper. I watch him, wondering if this is his excuse not to answer.

"I am going to answer, but I want to do it where we can continue this conversation uninterrupted. Can you wait until we're in my office?"

"Yeah."

He slides his hand out from under my skirt, and I button my blouse. I pull my coat around me more tightly as he raps on the window. Shane opens the door, then Dillan's offering me his hand to help me out.

"Do you need your computer?"

I look at Shane when he speaks and realize I'd completely forgotten he'd carried my bag out for me. I look at Dillan, and he nods. I guess I can get some made up work done while I'm here. Shane hands the bag off to Dillan after they both shoot me a look when I reach for it. Old world I guess. That's something I've noticed about all of them. They are chivalrous in a way that was likely drilled into them. It's reflexive.

Shane rides up in the elevator with us and follows us into the office suite. He moves to the reception area and sits on a sofa. He pulls out his phone and immediately appears occupied.

"I want to speak to Greta alone and uninterrupted. I won't answer my phone. Send a text telling everyone to contact you if they need me. But it better be life or death before you knock on that door. I have stuff to explain, and we need to figure out what to do next."

He doesn't wait for Shane to respond, instead putting his hand on my lower back and guiding me to a corner office. The blinds that hang along the glass walls are drawn and shut. The door is the only thing without a window. When we get inside, he goes to the desk, which has next to nothing on it. The entire suite is rather sparse. He picks up a remote, and suddenly, the windows tint darker. He offers me his hand, and we walk to the sofa. As we approach it, he's unfastening his belt and pants. When he sits first, I know why. Normally, he wouldn't sit before me. He pulls his boxer briefs down, and I straddle him. I slide down his cock, and it's heaven. I lean forward and close my eyes once my head is on his shoulder. He caresses my ass with both hands.

We need this. We need to be joined. We need the quiet. We need each other.

"There's no place I'd rather be than inside you. You are my other half, Greta. You are who and what completes me. You know we fit like we were made for each other."

"I know. I don't need or even want to get off right now. I just need you inside me. I've never felt this before. This isn't sex, and I've never had a guy inside me for any other reason than that."

I know his jaw clenches because I can feel it against my forehead, and I realize he hates me mentioning there have been other men before him. Considering how I felt learning about Maureen, I get it.

"Daddy, that's the past."

He eases me back so we can look at each other. His hands go back to my ass, now caressing my thighs too. My hands rest on his forearms.

"There is always a strong chance I will die. I can't help that. No syndicate man can. It happens. But I take every precaution I can. I will doubly do that now that I have you. I run errands and lead a regular life on my own. That said, if I think there's even remotely more than the regular simmering risk, I take at least one guy with me. Our vehicles are reenforced. The town cars have bulletproof windows and doors. The undersides are metal plated to minimize impact. Our SUVs are practically tanks. They are entirely bulletproof. The chassis are meant to withstand just about anything. The tires will still roll even if something punctures them. The front and back fenders are basically battering rams. If we're going out to do something, we carry extra weapons in the back."

Going out to do something. I can infer or deduce what that means.

"I know some scars look recent, but none are newer than

five or six years ago. Most are from my late teens, from fights that involved blades. A couple are gunshot wounds from a melee in high school."

My eyebrows shoot up. High school? What the fuck?

"A few of the Diazes insulted Maria Mancinelli. The Kutsenkos heard the brothers and came to defend her. Carmine heard it too and called the rest of his family over. Shane and Cormac taunted the Mancinellis that they needed the Kutsenkos and their Andreyev cousins to take care of Maria because they couldn't. I taunted *Tres J's* about being pussies if they needed to pick on a girl. One of them called Maria a bitch when she stood up for a friend. The brothers were teasing the friend because she liked one of them. We all got drawn into it, and it basically became a turf war at the party. We used to keep our distance and run in different circles once we were in high school, but we all wound up at the same party. It was a shit-show until we heard the sirens. Then each family broke off and scattered. Maria's the one who protected all of us. She spotted a cop whose father was *Cosa Nostra*, so she spoke to the woman. She told the officer who was there, and within seconds, the police cleared out. All of us would have rather been dragged in by the NYPD than deal with our respective leaders."

"Really?"

"None of us escaped severe punishment for our involvement. It didn't matter that I had two bullets taken out of me and a slash across my back. If anyone had been seriously injured or killed, there would have been an all-out war. We all learned from that. But that doesn't mean I haven't pointed a gun at members of the ruling families or been in their sights since then. That will never change. We use restraint, but we do trade bullets. The fucked-up part of this is that we used to trade lunches in grade school, and our moms and dads were the snack parents at our peewee games. We played on the same teams some years. Other times, the rivalry was already there."

I absorb all of that. It's a lot to take in and digest. My thighs squeeze the outside of his, and my pussy does a Kegel. It's as though I want to hold him in place lest someone takes him from me.

"When's the last time you got seriously injured?"

He watches me for a moment, deciding whether to tell me the truth or one of those lies. "About two years ago. Sergei stabbed me, and Anton's bullet grazed my ribs. It didn't leave a scar, but the knife did."

I suck in a breath that makes my stomach cave in. I didn't expect that. Somehow he didn't lose his shit knowing I was passing information to men who may not have meant to kill him but definitely intended to do him serious harm. I want to ask why, but that's prying into business that isn't mine. That's mob-bratva shit. I don't need to know, even if I want to.

"I know what you're wondering. It's because of shite that happened with Declan but after he died. I was no saint in the situation, Greta. I fought back just like them."

He says no more than that. He's not admitting guilt to anything. What I don't know, I can't repeat. I lean forward and rest my head on his shoulder again.

"Is this scaring you too much?"

"It bothers me immensely that anyone would make you their target. It scares me that you could die. I hate the idea that I could lose you now that I've met you. But none of it makes me want to walk away. At least, not unless you're with me. It just makes me want to hold on tighter."

"I'm not going anywhere unless you tell me to. But if you want out at any point, I will never force you to stay. None of the stereotypical shite. You will never be my captive. You will always have free will about whether we have a relationship."

"I fully expect shit to be hard at times. All relationships have their periods where they are. Ours may be doubly so because of this. But I intend to put the work in to make it last. Will you?"

"When you're ready for the next step, tell me. I'll already be waiting for you."

"What is that?"

"Officially living together as husband and wife."

That steals my breath. I sit back, just blinking. I finally find my tongue. "Is that your preference or a family tradition or because you're Catholic?"

"All of it, but remember, I will convert if that's what you want."

He was fucking serious.

"Can we just figure out what to have for lunch for now?"

"I'm opening the door to really talking about the future we mentioned last night. I'm not proposing here. Whether it's in a few days, a few weeks, a few months, or even a few years, when you're ready to talk about it, we will."

"Okay."

Before I can say more, my phone buzzes with a call. I reach for my purse and fish it out. I know Dillan sees the screen.

"Hi."

"Sergei and I need to see you now."

Chapter Nineteen

Dillan

What the fuck do they want?

I can't hear what Anton's saying, but I'm certain it's nothing I want to hear. If Greta wasn't Greta, thinking about them would make my dick shrivel. But being inside my girl-friend— the woman I'm more than halfway in love with —is where I belong. I'd spend all day like this. Yeah, I loved having my fantasy of her warming my cock with oral acted out. It was amazing. But this? Just sitting with her, my hands running over her thighs and arse. This is perfection. Especially when she leans against me. She's vulnerable, but she trusts me. She's accepting my comfort— which she only needs because of me — but still. She turns to me. She wants me. And there's nothing I won't do for her.

That's why I want to know what the fuck Anton and Sergei want.

"This isn't a good time."

Do they want to meet up with her? The hell they are.

Greta's quiet for a moment, but we're staring at each other. She must be listening. She has the phone pressed so tightly to her ear that I can't hear a damn peep. I want to snatch the phone from her and put it on speaker, or at least demand she do that. But I don't. I'm controlling as fuck, but that's too over the top even for me.

"I have nothing else to tell you, Anton. And I doubt there's anything you want to volunteer to me since you know I'll tell Dillan the moment you do."

I suppose it doesn't matter that she gave that away. It's not really giving something away when it's a fact we all know. I wait for what she says next.

"Bye."

That wasn't what I expected. She hangs up and tosses her phone back on top of her purse. I don't ask, hoping she'll volunteer instead.

"He said they had information I'd want that would change my mind about you."

"Do you want to know what it is?"

"No. And no, I won't call back at some point when I'm alone and ask to hear or see it. Honestly, unless he tells me you kick puppies or traffic people, what the fuck could he tell me that would make me think badly about you? I already know what your family does. I can already guess what you do to ensure your family stays on top. Don't ask me how I've made my peace with that, but I have. Probably because that version of you exists on the periphery of my world with you in it. It's there, but you aren't that man with me. Since you were born into this, I can rationalize what you do is a righteous cause to protect your family. But honestly, I just don't care as long as you remain kind to me."

"You're very philosophical about it."

"Or pragmatic. I don't know which. But right now, I don't

even care about lunch after all. I really want to take a nap just the way we are. I'm exhausted, but I'm so damn comfortable. And this position gives me an emotional security blanket I don't want to let go of. It's super soothing having you run your hands over me and being able to listen to your heart. I want to sit here and feel safe. Feel— I don't know."

Loved.

Maybe that's what she was going to say. I hope it is. That's what I want to say to her. Her acceptance makes me feel loved, and I want her to know she's the one for me. That I truly haven't been speaking in hypotheticals or wouldn't-it-be-nices.

"I could use a nap too, *cailín*."

I turn us, so I can lie down on the couch. I've taken more than one nap here. There's a table in front of it that has a drawer. I stretch to open it and pull out a blanket. She laughs as I spread it over us. We're both asleep before we know it.

It's been two weeks since I raced out of a meeting basically telling everyone to fuck off, so I could get to Greta. Shane texted me and freaked me the fuck out. I felt guilty as shite that I missed Greta's messages. I just didn't feel it vibrate in my pocket. Getting his, and realizing she'd already asked for help, made me want to jump out of my skin. I told the longshore-men's union rep that I'd pay some amount for someone to do something. I don't even remember, nor do I give a shite. I needed them gone, so I could go to Greta.

Since bringing her to my office for the afternoon, things have been quiet. So much so that I'm becoming paranoid. My cousins dealt with Misha and Pasha's bullshit. We got the vehicles back and even tipped off the Customs and Border Protection about the illegal imports they were planning to sell legally.

The feds would never give us back our stolen property, but it didn't hurt that the tip also came with proof we were supposed to import them aboveboard. That little nugget went to agents other than Spiegel and Jones, so they've had nothing new to harass us about since Customs is involved, and we look innocent. They've had a second shadow since Spiegel called Greta. We found someone in the ATF more amenable to believing we're the good guys and is spying for us. Amenable to the tune of 50K, but that's chump change in my world.

Neither Sergei nor Anton has reached out to Greta, but I'm keeping an eye on them. My focus has been on Lorenzo Mancinelli. He's up to some shite, and I want to know exactly what. Something's still brewing in Chicago and Kansas City, but we know more than Enzo does. More than any of the Mancinellis. Enrique still believes he's ahead of the game because he still has that twat of his infiltrating the Rizzos in Chicago. Been there, done that. In the few years since I took over, I have someone in every major crime syndicate across the country, and I have mostly reliable connections in the ones in Europe and Asia too. Fuck, I have men in the *Cosa Nostra*, the Colombian Cartel, and the Ivankov bratva.

I also have people on the payroll in the NYPD and NYFD. I've done several favors for people in the Justice Department, and I've bought a judge in most courts in the state of New York from municipal to federal. I've made friends with people at the FCC, SEC, and DOD. Pretty much, I have friends anywhere there are acronyms.

Either I'm making money off them, or I'm paying enough to keep the rest of my money. The moment I took over, I got men and even a few women in place to serve me. Salvatore, Enrique, and Maks have all been in power longer than me, but I made sure I slid my informants into better slots that can shut their shite down. Basically, I cock block them any time I can, and they're none the wiser. They're not stupid. They're just not as smart as me.

That makes me want to grin, but I'm sitting in a meeting with Seamus and a woman from the FTC. She's grasping at straws, trying to make a case against us for predatory business practices. She isn't wrong. We do that. But she has no evidence just a hunch. She's attempting to accuse us of fraud, but she can't pinpoint who we've defrauded or how we've done it. She thought she could trip us up. Between Seamus and me, there isn't much hope anyone can dance a jig around us.

The only person who might possibly give us a moment's pause is Laura Kutsenko. She and I went up against each other during the brief time I practiced. She's faced off against Seamus several times since she became the Ivankov bratva's in house corporate council. She's good. It always winds up as a stalemate with the bratva and mob both having to compromise. This woman in front of us, smart as she is, doesn't know what's coming. We're about to steamroll her.

I've been twirling my pen over my thumb with my arm partly extended on the table. I put it down and hold up my hand, my forearm still resting on the surface.

"Ms. Petrović, let's stop. You can continue to poke and prod only to waste your time. Or I can give you something better to investigate."

The brunette across the table from me looks utterly unconvinced. I don't blame her. I would be too. But Seamus did a full profile on her. We know her personal biases, and we will use them. She watches me, even more suspicious than she was when she walked in here. I'm about to rip a band-aid off.

"You lost your husband and two brothers in the Kosovo Conflict."

She flinches. The memory and the fact that it's "only" a conflict and not a war is painful for plenty.

"You and your children fled here when you were barely twenty-five. You sought asylum, but the Albanians found you here. Turns out your husband was a Serbian colonel who caused the Albanians a lot of headaches. The Albanians here weren't so quick to overlook that."

She remains silent, but I can see her discomfort. I just want her shaken long enough to gain the upper hand. If I draw this out too long, she'll resent me and shut down.

"You've gone after the Albanians several times, but you've gotten nothing to stick. How would you like Hoxha dropped off at your front door, so to speak? I can share information that would make it easy for you to file charges against them tomorrow."

"Why?"

"Because your investigation is slowing down business, which is annoying me. It won't stop me, but it will ruin your career. What I can give you on the Albanians is far more concrete than anything you can scrape together about my family."

"So you say. You don't know everything I have on your family."

Seamus grins and jumps in. "But we do."

He's so deadpan it startles her. He lists off the things we know she believes she can build a case off. Sean hacked this woman's cloud and read all her documents and evidence against us. I tasked him with that after he found the guy who leaked Greta's articles. I had a rather protracted conversation with the guy. It only took that long because he kept passing out from the pain. If his tolerance had been higher, it would have gone faster.

He wasn't the instigator, just the middleman. He didn't know on whose behalf he was sending the information. He just knew someone threatened his family, so he went along to protect them. He only had a decent life insurance plan, so it's a good thing his wife works. They're living off her income and Social Security now.

It could be Zef fucking Greta over because she rejected his advances. He's that fucking petty. It could be Zef trying to get to me through Greta because he noticed my attraction to her. Or that part could just be a coincidence, and he already thought she was a good mark. Any way you look at it, if he's the one behind all this, he went after her because he could.

The short time between finding out she was the leak, then taking her to our place— I one hundred percent think of it as ours now —for her punishment left her vulnerable because I wasn't thinking about who has a motive to hurt Greta. It was just long enough for someone to strike, and it could have been Zef.

Even if he has nothing to do with Greta, I still don't like him. He's outlived his usefulness.

"Mr. O'Rourke— either of you —come to the point, please."

She takes the bait. I can see the skin stretching over her knuckles as she clenches her hand around her pen. Seamus pushes a piece of paper toward her with a handwritten diagram.

"How would you like all the information you need to take down the Albanians and the *Cosa Nostra* for something as simple as drug conspiracy? You won't be able to do much under the auspices of the FTC, but we know you know people at the ATF. Your sister was married to Agent Mason Spiegel before they divorced, and he married his current wife. His second wife happens to be the Deputy Director of the Department of National Intelligence, which oversees such things as the DOJ, which has an antitrust department that works right alongside the FTC."

I point to the piece of paper.

"We drew out the tangled web for you. You were related to an ATF agent who is now related to the second-to-the-top of the DNI. The DOJ is under her purview, and the FTC works alongside the DOJ. So, you know plenty of people there. Wouldn't it be so useful if you could help the DOJ *and* the DNI? You could tell your contact at the ATF to tell his contact at the DNI to tell her contact at the DOJ to get involved. You'd have four agencies all coordinating through you. But—" I sit back. "The only way that happens is if you give us some space to breathe. If we can't breathe, we can't share what we know."

"You're extorting me."

My brow furrows, and I pretend to look confused. "How do you figure? We aren't asking you to do anything in exchange for that information other than giving us the opportunity to share what we know. We can't do any of that if you arrest any of us, and we lawyer up. We can't do that if any of us are locked up. Seamus and I are only trying to make things more convenient for you, Ms. Petrović. Are you confused and thought you heard a threat? Does my sitting at the far end of the oblong conference table from you somehow make you feel forced to look into illegal activity that should be prosecuted to the full extent of the law? Especially if the prosecution happens to punish a family connected to three deaths in yours. As you know, Zef's uncle shot your husband."

I saved that little nugget for the end. Her face goes white as a sheet, and she looks like she might vomit. We have a cleaning crew. As long as she keeps it away from my suit, she can puke all she wants. Seamus infuses concern into his voice I know he doesn't feel.

"Didn't you know? We assumed you did, and that's why you've been quietly trying to set them up to take the fall for anything you can think of. We know how you've asked Mason to investigate us, hoping you could tie us to them. Because if you took us down, they would go as collateral damage. Set the ATF and the FBI— so convenient that Mason's new brother-in-law is the director of the FBI —on the Mancinellis, and the Hoxhas will collapse too. Marco Mancinelli. That's who you want. Third most powerful man in that family and second in line to inherit. Not so high as to make him a martyr, but high enough to seriously imperil their syndicate."

The woman's still deathly pale as our gazes meet. "Do you play chess, Mr. O'Rourke?"

"Frequently." I don't. But I lie daily, and I'm good at it.

She only nods, and she must figure my chess playing accounts for why my mind can go in so many directions and see so many permutations. My mind already does that. That's why chess is boring. I win before most people can make more than two moves. It also means my mind is never quiet. The only reprieve I get is when I'm with Greta. My mind is idling more than whirling when I'm with her. It's still going, but it's coasting rather than revving.

"What can you give me?"

Seamus and I shake our heads. We look so damn much alike, and our mannerisms are the most similar, except for Shane and Sean. Nature versus nurture is real. You just can't teach some things. Ms. Petrović gawks for a moment before she catches herself. I know my cousin's smiling the same sexy smirk I have. She glances down at the table to compose herself. I just barely hear her clear her throat. I pick up my pen and twirl it around my thumb again as I answer.

"Nothing yet. Our memories will need some jogging. Right now, our attention is on how the ATF— Mason —is so singularly focused on Ms. Margaret McDonnell."

Calling her Margaret feels so incredibly weird. It's as though I'm talking about someone other than my Greta. But that's how most people know her. It's likely how Spiegel and

Jones know her, so it's the name the woman in front of me needs to pass along.

"What? I'm sorry, but I don't know what you mean."

"Let Mason know the information he's going to get from us through you will come a lot faster if I'm not focused on keeping Ms. McDonnell safe from your former brother-in-law."

"What's Mason done to her? He'd never harm a witness or even a suspect."

"He hasn't touched her, but he's harassing her."

Things may have been quiet for the last two weeks, but they haven't been silent. Neither Spiegel nor Jones has contacted Greta, but we know they've been following her. That's the ominous presence she felt following her right before we became a couple. They bugged her place. And they hacked her work and personal cloud. Fortunately, Sean expected them to do that and helped set things up for her to transfer all her personal stuff onto a server he operates. He also installed malware. There's no trace— at least no easily found trace —of her previous internet presence. Her social media remains and articles about her or by her are accessible, but her files all just whoosh— vanished.

The FTC investigator looks hesitant, but she pulls out her phone. She's making the call from here, so we hear it. I know Seamus trusts her as much as I do— which is very little at this point. She could make the call now, then make another one when she leaves that jacks shite up. But we'll tap her phone and hack her email. She'll get a shadow she'll never notice. If she dicks us over, we'll destroy her career.

That reminds me of how I thought I would handle things if a woman was the leak. When it turned out to be a woman, it also turned out to be Greta. Now I can't imagine doing anything intentionally to ruin her career, but her connection to me is likely to do it, anyway. I definitely don't want her to lose her job. If her time with the paper ends, it's because she decides that. I can intimidate Gary and the Editor-in-Chief to keep her, but that'll make her miserable. She'll figure it out.

I force myself to listen to the conversation Ms. Petrović is having with Mason. I didn't even notice Seamus telling her to put it on speakerphone, but now that I'm hearing it I realize he must have. I dart my gaze over to him. He senses it and looks at me. He dips his chin as if to say I got it.

"Draga, are they intimidating you? What are those pieces of shit telling you?"

Seamus and I laugh loudly enough that Mason must hear us. Draga— I knew that was her name, but I hadn't bothered to remember it —looks like she might be sick all over again. I speak up.

"Did you really think she would make the call without you being on speakerphone? We want to hear all of it. And if she thinks to call you back later and tell you something different, don't worry. We'll know."

I see her trembling. I won't touch her, but I see no harm in scaring her. It means I'll have to do much less in the long run.

"Mason, the O'Rourkes suggested you focus on Marco Mancinelli and Zef Hoxha."

There's a pause.

"You want me to target the Albanian mafia?"

"I'm relaying to you Mr. O'Rourke's suggestion."

"Suggestion. Bullshit. What are they threatening you with?"

"Honestly, Mason, nothing really. I'm sure they'll be watching me, but it's more of a career opportunity than a threat. We'd both benefit if you can help the FBI take down someone like Marco Mancinelli and the head of the Albanian mafia. Zef's no Salvatore, but he's still their *kyre*. Don't underestimate what it would do for us."

I love the smell of ambition in the morning. It smells like victory.

"O'Rourke, stay away from Draga, and you have a deal."

"I'll stay away from Draga if you leave Ms. McDonnell alone. You need to understand this isn't a debate over the chicken and the egg. It's clear. Leave my girlfriend alone, and I'll leave your family alone."

That makes Mason pause just like I knew it would. I've just reminded him that my reach is far longer than just this conference table. I can go after anyone I want, and there isn't shite he can do about it. If he wants to protect his former sister-in-law, his current wife, and his current brother-in-law-slash-lover, then he'll stay the fuck away from my woman.

"Fine. I'll tell Jones. We'll back off."

"Thank you."

I can be civil when I need to.

"Are we done? Should I hang up?"

I'm about to answer when both Seamus's and my phones ping. There's only one text thread that has a notification with sound. The rest are all on vibrate. He and I look at each other.

"Yes. Good day, Ms. Pretović. Mason, I'll be sure to follow up."

I stand and usher Draga to the door. Seamus is on my heels. He flips off lights as he goes. The moment the doors to the elevator close with Draga only in it, Seamus and I pull out our phones.

The group chat name is **911**.

CORMAC

Dill get home now. There's been an explosion.
M is fine but hurry.

Chapter Twenty

Greta

Agent Spiegel mentioning the Albanians got me to wondering about what the ATF wants with them. I felt conflicted about digging around for information about any of the syndicates now that I'm with Dillan, so I asked him. Not about information regarding the Albanians specifically. I asked him what I should do if another opportunity to do a story on a syndicate presented itself. He told me as long as it doesn't endanger *our* family, then he wouldn't object. He's been doing that for the past two weeks. Just subtle things like *our* place and *our* bed, and *our* family. The first two seem pretty natural since I'm still staying with him. We live together well.

It's not just the newness and being on our best behavior. We truly cohabitate well because we are so much alike. I remembered he pointed out we have the same dish towel. I'm certain he'd already noticed we have the same dining set down to the silverware. We also have a matching bedding set. So, our place and our bed make sense since I've practically moved in. But the 'our family part' catches my ear. I love it. We're not talking about children or even marriage in detail yet, but we're hinting at it pretty loudly since we had a conversation that basically declared we want to be together for the long haul. Neither one of us has retracted that. When he talks about the O'Rourkes and the McDonnells being our family, it makes me happy.

All of his cousins have rotated through being my bodyguard at least three times. Finn was the least certain about me, but I'd already sensed that. I realized earlier this week that the thaw came because he overheard a couple of conversations I thought no one else could hear. Hindsight being twenty-twenty, Dillan must have known. But he felt it was okay for his cousin to hear, so I refuse to be too embarrassed. But they were conversations where I genuinely wanted to know what I could do for Dillan.

Something went wrong, and he was away for a night. Cormac had to tell me he wouldn't be home. When he got back the next night, his knuckles were split and bruised. It doesn't take a genius to know he was punching someone. I'd found the first-aid kit in our bedroom when I was looking for a roll of toilet paper. While Dillan talked to Finn and Shane, who were at our place when he got home, I slipped upstairs and got the kit. I also got a bag of frozen peas.

When he said it was all right for me to be in the living room with them since they weren't talking about whatever happened, I sat silently next to him and took care of cleaning the cuts then put the frozen veggies on his hand. Finn and Shane said they were going to take off, and I thought they left together. Finn must have heard me asking if there was anywhere that needed tending. Dillan looked so damn exhausted I wrapped him in my arms and nudged him to put his head on my chest. I stroked his hair and told him silly stories from when I was a kid until he fell asleep.

The other two times were in the morning before Dillan took off to casinos they own in Atlantic City. There was something going on at one with slot machines not working properly and a dealer being loose with the cards or something. It was while we were saying goodbye. I asked him what he wanted for dinner those two nights since we cook together every evening. I promised to take a bath with him like we've started doing every night too. He whispered something in my ear that now I realize he didn't want Finn to hear because he could. I thought he was being funny, acting conspiratorial. Both times I wrapped my arms around his neck, went on my toes, and gave him a smacking kiss before I gave him a smack on the ass. That resulted in him squeezing my ass and kissing me properly.

All three were such normal couple things, and I think that's why Finn is finally okay with me. I think he understands I know I monumentally fucked up, and that it began my relationship with Dillan in a pretty fucked-up way. But I love Dillan. I'm certain of it. It's been two weeks of living together, but we've known each other two months. That's not a super long time, but it's not like we were some TV movie couple that winds up locked in a cabin in a blizzard and emerge twelve hours later in love.

The only thing that still feels outstanding is we haven't met each other's parents. I'm so fucking nervous about it. He seems completely fine meeting mine, but I've gotten a sense he's a little anxious. He just won't show it. I'm trying to be that brave, too. He's succeeding far better than I am.

"Finn, could we stop by my place on the way in? I need to grab a dress for tonight."

It's not Sunday, but the O'Rourkes are having a family

dinner for Sean and Shane's birthday. Dillan's taking me with him. He skipped one Sunday dinner because that was the night he was gone. He insisted Finn and Shane stay with me until he got home the next day. He skipped the other one because he had a meeting at 4Play. I had a pang of jealousy since I knew it was the first time he was going to one of his clubs since we started dating. I thought I hid it well, and maybe I did. But he took me with him, and I chatted with the girls between dances or when they were on their breaks. I hung out in his office when the Albanians came. He didn't want me anywhere Zef could see me.

"Sure. Then are you going straight to work?"

"No. I need to make a stop. I have an interview with someone. Finn, I need you to hang back. This person won't tell me anything if they see you."

I'm not telling him or Dillan that I'm meeting with Zef's ex-wife. The woman is only too happy to tell me everything under the sun about her former husband. She detests him. Apparently, he couldn't keep it in his pants. Shocker considering how he acted toward me. His divorce only finalized three days ago. She reached out to me.

"Do they know me?"

"They don't need to. You're huge and intimidating. That's enough to put anyone off from talking to a journalist."

"Thank you."

He grins, and I laugh as I get into the back seat of the SUV. Dillan insists I only ride in them when he's not with me. I don't know how he thinks I'm magically safer in a town car if he's there, but I don't argue. The town car affords us privacy, and I've discovered just how much I like to fuck in the backseat. We both love to fuck in the backseat.

It's a quick trip to my place. I already have the dress picked out in my head, so I grab it, shoes, and a pair of panties. I am not meeting his parents going commando. Not happening. And frankly, I hope it earns me a spanking after dinner. I like them. We've explored a lot more of our fantasies together, including various ways to have shower and bath sex. The most taboo was when he went down on me while I was on the phone with my parents. That was a serious test I nearly failed. My parents know about him. They know who he is, and they're not pleased. I need to get through tonight's dinner, then I can think about tomorrow night's. The one with my parents.

We're headed into the Bronx since there's a strong Albanian community there and in Queens. Zef lives in Queens, so his ex-wife, Aria, insisted we meet in the Bronx instead. She said she felt safe being in her community, but she doesn't want to be anywhere near Zef. I don't blame her. She moved back home with her parents and her three kids. They'll be at school, but her parents are retired. She told me they speak no English. Maybe they don't. Maybe they do. She was married to the *kyre*— boss —for fourteen years. She understands how to play this game better than I do. That's the whole point of the interview. She's not ignorant, and I guarantee neither are her parents. Her father must be affiliated.

Unlike the Irish in New York, which have branched out to every borough and every conceivable profession, the Albanians have remained incredibly insular. They stick to themselves, marrying within their community or to recent Albanian immigrants. They live by a code of honor— *besa* —that came over from the old country, which has strict terms about blood feuds and vendettas. From what I can tell, the Albanians have a far more hierarchical system than the Irish. They're more like the Russians and Italians— Sicilians. Dillan explained the difference to me the other night.

He also made sure I understand that only the Mancinellis are Mafia, and that's with a capital M. Other syndicates might be called that, but only the Sicilians truly merit the word since *Cosa Nostra* means "our thing." Zef is the Albanian boss of the *fis* or *fare*. The clan or extended family. Basically, the NYC branch. I admit I'm worried about Aria meeting with me since she's likely breaking that *besa*, which I looked up and learned means trust.

She agreed to tell me about Zef's business here in the city and his rivalry with the *fis* in Boston, along with his ties back to the head *kyre* in Albania. I don't know what she's going to share, but I pray it's worth the danger she's putting us both in. She approached me, not the other way around. I didn't know who she was until I casually asked Dillan if Zef had a wife who cared that he likes to touch other women. It took me five minutes to calm him down and convince him Zef hadn't found me and touched me. Then he told me about Aria, and it all confirmed what she'd said when she introduced herself over the phone.

I lean forward to point past Joey's shoulder.

"That one over there. At the end on the right."

Finn turns in his seat, and his face is stone. "You are not getting out of this car in this neighborhood. You are sure as feck not going into one of those houses. No. Dillan will kill me. Then he'll strap your arse until you have nothing left to ever sit on. Absolutely not."

I hadn't given them the exact address. I'd programmed it into my GPS and gave them one a few streets down but would bring us past my destination.

"Finn, it's the only place she would meet me."

"She? Márgrég, please tell me you are not meeting with Aria Hoxha." He clenches his jaw. "You are. What the feck are you thinking? Dillan is going to absolutely flip his shite that you're even in this neighborhood. Joey, let's go."

"No. This is work as much as it could help your family. Dillan said I could do pieces about the other families, and here's the first one."

I unfasten my seatbelt and slide to the door, but Joey doesn't stop. It's not like I'm going to tuck and roll from the vehicle. But I can make it clear I want him to stop. I wind down the window when I see a woman step onto the porch. Three kids run downs the steps before waving.

"Just stop here for a moment. Let me call her and see if she'll meet me somewhere else. Let her see that I'm really here. Maybe there's somewhere more neutral around here."

"It's the fecking Bronx. There's nowhere more neutral."

"You make it sound like it's a war zone. It's New York City, even if it isn't the good part."

Finn just stares at me as though I'm an idiot. I narrow my eyes at him, but he doesn't relent. I turn my attention to my open window.

"Aria!" I don't yell, but I call out to her. She sees me, and recognition flashes in her eyes. Then she takes in the black SUV. She shakes her head and backs away. I don't know how she knows it's an O'Rourke car or any syndicate's rather than a service.

"It's the hub caps. We have them customized at the same shop as the other three families. It's how we can tell them apart when we need to leave in a hurry. She recognizes them."

The Mancinellis, Diazes, and Kutsenkos. They're the other three.

"Let me out then. I need her to know I'm not trying to trick her or hurt her."

Joey stopped beside the end of the driveway. I'm just pulling on the door handle when there's a billow of heat, a bright surge of light, and the loudest noise I have ever heard. All of it pummels the car, pushing it across the street into a parked vehicle facing us. Finn grabs my shoulders and pushes me down, practically falling out of the front seat and onto me. There's another explosion then a third immediately after it. Debris is pelting the car, and it sounds like elephants landing on the roof. Then it's so hot. Scorching hot. So hot through the open window I fear I'm on fire.

"Joey?" Finn's reaching over my head as he speaks.

"Yeah, Boss. Let's go."

Before I understand what's happening, Joey's prying the door open on the opposite side from the blast. Finn's pushing as Joey pulls. Then Joey's yanking me from the car. Finn tumbles after me and crawls out. They nudge me into a sprint as we cross a front yard and run down a driveway.

"Aria? What about—"

"She's gone. There's no way. Run." Finn nudges me again. He's not rough, but it keeps me from slowing down. I do my best to look over my shoulder. The sight that's before me makes me stumble. I start to fall, but Joey hefts me up and onto his shoulder in a fireman carry. Finn's got his gun in his hands, and he's now running backwards every few steps, watching for anyone who might come up behind us.

"Is yours on?"

"Yeah, Boss. You?"

"Yeah."

I don't know what they're talking about. Finn runs past us, and I watch him scale a fence with ease. By the time Joey gets me there, Finn has it open. We run through the yard and into an alley behind the house. It isn't until we cross the street and another yard before they finally stop. Joey puts me down. I have a tree to my back that has a massive trunk. No one can see me. Joey and Finn are facing out, so I'm hard to see if anyone is looking at us from the front. They both have their guns drawn.

"Is what on, Finn? What the fuck just happened?"

Then it hits me. Reality. I shove Finn's shoulder. He doesn't want to move, but then he hears me gag. I shove again, and he grasps my hair as I puke on the grass. I swat at him, not wanting anyone to touch me when I'm sick. But I retch over and over until my belly and throat burn. I have my arms wrapped around me, so it's just as well he's holding my hair back. When I finally stop, he helps me back to the tree and eases me to the ground. Joey has a stick of peppermint gum for me. I don't realize I'm crying until I taste my tears.

"I almost died like my grandfather."

When I looked back, I saw the house ablaze, but so was the SUV we were in. Several of the cars on the street were. If we'd stayed another moment, the vehicle would have been engulfed in flames or too hot to get the doors open. We would have burned alive. Just like my grandfather. Wrong place, wrong time. Just like him.

"Ms. McDonnell, men will be here soon. Mr. O'Rourke and I turned on our trackers. They know to come for us. We just need to stay put if we can."

"If we can?" I shoot Finn a terrified glance before looking around. He squats beside me.

"Did you tell anyone you were coming here today?"

"No. The only other person who knew was Aria. She asked me to come because she's scared to go anywhere Zef might find her or his men might see her. He knows she's at—" I catch myself this time. "—he knew she was at her parents'. But I guess he promised to respect that as a safe place since their kids were there. Oh, fuck. They barely left. If they'd been five minutes later. Fucking hell."

I sob. Those kids have no mother and no home now. I don't

know if Aria's parents were in the house or not. But they're left with just a mobster father. Oh, God. Someone might say that about my kids one day if this happened to me. I could be a target as Dillan's wife if that happens. I—

"Márgrég, that won't happen to you. Zef did this."

I'm trying to understand Finn. Did I speak aloud? I look at him and try to piece together the last bit. "Zef killed his wife?"

"Ex-wife. That alone marked her in his eyes. He must have known she was meeting someone— possibly you —and timed it. He killed her for her betrayal."

He says it slowly, knowing I'm going to panic. I push to my feet and try to back away. Finn wraps me in his arms, and I try to fight him to free myself.

"Dillan would never do that. He would kill us if any of us tried to hurt you. He will pick you first. He will always pick you first whenever he has the power to. Listen to me."

He says the last three words with emphasis. His hold tightens enough that I can no longer struggle. I sob instead of trying to break free.

"I don't know what you have or haven't said to each other, but Dillan loves you. He's going to freak the feck out over this. We need to get you home before he gets there. You need to wash your face and change your clothes. If there's time, shower. Get the smoke out of your hair. I'm not telling you not to cry if you need to, but if he sees you like this, he's going to go berserk."

I look down at my clothes and see the ash and grime. I pull out my phone and tap the camera then spin it to selfie mode. Fucking hell. I look like shit.

"Finn!"

I peer past him to an SUV with a guy in it I recognize, but I don't know. He was Dillan's guard a few days ago. I saw him on the sidewalk when Dillan walked me out to the town car.

"That's Denny."

Denny. Danny. Joey. Tommy. Do these men never get grown up names? Why is that even what I'm worrying about right now?

"How'd you get here so fast?" It's Finn who asks, but I thought that same thing.

"I was at the station."

I look at Finn who climbs in beside me. Joey goes to the front passenger seat. Neither Finn nor Joey have put their guns away. Denny has one sitting in the middle console. Neither Finn nor Joey asks which station, so they must know. I don't get the impression I should. Denny looks at Joey then Finn before he speaks again.

"Anyone see you?"

Finn responds, and it doesn't reassure me. "I don't know. Maybe."

I watch out the window as we make the trek from the Bronx to Brooklyn. It isn't really that far, but it feels like it takes forever. My body is heavy, and I ache all over by the time we pull into the driveway behind Dillan's brownstone. Finn helps me out of the car, and I look down at my clothes. I feel like saying burn them, but that reminds me of why they're in this condition. That starts the tears all over again. But I'm not sobbing this time. They're just silently streaming down my cheek. The guys surround me and get me inside. I head up to the room I share with Dillan and straight into the bathroom.

I turn on the hot water and strip. I know there are large trash bags under the sink. I haven't asked why they're so big when the trash can is so small. But as I pull one out and open it to put my ruined clothes in, I suddenly understand. Ash and dirt might cover mine, but Dillan's must get covered in blood sometimes. Fucking hell. He could die just like Aria. I stand under the dual showerhead and try not to vomit again.

I don't know how long I stand there. I just let the water wash over me, but I do nothing to get cleaned up. I just let the bathroom fill with steam. I'm not thinking about anything. My mind is blank. I just keep crying even though my eyes are closed. I nearly jump out of my skin when arms wrap around me.

"Shh, *mo choi. Mo ghrá.*" My heart. My love.

I spin in Dillan's arms, and he wraps around me. Not just his arms. His shoulders round too as though he's shielding me from anything that isn't him.

"Daddy."

"Shh. I'm here. You're safe, and I'm here."

"Thank God. Finn said Zef did that to her. He said it was because she betrayed him by divorcing him and that he likely knew she was meeting someone since she moved out. I don't know if Finn meant a reporter or if Zef assumed a lover. But he said it was because she betrayed him."

He cups my cheeks and tilts my head back until I'm looking at him.

"*Is breá liom tú. Maróidh mé aon duine a thagann in aice leat. Cosnóidh mé thú go dtí go bhfaighidh mé bás. Ansin déanfaidh mé arís agus arís eile é sa chéad saol eile agus an ceann ina dhiaidh sin agus an ceann ina dhiaidh sin. Ní bhaineann aon duine leat, agus ní dhéanfaidh mé dochar choíche duit. Tá tú gach rud dom.*" I love you. I will kill anyone who comes near you. I will protect you until I die. Then I'll do it over and over in the next life and the one after that and the one after that. No one touches you, and I will never hurt you. You are everything to me.

He kisses me like he's afraid I might shatter. Like there's nothing more fragile than me, and right now, I feel that way. But the longer we kiss, the stronger I feel. I press my body against his and run my hands through his hair.

"*Is breá liom tú le mo chroí ar fad, Daidí. Tá a fhios agam nach féidir liom na rudaí is féidir leat a dhéanamh, ach déanfaidh mé tú a chosaint go bhfaighidh mé bás. Beidh grá agam duit arís agus arís eile sa saol seo agus an chéad cheann eile agus an ceann ina dhiaidh sin.*" I love you with my whole heart, Daddy. I know I can't do the things you can, but I will protect you until I die. I'll love you over and over in this life and the next and the one after that.

We keep speaking Gaelic because it feels natural. We've been switching back and forth, and words and phrases I'd forgotten are coming back to me with ease.

"Wee one, let's finish in here. Then I want you in bed with me while you tell me what happened."

He helps me wash my hair while I lather my body. My arms and shoulders are too sore to lift them over my head. Running my hands through his hair exhausted them. I feel physically weak, even if my mental strength returns. He helps me rinse off, then he wraps me in one of his fuzzy towels. I notice he brought his robe in with him. He knows I love wearing it. He wraps his towel around his waist and grabs my wide-tooth comb from the drawer where I now keep it. We walk to the bed, and I rub my hair with the towel I wrapped around it after slipping on his robe. I stick out my hand for the comb, but he doesn't give it to me.

I climb into bed, and he sits behind me, his legs bracketing my hips. He eases the comb through my hair, ever so careful not to tug.

"Colleen used to make me do this for her. Whenever she beat me diving for pennies or won at chicken, she would announce herself the queen of wherever we were. She loved being the Queen of Queens. As her minion, I had to comb her hair after we showered. She'd bang on my door, wait for me to say she could come in, then march over to me, and thrust the comb at me. If I wasn't quick enough, she'd wave it under my nose. I think she was probably three, and I was nearly five the first time she did it. And I agreed. I think I was probably twelve the last time I combed the Queen of Queens' hair."

I twist to look at him. He finished my hair just as he finished the story. I take the comb from him and put it down with the towel. I turn around and straddle him, pulling the robe open. We both know what we need. I sink onto his cock, and we hold each other. Somehow, we both know when we're ready to roll over, so I shed the robe before I'm on the bottom. He tugs his towel free and drops it on the floor. Then we're moving at an agonizingly slow pace. Our bodies rock together as we watch each other.

"I love you so much, Greta. I've never been so scared as when I got Cormac's text telling me to get home. That you were fine, but there'd been an explosion. That's all he said. I was frantic by the time I got to the car, and he answered my fifth call. I made my driver get in the backseat. I drove. I probably would have killed him for going too slow, even if he'd done the best he could. I didn't know I could take those stairs four at a time. Hearing you cry broke my heart. I couldn't get out of my clothes and to you fast enough."

"I didn't think I was making any sound."

"It was soft, but I heard it. I love you, *cailín*."

"I love you, Daddy."

We keep moving together until I can't keep from coming. He holds back until I'm about to have my third orgasm. Then he's filling me with his cum, and I'm clutching his ass, pressing him into me. He moves us again, so I'm sprawled across his chest as we catch our breath. His fingertips gliding along my spine feels divine. The way his hand always finds its way to my ass to just cup it is fucking erotic to me.

"We don't have to go to my parents' place tonight."

"Fuck. I forgot all about it. No. I want to go. I want to meet them."

I was frightened this morning that I'd make a fool of myself. But suddenly, it feels really urgent to meet them. To see Dillan with his family being a totally normal guy like I see when he's with his cousins. At least, when work isn't interfering. I need normality right now.

"Shit."

"What, wee one?"

"The dress I planned to wear was in the car."

"Do you have anything here you want to wear?"

"Yeah, but I was going to wear panties. Dillan, it feels wrong to meet your parents without underwear on. I don't have any here, so I grabbed a pair just before we left my place."

"And you knew that would earn you a spanking. I warned you from the start that I don't want domestic discipline, but I will punish you if you endanger yourself. Spanking you over the panties would have been foreplay. But taking my men to the Bronx without telling them the truth about where you were going, why you were going, and who you were going to see is dangerous for all of you. The fact that you were having a secret meeting with a rival syndicate's ex-wife... Fecking hell, Greta. You could have died. If Finn had let you out of the car like you wanted, you would be dead. I had to hear that second hand from Cormac who heard it from Finn. I could have lost you."

His voice wavers with that last sentence.

"I'll take whatever punishment you think I deserve."

"And I will give you one. But it'll be tomorrow. I can't do it tonight."

"Because you're too angry?"

What have I done?

"No. Because I'm still too scared something's going to happen to you. Because all I want is to put bubble wrap around you to protect you. Because all I want is to hold you every minute between now and forever. The bombing wasn't your fault. Even being there at the wrong time wasn't your fault. But you didn't let your bodyguards protect you properly because you didn't tell them the truth. That's what's earning you a hot arse."

"Can you forgive me?"

"I not only forgive you already, but I'm also marrying you."

Chapter Twenty-One

Dillan

I say I'm going to marry her like it's a foregone conclusion because it is. This isn't just a possibility that we're mulling over for some time in the future. Discovering she'd almost been killed today wrecked me. I've been scared way too many times to count. I've been terrified many times. But today was other level. I don't even have a word for it. It's whatever terrified is on roids.

"Um." She's not sure how to react to such a declaration. It's not just my words, it's my tone. She shifts to sit up next to me. Her physical distance, even if it's just beside me, makes me nervous.

"Greta, this is not how I'm proposing. I will do it properly and not an hour after something traumatizing happened. But I have never felt so certain about any decision in my entire life. This only gave me the perspective to see I will not waste any time wondering about whether my feelings are strong enough for a lifetime. I know they are, and I think the same is true about yours. I'm not going to demand we find a priest or a judge right this minute. I want you to think about it, and I want this to be a decision you don't feel coerced into. But this is what I want, and I want it sooner rather than later."

"Because I was in danger, and you want people to believe I'm untouchable?"

"You are untouchable regardless of whether you're my wife, my girlfriend, my fuck buddy, or my friend. You are the most important woman in my life. *Anyone* who comes near you better do it carefully. I won't trade your life and your happiness for anything. The rest of the world would be smart to catch on."

She stares at me, and I get a twinge of nerves. Then she smiles. Like a star shining down from the heavens. It's the biggest, brightest, happiest smile I've ever seen on anyone's face. She squeezes me as we hug. I think she agrees with the decision. I mean, I think she wants to make the same choice as I have. I've decided I want to marry her, but I can't decide for her whether or not she says yes. That has to be all her.

"Daddy, today's sucked bigger ass than I imagined possible. I was scared I was going to die. I was scared Finn and Joey would, too. But what terrified me— what still terrifies me —is this happening to you. And not just that, but it happening and me missing out on the time I have with you. I don't want to lose my chance. I know you take precautions, but this really hammered home the reminder that life is fragile, and it can be cut short way faster in this world. I want us to live together for real. Even before the wedding. I'm just staying here for now, but I want something official. I don't care if it's here, my place, or a tiny studio on Staten Island. Just together."

"We are not living on Staten Island. Yuck."

"You know what I mean. It could be Jersey if that makes it marginally better."

"It doesn't." I grin and tickle her. "But I know what you

mean. Where isn't as important to me either. It's the when. More specifically how soon. I'll move to your place, or you move here. We can make that permanent, or we can find somewhere new together. But I want it to be more than we're just staying at one another's place."

"Here is more practical, isn't it? You have your home office, and the guys meet with you here. It's also much bigger."

"Is that what you want? Don't say yes because you think it works better for me. It needs to work best for you. For us."

She looks a bit guilty for a moment, but then she nods. "I like my place, but it's not practical for several reasons. One is that I rent. That inherently makes it less reliable than being somewhere one of us owns."

"All right. This weekend, we get things organized."

"Are we going to tell people tonight? I'm meeting your parents for the first time. You haven't met mine. And it's Sean and Shane's birthday dinner."

"I'll tell the guys on the side. We'll get through us meeting both sets of parents, then we'll let all of them know."

"When we get married, I'd like a church wedding. But I don't expect you to convert, and it would probably upset your family if you did. I don't want that."

"*Cailín*, all of us have a complicated relationship with our faith. We all believe in the things we were taught. We all wish we could live by those rules. But it's hard to feel like you deserve redemption and forgiveness when you willingly commit the same sins daily. My dad's generation feels that way as much as mine. My mom and aunts don't have it any easier. They're married to and raised men who commit these sins. They accept them and turn a blind eye. We are Catholic, but we aren't very good ones."

"And I've given this a lot of thought. I know what it makes me to become like your mom and aunts. They were born into this, so they didn't have a choice. I'm making mine and coming voluntarily. Either way, we can regret the choices made for us or that we have to make for ourselves. We might feel remorse. We might even find satisfaction in them. But all the smaller decisions you make happen because the biggest one was made for you and your family generations ago. I can reconcile my faith with the monumental decision I'm making now. I've only seen you as the man you are with me. Forgiving. Kind. Honest. Dependable. Generous. I think you would be that man all the time if you could. That's why I can accept this. If my relationship with God and my faith changes over time, then it changes. It doesn't mean I think He's going away. If you want a church wedding, *mo stór*, then we will have one. It'll be an Episcopalian one since you don't have to be one to marry one in the church. If you don't want a church wedding, then we'll make other arrangements. Maybe one of your cousins could be ordained online."

"No. None of those feckers are marrying me to you. They can stand beside me at the ceremony, but I'm not giving them such a hallowed role. Uh-uh. I know too much about their drunken sex lives to want them saying anything about fidelity and a lifetime of love. I'd laugh at the most inopportune time."

She laughs along with me. My cousins really aren't that bad, but I could never take them seriously. And in truth, I'd prefer someone to marry us who has a healthy relationship with their faith. Someone needs to.

I watch her stifle a yawn, and it makes me realize how tired I am. I'm drained. I stretch and set my alarm clock.

"Let's take a nap, wee one."

She doesn't need telling twice. She snuggles close to me and is asleep immediately. As usual, my mind is still doing laps. But at least it jogs when Greta is around rather than trying to sprint a marathon. As I get closer to falling asleep, I know there's a meeting I need to have tomorrow.

⁂

"She's lovely, *mo chuisle*."

My mom has been called me her pulse since she was pregnant with me. She said I got the hiccups a lot, and the rhythm reminded her of having a second pulse. She also said that hearing my heartbeat on the monitor whenever she went to the doctor gave her more joy than she imagined. She said the same things about Colleen. Now there's only me. I treasure hearing it every single time. It will never get old.

"Thanks, Mom. Do you like her?"

We're standing in the corner of the living room together while the rest of the family fills the space and the kitchen.

"Yes, I do, and I'm not just saying that because I think I should. You know I would tell you the truth if I thought you were making a mistake. You wouldn't listen, but I'd still tell you. She's perfect for you. She reminds me of me when I met your da. I was only fifteen, but I knew. He's my other half. I hadn't realized I wasn't whole until I met him and felt complete. I can tell she does that for you. And you, more than anyone, deserve that."

"Me?"

"You've been leading this family indirectly since you were barely fourteen. It took a year for Donovan to recognize how influential you were and that he should listen to you. I tried telling my brother, but the man had a thick skull. You've shouldered tremendous responsibility because of it. I know you take every decision seriously, thinking of at least ten outcomes before you choose. That weighs heavily on anyone, and I know it does for you."

"It's usually only three, but yes, I do that. There's too much at stake to decide like Donovan and Declan did."

"I know. You're much more like your grandda than either of them. But even so, he made one too many bad choices, and my da paid for it with his life. If you believe she can enter this life and all the darkness and pain it brings, if you're willing to bring her into it, then we'll all stand by you both. She has your da enamored. He hasn't laughed like this since our Colleen was here."

There are little speech patterns my mom has that remind me how Irish we still are even though we've been here for four generations. I glance over at Da, and I know Mom is right. He lit up when he met Greta. He took to her right away, and they've had a lively conversation ever since. But it might turn sour in a few minutes.

"Mom, Greta and I need to talk to you and Da in private. Can we slip out?"

"Sure." She looks wary now, but she shifts her attention to my father. She sends him some telepathic message because he points to us, and Greta follows him. My parents have always done that. A look can convey everything between them. It makes me wonder if Greta and I will ever get to that point. I hope so. I slide my hand into Greta's, and we head to my mom's office. She's a mortgage broker and can work from home most days.

Greta and I discussed explaining how we met while we were in the car on the way here. She's nervous, but my dad's warm greeting helped put her at ease. Hopefully, that doesn't evaporate.

"Mom, Da, we'd like to let you know how we met. It's unconventional."

My parents look at each other again before my mom speaks.

"We know you met at one of your strip clubs. That Márgrég was a dancer there."

"She was never a dancer, Mom. Who told you that? Wait. Let me guess. Maureen."

"Yes."

I can feel the anger rolling off Greta as she sits beside me on a loveseat. I squeeze her hand. I'm about to explain when Greta speaks before I can.

"Mr. and Mrs. O'Rourke, I worked as a waitress there. But I wasn't truthful with your son or nephews about why I was there. I'm a journalist, and I was there to gather information. I wrote those two articles about your family that were published in the news."

I'm quick to jump in before my parents lose their everloving minds. It's not only that she told mob secrets. They'll see her as a personal danger to me. It'll be game over if they do.

"Greta didn't send them to publication. They were leaked. You need to know why she wrote them and what she chose to do with them. Peter killed her grandfather."

"Peter Doyle?" My father sits forward as he speaks a name we all wish we didn't know. He and my father didn't get along, so it wasn't a sad day to learn he'd been killed for real. It angered my dad to find out his own father-in-law faked Peter's death, but he was glad when he died in truth twenty-odd years later.

My mom settles her gaze on Greta when she speaks. "How?"

"He built and sold a bomb to the IRA that blew my grandfather up near a bus. He was in the wrong place at the wrong time. My grandmother, parents, and I watched it happen. I was five. It's my first clear memory."

I didn't know that. Fucking hell.

"We immigrated to the U.S. not long after that. It was too painful, and we didn't know if the IRA was going to do something intentional to us once we discovered who killed Grandda. My granny has Alzheimer's and lives in a care facility in Connecticut. She was having a particularly horrible day during one of my visits a few months ago. She sounded lucid, but I knew she was in her memories. She spoke as though we were still in Ballycastle. She railed against Peter for what he did. She unloaded all the pain and misery he'd caused. He— by way of the weapons your father sold him in Ireland —stole so much from my family. He stole years we didn't have with Grandda. He stole memories I never got to make, and neither did my parents or grandmother. He stole the means to support my granny back in Northern Ireland. He stole the love of her life. I wanted to take from your family just like he took from mine. But I wanted nothing to do with any violence. That's short-lived in many ways, and I didn't want to be entirely like him with that hanging over my head for the rest of my days. I wanted to ruin your family businesses. I wanted that before I met Dillan and your nephews. I thought I was so certain about who they were and what I wanted. Then Dillan made me fall in love with him. I kept waiting for something— some piece of information —that made them the monsters I believed they had to be. But they're not. They're six men who work hard, put their family before themselves and everything else, and provide for the people who work for them. They're funny and kind and so normal. Dillan found out I was trading information with one of your rivals. He believed I was the leak. It wasn't until after he fired me, and the second article came out that he learned I was the source and the author. But I did not send the articles for publication. Someone sabotaged me and wanted to hurt you. I'd already realized I couldn't follow through with my original plan. I couldn't because I was already falling in love with Dillan."

She unloads it all. She tells them pretty much everything short of our private moments together. My parents take it all in and remain silent. I can tell Greta wants to fidget, but she controls herself. Da's piercing blue eyes— the green is on my mom's side —bore into me before they do the same to Greta. The mellow guy from earlier is gone. The mobster is here, but I know he won't physically harm Greta. I'm not convinced his words won't.

"You did this to avenge your grandfather."

"I suppose. Maybe it was misplaced loyalty. But most of it was pure rage that your family hurt mine. It was retribution. I betrayed Dillan's trust by being at the club under false pretenses. I betrayed him by repeating things I never should have known. If I didn't speak Gaelic, I wouldn't have understood what I heard. I betrayed him by even putting words to the screen. But I did that because it was cathartic. I have never felt more conflicted than I did while I wrote those articles and in the time after. I thought they were going to sit in my cloud, and I would delete them. I thought I'd discover something more about Dillan that would make me feel justified in harming your family. Then they were out there for the world. I wanted to feel vindicated in my anger toward all things O'Rourke. All I did was make myself miserable for lying to Dillan, for writing anything when my conscience said I shouldn't, for wanting to hurt your family at all. Today made me realize the true extent of what I risked by betraying Dillan."

My mom's brow furrows before she speaks. "Today?"

Greta twists to look at me, her eyes huge. I guess she assumed they knew.

"Aria Hoxha was killed in an explosion. I believe it was Zef. He was angry that she divorced him, took his heir, and went to live with her parents. She and Greta had a meeting today. She promised to tell Greta everything she knew. Maybe

Zef found out. Maybe he believed Aria was meeting a lover. Maybe he's just as crazy as I've always said he is. But Greta, Finn, and Joey had just pulled up to her parents' home. Finn said Aria'd just said goodbye to her kids. She recognized Greta, but before anyone could do anything, the house exploded."

"She was about to go back inside." Greta interjects.

"Finn said it all happened in a matter of seconds from when she must have spotted the hubcaps to the explosion. Finn and Joey got Greta out and to safety before the SUV caught fire. Their trackers pinged, but I was in a meeting. I didn't check my phone. Instead, I got the alert from the group text. Cormac said I needed to get home because there'd been an explosion, and Greta was safe. That's all he said. I didn't know what it meant until I called Finn from the car."

I release Greta's hand and wrap my arm around her. If we weren't in my parents' home, I would lift her onto my lap. That's how close I long to be. I don't quite need the peace being inside her brings, but I want us to feel she's safe and unharmed. I remain quiet, holding her pressed against me as Greta continues to speak.

"Whatever Zef's reason for it, I realized just how badly things could have gone for me. That if I was involved with anyone besides Dillan, I'd probably have died just as violent a death. That or a bullet between the eyes. It also made me realize nothing I could do to hurt your family will bring my grandfather back or stop my grandmother from having days where she's trapped within her traumatized memories. I was scared. But what terrified me was knowing something could happen to Dillan one day, and I nearly ruined the one chance I have to be with him. I'll never risk that again."

My parents made me. I am the product of the two of them, so between the two of them, there's nothing I can hide from them. One or the other always knows what I'm thinking or feeling. Tonight, it's my dad.

"Dillan forgave you because he understands family is everything. He understands the need to protect it and defend it, to place it above all else. While you could have been a threat, he can relate to your reasons. That's why he's forgiven you. My son is the best judge of everything. Best judge of character. Best judge of situations. Best judge of the future. If he's made peace with how you met, and he loves you, then we accept you. I won't lie and say it doesn't make me wary, but you knew all along you'd tell us this. It was obvious how nervous you were when you arrived, but you've fit in so naturally I don't think you could have faked it. There are only a handful of people who could, and that's because they've been trained to. You have not."

That makes Greta shiver. She looks up at me, and I can read the question in her eyes. I lean to whisper in her ear.

"Nothing between us is fake. I've faked nothing with you. Not my suspicion. Not my hurt. Not my lust. And not my love. You are the only one who doesn't get some element of façade. Even my family does. You get the entire real me."

I kiss her temple as she continues to look up at me. She takes a moment, but she nods. Then she looks back at my parents, who are watching us like hawks.

My mom nods, and I know that expression. Her practical nature is about to take over.

"Right, so your family is from Ballycastle. I assume you're Protestant, but I know you might be Catholic. If you are Church of Ireland, you won't be marrying in a Roman Catholic one here. Dill, are you converting for the wedding or for good? It'll be an Episcopalian wedding, so I can leave my rosary at home. At least it'll be a proper Mass, so that's good. When is it? Do I have time to get a dress? I need my roots doing."

There's a pregnant pause before Greta laughs.

"I am Protestant, so I'd like an Episcopalian wedding. Anglican would be best. There's a church near my parents that I grew up in. I don't know how you guessed I'd rather not convert, and I don't know if you're okay with Dillan possibly converting. But I appreciate you even considering understanding it. You have time to get your hair done. We've talked about marriage, but neither of us has proposed yet."

"Neither of you?" My dad grins, and I can only imagine what's coming next. "Lass, don't wait for my son to propose. He'd do well to learn early that you're the real one in charge. Behind every man is a woman keeping his head out of his arse. My Siobhan was patient enough to wait until after I proposed to teach me that. But I also wasn't one to dither. I asked her to marry me two days after I met her."

"You are a daft sod. You asked me when we were fifteen. You kept asking until I said yes at twenty-three. It took me that long to housebreak you before I was willing to risk you piddling on the rug. Even then, I still had my work cut out with you. Our Dillan has more sense than you did. He'll be just fine. I raised him right. Though I'll tell you true, Márgrég, a rolled-up newspaper doesn't always go amiss."

I watch Greta's cheeks go red at the notion I might need a spanking. I haven't punished her, but we talked about it. We agreed to wait until the weekend because her arse is going to be so sore she won't be sitting much to work.

I think I might be saved by the bell when my phone buzzes in my pocket. I pull it out and check the caller ID. Motherfucker.

"I have to take this."

Neither of my parents looks surprised, but Greta watches me anxiously. I don't know if she's worried about me leaving her alone with my parents or concerned who might be on the other end of the call that I would interrupt our conversation for it. I get up, but I hesitate. I think about offering Greta my hand and walking back to the hallway with her. But I can't. I need to answer this now, and I want her to get comfortable being alone with my family. As I get to the door, I hear Greta.

"Thank you for being so kind, Mr. and Mrs. O'Rourke. I admit I was scared to be here once you knew."

My mom's voice reaches me as I step into the hallway. "Few would understand, but we're just dysfunctional enough to get it."

"Hello, Zef."

I answer the call and head to the basement. It's fully finished with a gym my dad uses daily. I often come over to work out with him in the morning if I don't meet the guys at the boxing gym Finn owns.

"Your woman got lucky today. It would have been a shame to waste a pair of tits like hers."

"If you know she's mine, you know how unwise it is to insult her. You might be fine blowing up your ex-wife, but come near my woman, and I will make your death far slower. You know I'm not exaggerating. What do you want?"

"Aria made her choices, and I made mine. Tell me what your woman—"

"Ms. McDonnell to you."

"Whatever, Dillan."

"It'll be Mrs. O'Rourke soon. I'd learn fast if I were you."

Zef chuckles, but I hear the tinge of fear. It's a laugh to cover his actual emotions. He didn't realize how serious Greta and I are, but now he does. By telling him she'll soon have my name, I've done far more than just stake a claim by calling her my woman. I've made her family. I've made her an insider. To an insular community based on family units, that means something to him.

"Tell me what Ms. McDonnell found out from Aria."

"Nothing. You murdered your ex-wife before she could speak to her."

"Aria said something to Ms. McDonnell to get her to agree to a meeting."

"Your ex-wife said she'd share your secrets. Neither woman was naïve enough to say anything valuable over the phone. That's why they were going to meet."

"You're lucky she wasn't inside when it happened."

"You're just as lucky because if you'd killed her— if you even look in her direction to hurt her —you will discover exactly what I'm capable of. Everyone believes the bratva are the cruelest because of their fucked-up childhood at Vlad's hands. But they're puppies compared to me. They have limits. I have none. Stay away from my future wife. I won't tell you twice, Zef. If I don't believe you right now when you swear to it, you'll wake up to every single thing but your kids being destroyed. Then we'll talk face-to-face for as long as you have one."

I'm not lying. I grew up surrounded by violence everywhere but in my home. There's been nothing but love under this roof. But I learned to kill when my father gave me my first knife when I was twelve. I started ordering hits on people when I was fourteen. I killed before I even had a driver's permit. My life is about as fucked-up as it comes. I didn't withstand the torture the Kutsenkos did, but I endured a lot.

I did it to protect Colleen from Declan. It also taught me I have no limits to the violence I can commit. I couldn't touch Declan when he was alive. But I sure as fuck touched everything that had meaning to him. He's dead now, but to this day, he's the only one who knows how twisted and sadistic I can be to protect someone I love. If Zef breathes in Greta's direction, he'll be the second.

"Calm down, lover boy. I'm not looking to fuck up our business arrangements. I need them more than I need those tits or ass."

He chuckles because he knows I can't reach through the phone and kill him. I step farther away from the stairs and switch the phone to speaker. I pull up my texts.

ME

I need the bag

"Why did you call, Zef? There's birthday cake I'm missing. If I don't hurry, there won't be a corner piece for me."

Cake is just a vehicle for frosting. I love it.

"You may think you got the feds off your back. But you still don't know who really leaked the articles. It shocks me you haven't figured it out. You're so sure of yourself and of them. You should have guessed by now. And if Sean were of any real use, he would have tracked it already. I'm only telling you because I want four mill shaved off the price of our deal. I want the coke for half the market price. I also want you to deliver it. I'm not sending errand boys to do it. You can take the risk of another transport."

JOEY

Do you want me to bring it to you?

ME

Yeah

"You are certifiable if you think I'm taking a penny less than what I told you to pay. If you won't follow through, then I'll move on to the next buyer. You are not the only person interested."

"But I'm the only one willing to pay."

"Is that what you think?" I laugh, but there's no humor in my tone.

"I know I am."

"What the fuck makes you think that?"

"Because you would have sold it to someone else if you could."

What a fecking gobshite. I can sell those kilos of coke to a cop and walk away if I wanted to. I'm selling it to Zef because it'll make him further indebted to me. He already needs the kilos because he owes the Mancinellis money. He can't repay them without selling the coke on the street. No coke means no repayment, which means Salvatore ordering a hit on Zef's favorite nephew. I know this because I tapped Zef's phone months ago. He does nothing to check his devices or accounts for hackers regularly. He thinks he's as untouchable as I actually am.

JOEY

Give me 20

ME

K

"Make sure you lock your windows and doors tonight, Zef. You're annoying me."

I hang up. There isn't shite that's going to keep me out of his house or any other I want to break into. I don't care if he's awake when I arrive. I'd rather he see me coming. I don't need the element of surprise. I want the element of dread.

Chapter Twenty-Two

Greta

"It's Siobhan and Tate."

I breathe a little easier when Dillan's da encourages me to use their first names. I'm not sure that I should before we're at least engaged, but I refuse to consider our relationship as anything less than permanent.

"Thank you." I'm not sure what to say now. Ummmmmmm.

"Did you study journalism?" It's a totally normal question for Tate to pose, but it catches me off guard, considering my occupation is why we needed this little chat.

"I did. I thought I'd grow up to be a war correspondent. I wanted one of the bulletproof vests that said Press on it. Even when I got older and understood why the vests were necessary and not cool, I still wanted to travel to help people know the truth about what happens in other parts of the world. To help inform and educate. By college, I knew that's not exactly how it works, but it's still my goal."

And that's why I tried to dick your family over. To inform and educate.

Fucking hell. For the umpteenth time, what was I thinking? I was thinking about a warped sense of justice and a Pulitzer or Peabody. I'd accept either.

"That's commendable."

I wait to see if Siobhan says more, but that's it. It makes me wonder if she believes the opposite.

"Some days."

I hedge, acknowledging my wrongdoing again, but not inviting further conversation about what I've done.

When she continues, maybe I missed the mark. "You were willing to risk a great deal to get your story. You were willing to risk even more by speaking to Aria. Zef isn't known for being rational. It's why she left him. He took his position rather than inherited it. He's ambitious, but that's his hubris. All the syndicates have been patient until now."

Is that what Dillan's phone call is about? Is he setting up a hit on Zef? Is he making plans to do it himself?

Siobhan looks past me to where I know Dillan shut the door as he left. She shifts her focus back to me, and I don't want to guess what she'll say next. "Has Dillan spoken to you about your role if you marry him?"

"He has. He hasn't told me what it would be in great detail, but I understand my duties are to support him and our community."

I want to make myself sound a part of it to maybe make me even more acceptable. Like it's already a done deal. But I also want them to know I want to belong. Tate softens his tone. But I still feel like I'm sitting in front of the grand inquisition.

"What did he say those duties were?"

"To stand beside him at events like weddings, baptisms, and funerals. I'm sure I'll also attend formal engagements since I know he goes to many charity and political fundraising ones. He said I would also help the women in the community with anything they don't feel they can approach Dillan about. Um— is that —do you do that for him now? If you do, I— Just let me know how I can help."

I nearly said 'if' as I stammered my way through that. If makes it sound like I'm an outsider, so I corrected myself. I wish I could have been more eloquent. Apparently, I can only do that typing.

"Has Dillan told you there are a lot of unexpected things that come up?"

"I know there's a lot he won't tell me. I know he'll lie. He doesn't like it, but he's admitted he will. He has people to protect, and that's a higher priority to him than satisfying my curiosity. I know he'll be gone a lot, sometimes for several days. I won't know where he is or when he'll be back. He told me if he's gone more than three days, for now, he'd like me to stay with your family. Once I know how things go, he doesn't think that'll be necessary. He told me there's somewhere they go to take care of business. It's a controlled environment for them. I don't want to know where that is or what goes on there. That's not the Dillan I know, only the one I know exists. He said there might be times when he comes home and needs space. He may tell me to go in another room before he gets home. I'm to wait until he's ready to see me. I know that means he either has to calm down or wash away— evidence. He already had to be away for a night. He told me some of this before he left and some after because he came home with raw knuckles."

Learning all of that had been a slice of reality larger than I thought I could digest, but it all went down. Having the night apart gave me perspective. It gave me a chance to see if I could live with knowing he was probably killing someone. Hell, maybe someones. It didn't faze me as much as it probably should have. That part gave me pause. How am I able to accept what he does so blithely unless I'm morally devoid too? I've always believed there's room for situational ethics. I just didn't think I'd ever be in this situation to realize the syndicates live by a rigid ethical code. It's just not the one the rest of the world understands or approves of.

Tate's been nodding along as I speak. Now he offers a little reassurance. "Dillan's told you the long and the short of it. Some things will come up that he's unprepared for because he's never been married before. They're things between a husband and wife that can't be explained. They can only be lived. But he's done well to tell you most of it, and you seem to have accepted it with aplomb."

"I was just thinking about that. None of what he said was shocking. It was more an explanation of what I already knew or assumed. Having him away for a night gave me a test to see whether I can resign myself to what he does, and I can. Nothing about Dillan strikes me as a man with a propensity for violence or an enjoyment of it. He does it because it's his job. He does it because he needs to live. He needs to live because of the people who depend upon him. I did more research than just being at the bar to eavesdrop. I don't know the inside story, but I know things Donovan and Declan did. I know how your father died, Siobhan. I have a hunch who did it, even if there's little documentation about it. I pieced together from police blotters what I believe was the retaliation for it. I can't pass judgement considering what I set out to do. I wanted to even the score not ride a moral high horse."

So much for steering the conversation away from my culpability. We may as well face it and move on. Siobhan's expression softens, and she even smiles before she talks.

"For someone not born to this life, you understand us. It's why Dillan loves you and wants a life with you. It's difficult to bring outsiders into this world. It's why none of the guys—Dillan included —have dated since college. I can't blame any of them for not wanting a woman who is already enmeshed in this, either. You understand us, but you also offer him a reprieve."

I look at them, and I try to understand them since Dillan seems a lot like them. But I don't know enough yet.

"You met when you were fifteen. Siobhan, your father led the organization, so you were certainly enmeshed. Tate, I know your side of the family was already involved. There doesn't seem to be a reprieve there."

Dillan's mom patiently explains it. "Look around. How is this home any different from a non-syndicate one? How is our family any different when we all gather? We created that reprieve. You have a choice to make, especially since Dillan works from home so much. You can let the mob consume every minute of your life, or you can decide home is like base in tag. You're safe there. You create the family you want. My father did that well until my sisters, brother, and I were teenagers. Then he believed we were old enough to see things as they were outside our four walls. Donovan was already involved, so it wasn't a secret kept from my sisters and me. Tate and I decided when we married we wouldn't keep our life a secret from the kids, but we would introduce it gradually. We also decided mob life wouldn't take over once Dillan got involved. My sisters and brothers-in-law made the same choice. It's why we're so normal when we're together. Yes, the mob is our life. Yes, it's the men's job. But we are more than just that. Dillan is, and so are you."

"Will your siblings be as accepting as you are? Will they let me join the family?"

Tate chuckles. "Dillan rarely flexes. He's still our son, and he defers to us as much as he does his aunts and uncles. But at the end of the day, Dillan runs this branch even if he isn't the oldest member of it. What he says goes, and no one is going to be stupid enough to get in the way of him being with you. It would be pointless. He's not just the boss, he loves you."

"My sisters and I are lucky we met our soulmates. It happened to be three brothers. None of us saw that coming until it happened. We want our children to be as happy in their marriages as we are. It takes work, and there are bad times. In the end, we chose who we want to make our families with, and that was no one's decision but ours. The same is true for Dillan, and the same will be true for the rest of the guys."

"Siobhan, you joked about getting a dress for a wedding, but I want you to know I didn't ask Dillan to convert. He offered. I admit I said I didn't want to, but before I said more than that, he said he would."

"You're more Irish than we are, even if everyone in our family keeps marrying people with only a hundred percent Irish blood. Despite what Americans may think, not all Irish are Catholic. If either of you wants to believe and practice any faith, then that's for you to decide. It so happens three of the four families are from countries known to be Roman Catholic. The other is Eastern Orthodox. We come from religious families. But each person must make peace with what they believe because none of us can be a perfect version of anything."

"Thank you."

I can live with that. Dillan didn't exaggerate. Siobhan, and probably her sisters too, have accepted who they married and who they raised. They've raised their sons to be independent despite being such a close-knit family. I feel better about this. It's like a check in the box on a very long list. Phew.

Before any of us can say more, the door opens, and Dillan appears. He takes in all of us, and it's clear he's relieved. I don't know what he feared returning to, but no one's yelling, and no one's crying. We're not even laughing at his expense about childhood stories. Those are things that could be happening.

He sits beside me again, and he immediately takes my hand. Something is different, though. What happened on that call? What did Zef say? Or did he take more than one call while he was out? I watch his parents for any cues, but I see nothing. They look as though everything is completely normal. I turn to Dillan.

"When do you have to leave?"

His eyes widen. "How'd you know?"

I shrug one shoulder. "I don't know. I just did. Something's off."

We both know we're not alone, so he sticks to kissing my forehead before he responds.

"I love you."

"I love you, too. I wasn't nervous a moment ago, but now I am. What happened? Never mind." I shouldn't ask, but it was reflexive.

"You can always ask. I just can't always answer. And I said I love you because I do. I love how well you know me already. That you can tell things about me that anyone who hasn't known me basically since my conception couldn't. I don't have to leave right now, but I am going to step out in about ten minutes. I'll just be in the driveway."

Dillan's parents live in Queens. Ironically, they live about five blocks from nearly the bratva *pakhan's* entire family, which is a neighborhood two streets over. The Italian don and his family live in the same neighborhood as the Russians. Apparently, the Russians didn't grow up in such exquisite homes, but they moved here once they each got married. The Kutsenko brothers had already moved their mother into a mansion, and they followed to be closer together when the brothers' and cousins' bachelorhood ended.

Dillan asked me if I would like to live somewhere like these neighborhoods. Just in style, not necessarily next door to his parents. I like their home. I love that it's big enough for everyone to visit, and everyone can even have their own room if they wish to stay over. It gave me the sense that if I have to spend the night at some point, I'm not intruding. They're already used to having a full house. It's far bigger than a couple with two kids ever needed.

I spied a photo of Colleen in the entryway, and there are more of her hung on the walls and framed on the mantle. There are just as many of Dillan. There're individual school portraits from every year. There are photos of the siblings together or with their parents. There are also photos of the entire O'Rourke family at different times. One more instance of how fucking normal they are. You'd never guess Dillan is likely leaving tonight to do something illegal.

Breda, one of Siobhan's sisters, pokes her head in the room. "Shane's threatening to eat all four corners of the cake if you don't hurry up and get in here."

"He wouldn't dare."

Dillan is out of his seat in a flash, and he's practically pulling me with him. Apparently, Shane's threat is to be taken seriously. And apparently, Dillan wants a corner piece too. I can't blame him. Cake is just a vehicle for frosting.

Dillan's parents follow us as he leads us to the dining room. There are two cakes set out on the table, Shane standing in front of one, and Sean in front of the other. I heard at dinner how hard Breda and her husband worked to make sure each twin knew he was a person independent of his brother. It appears like Shane's is red velvet, and Sean's is chocolate. As I observe, I realize there's a more practical reason for two cakes.

There are nine large men and four women here. One cake would never feed all the men, and the women wouldn't even get a slice. I anticipate a feeding frenzy at the zoo. We sing, and the brothers blow out their candles. There are some thinly veiled innuendos in Irish from their brother and cousins about what the twins wished for. Sean reaches for the cake knife, but his mother slaps his hand away. He pretends like it hurts. She ignores him. Instead, she looks at me.

"Márgrég, what would you like? And would you like a corner?"

I glance up at Dillan, and I can see he's anxious.

"*Mo stór*, even if I ask for a chocolate corner, you're still going to fight Shane for a corner of his. I won't narrow your chances."

Everyone laughs, and Dillan glowers. But it's playful.

"Auntie Breda, I'll give up my corner for Greta. She likes red velvet better. And Shane's just greedy. No one wants to see him throw a tantrum at his own party."

"Hey now!"

Shane appears duly insulted, but Sean elbows him.

"Don't think that because you're giving up a corner to Márgrég you're getting any of my corners. I already have to give one to Mom and one to Auntie Saoirse."

I cock an eyebrow and plunge in, hoping I don't make an ass of myself. "Do either of you really need to have more than one corner? I know neither of you went to the gym this morning. Finn told me."

The twins turn identical glares at their older brother, who in turn laughs at them. He snags the other cake knife and goes straight for Shane's cake. He's far enough away from his mother that she can't stop him. He cuts a massive chunk before he drops it on a plate. He smirks at his younger brother as he grabs a fork, looking like he's about to savor the first bite. But he hands the plate to me then crosses his arms.

"You never could share."

"*Póg mo thóin.*" Kiss my ass. Shane mutters, but his mother hears him.

"Would you like to leave with no cake at all? Finn, be nice to your brother for once. Shane, you'll be eating soap rather than cake." She looks at me. "I swear they weren't raised in a barn. They just spent all day there."

I lift my cake as I cut a bite with my fork. "Thanks." I grin as I put it in my mouth.

Shane looks like he would probably stick his tongue out at Dillan if he was five. "It's a good thing you're an improvement on all of them. I'll share with you and not because I have to. I like you. Dillan— well, at least now we get you when we get him."

Dillan's fast. He has a plate in one hand as he grabs the cake knife Finn put down. He goes for the matching corner on Sean's cake. He has the slice before anyone can stop him. No one expects him to then turn to Shane's and cut the opposite corner off. He grabs a fork, wrinkles his nose at his cousins, then turns away as though to shield his cake. He takes a bite that has a bit of both cakes on it.

"It's good to be king."

Sean thinks he's smarter than his brother. He mouths his response. "*Gabh transna ort fhéin.*" Go sideways on yourself.

It means fuck off.

"The only Irish spring you'll be seeing is the bar of it in your bathroom."

Breda puts her left hand on her hip as she wags her right index finger at Sean. There's humor in all of this. No one seems surprised at the guys' antics. No one seems surprised Breda threatens to wash her sons' mouth out with soap even though they're likely a foot taller than her. I think I might even see them both shiver with a healthy dose of fear. I feel like I belong. I'm an only child with no cousins near me. They say you can't miss what you don't know. I don't know what it is to be from a big family, but I missed having moments like these. Dinner at my parents' tomorrow night will be so different. Not bad. Just different.

But that gives me pause. I look over at Dillan. He might leave soon. Will we have to reschedule dinner with my parents? Hey, Mom. Hey, Dad. My mobster boyfriend needs to whack someone. Can we move dinner to another night?

How the hell am I going to explain half the shit Dillan does?

Chapter Twenty-Three

Dillan

My phone buzzes as we finish our cake. I'm not a glutton about much, but cake is definitely my Achilles' heel. But it has to be buttercream frosting. Whipped and fondant are gross. I don't need to look at my phone, but I do. Everyone's sitting in the living room, so it's noticeable when I get up. I'm okay leaving Greta alone with everyone since things seemed to go so well with my parents. As we left the dining room, we told my aunts and uncles that we'd like to speak to them soon, and that in the meantime, they can get an abridged version from my parents. I would rather tell them myself, but I'm going to have to leave tonight. I don't want them possibly left out for days.

I let go of Greta's hand, and she moves it off my lap. She looks at me, but she says or does nothing.

"I'll be back in a few minutes."

That registers surprise with her. She didn't think I'd return. I keep my comments only for her ears.

"*Cailín*, I will always do my best not to leave without at

least telling you if not with a goodbye. I'm not going now, but I will have to go soon."

"Alone?"

"For this, only Seamus will go with me."

I don't need the entire squad. But Seamus is a behemoth, and so is Cormac. I only need one of them, and it's Seamus's turn. I look over at my cousin, and when he senses someone watching him, he shoots his gaze to me. We exchange a look, and he nods. He won't ask anything until we're alone.

"Are you sure that's a good idea? Only one person?"

The moment the questions are out of her mouth, she appears horrified. Then scared. Then contrite.

"I'm sorry. I shouldn't have said that. I didn't think."

"You did think. You worried about me, and I appreciate it. I'm not going to censor your thoughts, wee one. And I'm never going to tell you not to ask me questions. The day you stop is the day I'll be scared you've stopped loving me. That you'll resent me not answering or that you've just given up. It's selfish since I can't always answer, but I want to know you care what happens to me or our family."

"I promise not to question you in public again."

"We aren't in public. My family always has plenty of questions and plenty of opinions. They help me be a better leader. I only need one person with me, and it's Seamus for his size. He's a reminder. If I thought it wasn't safe for just two of us, I wouldn't risk Seamus's life by going unprepared."

She nods. I can still see she's anxious, but it isn't about being out of line.

"Should I just go back to the brownstone?"

"Yes. The twins will take you."

"Are they going to go out and celebrate or something?"

"No. None of us party unless it's for work. This was the celebration."

"They're turning twenty-eight and cake with family is their way of celebrating?"

"Truly, we're all homebodies at this point. We had our wild days, and now we just like to go home to the quiet."

She nods as she looks around. My cousins are all handsome. They could live up the nightlife and get laid every night. They could just go out with the guys and drink. Hell, Finn owns a bar. But that's not our thing anymore. We've gotten that out of our systems. The one place we're all still willing to go is our BDSM clubs. We belong to different ones and are silent owners of the places we go.

"I'll be right back."

I know Joey's in the driveway by now, but he also knows to wait. He knows I can't always extract myself immediately. He and I have been friends since we were kids. It helps that we're related, so we see each other at larger family functions all the time. But we also just get along. I like his company and prefer him as my bodyguard when I have one. He's still the only person I trust driving Greta around if it's not one of my cousins.

"Hey. Thanks for bringing the bag." I scan the men patrolling my parents' property. We're behind a property gate behind a community gate. We still take precautions. I've thought about my living situation with Greta a lot. I like my place, and hers is nice too. But I don't like how easy it is to get into either of our places. I want to move to a neighborhood like this. Somewhere I can readily have more security.

"No problem. Do you want me to go with you?"

"Not this time. Seamus will."

Joey nods and turns back to the car. Since he knows the contents of the bag, he doesn't ask questions about what I'm preparing to do. I carry it back into the house and set it off to the side. I don't hide it, but neither do I leave it for someone to trip over. I return to the living room, but I catch Seamus's attention and jerk my head toward the hallway. He says something to Finn then joins me. We head into the kitchen.

"I need you with me when I visit Zef tonight. I can't kill him because he's still useful. But I am going to make sure he understands we are not equals. We aren't even playing in the same league. I'll also make sure he understands talking about Greta without respect is the surest way to cause his death. I'll bring him within inches of it.

"You need me to be the muscle?"

"Yeah. Keep other people away, and I may need you to help hold him down until he's tied up."

We won't take him to our place in the Bronx since once someone is there, they don't leave. We can't risk them ever narcing. It reminds me of a little ditty I learned in college from a friend from Boston. He came from one of the nicer parts. We met a douchebag at a party who was from a not so delightful town just outside of the city. Lynn, Lynn, city of sin. You never come out the way you came in. That's the best way to describe going to one of our places. You arrive in close to one piece, but you leave as ash or acidic ooze.

"Where's he at?"

I get my phone out and unlock it. I have several people I track on various apps who aren't my family. That's an entirely different means of tracking and for a different reason. I tap a few things, and I get Zef's location. "Go figure. He's at a bratva strip club."

"Do they know that?"

"The only way Maks or Bogdan are letting him through the door is if they're having a meeting with him. Hopefully, he lives long enough for us to see him. It also means we have to get him back into his neighborhood unless we wait him out. I'd rather not spend all night at this, but we may have to."

"Then I need to make a call."

"Plans?"

"Yeah." He's meeting someone at his club. He gives me no details, so that tells me everything.

"Sorry about that. Would you rather I take Cormac?"

"Nah. He has plans too. I don't care if I have to miss this."

Seamus is like I was. He has a standing arrangement with a couple of women. Sometimes they plan to meet. But most of the time, if the mood strikes, and he goes, then he'll scene with them if they're there. If not, then he'll do other shite short of actually fucking. None of us look for random people at the clubs. It's too risky. And not just for our dicks' health. It's too risky the wrong person will discover who we are. Since we own the clubs we go to, we have easy access to the member files. We can do background checks on the women we fuck.

We also don't get completely nude. Ever. Our tats are too distinct. If nothing else, the four-leaf clover with the O in the center screams who we are. But it's a rite of passage we all get after our first kill. I got mine younger than most. My mom cried for two weeks. Sometimes it was for what I did, but just as often it was because she said I was too young to mar the perfect creation she'd spent nine months making and twenty-eight hours bringing into the world.

"Let's give it an hour or two. See where he winds up. I want to take Greta home, too."

"She's doing really well in there. We're a big family. I know we're overwhelming when it's just the six of us. Adding all our parents is extra intimidating."

"It is. But she's getting along with Mom and Da, and I think that'll help tremendously when we tell your parents and Auntie Breda and Uncle Ronan."

"Are your parents going to warm them up?"

"Yeah. I asked them to as we headed back into the living room after the cake."

"You're an arse. Try that shite with my cake, and I'll stab you with a fucking fork."

"Be quicker than me then."

We all run. Some of us— like me —enjoy it. I ran track and field in high school and college. Others do it because it's good for them. It's often necessary. But I also have the quickest reflexes besides Finn and my mom.

We head back inside just as people are gathering their coats. I look for Greta, but I don't spot her. My heart races for a moment. What went wrong in the few minutes I was outside? She couldn't have left without me seeing her go past where Seamus and I stood talking. I look around and see her coat still hanging up on the rack. A moment later, she comes out of the bathroom. My reaction was completely irrational. But today's been intense even by my life's standards. A bombing and dinner with my parents. We say our goodbyes, then we're in the back of our town car.

"How do you feel that went, *cailín*?"

I ask as I lift her onto my lap. She curls up against me. My hand slides up her skirt as it always does now. This one is an ankle length pencil one. It's snug to get my hands up it, but it's worth the quest.

"Better than I thought it would. Your parents are so under-standing. At least, that's the impression they gave me."

"I told you my family would understand. And their happiness for us is sincere."

"I should defer to you in all things, Daddy."

She gives me a saucy smile as she unzips her coat. Then she's unbuttoning her blouse and pulling down her bra cups. With one hand under her skirt and one hand on top, I help her move to straddle me. She offers me her tits. Who am I to refuse?

"How long will we have before you have to go out?"

"Probably an hour or two. What're you thinking?"

"Something I ordered arrived today."

Her cheeks redden, and I can only imagine what it could be. No package comes into my place without the guy on duty checking it. Whatever she got, someone's already seen it. It embarrasses her, but not enough to have stopped her from getting it.

"Are you going to tell me what it is?"

"Nope."

"Will I find out when we get home?"

"Yup."

I suck her tits because they're there, and I can. Absolutely glorious. I wish we'd get home sooner. But my wish is to no avail. Not two minutes after we walk out the door and get in the car, *that* text message notification goes off.

CORMAC

Enrique's got Aidan and Denny. He'll trade them in exchange for carfentanil deal with the Culiacán.

Fuck. That's billions of dollars of potentially lost revenue if we give up that deal with one of the Mexican cartels. Carfentanil is a synthetic opioid that's about ten thousand times stronger than morphine and hundred times stronger than fentanyl. It's the kind that'll kill you just looking at it. It's also high value on the street. If we give up this deal, it'll piss the Mexicans off because no one's supposed to know we're doing it. It's more hush-hush than usual since the Culiacán have an arrangement with the Mancinellis because of family ties they gained when Luca got married. Zef thinks he's the one doing the deal because we've planted that belief. Enrique's been wanting it too thanks to us. I need to know how Enrique found out we're already involved.

ME

> Where does he want to meet?

CORMAC

> The bodega

ME

> Will Denny and Aidan be there?

CORMAC

> No. The guys' trackers say they're in Jackson Heights but not at the bodega. It's a construction site.

ME

> Are they alive?

CORMAC

> Don't know

Our men at a Colombian Cartel construction site likely means they're corpses. I'm watching Greta as I shoot these texts off and read the ones coming in. My plans for Zef are going to change, and that means so are my plans for tonight. I'll need to leave as soon as I drop off Greta.

Why can't we ever have anything nice? A delightful evening with my family followed by a delightful night with my girlfriend. Most people wouldn't think that's too much to ask for, but in our world that's like your birthday, Christmas, Hannukah, Kwanza, Easter and every other gift-giving holiday rolled into one. They're like a mythical unicorn. Maybe they exist— after all they are Scotland's national animal —but no one's ever seen one.

ME

> Don't come to me. We all go to Finn's

Cormac shoots me the thumbs up emoji. I lock my phone and ease it back into my pocket. We share a brief kiss as we arrive at the brownstone. We don't have much time because the guys will be at Finn's.

"There's something I got for us." It's in a package I brought upstairs with us. "Strip."

I unbutton and unzip my pants as she removes all her clothes.

"This is going to be quick and rough, Greta."

And that's exactly what it is. We're left breathless as I open the package and withdraw a vaginal plug and clit jewelry.

"You're going to wear this, wee one. You're going to keep my cum inside you until just before you fall asleep. When I come home, I want to see you just as you are now."

I slide the plug into her, and I use the double set of prongs to clip the jewelry to her pussy lips. I'm almost hard again at the sight she makes. I lean over to kiss her, regretting that we had so little time.

"Remember, I'm the one who makes you hard while you're gone."

My brow furrows.

"Greta, there may be times when I have to be at the strip clubs or even parties with practically naked women. I hate knowing that now that we're together. I also know you understand I have no limits to what I'll do to protect the people I love. The one limit I have that is absolutely unmovable is that I will never cheat on you. I will never fuck a woman to get something. I will never touch another woman or make her think I want to just to get what I need. There will always be another way."

She appears relieved, and I want to be upset that she didn't trust me. But what is she supposed to think? I won't outright say there is no limit to the torture I'll inflict, so I just say I have no limits. I can't blame her for thinking such a blanket statement includes fucking whomever I want to get what I want.

"Besides me not wanting anyone else, I really don't think any other woman could get me hard. Not after I know what you look and feel like. No one comes close to you, so my dick just isn't interested."

"Please don't test that theory." She whispers, and it breaks my heart.

I pick her up. Once I'm seated where she was just lying, I place her on my lap.

"I told you the truth about how I feel. But you've met my family now. Which member of my family do you think would forgive me for such a betrayal? Which one do you think would let infidelity go unpunished? No one in my family cheats. That is the only mortal sin we won't commit. The others pale in comparison."

"I'm sorry I doubted you."

"How could you not? I'm evasive on purpose. But I'm also figuring out what I can tell you. I don't know yet, so I'll err on the side of caution and say very little. I know that leaves you with a lot to speculate about."

"It does. But I know you, Dillan. I know you won't cheat. I just needed to know you'd still consider fucking for business as cheating. That it wouldn't fall into some justifiable gray area."

"My cock belongs to you. Plain and simple. It goes nowhere but with you. There are no shades of gray. Only absolutes."

"Good."

I go to my closet to change. I put on all black, including black cargo pants. I pull out my go bag. It has spare clothes and toiletries, but it also has cash and fake passports. We always take them in case something goes wrong, and we can't get home before taking off. It makes me realize something I should explain.

"The last time I was away, I was gone an entire night. It made sense that I arrived in different clothes than the day before. There are days when I'm going to come home wearing something other than what I left in. I'm not trying to hide perfume or lipstick marks. But there will be things on the clothes I can't risk being found."

She stares at me as understanding registers. "Makes sense. Thank you for telling me that. I would have wondered, but my immediate thought would have been you got injured. That it would have been your blood that you needed to get rid of."

I say nothing to confirm or deny, and it nearly kills me. As much as this is a lesson in her learning to live with the secrets and lies I'll tell, it's a lesson for me, too. It's never been this hard to keep something from someone. Not even my parents or Colleen. It feels like my heart is tearing in two, and this is the least of the things I'll keep from her. I have a new level of respect and empathy for my father and uncles. They don't go on missions as often as they used to, but if they're needed, they don't hesitate to come. They've been through this for more than thirty years. I'm struggling to make it through the first time.

"Daddy, I'll be all right. I have work in the morning, anyway. That'll keep me occupied during the day. I'll watch a movie or read tomorrow night. You have to go. I'm trusting you'll come home in one piece. You need to trust I'll be just as okay."

That does the opposite of reassure me. When she says come home in one piece, she doesn't know many times I've done that— just barely. I need her to be more than okay. She shifts back onto the mattress and opens her legs. I see the plug and the jewelry as she rubs her clit. She's not doing it to get off or even get aroused. She's doing it so I can watch. She stops, then stands.

"Remember that while you're away. It'll be waiting for you when you get home. Go. You're keeping the guys waiting."

"I love you."

"I love you, too."

I give her one last look before I walk out.

Chapter Twenty-Four

Greta

Dillan's been gone for two days. I haven't heard from him, but Shane's been assigned to me both days. He hasn't heard from his cousin, but he also hasn't heard from any of the guys either. He promises me no news is good news. He swears he'll tell me as soon as he knows anything.

What happened to Aria has me digging. As far as Gary is concerned, he thinks I'm investigating for another story similar to the unfortunate one I already wrote but about a different syndicate. I could. But that isn't happening. At least, I'm not putting a damn thing down on paper or my screen until I speak to Dillan and find out what he wants me to do with the information. What I'm learning is strictly for his family and him to use. Anything he feels is safe to share, I'll turn into an article. Maybe.

I'm working from Dillan's place— our place —I've been pretty good about thinking about it as ours, but sometimes I slip up —because of the secure wireless here. They have radio jammers and firewalls and whatever else Sean came up with. I learned he has a degree in national security and studied cyber warfare, among other things. It was Shane's idea I work here yesterday and today when I told him what I was delving into.

"Shane?" I call down the basement stairs to him. He's working out and has been for like three hours. He did the same thing yesterday.

"Yeah?"

"Can you come look at something, please? I'm not sure what it means, but I think it's something important."

I hear his heavy footsteps coming up the stairs, so I go back to where I'm researching in the living room. I've been sitting in Dillan's favorite recliner because it's crazy comfy. The man loves his creature comforts. That's for sure.

"I just came across this flight log. This plane is registered to Ardit Hoxha, but he's dead. Despite being owned by a dead man with no new legal registration, the plane's travel log has it going to and from Miami three weeks ago. Does this mean the FAA allowed a plane to fly illegally?"

"Yes."

"How does that work? Did Zef bribe someone to get it off the ground, and once it was up, there was nothing the FAA could do short of having it shot down?"

"Pretty much. You can see tracking planes is legal, and the flight logs are available for the public. But that doesn't mean the authorities always stop the planes before they make their trips. The FAA is like any regulatory body. It can't be actively in all the places all the time. They do the best they can to track planes in real time, but it's not impossible for a grounded plane — as in lack of registration or a maintenance issue —to take off. Especially if it's at a private airfield or simply not using an airfield."

"Not using an airfield. Do you mean like a cornfield or something?"

"It doesn't have to be that long. Most small fixed-wing aircrafts need about fifteen hundred feet to take off. Two thousand to truly be on the safe side, but it's not necessary. That's basically laying the Central Park Tower on the ground."

"Shit. When you put it that way, that doesn't seem long at all."

"It's not, but the plane's weight and speed don't necessitate more."

"How do you know this?" I'm not sure if I should ask that sort of question. But if he won't answer, he won't answer.

"You can guess one reason I'd know how much land a plane needs to take off and land, but I know because I'm a pilot. I enjoy flying and have since I was a kid. You only have to be sixteen for the FAA to allow you to fly solo in anything other than a glider or balloon. You can get your private pilot license at seventeen, so I did."

"Do you own a plane?"

He grins at me and wiggles three fingers.

"Three?!"

"Yeah. One's a glider. One's a VP-12 two-seater. And one's a biplane."

Fucking hell. I forget they're all billionaires. They like nice things for sure. Their custom-tailored suits. Their sports cars. Their nice watches and designer sunglasses. But that's about the extent of it. Dillan told me about how most of the other syndicate guys have or had penthouses scattered around Manhattan. It wasn't just about their wealth, though that was part of it since it bought them the best views of the city. Being on the top floor makes it difficult for an attacker to get to you. Short of coming through a window, they won't start the attack on the roof. And they'd take longer to get to you going up an elevator or stairs. With around the clock security, someone would intercept them first. But the O'Rourkes prefer their nice places to be less flashy.

Dillan has the brownstone here in Park Slope, one of the most expensive neighborhoods in Brooklyn. Finn has a loft in Soho, which is still Manhattan, but it's not a luxury condo by design. Sean and Cormac both have places in East Harlem not too far from me but in neighborhoods like five times as expensive as mine. Seamus is also in Brooklyn in the Boerum Hill area. That's a quiet and cozy place to live. Not quite what you imagine for a swinging bachelor pad. And Shane lives in Douglaston, a super expensive part of Queens. Pretty much, except for Finn, they all live in places designed for families. Yet, none of them— even Dillan —strike me as the type looking to have a family. Dillan might be now because we're together, but the other five definitely aren't. And that's making an assumption on my part because we haven't talked about when we might have kids or how many we'd like.

We haven't talked about a lot of things, yet it often feels like we've talked about everything. We know a lot about each other's families and childhoods. We've shared stories about college and the jobs we've had. He's told me about the businesses he owns alone and the ones in which he's a co-owner. That includes the BDSM club I already knew he went to but didn't know he was a silent owner. We discussed our memberships, and we decided that since he's also an owner of the one I belong to, we'd rather go to mine. He isn't thrilled about running into anyone from my past, but he was less thrilled about subjecting me to anyone from his. I don't ask about the businesses he owns on behalf of the mob.

But he still hasn't met my parents. I called to cancel and said he had an unexpected work trip out of the city. I think that's probably true if you consider "the city" to be Manhattan.

The place they go probably isn't in Manhattan but one of the other boroughs. He also told me a little more about how they have a controlled location that isn't on any records, and the few people in the surrounding area are mob affiliated or paid extremely well to forget they exist. He explained about not having his phone on, so no one can track him. He said they have beds, showers, and a small kitchen. I don't know what to picture, so I try not to.

I told my parents we'd set something up once he was back. It didn't go over super well. I'm pretty sure they guessed what I wasn't saying.

"If you're a pilot, then you know the laws. How did Zef fly in and out of these municipal airports with an expired registration?" I bring us back to the subject after my mind wandered for a moment.

"With plenty of money. Where was he going besides Miami?"

"Chihuahua, Mexico of all places. Why would he go there?" The moment I ask I know the answer. "Oh, for the same reasons as Miami, right?"

I look up at Shane as I turn my laptop toward him, so he can see the flight lists. His gaze meets mine, and I know he won't answer those questions. The silence is all I need to know I'm right. Drugs, at the very least. People as another possibility.

"Do you have the weight and balance records, too?"

"Um." I toggle over to another window and click a couple links.

"May I?"

I hand him the laptop, and he goes to the sofa. After a few minutes, he looks up at me, and he looks anything but pleased with what he found. He passes the computer back to me as he stands.

"I need to go up to Dillan's office to make a couple calls."

I nod. He can't stay down here because I'll understand anything he says in English or Gaelic. I discovered all the guys speak fluent Spanish with pretty decent Italian and more Russian than I would have guessed. My Spanish isn't great, but it's proficient. Whoever he's calling likely doesn't speak Italian or Russian. He heads upstairs, and I keep searching.

What's this?

Wait a— holy fucking shit.

This cannot be.

It is.

This is what Aria likely wanted me to know. It's probably what Shane figured out. I do a quick check at the browser history to see if he searched anything then closed the window. Nothing beside the website I showed him. Maybe he used an incognito window. He didn't click much and didn't type more than a few words.

I'm looking at a photo of Zef and a man the caption names as Jesus Espinoza. He's the *jefe* of the Culiacán cartel. The man is no joke. He's the type that leaves heads in town plazas to remind folks that the cartel is the real authority not the government. I don't know how this wound up in an online Mexican newspaper. The cartels pay a lot to stay out of the news. Then again, they also pay a lot to plant stories.

I skim the article, grateful my Spanish is as good as it is. Zef and Jesus went into business together. Zef apparently bought an agave plantation, and he's selling the harvested plants to Jesus, who has a tequila factory. I scrub my hands over my face. If Zef's doing deals in Mexico, then he wants to expand. He wants into the pot and cocaine markets. He might get stuff from Miami, but if he has a legit reason to have trucks crisscrossing Mexico and even crossing the border, it'll be much easier for him to run shipments.

I'm considering calling up to Shane to tell him what I just

discovered. But if he's on a call, he probably doesn't want a woman shouting his name in the background. I won't go upstairs because of what I might overhear. Even if it's nothing, things are still too new for me to do anything that might make someone suspicious. I already have to live down my eaves-dropping and spying. I don't want anyone to think I'm using Dillan.

My phone vibrates in my pocket. It surprises me to see who's on the screen.

A

"Hello."

"Hello, Molly."

The Russian accent is thick, but one thing I noticed about Anton and Sergei is their English is impeccable. I know one difference between Russian and English is their language doesn't have definite articles, so no "a", "an", or "the". Hence the whole strong like bull stereotype. These bratva members would pass for native English speakers if not for the Russian accents.

"What's up?" I try to sound casual.

"I know Sergei tried to talk to you, but you ignored his texts. We need to see you."

"Why?"

"Because there's more to what's going on than you realize. There are more moving parts than there were two months ago."

"I'm not interested. If it's that important, tell Dillan directly. You know I'll just repeat anything you say."

"We know. That's fine. I also know you're at his place with only Shane. Our connections on both ends are secure, so I'm not worried about our calls being tapped or traced. But it would be better to do this in person. Bring Shane."

"You don't issue me orders, Anton. We weren't partners, and we aren't friends. We did each other a favor for as long as it benefited both of us."

"I'm sorry if that's how it came across, but you need to hear what we have to say."

"Last time, you made it sound like you were going to tell me things to keep me away from Dillan. Now you're saying I should come with Shane. What's the deal?"

"I still have things to tell you that will warn you away from Dillan. But I know Shane's your guard right now, so you won't go anywhere without him. If I want to talk to you, then I have to deal with him listening."

"And you're going to speak poorly about his cousin right in front of him."

Anton chuckles before he answers. "I've been talking poorly about Dillan since I was fourteen and came to America. If I haven't stopped in almost eighteen years, I doubt I will today. Shane's used to it. I have nothing nice to say about him either."

"I don't find you funny, Anton."

"I wasn't trying to be. I don't like your boyfriend, and he doesn't like me. If the shoe were on the other foot, I'm certain Dillan would warn you away from me."

"Would he though?"

The line goes silent. I've just issued a silent threat, and I know it. I let the quiet hang there for a moment before I continue.

"Your silence confirms what I already suspected. I won't tell anyone, Anton. It's none of my business who you are or aren't with. Even if you weren't Russian, I wouldn't say anything. But it means you don't get to say shit about my relationship with Dillan. I'm not passing judgement on you, so keep your opinions to yourself."

"The difference is my partner will keep me alive. Yours is likely to get you killed."

"You have too much time on your hands if you're worrying about me."

I don't catch what Anton says next because the front door opens, and Dillan walks inside.

"I gotta go. Dillan's home."

I hang up without a second thought. I want to run to him and throw myself into his arms, but I don't know what kind of mood he's in. I rise slowly and put my laptop on the coffee table. I smile at him, but his expression shutters. Is he not happy to see me?

"Hi, Daddy." I keep my voice low, so it doesn't carry upstairs. I've missed him so much. It fully hits me. I've been ignoring the strength of that feeling to make it bearable while he's been gone.

"*Cailín.*" He breathes the term as he hugs me. I burrow against him, and all is right in the world again. I'm in his arms, and I'm safe. He's safe. I squeeze him before leaning back. Our kiss is one that no one should witness, so it's a good thing Shane is upstairs.

"Where's my cousin?"

That wasn't what I thought he'd say next.

"In your office. He had to make a call."

He glances up the stairs, then he's backing me into the kitchen. I'm in yoga pants, and they're down around my ankles before I know what's happening. Then he's lifting me onto the breakfast bar.

"Oh, Dillan. Fuck."

He's sucking on my clit, and I'm dripping in an instant. He's working my pussy with three fingers and his tongue. But he freezes just as fast as he started.

"Stay upstairs! I'll come up!"

My eyes are like saucers. I look out of the kitchen, but I

can't see the stairs or the landing from where we are. "How'd you know?"

"I heard him."

"I didn't."

"Good. That means I'm doing it right." He dives in again, and he's pushing me to the edge in an instant.

"Daddy, that feels so good... Yes... Yes. Just like that... More. Harder... Harder, Daddy. *Please*... Fuck. May I come? Dillan I need to come."

"Let me taste you, wee one. Come in five... Four... Three... Two... Now."

I never imagined I could orgasm to a countdown, but he knows me so well already. His command makes me shudder, and I feel the pleasure spread through my pussy and into my belly. I tense as I try to prolong the sensation. But eventually, it wanes. He lifts me down and pulls up my pants before leading me to the kitchen bench. He sits and draws me onto his lap to straddle him.

"Tell me how your last two days were, wee one."

He pushes up my shirt and sports bra before suckling. I explain how I worked from home and had found something interesting I shared with Shane and that I have more I need to show him now that he's home. He hums agreement a couple times, but he doesn't let up. We sit like this for a couple minutes before he finally sits back.

"I've missed you, *cailín*."

"I can tell. I missed you, too. I'm glad you're home."

"I wasn't sure if you were when I walked in. You finished your call, but then you hesitated to greet me."

"I didn't know what kind of mood you'd be in. I didn't want to crowd you if you were tired or wanting some space. You aren't used to coming home to someone in your place."

"Our place. And I was looking forward to nothing more

than finding you here. I admit I pictured you running into my arms and me twirling you around."

"You did not!"

He cocks an eyebrow, and I giggle. He might be a mobster, but considering how tender he is with me, I suppose I should know by now that he would be sentimental and romantic like that.

"Next time, Daddy. And all the times after that."

"Good, *mo stór.*

"I wish we could sit like this until we've both gone gray, but I need to talk to you and Shane. I just got off the phone with Anton, so that's one thing. But it's really about what I just discovered online. Did you know Zef is besties with Jesus Espinoza?"

Chapter Twenty-Five

Dillan

I still when Greta mentions Zef and Jesus Espinoza in the same breath. Jesus and I have a past, and it's one that nearly blew up in my face. I was so close to a huge score through him by double dealing and undercutting Enrique, but the fucking Mancinellis stuck their noses in. Well, in truth, I'm the one who wedged myself in. But if they'd stayed in their lane, there wouldn't have been a shootout, and I would have been several million richer. The truly complicated part is that Jesus Espinoza turns out to have an indirect connection to the Mancinellis through marriage. I knew, but I didn't want anyone else to. Now they do, so that means doing business with him is off the table.

However, Enrique sees no such problem. He's still trying to fuck Zef over by taking over the carfentanil trafficking from Mexico. It's why I've been gone. They can make the shite in Mexico, but the shite they're dealing comes from China through Mexico. The Culiacán have a smuggling system down pat through New Mexico because they're willing to go through the mountains. It means the Chinese drugs get into the U.S. with no one worrying about customs agents getting too nosy. There's already enough scrutiny over legal trade with that part of Asia. This is far more covert and, therefore, far more lucrative.

"What did you discover?"

"They've been meeting in Chihuahua off and on for about two months. I pieced together information from the flight logs I found for Zef's plane. It's still registered under Ardit, so that caught my eye. The weights and balances records suggest he's coming back with cargo he didn't leave with. Shane explained how little runway a plane Zef's size needs. I never imagined it was so little. Not even the size of a corn field."

"What else did you learn online?"

"According to the Mexican newspaper article with them together in a photo, they're making tequila together. Zef's also gone to Miami, too."

"I know. If I'd known you could sleuth this out so quickly, I wouldn't have been gone for more than an hour."

I smile to lighten things since I can't tell her the entire truth. I would have been gone an hour, then I would have left again. We have a guy in Zef's organization who we had to track down. Fucker went to ground, so we had to flush him out. He told us all of this and more. Zef didn't learn from Ardit and is still trying to run a human trafficking ring through Miami. I need to arrange a meeting with Maks to discuss that. I want nothing to do with that shite. Not after what happened to Maria Mancinelli and Misha Andreyev's sister-in-law in Miami. We did what we could to help, but we were still in the shite thanks to the Boston Albanians.

Maks will go ballistic on Zef when he finds out. They don't have a good relationship to begin with, but the bratva here in New York has negative one million tolerance for any type of sex trafficking. The Moscow bratva nearly pushed their moms into it when the women were younger. Their dads did some shady Soviet Union-KGB psych-ops shite back there to protect their wives. If Maks doesn't kill Zef, then Zef will take it up the arse and be Maks's little bitch until one of the bratva or even the *Cosa Nostra* finally can't stand him and off him.

"I only just found out. I was about to tell Shane when Anton called, then you came home."

"What did Anton have to say?"

"He still wants to talk to me. He said Shane could come too. I wasn't interested."

"I'll deal with them. I'll make sure they leave you alone. I'm so glad I'm home, wee one. I missed you more than I even imagined."

And I did. I hate the part of my job that I did this week. The tracking people down. The beating confessions out of them. The trailing others and watching them. The bribery and extortion. I may be good at it, but it doesn't mean I enjoy it. Now that I have Greta in my life and am sharing a home with her, I doubly despise it. What a fucking waste when I could be with her.

"I feel the same. I know I'll survive while you're gone. I don't want you to fear I can't or that I'll become needy and demanding. But I still prefer being with you."

"You can demand away, *cailín*. Your wish is my command. I—"

I'm interrupted by pounding on my door and the doorbell buzzing over and over. What the fuck? Greta and I look at each other. I help her onto her feet, and she fixes her clothes to make herself presentable. We're coming out of the kitchen as Shane rushes downstairs.

"NYPD."

He announces it as he meets us in the foyer. What are

they doing here? They *never* come here. The way they're banging on my door sounds like they have their battering ram.

"Coming!" I call out then turn to Greta. "Go up to our bedroom. In the back of the closet, there's a little latch behind the clothes' rod. Press it. A door will open. There's a panic room there. Go."

She doesn't hesitate. She bolts for the stairs. I wait until she's out of sight and count to twenty. Then I walk to the door and open it.

"Dillan O'Rourke?"

"Micky, you know who I am."

What the fuck is Micky O'Toole doing standing on my stoop? The man is secretly close to a millionaire from how much we pay him.

"Is Margaret McDonnell here?"

"Why?"

"That isn't the answer to my question. Yes or no."

"Why?"

"Dillan—"

"I'm not obligated to answer your questions while you're on private property without a search warrant or a warrant for my arrest. But you are obligated to answer mine. Why?"

He pulls a piece of paper from his pocket, and as he does, he nods to the men and women with him. Shane and I can do nothing. We're pushed out of the way as officers flood my home. I'm not worried that they'll find anything. That's why I have a panic room. Anything that truly can never see the light of day is in there. The things I keep in the safe are there more to be protected from fire or to confuse law enforcement than to hide it. My computer is so fucking encrypted only the NSA or CIA could crack half the shite.

"What is going on?!"

I'm fucking enraged. I can't turn to look up the stairs in case any of them take that as a hint to where Greta is.

"I have a warrant for Mar—"

There's an earsplitting— heart wrenching, in my case — scream. I don't wait to hear what Micky has to say. He's here to arrest Greta, and they just found her. She must not have found the latch in time. I know where it is because I was there when Shane installed it after building the panic room. At least, his construction company did.

I take the stairs three at a time and get to the landing as two women drag a flailing and kicking Greta out of our bedroom. Two male officers follow them out.

"Dillan!"

There's a red mark on her face, and I see red.

"Get your motherfucking hands off my fiancée! Now."

I take a menacing step forward that makes both women stop. I don't know if it's my reputation, if it's that and hearing me call Greta my fiancée, or those two things and my expression. It could be any or all of them.

"I said let go of her. I won't say it a third time. You will do as I say."

There are few people in this city that can give a command like that and be obeyed by pretty much every cop on the force. Maksim, Salvatore, and Enrique are the only other ones. But my word carries even more weight since it's no secret how many Irish Americans are in the NYPD. If they aren't on my payroll or they don't have a family member who is, they've at least heard of me. Plenty of them insist they're true Irishmen when the only Irish thing about them is their last name and their corned beef on St. Patrick's Day.

This time, Greta doesn't hesitate to fling herself into my arms. I wrap mine around her for a moment, then I push her back. I cup her jaw and whisper.

"Which one did this?"

Her eyes widen in terror. She's never seen this look in my eyes. She knows what it means. I can tell she's scared on the man's behalf. But the longer I keep my gaze locked with hers, the more she knows she can't keep this from me.

"The one on the left."

I look over her shoulder at the man. I say nothing. I don't even show any emotion on my face. It's all in my eyes. He knows. He knows it won't be today or tomorrow or even next week or next month. But he knows his death is coming. He knows I will make him live in fear. Toy with him until I'm ready. Then it will be painful. That's my reputation, and it isn't built on myth.

The officer on the right decides to show he has some balls. Ones I'll cut off and shove down his throat.

"Let go of our suspect. You're interfering with police business."

I shift my gaze to him, casting my eyes up and down. I let him see how unimpressed I am. The two women have wisely remained quiet and out of the way. I lead Greta downstairs to where Shane is still waiting with Micky. He and I are both wearing suits, and he and I both have guns holstered at our lower backs with knives in our pockets. But no one has patted either of us down. He and I won't be pulling our guns when we're this outnumbered, but I will if it's Greta's life at stake.

"Let me see the warrant."

Micky hands it to me, but he doesn't meet my gaze. He's looking between Shane and me, toward the living room windows. I unfold the paper with one hand while my arm remains wrapped around Greta. It has the time and place on it, which makes me look back at the top of the document. It's not really NYPD here to arrest Greta. I look out the still open door.

"Mr. O'Rourke, let go of our suspect."

Mason Spiegel climbs the last step before walking through my front door. I ignore him and look back at the warrant. The charges are listed, and there are plenty. They're ridiculous, but they're printed right there in front of my eyes.

The list starts with providing false information to acquire firearms illegally. Owning unlicensed firearms. Carrying the illegally purchased firearms across state lines with the intent to sell— that's for a pistol. Purchasing firearms on behalf of another person. It lists the other weapons as machine guns and weapons over fifty calibers. But here's where they are really building the federal case. They don't name me specifically, but it charges her with trafficking guns for the O'Rourke Organized Crime Group.

Fancy.

We simply go by the mob.

They are trying to bring me down by going through her. They want to back me into a corner and expect me to give myself up for her. I will if I have to. But I'll take every motherfucker in the ATF, FBI, and NYPD down with me. I can only see ATF agents out there, but knowing what I do about Spiegel, I'm certain the FBI is waiting in the wings.

I thrust the warrant back at Micky and look at Mason.

"What's the probable cause? You have a warrant for Ms. McDonnell's arrest. You did not provide a warrant to search my home. There's no emergency here where I'm incapable of giving consent, so you've violated my rights. You're awfully young to retire. I hope you've saved enough."

"We searched Ms. McDonnell's residence and found the stockpile of weapons."

Greta remains silent, but I see her eyes widen from the corner of mine. She twisted enough in my arms, so she could read the warrant while I did. Now I can see her face more easily than when she stood directly beside me.

Micky pulls handcuffs from his belt and steps forward. "Margaret McDonnell, you have the right to remain silent..."

I've heard the Miranda rights enough times to repeat them in my sleep. The NYPD has only arrested me a handful of times, and not since I was a teenager. But I've been around plenty of people who have been.

"I accompany my client in one of your SUVs. You will not question her without me present."

"You can't be her lawyer." Mason practically spits the words at me. I raise both eyebrows, waiting for him to give some ridiculous explanation that won't matter. "You're sleeping with her."

"How do you know that?"

Greta goes rigid beside me. But Mason will have to admit spying on her if he gives any concrete evidence that he's speaking from more than speculation.

"You're engaged."

"And I'm Catholic. We're not married."

Utterly laughable what I imply, but I didn't lie to federal or local law enforcement when I said that. But Spiegel gave me the opening I really need.

"And yes, we are engaged, which means my romantic relationship with Ms. McDonnell predates my time as her attorney. It isn't a breach of conduct to have a romantic and/or physical relationship with a client if it began before the time when the professional relationship began. I can pull up the ABA guidelines if you want. I have it bookmarked on my browser."

You better believe I have that shite nearly memorized. I know exactly how far I can skirt the law and the codes of conduct to keep from being disbarred. I turn to Shane.

"Call Cormac and Seamus."

Cormac specializes in criminal law, and Seamus specializes

in corporate. We all know how the federal legal system works. The common denominator is no agency wants the three of us walking in together to defend one suspect.

I don't stop Micky when he eases Greta away from me because he's gentle when he takes her arm. I know he's handling her with kid gloves because I'm watching his every muscle twitch. He draws her hands behind her back as she watches me. I hope she can read the reassurance in my eyes. I follow Mason, Micky, and Greta out of the brownstone and down to the street. I can hear Shane issuing orders to the NYPD to get out. He'll deal with my place, and he'll get our cousins down to Manhattan Central Booking. They did that on purpose. They want to intimidate the shite out of Greta. They want to make it seem as bad as it can possibly be. They're going to toss her in gen pop while her paperwork processes. They're going to try to keep her overnight.

Micky's careful as he helps her into one of the NYPD SUVs. I wait until he steps back before I get close enough to lock eyes with him. He mumbles, but I understand him.

"My girls."

He has three daughters. Three, five, and eight. His wife died of ovarian cancer a year ago. Spiegel has something on him. If that's the case, I can't blame him for doing what he has to, to protect his family. I dip my chin, then I shift to watch Mason walk to a black SUV.

"Should I call Director Hollands at his office or at home?"

The ATF fuck face whirls on his heels. Rage pulsates off him. Good. He understood the mob threat.

"Well, which one?" I pull out my cell phone and unlock it. Then I hold it up so he can see I pulled up my contacts. He stalks back over to me.

"You don't need to call the FBI. They're already here." He points down the street.

"I'm not interested in getting the FBI involved. I'm interested in getting Hollands involved."

We stare at each other, and he realizes I more than know about their affair in passing. He knows I know all the sordid details. I made sure I do.

"Fuck you, you Irish piece of shit."

"And I was thinking I should be hospitable and invite the Director over for a glass of whiskey. But pieces of shite don't have the good graces to do that. No. We fling muck and make sure it sticks. Does your wife have a good dry cleaner?"

I don't wait for his response. I slip into the vehicle beside Greta. If we were in one of my town cars, I would pull her onto my lap and hold her. If we were in one of them, and she had handcuffs on, it would be because I'm about to fuck her senseless. Instead, I rest my hand on her thigh. She knows enough to remain silent the entire way to Central Booking. I escort her in, but they separate us immediately.

The next three hours are excruciating. They're keeping us apart intentionally, even after they do the initial paperwork and fingerprinting. I have no way of knowing what's happening to Greta. She should have her hands free, but some sadistic piece of shite could have put her in a holding cell with a dozen other women with her hands still cuffed behind her back. They will have stripped her and searched her, then forced her to wear a jumpsuit. All of her possessions will be in bags. They didn't take her purse because Shane texted to say it was still at the house, so they don't have her ID. I slipped her phone out of her yoga pants' thigh pocket before we got here. I have it in my left breast pocket.

Cormac and Seamus are sitting on each side of me in an interrogation room while we wait. They said they'd bring her in five minutes ago. They got tired of us drawing so much attention in the waiting room. It was scaring people. Not being in the NYPD holding center to see whomever they're here to see. It's three mobsters glaring at everyone in uniform. People are demanding and yelling just so they can finish what they're doing and get away from us. If Finn were here, we could be the Four Horsemen of the Apocalypse the way everyone acts.

The door opens, and a female officer steps in with Greta following her. Another woman walks behind *mo cailín*. My little girl. That's what she is. She's not a child, nor do I think of her at younger than she is. But she is mine to love and take care of. Seeing her in the orange jumpsuit with a bruise on her face from where the officer slapped her makes me feel like a greater failure than I ever have. She's here because she's with me.

"*Ar ghortaigh aon duine eile thú, mo ghrá?*" Did anyone else hurt you, my love?

"*Níl.*" No.

I want to demand to know whether they gave her any ice to take down the swelling, but I know they didn't. The officer who led them in guides her to a chair. She attaches Greta's handcuffs to a set that's attached to a bar on top of the table.

"Really?"

The officer doesn't answer me, so I look at the two-way mirror, knowing there are people watching us. They're going to keep her chained to a table like she's the threat in this room. I don't know who's there, but I will in a minute. They won't keep us waiting now that she's in here.

Sure as shite. The moment the door opens to let the female officers out, two detectives walk in. I know them too. They look far less than thrilled to be here. I know we're being recorded since I immediately spotted the camera in the corner, mounted to the ceiling. The red light was flashing before we came in. They wanted to record my cousins and me, and they wanted to record how I reacted to her coming in.

"Ms. McDonnell, I'm Detective Fleishman, and this is my partner, Detective Monahan."

She does nothing. She doesn't dip her chin. She doesn't say anything. She doesn't even acknowledge they entered the room. She's watching me.

"We have some questions to ask you."

She still doesn't look at either of them. She doesn't need to. She can see their faces in the reflection. She just keeps looking at me.

"Ms. McDonnell, what's the nature of your relationship with Dillan O'Rourke?"

It's as though no one spoke. She doesn't register hearing anything. Her expression is so remote I'm wondering if more happened than I know. Has she completely shut down? Has she retreated so far into her mind that she doesn't hear anyone?

"*Is féidir leat é sin a fhreagairt go fírinneach.*" You can answer that truthfully.

"*Tá sé de cheart agam fanacht ina thost, mar sin táim chun.*" I have the right to remain silent, so I'm going to.

"Ms. McDonnell, we are conducting this interview in English. Please respond to the questions in English."

"She doesn't have to. She has every right to use a preferred language, and she's chosen Irish Gaelic."

"You're her legal counsel. You can't be her interpreter."

"Any Mr. O'Rourke can. Only I'm listed as her lawyer on the intake form."

"They're your co-counsel, or they wouldn't be here." Fleishman isn't a happy camper. I shrug.

"She's invoked her Miranda rights. She doesn't have to say anything."

Monahan taps in when Fleishman sits back in annoyance. "If she has nothing to hide, then why not tell us?"

Cormac snorts and leans forward. "If she has nothing to

hide, then she has nothing to say. We don't need our criminal justice degree to do basic logic."

I look over at Cormac in surprise.

"Oh, yes. Billy and I were classmates at John Jay. We took forensic psychology together. I believe the professor caught you trying to cheat off my final exam our senior year. If you didn't already have enough credits, you wouldn't have graduated on time. And here you are, a law enforcement officer who violated conduct ethics. Hmm."

I shift my gaze back to Billy, who looks ready to lunge across the table at Cormac. He can try. Even without cameras on, he wouldn't. My cousin is twice his size, and Billy Monahan isn't a skinny guy. He hasn't been since we were thirteen, and he gained like forty pounds in one semester. I didn't know where he went to college, though. I'd heard he was on the force, but I haven't seen him in at least a decade. It wasn't hard to recognize him.

This isn't amusing Fleishman. He snaps at us. "Can we get back on track?"

It's Seamus's turn to pipe in. "What track are we supposed to be on? The train isn't coming into the station. Our client has invoked her right to remain silent. There's no point in waiting around for something that won't happen. Why haven't you sent anything to the DA?"

Fleishman's a fucking idiot. "What makes you think we're holding anything back?"

"Because my second cousin's wife is a clerk there, and nothing has come in. That means you're either holding onto it to force Ms. McDonnell to remain in your custody, or you have nothing to file. My money is on the latter. You convinced Judge Hartman to issue the warrant because the man lives and breathes to harass our family. But now you have nothing because there is nothing."

Judge Herman Hartman has a hard on for trying to catch anyone affiliated with a syndicate. Except the dumbass always bets on the losing horse. He issues the search and arrest warrants because he takes money under the table. Then they never come to fruition. Either there's nothing to find, or we're so slick they can't even catch us. He does this to all of us. All the apex predators. My family, the Mancinellis, the Kutsenkos, and the Diazes. He goes after some of the smaller fish, and sometimes he gets a nibble. But one of these days, he's going to wake up to find himself the prey.

Billy turns back to Greta and tries again. "Ms. McDonnell, we know you don't want to be here. We don't want to keep you here. Answer our questions, and we may be able to let you go."

She finally turns to look in the detectives' direction. The look she gives Billy screams she thinks he's too stupid to live. He is. He'll regret having anything to do with this case. He knows who we are. He should have gotten himself far, far away rather than walk in here. He's done nothing to help Greta, so to me, that's enough to put him on my list of people to blame.

"Dá mbeadh na hairm sin go léir agam agus má chuardaigh siad m'áit cheana féin, cén fáth a ndéarfadh siad go bhféadfainn dul dá gcuirfinn freagra ar a gcuid ceisteanna?" If I had all those weapons and they've already searched my place, then why would they say I could go if I answer their questions?

"Chun trick tú." To trick you.

That sounds enough like English to make the two detectives uneasy. I know Billy doesn't speak Irish, so I'm not worried when Greta and I continue in it. She's watching them now as she speaks to me.

"I'm spending the night here, aren't I?"

"Probably. I'm so sorry."

"Don't apologize for other people's stupidity."

She turns her head to look at me, and the resoluteness in

her gaze reminds me of why I know she'll be perfect alongside me as my wife. She gives nothing away, but when they translate the audio recording, they'll know she's not ignorant of what's going on. That makes her far more dangerous than they realize. If she was willing to take on my family and me, they've sorely underestimated her.

Cormac's phone buzzes, so he steps out. It must be important for him to take it. It makes me wonder who it is and whether it's about this or some other shitstorm brewing. No one speaks since there's nothing more to say. When Cormac returns, he glances at Greta, then looks at me and nods. He's set things up to ensure she's safe while she's here. Billy shifts in his seat, and I realize he did it to catch my attention. His eyes shift sideways toward his partner before he raises his right eyebrow. Then his chin dips. He looks over at Cormac, then back to me.

Ahh. He was stalling, and he's the one who made sure there are guards and women in place to protect Greta once she's in her cell for the night. Whoever he had taking care of this called Cormac. Billy pushes back his chair.

"Ms. McDonnell, if you aren't willing to cooperate, then we have nothing more to say. Officers will take you to your cell. Dinner's at seven and lights out at ten. Sleep well."

Fleishman stands too. Greta cracks a smile as the second detective rises. Fuck me. What's coming now?

Chapter Twenty-Six

Greta

"Drew, who're you going to ask to leak this story since you obviously can't ask me?"

All five men stare at me, but I don't take my eyes off Drew Fleishman. I've remained silent because I didn't want to answer their questions. It didn't mean I don't want to ask my own. I make sure I speak loudly and clearly. I'm certain this entire dud of an interrogation is being recorded. I saw the red light on the camera, and I know they record the audio too. I twist to look straight at the two-way mirror. I keep my expression neutral, but let whoever's watching see me now that I left that little bomb dangling.

Dillan sounds somewhere between shocked and angry when he speaks to me.

"*Tá aithne agat air?*" You know him.

"*Sea. Tá sé ina fhoinse istigh agam ó thosaigh mé ag an bpáipéar. Rinneamar dhá mhí ar an dáta, ansin dhumpáil mé air. Ach táimid fós úsáideach dá chéile.*" Yeah. He's been my inside source since I started at the paper. We dated for two months, then I dumped him. But we remain useful to one another.

If it didn't piss Dillan off before to find an Irish American cop in front of us who went to school with Cormac, he's definitely pissed now. I'm pissed too. I don't bother lowering my voice because I want this part clearly translated.

"*Tá sé cac sa leaba.*" He's shit in bed.

That's no lie. I wanted to like him, but he was boring. I could have overlooked that since he's attractive, but he couldn't fuck his way out of a whorehouse. It makes Dillan, Seamus, and Cormac laugh. Billy sounds like he nearly chokes. I'm certain he isn't a fluent Gaelic speaker or Dillan would have let me know. But it's not a hard sentence to understand.

"What? What'd she say?" Drew demands to know, looking at all four guys then at me. When he narrows his eyes and leans forward, my three guys shoot out of their seats. Dillan puts his hands on the table and leans toward Drew, so he blocks me from the douche. He says nothing, but that's far more intimidating. Drew backs off. At least he got one thing right.

Drew and Billy leave without a backwards glance, and that's fine by me. I suck in a deep breath and steel myself for what's coming next. They're going to separate me from my avenging angels.

"Turn it off. I want to speak to my client." Dillan's looking at the mirror, but I'm looking up at the camera. The light goes off, but no one says anything until they've pulled their chairs close to me. It's Cormac who speaks first.

"Billy put things in place. There are three women guards who'll watch out for you. There will be one outside the cell anytime you're in there. Turns out we have three women in here right now for possession, drunk driving, and forgery. None of them are bad people. They just make shite choices. They'll keep you safe in the cell. Stick with them."

He pulls out his phone and shows me three pictures, telling me each woman's name. He's just finished when the same two female cops come back. They unfasten me from the table, and I turn to Dillan. He glowers at them, and they back off. Then he pulls me into his arms. He kisses me, and it'll be enough to sustain me until I see him again. Hopefully, that'll be in the morning.

I'm sandwiched between the women as they lead me out. I don't look back since I know people are watching us. I lift my chin with as much arrogance as I can muster. Let these fuckers see me. They know who I am. I'm Dillan O'Rourke's woman.

Ally, the drunk driver, Stace, the one in for possession, and Lily, the one in for forgery, all look out for me. I get to the cell that's probably fifteen by twenty and overflowing with women. Ally introduces herself and leads me over to a cramped spot on the floor where the two other women make room for me to sit with them. I wonder why they're on the floor. Why wouldn't they want a spot on a bench? The floor is— if I think about it, I'll be sick. The entire place stinks of piss. Like they hang piss-scented air fresheners or pipe the scent of piss in. It's overwhelming. The only reprieve is a whiff of someone's B.O.

Stace explains it to me without me having to ask. We're all keeping our voices hushed. "The benches are horrible to try to sleep on. You're better off trying to catch a couple hours on the floor. Tomorrow's going to be a long day for you. Do you know what to expect?"

"I know what's going to happen. I'm not so sure I know what to expect. They'll cuff us together like a chain gang, and we'll go over to another holding cell they call a waiting room. Our attorneys will discuss what's happening while we wait to be called for arraignment. Some people will plea out and pay fines, then go free. Others will be there until they get moved somewhere pending trial."

Ally offers me a smile that's more like she's going to explain something to the village idiot than offer me sympathy. "We know you're Dillan's woman, but you may go nowhere in the morning. They may keep you here. Or you could go over there, but they won't let you see your attorney for a couple days. Just because you're with Dillan doesn't mean there's a guarantee they'll process you faster. The opposite is more likely. They'll keep you here to punish you and Dillan."

"I thought they couldn't hold anyone for more than thirty-six hours."

All three of them now give me that same smile. Lily shakes her head.

"Due process ended at the door. What's anyone in here going to do? Most of us are waiting for an overworked, under-paid public defender who couldn't give a shit beyond making it through the day without pissing someone off so badly that they get shanked. I've already been here thirty-eight hours, and that's just in this cell. Who knows how long I'll stay here or the holding cell in the courthouse? Ya know, it is New York. The dockets are awfully full."

She says it with mocking sarcasm as though she's heard that plenty of times from someone with authority. It makes me look around at the other people here. Short of the uber wealthy, there are all walks of life here. That makes me wonder how the rich get arrested. What would happen to Dillan? He's got more money than most, but because of his position, this might be the exact place they'd love to toss him if it were filled with men.

Well, fuck. The women would love it if he were tossed in

here. It would be a fucking feeding frenzy. Because he's so wealthy, would that buy him better accommodations? If I get arrested after we get married, would I get better ones? That's a question I didn't imagine I'd ask myself two weeks ago.

PB and J sandwiches for dinner then dry cereal for breakfast. The night stretched forever with way more sounds than I'd like to examine, and this morning has been little better. It's nearly eight-thirty, so if they're going to take me to be arraigned, then I'll be doing the perp walk shortly. I remember what Lily explained to me last night. Just because I get out of here doesn't mean I'll be getting out of lock-up anytime soon.

"What're you looking at, cunt?"

I don't realize the woman near the metal bars is talking to me. I was looking in her direction, but not at her. She only came in an hour or so ago. She's been eyeing me, but I hadn't acknowledged her. I guess she's tired of being ignored. She pushes away from the sliding door and walks the short distance to where Ally, Lily, Stace, and I are still sitting. The female guard calls out to the bitch.

"Dolores, back off."

Dolores flicks the officer off over her shoulder. She keeps approaching. I ignore her. Ally and the other two women shift to block me, but this bitch could knock all three of them out with her flabby underarms waving around like fucking sails. I'm feeling a bit more than just pissy right now. I'm tired. I'm dirty. And I'm fucking scared.

Dolores tries to reach between Ally and Stace to get to me, but they both stand faster than I expected. Lily's inching away, but I realize she's getting around Dolores before coming to her feet behind the woman. Ally gets in front of me and in Dolores's face as I stand, too.

"Do you know who she is?"

"Yeah. She's fucking Dillan O'Rourke. Big fucking deal."

"If you know that, then you're stupid to get in her face."

"You ain't paying me to stay out of it. But I am getting paid to get in it. Move."

Dolores tries to push Ally out of the way, but the girl's sturdier than she looks. Ally puts both hands on Dolores's chest and shoves her hard. The bigger woman stumbles back a step, but not before she takes a swing. She misses Ally, but she nearly hits Stace, who is having none of it. Stace's nails claw down the side of Dolores's face, leaving trails of blood. When Dolores takes another swing, this time aiming at Stace, I reach out and grab her fist. My other hand wraps around her wrist and squeezes as hard as I can. I push my weight toward her with a wide step forward. It allows me to get her arm behind her back. I take Lily's spot and yank the cunt's arm straight up behind her. She bellows in pain. I kick the back of her knee, and she goes to the ground. I follow her down with my knee on her cheek. I grind my bone against her bone, and she whimpers.

"Who the fuck sent you?"

Dolores tries to fight to get me off, but my weight is practically crushing her face, and I have her arm still pinned behind her back.

"Who the fuck sent you?"

I ease my weight off her just enough to be sure she can speak. I can't understand when she does, so I grab a handful of her hair as I take my knee off her cheek. I lift her head, but I'm poised to smash it face first if she doesn't cooperate. I hear guards yelling, and other women are placing imaginary bets. I hear the metal door rattle, and I know it's going to open soon. I lean as close as I dare and whisper to her.

"Answer me, or I will make sure the only way you leave here is in a body bag. If you know I'm Dillan O'Rourke's woman, then you should ask yourself just what kind of person I am." I drop my voice even lower. "I'll motherfucking kill you, then have tea with my granny."

Something about me makes her realize I'm not joking. If it's her or me in a fight, I'm fucking picking me. I'll snap her goddamn neck if I have to.

"Zef."

I let go of her arm as the door slides open. But I take the opportunity to drive my foot into her mouth. She screams, and I laugh. At least, I look like I am. I don't make a sound. They're probably recording video and audio for this whole place.

I put my hands up and back away. They uncuffed us all just before dinner, and they haven't put them back on yet. They must know this means fights'll break out. But it doesn't stop them from leaving us free to move our arms.

"You all right, Ms. McDonnell?"

I look to my right as the female guard who was outside the cell approaches me.

"Yeah. I'd like to see my lawyer."

No one was eager to fulfill my request, so I've been waiting in the holding cell in the courthouse for twelve hours. It was a short walk with the rest of the chain gang, and this place smells just as bad as the cell in Central Booking. Really, the only difference is that it's noisier and even more crowded. Clients sob to or argue with their attorneys seated at the tables in the middle of the large cement room. Those of us with no one to meet with are relegated to benches against the wall or standing around. It's boring as fuck. I like people watching, but this sucks ass.

I've been in custody for nearly twenty-four hours now. Two more people have tried to pick fights with me on the walk over, but I think only Dolores was sent for me. Guards intervened much faster, and I heard Dillan's name whispered among them as they broke up each encounter. One guard got me a space on a bench and has been hanging out near me, one hand on his gun. I guess I'm untouchable in here.

Each time I hear Dillan's name, I wonder how he's doing. He's probably ready to burn the city down. He's a man who craves control because so much of his life is beyond his. This is his worst nightmare. It's the ultimate reminder that try as he might, not everyone and everything will bend to his will. All he's wanted is to protect me and take care of me. He's going to feel like a failure, and I hate that because he isn't. None of this is his fault.

"Margaret McDonnell!"

I look up at the sound of my name. I see Dillan across the room as though I conjured him with my thoughts. I get up, and the guard nods to me. He leads me over, and two more fall in behind me. I have a personal escort. I'm not sure if people think I need the protection from everyone in the room or if everyone in the room needs protection from me. I think anyone who recognizes Dillan believes it's the latter.

"*Cailín.*"

Dillan hugs me, and I sigh. But I pull away and whisper.

"I'm gross, Daddy."

"You're the most beautiful sight I've ever seen. Let's go home."

I look around, and my brow furrows. "What about my arraignment?"

"They dropped the charges."

I look at him for a long moment before I sweep my gaze around the room. I spot Stace, who was the only one of the three to walk over with me.

"What can you do for Stace, Lily, and Ally? They really helped me out last night and this morning."

"I heard. All three of them will be out within the hour."

"You heard?"

"Of course. When your fiancée knocks four teeth out of a biker bitch while in Central Booking, people make sure you hear about it fast."

Fiancée. He's not saying it because people are listening. He could call me his girlfriend or even his woman. Misogynistic as that term is, I gotta admit I enjoy hearing him call me that. I feel cherished. He's just the right amount possessive. But I can tell from the exhaustion in his eyes he doesn't feel like he's been the right amount protective.

"When we leave, could we stop by Finn's? I know it's not that much farther to get to Brooklyn, but I really want a shower."

We're at the Manhattan Central Booking, so we're near Soho. Only a few blocks. I know we could get into Brooklyn without much of a drive, but I just feel so fucking disgusting.

"I already planned for it. I have fresh clothes waiting for you in the car. Finn knows we're coming."

"Thank you, Daddy."

We have to sign shit, and I get my clothes back. I'm glad to get out of the jumpsuit and stupid shoes that don't fit. It's not until we're outside that we really kiss. I still feel disgusting, but it's like it breathes life back into me. He kisses my forehead over and over once we pull apart to catch our breath. I have my left cheek pressed against his chest. I can see my breath, but I can also feel the heat coming through his shirt. I hear his heart beating, and I instantly calm.

"You're safe now, baby. Let's go."

I let him guide me to the town car, and I smile at Joey. He nods to me, and that's about as much happiness as I'll get out of him. But just as I'm about to bend to get in, he winks at me. I hear Dillan growl. That just makes me laugh as I scoot in. The moment the door closes, he's lifting me onto his lap. He nuzzles my neck, then he's resting his head against my chest. I stroke his hair as I feel him shudder.

"I'm so sorry, Greta. So, so sorry. Please don't—"

His voice catches. I lean back and cup his jaw with both hands.

"Dillan, I am not going anywhere. You may not have officially proposed, so I will. Will you marry me?"

"I am going to marry you, but you did not propose."

"I'm pretty sure I did."

"How about we have a few hours between you getting out of lock up because of me and you pledging your life to me?"

"Why? Do you think I'm asking because I'm so grateful to be free? Am I asking so I won't have to go back there if I'm your wife? Do you think I'm delusional from lack of sleep?"

"No. But I think it was something traumatic, and I'd rather our engagement not start on the tail end of your being tossed into jail for nearly twenty-four hours because of me."

I look at him, and I realize how pointless this argument is. There is nothing to be gained over arguing about who's proposing to who. The bigger issue is what he's telling me, not what he won't agree to.

"Dillan, I do not blame you for this. It wasn't your fault. Zef had a woman inside."

"What was the woman's name?"

"Dolores something. I don't know. She knew who I was, but I didn't know who she was. But I kicked some of her teeth out."

"You really did that? I heard there was some altercation with a biker, but I thought the guard was exaggerating."

"Yeah. Stace, Lily, and Ally tried to defend me. She went after them too, so I blocked a punch. Then I grabbed her arm, twisted it behind her back, kicked her knee, and when she landed on the ground, I put my knee on her cheek. She finally admitted it was Zef who sent her after me. When I stood up, I kicked her as hard as I could in the mouth. Last I saw was blood coming out of her mouth and some teeth on the floor. They got me out of there soon after that, but then I had twelve hours in the courthouse holding cell."

He sighs and looks out the window. "I can't do anything about her because she's a woman. At least, I can't personally. I'll make sure some guards make it clear that when she gets out, she stays away from you. I can't do what I wanted to Zef because there's more at play. But I called Maks this morning. He was pretty fucking pissed at hearing Zef's doing business in Miami. I followed your lead and gave Maks a shit ton of information about what Zef's been investing in down there. Maks will deal with him one way or another."

There's nothing more for me to say. I can't ask questions because he won't answer them. Rather than put him in a position to lie or just go silent, I opt to leave it alone. I sit back against him, still feeling disgusting in my clothes when he's in a fresh suit. But he tightens his arms around me, and I know he needs this as much as I do.

It's not long before we reach Finn's, since it's only a few blocks. Though in Manhattan, a few blocks can take thirty minutes. We head up in the elevator to the penthouse. The loft is a converted warehouse. I can tell there's been a lot of work done to make it a luxury condo building. We walk down the hall, and Dillan unlocks the door.

"Finn?"

"Yeah. I'm just leaving."

He appears from a room across the loft. The place is enormous for a single floor. It must be at least three thousand square feet. It surprises me to see how many books he has. There're at least two bookshelves that look like they must have antique collections. There are others with books on various places around the world. Some look like coffee table books, and others look like travel guides. There's a bookshelf that appears to have textbooks that all look finance and accounting related or software design. He has a massive sectional that screams "take a nap on me" or "watch a movie here." His TV is practically a theatre screen. I look over at Dillan.

"We like rugby."

My brow furrows, then I look back at the TV. I bet it's like being on the field when you're watching sports. The kitchen is completely gourmet. The stove has eight burners from what I can see, and there are two ovens. One beneath the stove and one in the wall. The fridge looks nearly industrial.

"Finn's the best cook of all of us. We may conduct business at our place, but we eat here."

"Yeah. You owe me at least ten pounds of steak. Don't think I forgot."

Finn walks into the living room and looks me over. He offers me a loose hug and a kiss on the cheek.

"Are you all right? Who did that to your cheek? Was it a guard?"

His rapid-fire questions surprise me. He sounds like he's ready to ride into battle in my defense. It's so different from a couple weeks ago when he clearly didn't trust me and didn't want me around his cousin.

"No. It's from the cop at our place. But some chick Zef sent thought she could intimidate me because she's bigger than me. She's going to need a set of false teeth now."

"You punched her teeth out?"

"I wish. That would have been something to brag about. I kicked her."

I can't imagine packing the strength needed to use my fist to do that kind of damage. But considering who I'm talking to, I suppose it would be the most obvious way to do it.

"Good. There's everything you should need in the guest bathroom in the room to the right. I just double-checked. If there's anything else you need, tell Dillan. He knows where everything is. Use whatever you want. You're probably starving. The fridge is full, so take what you fancy."

"Thank you, Finn. I really appreciate it. I'm sorry if we're chasing you out of your place."

"You aren't. I have a meeting." He says nothing more than that, so I just nod. I look toward the bedroom, then at Dillan.

"Go on. I'll be in there in a few minutes. I want to talk to Finn about something."

Chapter Twenty-Seven

Dillan

"Finn, I want Spiegel on a fucking platter. He put Greta in there. I want a fucking apple in his mouth and him speared on a skewer. Then his roasted arse on a platter I can serve to motherfucking Hollands."

"I know. I'm working on it. I have the information we need about the Rizzos and Grassos. I'm finalizing the deal to get the supplies the Grassos need for the meth. Once that's in place, I'll make sure Enzo's the one who has to deal with it."

"But I want the heat on Marco. Get Spiegel off my arse and Greta's."

"How much are you willing to pay?"

"Jack shite. Tell Spiegel if he'd like to keep his marriage and his job, then he'll cooperate. If he wants Hollands dick up his arse or the other way around ever again, then he'll do as he's told when he's told. Otherwise, he won't be talking to you in private. He'll be talking to my motherfucking brass knuckles."

"The shite with Enzo's going to take some maneuvering.

With Luca, Carmine, Gabriele, and Matteo now married, Enzo's the most likely to go. If we're really lucky, then it will be Marco. But it shouldn't be too hard to make the Rizzos think they can make a move against Salvatore on the sly. They still think Luca nearly marrying the don's daughter bought them some peace."

"Dumb shite. All that did was cause them no end of trouble. Now they have Salvatore watching every breath they take, and Niko's ready to launch a full-scale attack if a single one of them leaves their time zone."

"You know that. I know that. We all know that here, but they think they matter. They're in the middle of the country in some city that believes because it produced Al Capone it can compete at our level. Fucking chumps."

"Let me know what happens. I need to speak to Maks to make sure Zef's dealt with like he promised. I want to do it now while Greta's in the shower."

"I'll get out of here."

"Where are we with the DEA and the Diazes? Does our contact know Enrique's trying to take over Zef's deal with Espinoza?"

We're going to have to let our potential profit go. But I can live with that, knowing it's going to fuck over the Colombian Cartel.

"Yeah. I took care of that last night."

"Good. I wanted that carfentanil, but if we can't have it, then let Enrique take the fall for it."

"We could always plant it on Misha and Pasha for what they did with our legal imports."

"No. I'm doing Maks a solid by telling him about Zef. I'd rather they owe me than go tit-for-tat right now. Where are Sean and Shane?"

"They're on their way to New Mexico in the jet. They're

going to intercept the shipment to make sure Espinoza knows we control the terms of their deals. They'll make sure we get the next shipment and send it up to Canada. Then they'll make sure Espinoza gets on the phone with Enrique."

"Good. Drop a hint to Marco, but let him think he's stumbled upon a possibility. I'm not ready for him to know yet. Not until we're certain we have Spiegel on track to bust him. I know it goes without saying, but make sure your brothers know not to be within a fucking mile of that carfentanil without a gas mask and a full-on biohazard suit."

"I'll let them know you care. If you need anything, call or text."

"I'm going to take Greta home once she's cleaned up. We'll go from there."

I watch my cousin walk out of his place. As I look around, it strikes me for at least the trillionth time how fortunate I am to have the family I do. Yeah. We have fucked-up lives. We do majorly fucked-up things. But if I had to be born into a mob family, I'm glad I was born into mine. Not everyone in mob families is as fortunate. The organization always comes ahead of all else. But the only way we can do that is by putting family first.

I pull out my phone and dial Maks. It rings three times, and I wonder if he's considering sending me to voicemail. When he finally answers, it's with a wailing toddler in the background.

"Konstantin, you're all right. Your sister will give it back when she's done. Mila, be nice to your brother. Hello."

"Domestic tranquility suits you, Maks."

"Fuck you."

"Not unless you buy me dinner first."

"What do you want? The twins are ready for their naps and are getting fussy. Unless you want Laura calling you to know why I'm late putting them down, speak fast."

"You know what we discussed earlier about our micro dick friend. I found out he set someone up to be in Central when Greta was there. She went after Greta with a warning Zef isn't done with her."

"Is Greta all right?"

"Yeah. She's fine, but that woman isn't. Dolores someone or other."

"Dolores Dervishi?"

"Maybe. I don't know anyone named Dolores."

"Biker chick type?"

"Probably considering the woman was ready to go up against Greta and three of our women I knew were there last night."

"Yeah, that's her. She's Zef's cousin-in-law. She's dangerous, Dill. If she's set her sights on Greta, watch her. She's not quick to forgive."

"Thanks. Do you want Zef for sure?"

"Yeah. He still serves a purpose."

"To you he does, Maks. If he comes near me or my family, I'll stop him for good."

We run radio jammers and regularly sweep for bugs in our places. All the other syndicates do the same. But we're still cautious when we discuss anything. We never know if one of the other families is taping us. I hear a toddler voice asking for Papa.

"I'll let you go. I'm giving you Zef as a courtesy. The moment he stops being useful..."

"I know. I know."

We say our goodbyes and hang up. That's about the most normal conversation we've had since we were in high school and played soccer on the same team. We were fucking co-captains together. We'd already stabbed each other a couple times and shot each other once by senior year. But for the sake of the team and our competitive natures, we could get along well enough to lead our team to state champion. The day after, we nearly put each other in the hospital. It was just a friendly reminder that we aren't actually friends.

I head into the bedroom just as the shower turns off. I walk into the bathroom and pull a towel off the rail. Greta jumps when she pushes back the curtain and finds me there. I open the towel to her, and she steps into it.

"I wanted to join you, *mo ghrá*, but you finished faster than I could take care of a call."

"That's fine. I really just wanted to scrub myself clean. Maybe a bath tomorrow night."

"Definitely."

She has no idea what I have planned.

✳

Greta and I went back to the brownstone, and she passed out for nearly fourteen hours. I got nervous and called my mom. She told me not to dare disturb her. It was obvious she needed the sleep. Then she proceeded to be an absolute Irish mother and sent my da over with Irish pasties, which are sort of like the old McDonald's apple pies, but with beef, potatoes, and gravy in them instead. She also sent fish pie, which would be called a casserole by most Americans, colcannon— mashed potatoes, cabbage, scallions, with about a gallon of Irish cream. To finish it all off, there was apple cake. Stick to your ribs food as Nana used to call it.

"Dillan, I truly cannot eat another bite. I'm so full. If I eat any more, I won't have room for dinner with my parents."

I know we can't put it off any longer, but I'm not exactly enthused to meet her parents the evening after she was in jail. We've already discussed how to handle it, but there is no way this is going to go over well. We don't want to avoid it because it's inevitable it will come up somehow.

"What do you want to do?"

She grins and gets up from the table. She dashes to the stairs, and I'm hot on her heels. She was so tired last night, and I was so relieved to have her in bed beside me that I just held her while we slept. Now she's laughing as she gets to the bedroom just before me. I could have caught her, but she's giggling, and I love the sound of it. But I realize my mistake when she closes the door on me and locks it.

"Wee one." I infuse warning into my voice, and all I hear is another laugh.

"Patience is a virtue, my love. Give me a moment."

I hear movement through the door, but I have no idea what to make of it. I hear packaging opening, then it sounds like she's assembling something. It goes quiet for a couple minutes. The anticipation is nearly killing me. This is better than every Christmas I've ever had.

"Daddy, I'm unlocking the door. You need to count to twenty— slowly —before you come in. If you don't do it, I won't let you play. You'll have to watch me."

"Are you giving me orders, *cailín?*"

"Yes!"

I hear the door unlock. I put my ear to the door as I count.

"Eighteen, nineteen, twenty. Ready or not, here I come."

I open the door, and the sight that meets me assures me I'm going to come. Jesus, Mary, and Joseph. I kick the door shut. Then I'm pulling my T shirt over my head and practically falling over in my haste to get my pants and boxer briefs off.

"Do you like your surprise?"

All I can do is nod. I suspect my tongue is hanging out of my mouth as I pant. Fuck me. I have the most gorgeous woman in the world waiting for me, reclining on a sex swing. She's got her legs in the slings already, and the sight that meets my eyes is ready to make me blow my load already. She has the vaginal plug in, and the jewelry clipped to her pussy lips. But it's more than that. She also has a vaginal spreader, so I have the clearest view of the plug filling her.

As fast as I stripped, I'm slow as I prowl toward her. She's swaying already, her pussy gliding toward me, then away in the most tantalizing way. I want nothing more than to shove my dick in her and pound her until my neighbors wonder what's going on.

"Is this the surprise from the other night?"

"Yes."

I take in the swing frame. It snaps together, so it wasn't any harder to assemble than a pop-up canopy. I study the swing and realize it's the type I could suspend from the ceiling if I put it into a beam. I'm nearly two-hundred-and-thirty pounds. It's likely the frame is designed for up to three-fifty. I won't be able to swing with her, even though it's designed for that. But I'll be able to once I have it installed permanently.

"Baby girl, look in the mirror."

I shift, so she can see into the mirror over the dresser. It's the long style with four wide drawers. The mirror is the width of it and hangs above it. I step behind her, so we can see each other in the reflection. I gather her hair in my left hand and lean over her right shoulder to lick her nipple. When I straighten, I pinch both of them.

"Do you see how desirable you are?"

I stroke my cock. She's slow to do it, but she nods.

"Do you have any idea the restraint it's taking not to yank the plug out and fuck you until you beg me to stop because you can't take it anymore?"

"You know I won't beg you to stop. You know I won't safe word. I'll only beg you for more."

I walk back around her and examine the harness and pulleys. I adjust the straps over her shoulders and tilt her forward until she's face down but suspended. I fist my cock, and she leans even farther forward until she can lick me. I guide my length into her mouth. My left hand presses away on her shoulder while my right hand gives her arse a light spank. It's just enough to push her forward without ramming my junk down her throat. She sucks so hard she pulls my hips forward as I push her back. We do this over and over until there's spit around her lips, and I'm fighting for control. I adjust the swing again, and now she's reclining even farther than she was when I came in. I pull the plug out, and it's coated with the evidence that she's just as aroused as I am. I drop to my knees and feast. My hands on her hips help her sway to the rhythm I want.

"Daddy, may I come?"

"Yes, *mo stór*. You don't have to ask today."

"I want to. I want you in complete control, Dillan. All of it. The swing is the way I want it, but you decide how we do it."

That threatens to unleash a beast in me as I work her clit until she cries out. I did that with only my mouth. I thrust four fingers into her. Between the plug and the spreader she's still wearing, I can easily slide all of them into her. She's so slick and warm. I work her over and over, watching to make sure she's still enjoying it.

"Will you give me all of it?"

She phrases it as a question since she said she wants me to decide. I know what she wants. I press harder with all my fingers and thumb easing into her. I inch closer on my knees. Her shins rest against my shoulders and pecs.

"Rock against me. Control how deep you want me, Greta. I'm going to fist you, but I'm worried about hurting you. I have large hands, and you're still really tight."

She's always been that way, and despite how it looked

when I kneeled, beyond her entrance, she's still as narrow as she's always been. Knowing that makes my dick jump. I stroke near her cervix and along her g spot. The thumb on my free hand rubs wide circles on her clit.

"Ahh... Shit.... Fucking hell... That's so big. Fuck, it feels good... Oh!... Yes. Just like that... Daddy, may I come?"

"Yes."

I feel her contract around me, and I see her abs flutter. I keep rubbing her clit as the fingers on that hand press from the outside while my other set of fingers stroke from inside. She uses her shins to make the swing move faster. Her head's flung back, and her eyes are closed. Her hands clutch the straps. I ease my hand out, and she whimpers with dismay. I'm studying her to make sure it's never in genuine pain. I remove the jewelry and the spreader. Then I grasp her hips.

I guide her onto my cock with a thrust that jars her pubic bone against mine. She screams. Good, but not loud enough for my neighbors to hear. I push her body away from mine with each thrust, and it follows me back with each withdrawal. I want to tell her I can't wait until I can swing with her, but I don't want to bring up the fact we can't with the weight limit of the stand. I'm the reason we can't, but I know it'll make her think about herself in a way I don't want.

"Wee one, you feel so good."

"You do, too. I'm close again already."

I pull out, and she wails. "The moment you come on my dick, I'll be done. And I'm certain I'm going to come so hard, it'll take me more than a couple minutes to recover. I'm not ready for this to be over."

"I want to feel you come in me. I want all your cum inside me with the plug to make sure not a bit drips out of me."

"You will, but not yet."

We go back and forth, changing her position over and over

until I'm certain she's on the cusp of being too sore to enjoy what we're sharing.

"Come, Greta. I'm going to fill you."

She does a Kegel, and then I know she's coming from the way her body stiffens, and she trembles. She holds her breath, and I see the cords in her neck strain. I sink my fingers into her fleshy hips and jackhammer her until I shoot every ounce of cum I have inside her.

"You are going to wear that plug tonight at your parents."

"What?!"

"You heard me. You are going to wear it and know that while we're having a pleasant dinner with your folks, I'm still inside you."

She looks speculatively at me for a moment. "Do you truly want kids one day?"

"I didn't until I met you."

"Because you need an heir?"

That surprises me, and it must show because she looks relieved. We've talked about kids, but it's always been a very general sense. We've never said when or how many. We haven't even said we will definitively. It's always been more about affirming we want our future together than exactly what that future will look like. More like suggesting we'll be the yuppie couple with the house, picket fence, and two-point-five kids than actual family planning.

"No. I have five cousins who might one day marry and have kids. If I need an heir, there's bound to be one among their spawn. It doesn't have to be a son to inherit. I proved that. But if we have children, it would be a blessing. Why?"

"Because I'm not sure if I do. But if we decide to, I'd like to think we'd conceive on a night or day when you plug me full of your cum."

"I'd like to think that, too."

I help her off the swing, and we both look at the clock. Far more time has passed than we thought. It's time to get ready for me to meet the parents.

Torrin McDonnell opens the door before Greta can put the key in the lock. He's bigger than I pictured. He's close to my size. Not quite as in shape, but I don't get any hint of a dad bod.

"Welcome. Come in." He gives Greta a hug and kiss on the cheek.

"Hi, Da. This is Dillan."

"It's nice to meet you, Mr. MacDonnell."

"Torrin."

A voice comes from farther inside the house. "Mair?"

That's a nickname I haven't heard for Greta, but it's certainly better than Molly.

"Yes."

An attractive woman who is clearly Greta's mother walks down the hall from the kitchen. The resemblance gives me a view into my future with Greta. Seeing her parents together is like a glimpse at an older us.

"Mam, this is Dillan."

She's always referred to her mother as Mom. I wasn't expecting the traditional Irish term. It sounds odd to most American ears. It's why no one in my family uses it.

"Mrs. McDonnell, thank you for having me for dinner."

Fuck. That sounds like I'm the one who's about to get roasted on a skewer.

"Sorcha, please."

I smile at her parents as I help Greta take her coat off. I hang both of ours on the rack and follow them into the living room. The moment we step into the better lighting, her parents freeze. They turn raged-filled glares at me. Greta shifts in front of me. We thought the makeup she put on was enough. I guess not.

"Dillan didn't touch me. He would never, ever, ever slap me. He would never lay a hand on me in anger. I know that to be as true as the sky is blue and the grass is green."

"Then what the devil happened to your face?"

Torrin demands an answer from Greta, but he's still glowering at me. I can't blame him. Sorcha steps forward and peers at Greta's cheek. Neither of them misses that she's still standing in a defensive position. She even shifts when I come to stand beside her. I slip my hand into hers and run my thumb over the back of hers. She immediately relaxes, and her parents notice that too. It cools their anger when they see she wants to be close to me to ease her anxiousness.

"There was an incident, and I wound up with an angry woman in front of me. She wasn't pleased to see me, so she lashed out."

Sorcha's now looking at me as she speaks. "What sort of incident?"

"Mam, I told you about the articles and who Dillan is. You swore not to say anything because you'd already guessed. You need to know that what happened wasn't because of Dillan. Someone tipped off federal agents about my stories, and I'm fairly certain who. But those agents have been pressuring me to tell them more. I've refused. Because they haven't been able to coerce me into meeting with them or give them any additional information, they staged a raid on Dillan's brownstone two days ago. They arrested me. I spent a night in Manhattan Central Booking."

She stops there because we agreed they shouldn't know anything more than what's public record. She observes them, unsure how they're going to react. I caught what she said about having an idea about who sent the feds after her, but I can't ask what she means. Torrin looks at me.

"Why didn't you get her out sooner?"

"I tried. The judge who issued the warrant is getting paid by several precincts to issue warrants for members of all four major syndicate families. The ATF knew they had no grounds to arrest me without causing a media frenzy. They created trumped-up charges and found a judge willing to serve a federal warrant. They thought they could scare Mair into confessing things she truly doesn't know. They thought they could intimidate me into turning myself over."

I look down at Greta, who's staring up at me as though I've sprouted a second head. She has been since I called her Mair. I'm not convinced her parents would welcome hearing me call their daughter something no one else does.

"If I didn't have other people who depend on me, I would have lied my socks off to trade places with Mair. I—"

"Dillan, it's Greta. Only my parents and Granny call me Mair. You know everyone else calls me Molly. Your family can actually say Márgrég. Please call me what you always do."

Her parents watch us, and I feel uncertain about what to say. That's an unusual state for me to be in. The one thing I absolutely can't call her in front of her parents is *cailín*. I won't even do it in front of mine. I'm pretty sure the other guys have heard me, but it wasn't intentional. I'd have kept that entirely private, but I know I've slipped up. Very unlike me, but I don't always think in a million different directions when I'm with Greta. She steals all my attention.

"I would have traded places with Greta. I did what I could, and I can guarantee it will never happen again. It took time to ensure that."

I observe them as much as they're doing the same to me. Greta breaks the trance and leads me to a sofa. We sit together, but I keep a respectful distance between us, our joined hands resting on the cushion between us. I'll take my cues from them since I don't know what to say now. It's Torrin with his thick accent who speaks next.

"I'm certain you've run a background check on us. If our families are to blend, then I can't blame you. I've done my own research on you. We're from Ballycastle, but I have plenty of old connections throughout Ireland. I asked some discreet questions. All the answers came back the same. I shouldn't cross you if I want to see my grandchildren. But you're also an honorable man thrust into a shite situation when you wound up where you are. You've been working to right wrongs done before you and to restore your family to what it was during Liam's early days. The days before Peter left New York. You are not Liam O'Rourke. Neither are you Donovan or Declan. You're you."

Sorcha has her own thoughts to share. "Having access to millions of articles online also made it easier to learn about you here in New York. There's not much that names you specifically, but I don't need Mair's journalist skills to piece it together. What are you going to do to ensure our daughter's safety?"

"Greta has around the clock protection. There are several men staked out each night in my neighborhood and hers. She has at least one bodyguard from my immediate family with her every day. She will always have the freedom to go where she wants and do what she wants, but I have a tracking bracelet that will arrive by tomorrow night. It has a special clasp that only a custom key can unfasten."

That explanation doesn't sit well with Sorcha. "You're going to track her whereabouts all day?"

"I could, but I'm not going to. Everyone in my family wears them." I unfasten my watch. "Do you see how this has two knobs. This bigger one isn't what controls setting the time. If I push it, it signals an alert that goes to my cousins, da, and uncles. No one spies on each other. No one monitors each other's coming and going. We have them as a precaution."

Greta and I agreed not to tell them about the explosion yet. We know it'll likely cause a massive argument when it eventually comes out. But jail for nearly twenty-four hours is about the only bomb we can contain tonight.

Torrin nods, but he isn't satisfied. "What else?"

"While I feel my home is safer than her apartment, I'd like us to move to Queens and get a home in a gated community there."

This is news to Greta, but she hides it well. We haven't spoken about our living arrangement in a few days. There's been plenty of other stuff going on. I explain to them what type of community I'd like us to live in and the type of security it would have. It eases much of the tension, and we soon move into the dining room. Dinner is amazing. Once the initial suspicion dissipates, we have a meal nearly as lively as the one with my family. Her parents warm to me, and I can tell it's genuine because Greta's having a good time. Her parents tell me tons of stories about her, and I share ones about my family and me. It's idyllic, and the time flies.

I feel my phone vibrate as we finish dessert. I pull it from my pocket and notice it's Seamus. They all know I'm here, so it must be important to interrupt.

"I'm sorry, but I have to take this. It's one of my cousins. They'd only call tonight if it's urgent."

"My room is at the top of the stairs and to the left. The second door."

Greta twists in her seat to point. I pull my phone all the way out and hurry from the room. I hear the silence, but when I reach the stairs, I hear laughter again.

"Hello."

"Dillan, you will never believe this shite."

"What the hell? Why are you interrupting my first dinner with my future in-laws?" I practically hiss the questions. Is he setting up a joke?

"Dillan, they arrested Enrique."

I nearly drop the phone.

"You cannot be serious."

"Oh, I am. It's the DEA. Our tip went a lot further than we expected."

"Where is he now?"

"They have him somewhere, but we don't know where. Pablo and Alejandro are looking for you. You need to get home."

"I'm with Greta. They wouldn't strike with her along with me, would they? They know how Enrique feels about that. He knows Laura would never forgive him, and he's spent nearly three years trying to work his way back into her good books. She's still threatening to take a rusty knife to that tattoo with her initial and her sister's."

"You don't need to tell me what I already know. I don't think Enrique would sanction it, but Alejandro's a sociopath, and Pablo just hates you. You need to get home."

"Fuck." I run my hand through my hair. "Give me twenty minutes to make some calls. I'll text you when we're leaving. I'm up in Greta's room. I'll have to make it quick."

We hang up, and I pause to think. We wanted the DEA to harass and threaten Enrique for a few months before making any move. We wanted him dangling for a bit, knowing shite was building. Now the DEA's screwed the pooch because there's no way they have anywhere near enough information to get an indictment. It'll be Greta all over again. It won't even go to arraignment. But on the off chance it does, I need to be prepared.

"Mary Lou, put me through to your boss."

"Hello, Mr. O'Rourke. He's—"

"Nope. I called you, so he couldn't dodge my call. Put him on the line."

I hear a muffled sound, then there's a man's voice.

"What do you want, O'Rourke? It's awfully late."

"And you're still in the office. Does your staff know your wife kicked you out for having an affair?"

I hear Taylor Hollands suck in a breath. Good. Be scared. It's only going to get worse.

"Do you think your sister will do the same thing to Spiegel when she finds out he's having an affair?"

"You wouldn't."

"If that were true, would I have called?"

"You're just trying to intimidate me."

"Of course, I am. But you know I'll follow through, Hollands. You and Spiegel can fuck each other every day until the Second Coming. I don't give a shite. But you will have the DEA release Enrique Diaz if you want this little secret to stay among the three of us. If you don't, Taylor, you and Mason are going to find out with your arses just what it's like to have an open relationship when you're in jail. Deal with it by sunrise."

"I can't tell the DEA what to do. I'm the Director of the FBI not the DEA."

"But you were college roommates at Yale way back in the day. You had lunch with him three days ago. And while you're cozied up with a little pillow talk with Mason, make sure he understands the task I assigned him is non-negotiable. You and Director Watling over at the ATF are going to get up close and personal with Marco Mancinelli."

"You want me to tell the DEA to drop a case. You want me to create— what? A joint task force with the ATF to go after your rival?"

"And if you don't, then everyone will know you're fucking your brother-in-law."

"You motherfucker—"

"I'm not the one with questionable taste in bed partners. Say another word about my mother, and you'll find yourself put out to pasture by sunrise. You know I don't make idle threats."

I also know I have my VPN activated on my phone and my GPS off. We never have our GPS on unless we need directions somewhere specific. Then we screen shot the steps. The GPS goes back off immediately. He definitely wasn't prepared for this call, and I made it through his secretary's landline. He isn't recording it, but he'll start if I don't get off soon.

"Take care of it, Taylor."

I hang up. I head back downstairs and slide back into my seat. We pick up the conversation where it left off. We stay for another two hours before it gets late enough that I'm glad I have a driver waiting for us.

"*Cailín*, what did you mean when you said you thought you'd figured out who started all this?"

"I think Anton and Sergei were the leak. They said they didn't know who did it, and they were looking into it. I think they meant they didn't know the articles were going to run as soon as it did. I think they intended whoever they had at the newspaper to wait a little longer. I think that's what they've been wanting to tell me."

"I thought it might have been them, but a lot's happened that you know I can't tell you. It distracted me and made me look elsewhere. I won't be distracted in the morning."

Greta watches me for a moment before she nods. She leans against me for the rest of the ride home. We're both more tired than we realized, and after our fun with the swing earlier, we're happy to just climb into bed.

It takes me an hour after Greta falls asleep for my mind to

calm enough to sleep. I have shite on track to deal with Zef. Shite's in the works to deal with Enzo and Marco Mancinelli. That'll get the ATF to lay off Greta.

My phone buzzes, so I reach for it on the bedside table.

ENRIQUE

I know what you did, cabrón. Maybe you should put Sergei and Anton in your crosshairs and leave me the fuck alone. You trust them too much not to go near women. They let yours be a casualty of war.

I look over at Greta. I should have listened to my gut. I was a fool not to. The Kutsenkos and the Andreyevs on their fucking moral high horses. They were the ones to hack Greta, and she figured it out. She said as much during the car ride home tonight.

But there's way more to it than that. Sergei and Anton were the ones to get the ATF involved. They wanted the articles to work, so they pointed the feds in her direction and let them go to town hacking and harassing. They counted on Greta being willing to narc on us. She said they both tried contacting her, telling her they needed to meet. They may have wanted to warn her, but they didn't care enough about their no women and children policy to keep her from being collateral damage. Just because she came to no physical harm doesn't make this shite okay. Those motherfuckers.

I ignore Enrique, but I tap Sergei's and Anton's numbers to create a group chat.

I won't be able to deal with them in a day or a week. What I have planned is going to be slow. I'm going to strip them bare piece by piece unless they come up with something that redeems them. It really may take the Second Coming for that.

"Daddy?"

"Yes, *cailín*."

"Who are you angry texting?"

"Angry texting?"

"You sound like you're about to crush your phone from the way you're pounding on it."

"It's nothing. I'm sorry I disturbed you."

She rolls over before I can lock the screen. She grabs my wrist and looks at my phone. She looks up at me.

"What're you going to do?"

I look at her for a long time. "Whatever it is, you can count it as a wedding present."

She shakes her head and sighs. But she also sits up enough to cup my cheeks and press a tender kiss to my lips.

"You're the boss. I love you."

"I love you."

Epilogue

Greta

I look over at my husband of a month. We're on sun loungers on the beach outside the bungalow in Crete Dillan rented. We ran away from the remaining cold weather in New York and have been on an extended honeymoon. I pooled all my vacation and sick days to have the time to take off for this. I'd accumulated plenty since sick days aren't necessary when you can work from home. I'm back in Gary's good graces because the series I did on the Albanians benefited him since it drew just as many clicks and read throughs as the two articles that started the shitstorm that turned into my happily ever after.

"*Mo stór*, are you ready?"

"I don't wanna."

Dillan read each article before I submitted them. He was my CI for most of it. I don't know how he did it, but Sergei and Anton apologized and even gave me some info, too. I didn't ask, so none of them told me what Dillan did. It took us a month to get married because Dillan had to be away for two weeks. It was unexpected, so I stayed with his parents. I absolutely adore them. My parents are actually really similar to his, and they hit it off when they met. They've gone out together a few times to have dinner.

"We have to go home at some point."

"But do we?"

We got married in the Episcopalian church that I've gone to since we moved to America. We spent a week in Ireland touring around the country to see Dillan's family. He did a little work, but not much. Then we crossed over to Northern Ireland to see mine. Needless to say, we raised a few eyebrows at first, but it didn't take long for everyone to see I fit in with his family just as well as he fit in with mine. Then we spent a week touring Morocco, and now we've been in Crete for a fortnight. My real Irish comes out sometimes. I smile to myself.

"What has you grinning when a moment ago you looked ready to pout?"

"I was just thinking about how amazing this month's been."

"It has been grand."

Now I truly laugh. My accent came back heavily during our week in Ireland, and Dillan gained a bit of one since we switched back and forth between English and Irish all the time. Expressions I'd forgotten came back to me too, and Dillan adopted some just to make me laugh. That was one of them.

"Do you think we can come back here?" I look at the tan I've gained, and I much prefer it to how pale I usually am in winter. I've always been fine in the sun, rarely burning despite my dark red hair. I wasn't so sure about Dillan with his lighter red hair and freckles. But he hasn't burned either. We both look sun kissed.

"We'll definitely be back. We have a house here after all."

"What?" I jerk upright on my chair and look at the place

we've been staying. I've mentioned a few times— okay maybe a few dozen times —how perfect it is. "This one?"

"Yes, *mo cailín*. Just a little belated wedding gift."

"Little? Belated? Wedding gift?"

I punctuate each word and phrase. This is outrageous. I know no one else who gets a house in a foreign country as a wedding gift. That's how the other half lives. When I look at Dillan's bare chest, abs, and toned arms and legs, I think about how hot he looks in everything, from just his skin to his tailored suits. That reminds me I'm now part of that other half. The wealth I've stepped into hasn't fully registered despite flying on the O'Rourkes' private jet.

"Yes to all the above. Come on, sweet cheeks. We have just enough time for another round of shower sex, then we have to go. The plane'll be ready in two hours."

To most people that would sound like a ridiculously long time to need to get ready, especially since we're already packed. But our shower sex has turned into a decathlon.

I stand and turn toward my chair, deliberately sticking my ass out as I grab my towel and hat. I shake it. I wasn't so sure about the bathing suit I picked out once we got here. I got nervous and nearly chickened out. But Dillan spotted it and begged me to try it on. I thought he was going to rip the string right off it in his hurry to get me out of it. It's been the only one I've worn while we're on this private beach.

I lurch forward as his hand lands across my ass, but his arm is already sliding around my waist to keep me from falling. He pulls me back against him, and I can feel him getting hard. I rub my ass against him. That gains me another spank before he hefts me over his shoulder. I clutch my stuff as he continues to land one after another as we enter the bungalow through the bedroom. We made the mistake of going in through the dining room on the third day, and I nearly died of mortification when

Finn, Sean, Shane, Cormac, and Seamus saw me in this suit. Or rather glimpsed me. I ducked behind Dillan, who put his hands on his hips to shield me. Five chairs around the dining room table scraped the floor, then I heard five sets of shoes practically run from the room.

"I'm not the one who took so long Finn had to come knocking last night to make sure we left in time for our dinner reservation."

I wag a finger at him as he puts me down in the bathroom. We strip and step into the shower. The dual showerheads are like the ones in our bathroom in the brownstone. We're moving into a house in Queens when we get back. For now, things are practically storybook perfect.

"And my cousin would have lost that hand if he'd knocked one more time. No one rushes me when I'm taking care of *mo shíorghrá*." My eternal love.

"You say the sweetest things."

He hums his agreement as I kiss him. I pull back and lock gazes with him before I speak again.

"*Is ceol mo chroí thú.*" You're the music of my heart.

Don't miss Finn's story when the mob's second-in-command falls for the sexy, intelligent doctor with a past she'd rather keep secret.

Preorder your copy of Mob Star and have it waiting for you on release day.

Would you like an extra sex scene with Dillan and Greta? Subscribe and get your free download here.

Don't miss the next installment

You're a fool to underestimate me.
I do more than just run numbers.
I do more than just work for my family.
There's nothing I won't do for her.
Touch what's mine, and you won't live to regret it.
She's more than I knew I wanted and everything I need.
She's light where I'm darkness.

She's kind where I'm ruthless.

My pleasure comes from her pleasure, and I'll give her more than she imagined.

There's no one and nothing more important than her.

Get a bonus epilogue

Enjoy this free bonus epilogue with a scene from *Mob Boss* where Dillan and Greta have just left Shane and Sean's birthday dinner. You know they can't keep their hands off each other in the car. Join them for the ride home and some kinky sex once they're there.

Check out this extra sexy scene with Dillan and Greta. Get your Copy here.

Thank you for reading Mob Boss

Sabine Barclay, a nom de plume also writing Historical Romance as Celeste Barclay, lives near the Southern California coast with her husband and sons. She loves her days at the beach soaking up way too much sun, a good Netflix binge, and a strong hot chai. Her heroines are independent women who can defend themselves but love their Alpha heroes who want nothing more than to protect their soulmates in her Mafia Romances. She's Gen Y/Oregon Trail and loves creating engrossing contemporary romances that will make your toes curl and your granny blush.

Subscribe to Sabine's bimonthly newsletter to receive exclusive insider perks.

www.sabinebarclay.com

Join the fun and get exclusive insider giveaways, sneak peeks,
and new release announcements in
<u>Sabine Barclay's Facebook Dubious Dames Group</u>

Do you also enjoy steamy Historical Romance? Discover
Sabine's books written as Celeste Barclay.

The O'Rourke Brotherhood

Mob Boss

Mob Star

Mob Princess

Mob Saint

Mob Bride

Mob Knight

Do you also enjoy steamy Historical Romance? Discover Sabine's books written as Celeste Barclay.

The Ivankov Brotherhood

Bratva Darling
BOOK ONE SNEAK PEEK

LAURA

As I sit across from the four Kutsenko brothers, I press my lips together to keep from drooling. No four men should be so strikingly handsome. Not all from the same family, anyway. I fight a valiant battle against letting my gaze drift toward the eldest, Maksim, whose ice-blue eyes bore into me. After years of negotiating billion-dollar investment contracts while facing countless ruthless businessmen, I've learned to keep my expression studiously blank. But it's a true struggle today. Instead, I focus my attention on the squirrelly lawyer sitting across the conference table. While he's disingenuous with each comment, he's a good negotiator. But I'm better. How cliché am I?

While I feel Maksim watching me, I focus on Dmitry Yakovitch as he continues to argue the merits of the venture capitalist company I represent, RK Capital Group, merging with Kutsenko Partners. What he means is the merits of

Kutsenko Partners acquiring RK Capital Group, then stripping it and making it another money-laundering shell corporation. While most people in New York have little awareness of the Russian mafia, I do. The Kutsenko brothers' names appear on no titles or deeds anywhere in New York City, but it wasn't difficult to determine which shell companies likely belong to them. Their assumption that I'm unfamiliar with them is proving beneficial to me as they continue to whisper amongst themselves in Russian. I think they may even believe they're convincing me that they don't speak much English.

The senior partners of RK Capital Group know who I'm negotiating with, though they may not know I'm aware of these Russians' more nefarious operations. They've given me the go-ahead to agree to a merger with an eventual acquisition, but only for the right price. A price to the tune of twenty billion dollars. Considering an investment firm like Goldman Sachs is worth nearly one-hundred-and-twenty billion dollars, my clients' asking price appears reasonable.

"Mr. Yakovitch, I shall stop you now." I raise my left hand, pen caught between my index and middle fingers. When I have his attention, I lean back in my chair and casu-ally twirl the pen over my index finger and thumb. "Fifty billion is my clients' asking price. You know that. Your clients know that. RK doesn't oppose the merger. What they oppose is the insulting offer you've made. It's nearly noon, and I'm hungry, Mr. Yakovitch. I have a delicious ham sandwich waiting for me. I even have three chocolate chip cookies waiting for me. If we aren't going to make any progress, I shall let you go, so I can move onto my eagerly anticipated lunch."

I cant my head just enough for me to appear as though my gaze rests solely on the opposing attorney's face, but I can see each Kutsenko brothers' reaction. My face battles yet again against showing my emotions as I fight not to smirk. Their muted but surprised expressions confirm what I already know.

"Please tell your clients to make a reasonable counteroffer, or I will conclude this meeting and enjoy my ham sandwich and cookies."

Dmitry glares at me before turning to Maksim and his three brothers. In rapid Russian, he doesn't interpret my suggestion. Oh no. There's no need for that. I can't catch every word because his voice is too low. But I catch something along the lines of "The bitch refuses to budge. What now? A fucking ham sandwich. More like a stick up her ass."

Maksim swivels his chair to look at his brothers. In Russian, he says, "Fifty billion is ridiculous. She's not so stupid or naïve not to know that. My guess is they'll settle for twenty billion. We offer fifteen."

"That's barely better than what we already offered," Aleksei, the second-oldest brother, argues. "She'll be eating the fucking sandwich and dipping her cookies in milk before we walk out the door. We need the buildings."

"We offer twenty, Maks," Bogdan, the youngest, insists.

As I watch the brothers discuss, their voices barely lowered, I pull my lunch sack from the black leather satchel by my feet and set it beside my laptop. It's a ridiculously pink floral bag with an embroidered monogram, the L and D overlapping. It's an empty prop, but they don't know that. I watch as five sets of eyes narrow. I offer a smile that would appear innocent in any setting other than this meeting. It's patronizing, and I know it.

Bratva Sweetheart

Bratva Treasure

Bratva Beauty

Bratva Angel

Bratva Jewel

The Mancinelli Brotherhood

Mafia Heir
BOOK ONE SNEAK PEEK

Luca

This asshole is pissing me off. We've been going around in circles for five minutes, and the longer we stand out here, the greater the likelihood someone will spot us. I have a sixth sense about these things. It's why I'm still alive at the ripe old age of thirty-one.

"Espinoza, enough already. Either sell to us or don't, but we set the price. Your tequila is good, but it isn't nectar from the gods."

I'm watching Carlos Espinoza, some lackey for the Mexican Culiacán Cartel, try to maneuver me into paying more than the agreed upon price. I know it's so he can skim off the top.

"It's as close as you're going to get. You've upped the order, so the price per case goes up."

My uncle, Salvatore Mancinelli, is the New York don. He

negotiated this deal, and I warned him it was a bad idea. But what do I know as his underboss and heir? I'm not backing down.

"Haven't you ever heard of a bulk discount? The more I order the better the price should be. No one else around here is buying from you. You know we're your only choice in three out of five boroughs. You aren't going to the Bronx because you won't get more than pennies there. You aren't going to Queens because you don't want to run into the Colombians. You aren't going to Manhattan because then you face the bratva along with us. And what are you going to do in Staten Island? Sell to us anyway? We control Staten Island and Brooklyn when it comes to liquor stores, so take the money and go."

"Luca, there are plenty of liquor stores in Brooklyn that aren't owned by Italians. I'll go there."

We aren't friends. He's patronizing me by using my first name. Fuck him and the horse he rode in on. I have other solutions for this shit.

"And I'll just take what I want from them for free. That's not a half bad idea. The deal's over. Take your shit with the worm in it and go."

"Motherfucking racist. Not all tequila has a worm in it."

"You're selling Mezcal. It's known for the fucking worm. I wouldn't start calling me names, you *penche hijo de puta.*" Fucking son of a bitch.

He has twenty-five crates of stolen tequila that he's trying to offload because he knows he can't sell it at his own liquor store.

"What did you call me?"

Carlos takes what he thinks is a menacing step forward, and his two bodyguards do the same. Not smart. Neither of my two bodyguards nor I react, but the three men in each of my cars open their doors. They won't do more than that. It's just a reminder that the Culiacán can try, but the *Cosa Nostra* still run New York City.

"This is the third and final time I say this. Sell or leave."

Every head turns toward the liquor store's back door as it opens. A gorgeous blonde steps out, and I wish I had the time to appreciate her beauty, but she's about to die. Carlos and his men draw their guns and pivot toward her. My men pull their weapons too, but we keep them pointed at the Mexicans. The woman stands like a deer in the headlights for a second before ducking behind the industrial garbage dumpster like a frightened rabbit. Three shots hit the metal almost at the same moment. That's all it takes for my men and me. The two bodyguards standing with me aim for a guard each, and I set my sights on Carlos. We squeeze our triggers, and the men fall.

Screeching tires tell me Carlos's driver takes off. I hear more gunshots as at least one soldier in my cars tries to shoot the escaping vehicle. Glass shatters, but the sedan keeps going. I hear more tires squeal as one of my SUVs takes off and chases the guy. I holster my gun and wave my men to do the same.

I inch forward toward the trash can, but I see the shadow shift. The woman bolts from the other side. She's still the frightened rabbit, but I'm the fox pursuing her. She's fast, I'll give her that. But she has to be at least a foot shorter than me. My legs are a lot longer and cover a lot more ground with each stride.

She weaves among the cars, most likely believing it's harder to hit a moving object. She isn't wrong, but I have no intention of shooting her. I push myself harder and pounce as she darts out and tries to cross the last stretch of parking lot to reach a better lit area near a bus stop. I lunge.

"Stop running, *piccolina*. I won't hurt you."

I wrap my arms around her and pull her back against my chest, but I'm quick to spin her around and put space between us as I grasp her arms. Of course, she fights me.

"If I wanted you dead, I would have shot at you, too."

"It doesn't mean you won't kill me after."

She's breathless as she continues to struggle. I almost let go to take a step back, insulted at what she implied. But I can't blame her. If I were a woman, I'd be terrified of the same thing.

"I'm not going to rape you. I'm going to talk to you."

"Talk? You are not a man who talks if you just killed a guy."

"To keep him and his men from killing you. I told you, if I wanted you dead, I would have shot at you too. And I wouldn't have missed."

She stops struggling against me, but her eyes continue to dart from one place to another, trying to find somewhere to flee. I know I can keep her in place with only one hand, so I release her left arm. I still have a firm hold on her right one, but I haven't held it nearly as tightly as I could.

"I'm Luca. I know you figured out you interrupted something you shouldn't have. Did that man know who you are?"

"Yes."

"What about his driver? Would he know you?"

"Yes."

"Do you have a name?"

"Yes."

"*Piccolina*, we won't get very far if yes is all you can say. Are you willing to answer me with more than one word?"

"No."

I knew that was coming, and I grin. I can't help it. I wasn't wrong about her being gorgeous, but I doubt she wants to know that's what I think. At least, not if I want her to know I won't assault her.

"Fine. I have more than twenty questions I can ask that you can answer with one word. Do you work at the store?"

"Sometimes."

Ah, an improvement.

"Did Carlos know you were still working?"

"No."

"Do you have a car, or do you take the subway or bus?"

She raises her chin and remains silent. Smart but counter-productive.

"The subway or the bus will get you killed. You're too easy to find and follow. Do you have a car?"

"Yes."

"Can you stay with someone instead of going home?"

She refuses to answer.

"If that man knew you and you sometimes work in the store, then he knew where you live. If he found that out, so will someone in his cartel."

"I know. Let me go. The longer I stand here, the more likely someone is to come back for me."

"No one will touch you while I'm here."

"Arrogant. If he shot at me, he would have shot at you."

"And he would have died, anyway. What's your name?"

"Jane."

"Look, I know you won't get in one of my cars and let me drive you somewhere. In most cases, I would say that's a smart move. But you did nothing wrong tonight except for leave work at the wrong time. I know that, and you know that. But the Culiacán won't see it that way, *piccolina*."

She freezes for no more than five seconds before she trembles so much that I can see it. I don't know what drives me next, but it's the same instinct that's made me call her little girl three times. I pull her to my chest and tuck her head against it. I stroke her hair down to her shoulders, rubbing my hand up and down her back. This is the most inopportune moment to notice she isn't wearing a bra. I will my body not to react.

"What does that mean?"

Her voice is barely more than a whisper, but I know what she's asking.

"It means little girl."

"I should be insulted, but the way you say it…"

"It has nothing to do with your height. I know you're not a child."

God, do I know she's not. She feels amazing. Her tits are soft as they press against me, and I can see she has the most delectable ass. I'd love nothing more than to cup it and squeeze until she goes up on her toes and begs for me to wrap her legs around my waist and fuck her. For fuck's sake. Stop, you disgusting asshole. That is not what you need to be thinking about.

"Why didn't you shoot me? Whatever you were talking about, if it was with a Cartel member, then it wasn't completely legal. Carlos didn't want me alive to talk about seeing you together. Why are you letting me live?"

"I told you. You did nothing wrong but try to leave work. He should have checked the building before starting the meeting. That was on him. The only thing I take issue with is you leaving by yourself and walking into a dimly lit parking lot. I suspect you do that often, and that's too dangerous. Jane Doe, I don't hurt women."

Mafia Sinner

Mafia Beauty

Mafia Angel

Mafia Redeemer

Mafia Star